Praise for
The Late Bloomer

"I fell deep into the postapocalyptic and ad
Bloomer and didn't want it to end. Not only
but the voice of the central character had m
Kevin March became a person I cared about
page was finished."

—**Dan Chaon**,
author of *Ill Will*

"Like a sharp, winding staircase that narrows as it turns, the claustrophobic world of *The Late Bloomer* hems the reader in page by page."

—**Tal M. Klein**,
author of *The Punch Escrow*

"Harrowing, unsettling and exquisitely written, *The Late Bloomer* is part *War of the Worlds*, part *Twilight Zone*, and part Shirley Jackson. It is an unforgettable, unforgiving vision of the end of the world, of those who attempt to survive and those who wish to stop them. The images conjured here will haunt you long after putting it down. Good luck, dear reader."

—**Louisa Luna**,
author of *Two Girls Down*

"We classify some prose as genre, some as literary, and 'never the twain shall meet.' *The Late Bloomer* is both. Falkin gives us all sorts of Stephen King (story), meets the oft-mentioned William Golding's (character), *Lord of the Flies*. Experimental in its style, protagonist, writing protégé Kevin Gabriel March, possible future guide of the new world, dictates the old world's ending into a stolen voice recorder. Establishing a *Stand*-like setting, *The Late Bloomer* morphs into full-on textbook lit, like, for the ages literature. Like man versus all seven narrative conflict themes. Like drilling deep for symbolism and allegory. Yes, literary devices and shit. This novel overflows with rich language and divine sentences. *The Late Bloomer* is giving me *everything!* After the end someone must tell the tale, dear Reader. Why not our Kevin Gabriel March?"

—**Teffanie T. White**,
African American Literary Award-winning author of *Dirt*

"An apocalyptic coming-of-age tale the likes of which you've never seen, Mark Falkin's *The Late Bloomer* channels the heart of Ray Bradbury, the sensibilities of Rod Serling, and the grim despair of Cormac McCarthy, all wrapped up in Falkin's unshakable, inimitable style. Both beautiful and horrific, this is a young adult novel that even the most case-hardened fans of speculative fiction will find riveting and deeply moving. Highly recommended."

—**Ronald Malfi**,
author of *Bone White* and *Little Girls*

"With dark humor and taught prose, *The Late Bloomer* takes the reader on an apocalyptic journey that is hurried, furrowed and in Mark Falkin's skilled hands, all too real. Literary horror at its finest."

—**Bethany Hegedus**,
author of *Alabama Spitfire: The Story of Harper Lee and To Kill a Mockingbird*

"If you're a fan of dull, weary storytelling with characters you've seen a million times doing the things you've seen them do a million times until you pass out from boredom, then this isn't the book for you. If, on the other hand, you're into roller coasters, laughter, fear, surprise, and characters who keep going against all odds, then *The Late Bloomer* will suck you down its twisted literary throat through its very last word."

—**Jason Neulander**,
producer, director and creator of *The Intergalactic Nemesis*

"With pitch-perfect prose, Falkin has penned an irresistible and audacious coming-of-age novel that plumbs the depths of adolescence and global cataclysm in equal, page-turning measure. I predict *The Late Bloomer* will take its place on the post-apocalyptic bestseller list, next to *Station Eleven* and *The Stand*."

—**Will Clarke**,
author of *The Neon Palm of Madame Melançon* and *Lord Vishnu's Love Handles*.

"With *The Late Bloomer*, Mark Falkin has created a visceral, classic adventure story updated for our dystopian times when many of us long to push the reset button. Read your Jackson, your Golding, your King, and your Falkin, and be careful what you wish for."

—**Michelle Newby Lancaster**,
Contributing Editor, Lone Star Literary Life

"An apocalyptic tale unlike any other, *The Late Bloomer* is smartly written; with shades of Stephen King meeting Cormac McCarthy, a blistering pace and lyrical prose, it demands to be consumed. Falkin's take on the end of the world is intriguing, beautiful and tragic—a must-read."

—Kristen Zimmer,
Amazon #1 bestselling author of *The Gravity Between Us*

"With *The Late Bloomer*, Mark Falkin has written a *Blair Witch Project*-kind of novel, a dystopian nightmare that sends his characters racing to escape a killer that always seems to be waiting just ahead of them. It's a gripping rush of literary adrenaline."

—Michael Noll,
Program Director, Writers' League of Texas
and author of *The Writer's Field Guide to the Craft of Fiction*

"Imagine nature itself seething with Holden Caulfield's rage at adult phoniness. Now imagine what happens when a decimated humanity inherits the planet. With *The Late Bloomer*, Mark Falkin combines an authentic portrait of twenty-first-century adolescence with a terrifying, and unsettlingly plausible, vision of the end of humanity as we know it."

—Christian TeBordo,
author of *Toughlahoma* and director of the MFA Program and
Assistant Professor of English at Roosevelt University

"*The Late Bloomer* is a standout novel—a contemporary end-of-days novel that grabs you by the throat and won't let go. Narrated in the unforgettable voice of Kevin March, the unlikely and resistant teenaged 'late bloomer' whose prophetic dreams have marked him for leadership of those who survive a world apocalypse reminiscent of the great floods, *The Late Bloomer* is an important cautionary tale that will haunt you long after you've finished the last page. With themes of good versus evil, the horrors of mob mentality, and the necessity of human empathy, *The Late Bloomer* gives strong nods to *The Hunger Games, The Terminator,* and *The Lord of the Flies*, wherein the beast resides within us all. The story's unexpected climax is a chilling perspective of a political era where it may seem that only our youth can be entrusted with society's moral compass."

—Martha Louise Hunter,
author of Painting Juliana and host of KOOP's *Writing on the Air*

"Imagine a dystopian vision in which Stephen King's *The Mist* meets Jeff VanderMeer's *The Southern Reach* trilogy, and Margaret Atwood's *The MaddAddam Trilogy*. This is the world Mark Falkin conjures up in *The Late Bloomer*. Like the best postapocalyptic novels, *The Late Bloomer* is a tale of horror derived from the stuff of everyday life. A dark menace haunts these pages, lurks in the shadows, and the beauty of this novel is that it makes you seriously wonder: could this happen to us? A smart, sophisticated YA novel, *The Late Bloomer* will grab you by the scruff and pull you along for a wild ride."

—**Kyle Semmel**,
2016 NEA Literary Translation Fellow
and Executive Director of Writers & Books

"In *The Late Bloomer*, Mark Falkin's postapocalyptic young adult novel, the world as we know it has imploded. A small band of teenagers are the only ones left to figure out what has happened and try to piece some semblance of their world back together. Beautifully written and action-packed, *The Late Bloomer* is narrated by a teenager who is at once jaded and hopeful, a voice you're not likely to forget any time soon."

—**Suzanne Greenberg**,
Professor of English at California State University and winner
of the Drue Heinz Literature Prize for *Speed-Walk and Other Stories*

The Late Bloomer

The Late Bloomer

Mark Falkin

A California Coldblood Book
Rare Bird Books
Los Angeles, Calif.

THIS IS A GENUINE CALIFORNIA COLDBLOOD BOOK

A California Coldblood Book | Rare Bird Books

453 South Spring Street, Suite 302

Los Angeles, CA 90013

rarebirdbooks.com

californiacoldblood.com

Copyright © 2018 by Mark Falkin

ISBN 978-1-947856-54-7

FIRST TRADE PAPERBACK ORIGINAL EDITION

For more information, address:

Rare Bird Books Subsidiary Rights Department,

453 South Spring Street, Suite 302, Los Angeles, CA 90013.

Set in Minion

Cover art and typesetting by Leonard Philbrick.

Author photo © 2018 Mike Mulry/XCELARTS

Printed in the United States

Distributed by Publishers Group West

Publisher's Cataloging-in-Publication data

Names: Falkin, Mark, author.

Title: The Late Bloomer / Mark Falkin.

Description: Los Angeles, CA: California Coldblood Books,

an imprint of Rare Bird Books: 2018.

Identifiers: ISBN 978-1947856547

Summary: The world experiences an unthinkable cataclysm and Kevin March, high school band trombonist and wannabe writer, embarks on a journey that promises to change everything.

Subjects: LCSH Horror. | Texas—Fiction. | Friendship—Fiction. | Apocalyptic fiction. | BISAC YOUNG ADULT FICTION /

Apocalyptic & Post-Apocalyptic

Classification: LCC PZ7.F18852 La 2018 | DDC [Fic]—dc23

From across the valley the thud of an axe
arrives later than its strike
and the call of goodbye slowly separates itself
little by little from the vocal chords of everything.

—Galway Kinnell, *The Silence of the World*

DOCUMENT TRANSMITTAL NO. 2351-ND21
CLASSIFIED - UICO EYES ONLY

DOC. DESC.:
Transcription of digital audio recording of
Kevin Gabriel March, October-November 2018

SUB. DATE: ND21-122
RE: RE:Day Of Events & Aftermath
REF. TITLE:No Go

TRANSCRIPT#:0001
DOC. RATING:***URGENT***
ACTION REC.:WIDE AND IMMEDIATE CIRCULATION

SOURCE MATERIAL CUSTODIAN:
INSURGENT OFFICER MARCH #456771/NDBY2018

TRANSCRIBER:
INSURGENT OFFICER MARCH #456771/NDBY2018

EDITOR:
INSURGENT OFFICER MARCH #456771/NDBY2018

TRANSCRIPTION OF AUDIO RECORDING OF
KEVIN GABRIEL MARCH
OCTOBER/NOVEMBER 2018

PLEASE, GOD, DON'T LET HER DIE.[1]

SO, PROLOGUE.[2]

MR. E, YOU'D LIKE THAT *I'm trying to do this. Instead of videoing everything and narrating over it. I couldn't have done that anyway. There was no time to be a reflective documentarian. Now that I've got some time, maybe I can process all this and tell you what happened.*

In fact, doing it this way is how I process it.

I know you'd prefer this to, well… you were such a supporter of my writing, a mentor. And so telling this with the intention of writing it down instead of filming it…I know you hated the world of screens we'd come to live in. I tend to agree with you now, though at first I thought you were being a crabby old teacher who didn't get it and stubbornly didn't want to. Referred to yourself as a Luddite. I had to look it up.

---

1 Kevin Gabriel March (KGM) utters these words in whispers. Another sound appears here, a wheezing, emitted from another person in the room—Kodie Janine Lagenkamp (KJL). While these words are unintended for inclusion in the overall purpose of the recording and are wholly disconnected from its structure as depicted in the following transcribed pages, as such is specifically mentioned on page 172, they are included herein by reference.

2 Transcriber/editor attempts to indicate and include dramatic pauses, sighs, various vocalizations, obvious emphasis (wherein italics are employed), and paragraph breaks like this one. Editor places the entire prologue in italics, as such was common in old-world literature.

But it's me who gets it now. I was getting it then, the way you saw things, which wasn't negative at all. I got that you were trying to show me that through storytelling I could show readers that the world is a beautiful place, that life is a beautiful thing, even when we're scared and we don't understand what life is and who we are and why we live and what happens after we die. "Don't let anybody tell you they know, because they don't," you'd said. When I repeated this at the dinner table to my stepdad, Martin, he said, "Sounds like your typical liberal school teacher who can't hack it in the real world so he teaches, warping minds with his embitterment." Pretty poetic for an asshole like Martin, I have to say. I remember offering him a brittle smile when he said that, nodding my head, and muttering to myself, "Embitterment, hmmm."

And what you said about stories. I really get that now, too. You'd said they weren't just about filling time, entertainment. Not that that's wrong, a story can be both meaningful and entertaining, you'd said, should be both for it to resonate. You told me that stories connect us, make us understand ourselves and each other a little better. That stories make the world a better place because they are empathy engines.

I like that. Empathy engine. Vroom vroom.

It's a noble cause, storytelling, you'd said. Noble work.

So, here I go with being noble.

This is for you Mr. English, probably for you more than anyone, except that it's really for you, dear reader.[3]

OKAY, SO, EVEN MORE PROLOGUE. *Of the housekeeping ilk.*

I'm using a little handheld digital micro voice recorder[4] to talk this book into being. I took it when we broke into RadioShack. The box[5] it came in said Capture Your Stories *with that circled R trademark thing next to it. So, that's what I'm doing: capturing my story. I'll shape it later, if I make it.*

I hate that I even have to say that. If I make it. God. I want to unplug that part of my self. Got to keep my spirits up. I know that part of me is the least

---

3 Section breaks such as this indicate that KGM has stopped recording. The next passage or paragraph indicates his resumption of recording.

4 Olympus WS-822 Digital Voice Recorder with Intelligent Functions, mfg. China 2017

5 Photo of box attached as Exhibit A

Kevin. I don't know. He's the one just trying to survive. To tell it the way things are. The reason…why things are what they are. Heh.

I'd sit and write it properly, this book, a narrative non-fiction they'll call it, because even though it's got a novelish, fictiony feel to it, it's all true. Or maybe it's a memoir. A memwah. *That's what it is.*

Whatever. Point is, I can't just sit and write it all down because if I don't keep moving…well, I don't know what they'd do. But she's waiting for me, so I can't stop. And doing this keeps me company. This and Maggie here. Isn't that right, girl?

I mean, I always wanted to be a writer. Here's my chance. Maybe my only and last, but.

In case I don't get too far along doing this, I have to say that although I've got my reasons for going down there, I can't say I feel like I'm truly going to save them. But maybe I can help them. It's all a big fat maybe, as it has been from day one. They seem to think differently. Kodie says they do, at least. But I don't know. We're just too different now. There's something, what? pernicious about them. Sure, because of what they did, but mostly it's in the way they move, the way they flock…

If I repeat myself or if this sounds clunky sometimes, just know that this is raw raw raw. I'm going to really write this someday. I need to 'capture my story' now because I don't know about tomorrow. Tomorrow is so far-seeming. After all that's happened, it would be foolish to say you're going to know what happens next.

But I think this book will be important because I think I may be the only one left. It certainly feels that way. Unless she really is there waiting for me like she says she is.

OH, DUH—GOT OFF TRACK THERE. Let me get this out of the way. Okay, I'm Kevin Gabriel March and I live in Austin, Texas. I'm not sure what day it is, the day I start this recording, November something, but all this started the morning of October 29, 2018. I'm a, I was, a high school junior and I'm seventeen years old. Birthday's December 24. Always hated that timing. We get the gift-shaft, we who are born so close to Christmas. You just don't get celebrated. You get overlooked.

1 Dreams and visions swirl. They're *heavy and seem important. Not just*
2 *my brain firing, my mind reacting to conscious life. So many feelings, sights*
3 *and sounds, but this one's been a repeater—a beach; a big sound of something*
4 *rubbing up against an object in the water, a wooden pier, maybe; nightfall*
5 *and fires in a row, dancing silhouettes; in midmorning light, a blurry presence*
6 *perched on the sea's horizon.*

7 They can do the jobs *of armies. Odd thing is, they don't seem to act at*
8 *the behest of a leader. They move as quicksilver, like one organism, a massive*
9 *flock of birds abruptly lifting into the air, undulating, twisting, graying the*
10 *sky; or like a school of fish winding and turning all shiny in shafts of light*
11 *knifing down through the water. A content and contiguous group, a single*
12 *entity moving and working and living en masse, seeming to move toward a*
13 *moment. Moving inexorably toward it.*
14 *As am I.*
15 *Right now, I don't watch them. Now I move. It's just dawn, best time to move.*
16 *Yesterday morning, from atop of the W Hotel, I saw them through my*
17 *$1,000 binoculars. Per usual, they were out in the open, a beige wintering*
18 *Texas field beyond the floodplain south of the city. I wonder now if they are*
19 *the ones following me. No, I don't think they do it that way. They don't need to*
20 *follow me. I think they relay the message ever-forward: here he comes.*
21 *It was predawn, just when the rim of sky in Austin went that violet*
22 *crown attributed by O. Henry, (Does this matter, Mr. English, the color at*
23 *dawn? Sometimes I just want to describe the beauty and the horror because*
24 *that's what life is. Guess that's why you said I'd make a better poet than a*
25 *novelist. I remember asking, "Can I tell them what happens next but with*
26 *lyrical writing?" You smiled so big and your eyes shined.) I saw their bellies,*
27 *all of them together in total synchronization, of course, swelling and deflating*
28 *rapidly though they're asleep. Maybe they're having bad dreams in that deep*
29 *REM sleep?*
30 *But what would they dream about?*
31 *Anyway. Enough of this. Let's start from the beginning.*
32 *Okay. Deep breath. Here goes...*

To be truthful, when I first heard the sounds, I was lighting a bowl of pot.

Most of the western hemisphere lay gripped by predawn sleep, and there I was, sitting cross-legged on a boulder at Mount Bonnell, overlooking Lake Austin. Yeah, that's me there in your mind's eye, the silhouette of a young man holding a blue finger of flame in the dark.

The bowl blooming orange, that's when it happened. Holding the smoke in my lungs, I hear this…sound.

Sure, I'd be thinking it, too, if I were you: the guy's a burnout, he's hearing stuff. Yeah.

But if you're reading this, the very fact that you're reading this, you know exactly what I'm talking about and so you know a couple of hits of low-impact smoke had no role to play in what I was hearing at dawn of that morning, the morning of the day of. So let's move on.

But just so you know, no, I am not a pothead, a burnout. Not being defensive, but I'm not. In fact, I was still new to the whole smoking-pot thing. Sure, when you're waking and baking alone at an urban overlook, you've moved out of novice territory, but still.

Really what I was on that morning was a heartbroken and stressed-out trombonist.

So, I keep holding it in. I stifle a cough, feel my face go red, ropey veins popping out on my neck. I'm listening, lungs full of smoke, eyes toggling.

At first, I thought they were testing the tornado sirens. The sounds started with this low shuddering boom, then came a wailing siren. A bomb blast followed immediately by sirens? Something over at the military installation, Camp Mabry? They do battle reenactments over there. But at dawn? Couldn't be. No storm, no bomb, no war games. Had to be a test. But why at the stroke of dawn, waking up the city? Can't be.

Within seconds, the sound became so loud that I coughed out the smoke and stood up on the boulder. Smoke wisped above my head. I faced west, looking out over Lake Austin. What was called Lake Austin was really the dammed up Lower Colorado River. Moving south beyond Lady Bird Lake, the river flowed southeast through LaGrange, Bay City, to the Gulf of Mexico, dumping into the Matagorda Bay between Corpus and Galveston. The sound came from the downriver direction, my left. And the sound now, though constant and siren-like, was the deep and mournful tone of what I thought were the sounds made by whales. Whales in extremis.

Whale sounds. In Austin, Texas.

More than whale sounds. Otherworldly sounds; countless whales not just moaning and sighing and singing, but crying out.

Screaming.

I HEARD A DISTANT TINNY crash. To the upriver right, on the Pennybaker Bridge, this big rust-colored double arc, there are flames. So far away that it looks like an orange wink between two dots. The dots were cars and the fire bloomed. Had to be a big wreck to create a fire I could see from miles away. The sounds waned then fell off as quickly as they had come. The arc of first light was just up in the east, soon to be a red ball hanging next to the University of Texas clock tower like a counterpoint. Muscles in my shoulders relaxed from being hunched against the sound. I looked at the pipe in my hand, incredulous. *What am I smoking, my God?*

I closed my eyes and shook my head with vigor to clear it. Surely, I was hearing and seeing things.

Kept my eyes closed for a beat, another.

A hawk cried down in the valley. I felt the breeze on my cheeks. I heard the whelming hum of a waking city. With your eyes closed you can really hear it all. The metallic clacks and low roar of a city all around you.

I opened my eyes. Down on the bridge there was a line of smoke rising to the sky and in the distance I heard emergency sirens. Car and home alarms everywhere.

Now something caught my eye to my left. It looked like a ripple coming up the river.

Slowly fetching upriver, maybe five feet high, stretched entirely across in an even line. Weird because the Colorado is dammed in several places between here and Matagorda, including the big one right down there, the Tom Miller Dam. I'd kayaked around Red Bud Isle often with Martin and Johnny. Tom Miller is pretty high, maybe one hundred feet.

Coming. Close, close, close.

Trying to beat it, I jumped down from the boulder and ran up the rutted stone trail to the limestone overlook and watched it come. Riding, *gliding* on top of it was a large, pointed shadow. I glanced up to see what kind of cloud made that shape, moved that fast. Nothing in the sky but dawn's blue.

The wave rolled past. It lapped up onto the straight-edged shorelines. The water swept over jutting docks, leapt up and collapsed onto the golf-green yards, the water's-edge swimming pools, the driveways and outlooks where cocktail parties were had.

It just rolled by—so quiet. The shore got wet, the docks rose and fell, nothing broke, no noise.

On it went toward the bridge with the line of smoke fingering the sky like calligraphy.

As that wave came, I noticed a balding man across the lake walking out in his tighties. Skinny guy, knobby knees and elbows with a pot-belly. Stood out in his yard with his arms crossed. The water spread across his grass and must have inched to his toes because he backed up a step.

Here's where my heart begins to race.

I'm really wishing I'd not come up here to toke as I told myself I needed to stop doing. Mr. English knew I was habitually smoking. He brings out the truth in me, even now, as I talk this book out, the very act of doing this the only thing keeping me sane.

His body looking the size of an apple stem from way up here, the man lifted his chin to look up at me. When his face locked on to mine, he waved at me real excitedly like a little kid who recognized me and was about to go down a big slide. Kind of a hey, watch me! I could just make out his smile. It was grotesque and wild and I turned my face away.

What I saw fifty yards up the path was what looked to be a purple-green (scaly?) firehose being pulled into the brush, a hose that tapered and ended in a black tip that swayed and flicked before it disappeared. Much like a tail.

I blinked. I swallowed hard.

When I looked back down at the man, he was returning to his house. I'm staring down at his yard and thinking, *what the hell have I just seen?* when I hear a pop and see a flash in the grass. A firework-sounding pop that echoes up the ridge. I know it's a gunshot, having been out with Martin pheasant hunting twice, neither time liking it.

That flash in the grass, that faraway pop. It came from that guy's house.

Granted: a little high, but not stoned. The weed's not that good. Stuff me and Bastian grew ourselves and we don't know what we're doing at all. Yet I'm reeling. Did I just see a twenty-five-foot-long tail belonging to fuck-knows-what slither into the cedar pines and that man way down there wave at me and then go inside and shoot a gun? Did I just hear that huge sound at daybreak?

That sound. The thing swelled, crescendoed, then wound down beyond hearing, yet I knew it didn't stop. It had moved on. Like a siren, turning its blare at you, then away. Like a wave.

Car wrecks happen on bridges. Emergency sirens come with rush hour. But this rolling, shadowed wave? This waving dude? His gun's report. Indeed, what did it report? It reminded me very much of a race's starting gun.

Oh, how prescient. Because I haven't stopped running since.

AND THAT WAVE? A TINY tsunami, the aftershock of a giant heave. But I hadn't felt an earthquake. Even if that was the cause, how in the hell did that wave come here from the sea? All the way up the Colorado, hundreds of dammed-up miles?

How would I assume it came from the sea? It just felt that way. No matter how improbable it was for me to be standing at Mount Bonnell in Austin, central Texas, to have experienced what I did, I did. And something deep within me knew—down there in the "mandala of my solar plexus," what Mr. English called it, my visceral reaction—it came from the sea. Every instinct cried out that truth.

IT DID. IT CAME FROM the sea. I know, sounds like a fifties horror film. But what proceeded was exactly that, and worse because it didn't end, hasn't ended, the terror. The not knowing, which is so much worse than knowing. Things being over, as awful as the over is, is the better place to be. I know that's true if I know nothing else. Because right now I really don't know what's going to happen to me, but I know it's a when, not if. And that's the terror.

I WASN'T LATE FOR SCHOOL, but a tight panic in my chest made me feel like I was late. The eeriness of faraway sirens and the otherwise quiet of the mountain pervaded, spooked me, and I grabbed my bag of shake, stuffed it, my lighter, and pipe into my pockets as I ran past the viewing platform to the stone stairs.

I remember looking at my watch, 7:47, and I thought: airplane preparing for takeoff. That's what I did. One hundred limestone stairs, burnished by time and many soles. Flying down those steps two at a time, my hand on the rail running down the middle, a canopy of oaks forming a tunnel which would lead me down into another world, my life as I knew it not only altered, but erased.

Normally, in a half hour or so, people, alone or breathlessly yammering with a friend, would be running these stairs. The moms in their tight lycras. Tourists mounting the steps, looking up to see how far they still had to go and would-it-be-worth-it on their faces.

These people weren't coming today.

I'd be hearing the marching band practicing soon. Hoped I would.

Whatever buzz I had acquired was gone, my adrenalized blood having overwhelmed the THC. I had to get home. Though it was my job to take Johnny to middle school and on the way pick up his classmate Travis, a nice kid but a confirmed nose-picker, this wasn't a regular day anymore. Friday's morning rigmarole no longer applied.

I RAN DOWN MOUNT BONNELL road to where my car was parked on a side street so as not to invite a cop's attention. I jumped in my beater beige Accord, fading and peeling W window sticker from however-many-years ago included. Martin had agreed to give me his car if I'd pay for the amount insurance went up because a man-child with a nascent brain was its driver.

The ignition keyed, I'm reversing, and immediately two police cars with sirens howling come whipping around the curve blowing by me. My heart thudded and rose in my throat as they came because of the old-world fears of being busted for having a baggie of shake and stinking paraphernalia on my person. So relieved when they blew past. Then it hit me why.

They ignored some kid who, because he got kicked out of marching band despite being the key trombonist high-stepping on Friday nights, has been smoking bad grass before school lately, twice a week. They're not stopping for that kid who works at the Dollar Tree to pay the man-child insurance premiums, that college-bound kid with the grades to qualify for automatic entry into UT, that kid with the sort-of girlfriend Kodie who also works at the Dollar Tree. Nobody of authority cares about that kid, won't ever again. Not after what happened at dawn the day of.

I SNAPPED ON THE RADIO and found news-talk, expecting to hear bulletin voices. What I heard winding through the tony Balcones neighborhood of wide yawning lawns was a jolly jingle for some auto collision repair company. Then another for Thunder Cloud Subs. On every station an ad. No music, no talk. Not even on NPR carrier KUT, or the classical station, both airing calls for fundraising. No programming, no content. All smiles and jingles and shaking the moneymaker, we'll be back in a moment after these brief words from our sponsor, nothing weird going on.

In my rearview came a massive Suburban with blackout windows. It swerved around me and gunned it up the hill and gone. I gulped, put two hands on the wheel, and drove over to the right a bit. Another blackened SUV did the same thing, but this one honked once, then jerked around me.

For a stretch there were no trees. I could see the whole sky. Though I didn't know what was happening, I knew it was bad and I wondered how catastrophes happened on gorgeous blue-sky days like this, autumn crisp and perfect.

At the first lighted intersection I get to, two cars are crumpled at front ends, steam hurling from under rent hoods, driver doors open. No drivers slumped in either car. As strange as this is, what's more strange is that I'm the only other car here, save for yet another police car which just blows by.

I pull over next to the coffee shop which is usually packed at this hour but which is deserted, no life but the neon blinking OPEN sign in the shape of a mug. I flip on my hazards and walk over to the first hissing car I come to and peer inside. The door chime dings and the radio blares a jolly jingle. In the other car, a yippy little dog with a studded collar snarls at me, hunching down and baring its teeth.

I considered the right thing to do here. Call it in? Nobody's even here. No crowd streams from the coffeehouse to onlook. Nothing. Just this growling dog who now leaps at me, its teeth and nails scratching the window, its spit smearing the glass.

Up the street I see a blue city bus parked at the side of the road atop the bridge crossing the MoPac expressway. Tall chain-link fencing curls over the pedestrian walkway.

Dueling jingles going, apoplectic dog. I blinked my eyes hard at that fencing. It's a couple hundred yards away and the sun is right there so I'm not sure, but what I think I'm seeing is something crawling, several somethings, crawling up the fence. From here it's just black dots advancing upward.

The way home is over the bridge so I run and jump back into my car and take off in that direction. In seconds I see that it's people—people probably from the bus, which I see has its doors open—climbing the fence.

Why in the hell are they climbing the fence?

This sight made my heart thrash about inside me like it wanted out, that it knew something I didn't yet and wanted no part.

I stepped on the pedal, mounted the hill, engine roaring. Ten of them, giggling and laughing. I remember how confusing that was. I remember my mind doing flips and thinking to myself that I'd smoked someone else's weed by accident and it was laced and now I'm seeing shit because this is insane, what I'm seeing. I jump out and yell up at them, "Hey! Hey!"

None look down at me save one, a woman in green nurse scrubs. She looks down at me under her armpit as she reached up to get another hand hold of chain-link.

The smile on her face, the wild glamour in her eyes.

I remember how bright and insane her lipstick was, as if she'd applied it thickly just before departing the bus. I can imagine her giggling and huffing with delight on the bus, looking with wonder out the window at the MoPac below, applying her lipstick, laying it on so hard that it smears and then she rolls her lips over each other to spread it and gives these big satisfied smacks when done and she drops the lipstick and it rolls on the floor to the front of the bus, following her under the seats as she shuffles to the door.

And I remember her wide eyes saying nothing but *yes!* Yes to what, I didn't understand. I guess the look on my face questioned her. She nodded exuberantly. She reached out her hand and her eyebrows went convex with imploring.

"Join us!" she yelled. The wind whipping her hair to and fro. She didn't implore long before she was scaling again, and about to reach the part of the fence that curls back over the pedestrian walkway.

"Hey! What are you doing?"

Over the bus rattle I could hear them struggling with effort. These people were not young. A few were not thin. A couple of the men wore cheap suits and Florsheims which slipped in the chain-link diamonds. The driver was up there too, fat ass swaying back and forth with each frenetic step up, arms shaking from the effort of maintaining his girth against gravity. Their determination frightened me. I couldn't wrap my head around what was happening. I didn't have time. Everything I did was a reaction and my heart raced and my head cleared from any concerns other than the right now. That's really where I still am today, except when I'm talking into this thing. I'm right now, past and future extending in both directions away from me, totally and equally unknowable.

They climb and I watch, shouting, asking what's going on, why. I ran to the bus door where I see a little girl, toddler age. She'd dropped her stuffed animal. I picked it up and tried to give it to her. She just looked at me.

That's when it really hit me. A mother climbing a fence over an expressway as her child stands abandoned in a bus door, the chug and exhaust of the bus and the expressway roar. This dead-eyed child.

I had come down Mount Bonnell into a nightmare from which I would not escape. That's what hit me with a flood of adrenaline flushing my brain and making me go a little weak in the legs, tingling at the extremities. I was in this now, whatever this was, until I was dead. Only then would it end.

I thought my life had sucked before—unsure if Kodie felt about me the way I felt about her; getting kicked off the marching band squad (we were to play the Macy's Thanksgiving Day Parade!); Martin riding my ass; Mom not caring that he's riding it, her disappointment in me; Dad two thousand miles away and caring even less; Mr. English so pissed at me that he's no longer pressuring me to submit my stories to journals; the SATs coming up; a stack of college applications on my desk.

But now I would learn what fear was, as one of the younger men got to the top of the fence and sat in a crouch above MoPac and bobbed up and down as if he were attaining the momentum to—

No.

(I didn't yell it. I thought it: *[no!].)*

(Not a *no* for this man. A *no* that feared what this act meant.)

— jump. Which he did. As if into a pool, a swan dive thirty feet down. He plummeted, I ran to the fence, heard tires screeching and I saw this man faceplant into the windshield of a swerving car. A doll crumpling, tossed, and car pulped.

Yet the rest of them kept climbing.

And a police car raced past this scene, too, followed by big black Suburbans, a black helicopter tracing the sky above them heading in the same direction.

Then it's the nurse who manages to get on top, having scratched herself bloody on the fence's metal. She sits like a gargoyle right above me on the rounded top of the fence, bobbing in pre-dive. I shook my head fast, called out *no* and *why* and I cried out a wordless cry. She looked down at me and smiled that bright red smeared lipsticked smile, mouthing to me while vigorously nodding, *it's okay, it's okay.* Then she lifted her chin proudly, her eyes scanning the horizon, and jumped.

Tires screeching with temerity and the metal crunching. I vomited.

Remembering back now, what made me vomit was the sound that came from her as the first car hit her. It sounded like she had been punched in the stomach. Just had the wind knocked out of her. *Whuh!* Because I didn't watch. I had turned my head and closed my eyes, but when I heard that sound along with the thud of her meat and bones slamming onto the vehicle. My mouth rushed with salt and I threw up and in there somewhere I cried but sucked it up quick.

THOUGH I DON'T REMEMBER MUCH after that until I got to my street, I do know that I had no qualm leaving that toddler. I left her on the MoPac pedestrian bridge, standing there continuing to watch the space in the blue autumn sky where her mother had just been.

I do remember the cemetery on the way home, the big one where Michener's buried. The blond rays cutting through the trees to spotlight groupings of markers, the obtuse slants of the headstones' shadows. And, though I thought nothing of it at the time because I was hauling ass home with more on my mind, now I remember seeing children meandering around in the parking lot of the little Montessori school across the street from the cemetery. Johnny went there for a couple of years. It's a seventies strip mall converted into a school. Shops became classrooms. Oftentimes I saw them being led to the playground by their teachers, all walking in straight lines along the breezeways.

But this morning there weren't any teachers. The kids wandered around the parking lot looking dazed. The line of cars by the orange cones where the kids get dropped off stood still. An Odyssey had on hazards, the auto-sliding door wide open. A motionless woman's arm hung out of the window of a silver Volvo midsize SUV.

MY STREET WAS PARTIALLY BLOCKED by a garbage truck. Being Friday morning, the city trucks should be rushing through the neighborhoods, their breaks squealing, their motors roaring, but this one on my street was stopped in the middle, its huge robotic arm frozen mid-grab. The doors of the truck were open and that beeping noise came from it. I could just squeeze by, my tire scraping the curb. As I got even with the truck's cabin, I slowed. On the CB I heard a man's voice screaming through static. I slowly slalomed down my street around felled trash containers, my teeth set on edge at the static-laced screams. Countless asynchronous sounds of car and home alarms filled the morning air now.

In my car, the radio jingles had finally given way to someone speaking. The guy who normally read the morning headlines did so again but there was a personal, conversational tone to his voice. I turned it up. He said, something has happened this morning…everybody, something is definitely happening…this reporter can't even begin to tell you what and I don't even know if any of you are listening, or something like that. Then he said, "But something dire has befallen us and it isn't just happening here in Austin. My station crew isn't here. It's just me. I don't know where to begin and frankly I think I'm going to have to go. All I can tell you is that I've received reports that people are dying, and that there are mass numbers of accidents occurring, and, we, I don't know if this is some sort of biochemical attack or a fast-acting virus…so this is probably my last broadcast for some time. I'm so sorry. I don't know what else to say." And that was it.

Way up the street I see this man in gray coveralls and yellow reflective vest. A trash guy swaying curb to curb. I drive up slowly. He turns his head and there's a rill of blood running down his face, staining his coverall, bright on his reflective vest.

I asked if he was alright. My heart surged and snagged as I waited for the limping, bleeding, large garbage man to either answer me or lurch in my direction with his hands outstretched.

What I really waited for in those seconds, I know now, was the smile. Would he smile or not.

"Yeah, I just…hit my head. I got to get home. Don't feel well." He stopped walking and I stopped my car. "You know where home is?"

"Yours?" I said out my window.

"Uh-huh. Mine." His voice, I remember, was higher in register than I figured for his size and it sounded injured. He was alone. Where were the other trash men?

The one good thing about him was that his eyes weren't wild and he wasn't smiling.

"No, sir. I'm sorry, I don't."

"S'okay. I'll find it. You need to go find yours." He lifted his arm to point ahead as if he knew my home was down the street. He took a step closer to the car and I got a good look at his face. At the corners of his mouth, a white congealed spit seemed to keep his lips from moving fluidly. A step closer and I could see that the spit almost looked like webbing. When he spoke, his lips slicked with blood, it spread and striated but held fast.

"You need to get home." Close now, his breathing was stertorous. He sweated profusely. And though there was no glee in his eyes, they were wide and white with suffering.

He reached inside and patted me on the shoulder and he said go on as if a finish line lay ahead and I was almost there but that he would never make it. I drove on, my house just up another two blocks. In my rearview mirror I saw the trash man bend over, hands on knees, shaking his head side to side like he adamantly told the street no.

EVERY TRASHCAN TOPPLED INTO THE street. Five houses before mine the man who I only knew as a retiree living alone stood stock-still in his robe holding his bundled newspaper in both hands. His front door gaped open and his head turned with my car as I passed. He didn't move but for his head. The cool autumnal breeze that had whipped the nurse's hair ruffled his robe around his legs. After passing him, in my side mirror I saw he still looked at my car, jaw agape, unmoving.

A fully dressed woman lay flat on her face in the yard across the street from my house. God, it must have been Mrs. Fleming. I couldn't remember what she did, I want to say something at UT, maybe in the Spanish department? That doesn't seem right. She tutored me in Spanish some in grade school. She left for work at about seven forty five every morning. We'd always exchange waves as I left at the same time. It looks like she was walking to her little grey wagon like she does every morning, keys out, and collapsed facedown in her yard. One of her legs was bent at the knee like she was taking a nap, but her arms weren't visible underneath her. Her purse lay a yard past her head. Her woolen skirt flapped up onto her buttocks revealing tussled, and soiled, undergarments.

Any other morning I would have run over to see what was wrong, or I would have run into the house and yelled out at Mom that something was wrong over at the Flemings'. But this morning...everything everywhere was already wrong so yelling about one thing across the street seemed pointless.

My concern then was what would be wrong at my house.

Mom and Martin were used to me being out of the house early on Friday mornings because they're game days (today is homecoming), and the marching band always got together before school on early Friday mornings to practice new routines. In this case, it was the one we were going to do at the Macy's Thanksgiving Day Parade. Mr. Yancy, the band director, was all excited and so were we all. We didn't mind early rehearsals while having New York on our minds.

But I haven't told Mom and Martin that I've been kicked off the squad. To keep up appearances, and delaying reality, I got up early and, instead of just going to sit in my car somewhere as I've done the last couple of Fridays, I got it in mind to drive up to Mount Bonnell. I had to tell them and was going to today because I knew Mom was trying to get time off and book a flight and hotel. Not Martin, though. He was to stay in town with Johnny and said he was going to watch on TV from his folks' place on Thanksgiving. I doubted he would. He'd make a point to watch the pre-pre-game football nonsense, grown men in suits tossing the ol' pigskin around a studio-sized gridiron, yucking it up like the overpaid idiots they are. But I knew Johnny and Grandma would sneak into the back room to watch.

I got up early and made like I was going to band practice but instead went up to Mount Bonnell to smoke my crappy weed.

This is why I got kicked off the squad. The crappy weed.

Mr. English was not only my AP English teacher but he was also my advisor, so when Coach Numbnuts had me by the elbow in one hand and my pipe in another as we marched into his office, his face fell, more from fatigue than from disappointment. A little of both. Maybe disappointment that he had to deal with such petty little things instead of revising his big important novel.

Coach Numbnuts is a moniker Bass first applied to Assistant Coach Weir. There was this Oklahoma-committed lineman who declared kicking off was easy and that kickers were pussies. Numbnuts gave this lineman several chances to kick off at practice, each one shanking like foul shot from the sky. The last hit Weir in the balls so hard that he fell down and didn't talk much the rest of the season.

We were all trying to work it out, but as of now I was off the squad. Maybe, just maybe, I could get back on. Numbnuts wasn't so mad much as he said his hands were tied. If he didn't report the incident, he'd be fired. The incident: He found my reeking pipe in the pocket of my jacket in the locker room in front of my locker. The jacket didn't have my name in it, but he stood on the bench in the locker room before practice and held the jacket up in the air and threatened to cancel our parade trip if somebody didn't fess up right then.

His hands were tied.

I fessed up.

THIS IS WHAT I'D HOPED to see: Mom's and Martin's cars gone and Johnny on the porch with his backpack waiting for me to pull up to take him and his nosepicking friend to school. But Mom's car was still there, and Johnny wasn't, and if I wasn't scared before, and I was, now it was official and now it was really real because as out of touch with my family as I'd become, it, whatever was going on, had touched my family, my home. My bowels got heavy and that awful adrenal buzz hit me again. Johnny wasn't there waiting for me with that put-out look of his. A look I now wanted to see more than just about anything.

I pushed open the ajar front door. It creaked and moaned in a way it never had before. I remember thinking at that time of acute stress that this was a joke, the creaking door, somebody's putting me on.

Please somebody say they're putting me on.

Martin's always out the door before me, off to his job as a commercial real estate inspector. When the economy dove in 2008, he started his own business. You had to give it to Martin; self-made. An asshole, yes, but a formidable salesman. Maybe his assholishness paid dividends there. Type A personality. A for Asshole.

So Martin wasn't there as expected, his car gone. The silence of the house on a busy fall Friday morning jarred me. And the overall tenor of the house, the darkness, a pall over everything. That morning it felt like the very air carried an extra charge, that in it floated newness, stardust. Something was wrong here and I braced against what it could be.

It's not a big house, a well-appointed fifties ranch style, original wood floors throughout, with three bedrooms, two baths, an open galley kitchen great for entertaining (talking in Martin-speak now), newish deck, updated windows, a utility room and mudroom off the kitchen boasting a big yard for midtown, enjoying a canopy of large old live oaks and cedar elms.

Martin, a couple glasses of wine in him before dinner, told me he'd bring me into his inspecting business, it was going so well. Hmmm. Let me think long and hard on that one, Marty. He hated it when I called him Marty. He glared, took a pull on the white he and Mom drank before dinner 2.5 times a week.

My eyes found items on the entryway table. Yesterday's junk mail stacked for trashing. A half-full coffee mug, probably Mom's because Martin took a stainless tumbler with him like a toddler does a blankie. Mom's phone.

I make my way down the short hall, going straight to Mom and Martin's bedroom, bypassing Johnny's closed door. I flip on the hall light because though the sun is up now, this hall is dark. Way darker than it should be at eight on a weekday. Usually the house is an absolute hive of commotion; Mom's hairdryer whining last-minute, me and Johnny quickly pulling on clothes, brushing teeth, scarfing down something passing for breakfast, news radio on.

I could hear the clock radio through the bedroom door. Probably the fall pledge drive woman on public radio, talking gravely into the microphone. Nothing about making their fundraising goal for the eight o'clock hour. I stood outside the door and welled up, thinking about Mrs. Fleming laying in her yard across the street. Would Mom be sprawled on the bathroom floor under the glare of its lights?

I knuckled the door open. A wedge of bathroom light fell into the room, against the unmade queen size. The radio woman saying she didn't know what to say ladies and gentlemen it's beyond words. A snatch of curled black electrical cord lay on the floor in the bathroom doorway. The hairdryer cord.

I gulped and dashed to the bathroom. Empty. I checked the space between the bed and the far wall. I sighed short-lived relief as I remembered that her car was still in the driveway. Panicked, I hurried out to the car to see if she was sitting inside having gotten farther than Mrs. Fleming. But it, too, sat empty.

I quickly went back to Johnny's room. I envisioned him curled up and snug in bed under his red Manchester United bedspread, his life-sized precision-cut vinyl poster of Wayne Rooney looming over him. Wayne's eyes are closed and he strikes the messianic pose he executed after his famous (in football circles) 2011 bicycle kick goal against Manchester City.

I opened the door and flipped on the light, my heart absolutely pounding to where I almost couldn't catch my breath. He wasn't there. The room exuded the afterburn of exhausted energy.

I swallowed hard, yearning to have a reason to say a version of what I always did: *It's five 'til, dude. Forget breakfast. Gotta shit and get, go get Nose Gold. His Mom'll wig if we're late.*

On the floor at the foot of his bed stood a pile of athletic balls: a base of three basketballs and a few flat soccer balls, a found cherry ball, a couple of volleyballs, a bunch of tennis balls grayed with age and weather, a few of Martin's yard-putter golf balls on top, the whole thing forming a pyramidal shape two to three feet high. I didn't give it any thought. Just some silly thing he'd constructed out of boredom.

Not weird at all for him, really, with all the sleepwalking he'd been doing over the summer, coming into my room with his hands behind his back and mumbling. My head would hurt each time, a pounding above my right eye. Sometimes I could make out what he was saying: *coming coming…close, close, close.* His somnambulism eerily coincided with the vivid, recurring dreams I'd been having. One time I woke up suddenly to Johnny standing, seeming to hover, over my bed. I was so startled that I cried out. In glassy-eyed response he'd said, "It's only me, brother. No other." When I told him to get out, he peed down his leg. This scenario repeated itself several times last summer. One stretch in June it was every night for a week. Every night: *It's only me, brother. No other*, in this mellifluous voice.

Though at that moment I felt pulled in several directions, the urge to find my brother tugged hardest.

Through the window I could see Mrs. Fleming's skirt flapping in the increasing wind. It looked like she'd keeled over from a heart attack. We felt well-versed in sudden heart attacks as Martin's father had died of one on Martin's forty-sixth birthday. The candles had been lit and the song had been sung and then the phone rang and Martin had said, "Ignore it, I'm blowing out my candles here." Then came the hectic message on the machine. Martin had a glittery conical birthday hat on. Smoke rose from the wicks.

Vehicular emergency sirens wax and wane, the day brightening into full morning now out the window.

Johnny gone, Martin gone, Mom gone, and out the window the trashman staggering down the street, his bald head a cap of blood, the edges of it looking like melted wax oozing down. The radio woman's voice muffled and caught.

I tried the TV but the cable was out. Mom's phone at the entry table, I decided to try her at work. Sad to say that at that moment I didn't even think to call Dad. Dad was too far away to help and it was in that moment when I fully realized that physical proximity may be the most powerful relationship element of all. Just how simple it all is.

My room was neat as always. Stacks of paperback pulps and dreadfuls I'd digested stood along the far wall like columns. Bed as I'd left it, made and taut, if not to military hospital standards.

For a burgeoning pothead with extracurricular activity attendance issues whose de rigueur look was rakish longish hair and post-ironic T-shirts from Goodwill and whose public posture and gait was meant to suggest slack casualness, in other words, *cool*, my room, my school lockers (my jacket on the locker room floor really chapped my ass because that sort of disorder was not me), all my spaces, are tidy and organized. My phone sat on the desk next to an SAT prep book. It's here and not on me because I'm not one of these people who needs to be tethered to the device jacking us into the matrix all the damned time. Or maybe I'm just aping Mr. E. I had started ostentatiously leaving it on my desk for Mom to see should she lean in to glance around, as all Moms do, every day, we know.

Wind busts on the window, a low-hanging tree branch dips down to scrape the glass. I stiffen, rub my sweaty hands together. I pick up my phone. The messages are from Kodie and Bastian. Kodie's text from twenty minutes ago—WHERE ARE YOU? MEET ME AT DT ASAP. Bastian's—WE'VE GOT TO GET OUT MEET ME AT TERRAPIN STATION. My throat flushed with adrenalized blood.

*She's out there stumbling around with something going wrong with her mouth or there's nothing wrong with her mouth because she's smiling and...*I couldn't believe I had those thoughts. Especially about my own mother, but I guess that's the thing about the survival instinct; you start distancing yourself quickly. No time to cry, knowing that the time for that had to be later if the now was to be survived. Like, I guess, if you're a soldier at a battle line and in the concussions all around, you fail to notice that the guy next to you is still, and when you turn him over he's got no face, you don't break down right there and weep. The urge just isn't there because you want to keep your face.

Urgent texts from Bastian and Kodie were not what I needed right now. I needed to know that Mom was at the hospital where she worked as an administrator, that she was about to sit down and do some administrating after blowing the heat off the top of her coffee, glancing at the desk photos of her life, then the blinking cursor and somewhere deep inside smiling that she had this job in this place she knew so well and maybe even she believed she was doing some good in the world. I'd only heard from friends. I needed to know that the grown-ups were in charge, and, though Mrs. Fleming lay face down in her yard, emergency vehicles yet to arrive, the adults would take care of things. The shit had hit the fan and hit it hard, but, eventually, the grown-ups were out there Working On It. That they were Taking Care of Things.

But they were in their yards, facedown. *Cara abajo.*

All I had on my phone were texts from a fourth-string football player and the girl who I think I'm in love with. Yeah, it's love. Even then I knew it was. To think, two weeks ago, I had sex for the first time, I was practicing for Macy's, and clocking in at 1250 on my SAT practice tests. I could smell victory in my life.

Mom's work voicemail. Her voice sounding clear and upbeat—I can see her at her desk with her clipped-on ID card, JANICE MARCH, her long brown hair greying at the temples contained by the tortoise headband she always wore at work, her large brown eyes narrowing at some item on her screen and having to lift her reading glasses to her face, wearing a shawl because the office was always so cold—a mother in the prime of her life, her offspring growing up around her, her daily work meaning enough, her mate companion enough.

If my brain wasn't bathing in chemicals fire-hosed on so as to increase the chances of my body's survival, I wouldn't've caught the emotion in my throat at hearing her voice. Instead, I left a perfunctory message she'd never hear in a strong assertive voice. Pretending to be communicating with Mom soothed, if only for seconds. "Hi, Mom. I know you're probably just getting in but, give me a call back when you can."

I put my palms on the windowsill, nose pressed against the glass, steaming it in expanding and ebbing blooms as if each contained a thought which got sucked back into my mind. My face went placid staring out across the street.

Mrs. Fleming lay in her yard. Flapping skirt. Mom lay somewhere, a yard, a stairwell, a street. I whined and fought back tears. Burst out with it, once. Emergency sirens lowing in the distance where tires squealed.

I wondered if any of those squeals were made by Martin. This guy I've been forced into knowing. Sometimes I like him. Sometimes I don't. I'd say it's a mutual tolerance borne out of love for Mom. I love my brother even though he's half Martin. Sometimes when Johnny says *Dad* my emotional wires cross and fuzz with smelting heat and break apart because Johnny belongs to me and Martin doesn't. There's that split between us, and that split always causes me pause.

WANTING TO TRY MY LAPTOP in the other room, I started to walk down the hall. I was going to catch the coverage of the world coming apart online. Finally, I'd get at least some answers, see somebody, even if only on a screen.

And then the rumbling.

The family pictures on the hall wall clattered. In one, Johnny's missing teeth, Martin's less sunken in and with darker hair, that wheelin'-dealin' smirk and bullshitty gleam in his eye. Mom's hand is on Martin's shoulder, her wedding band sparking in the flash. The photographer kept saying *stand over by Dad, no, no by your* Dad, *there, over* there, *stand over there* and I said no. Unexpectedly, Martin had smiled. Maybe he was pleased that I stood my ground on that blue drop cloth next to the light umbrella. Rarely was he pleased with anything I did. But in that mall studio, an infant wailing in the waiting room, Martin was pleased.

The rumbling. I thought of the wave down the river and sounds that preceded it. Was that all this was after all? Aftershocks of some fracking-induced earthquake?

The waving bald man, the jumpers, the bleeding trashman, cops careening past.

Mrs. Fleming's flapping skirt.

That scaly tail's slither into the brush.

Earthquake? Yeah, right.

The low rumble got louder and the house shook.

I heard something in the rumble. A high whine. Mechanics gone wrong.

I dashed outside against all logic to see that what made this horrible sound was a machine losing its battle with gravity. There in that blue sky came a transcontinental jetliner with its nose pointing down at an angle too severe to be anything but crashing.

It came from the north and was going to crash in our neighborhood. I understood the phrase "deer in headlights" because I just froze. This behemoth hurtled at me. I say hurtling but really it was weird how slow-moving it seemed, how destined. It boomed and shrieked as its gossamer shadow passed over. I clamped my palms over my ears and winced and turned to watch it glide over the house. It got even louder then, the failing turbines shooting sound at me. I took my hands away in time to hear the ineffable crash and explosion, one, two, hitting me in the chest. I stumbled then righted. The fireball looked fake above our treetops.

I heard crackling but nothing else. No screaming and no emergency sirens pouring this way. Stunned on my heels, I watched the sky fill with black smoke, then the wind carrying some away.

My mind trilled, go see! But I knew seeing it wasn't going to change anything, that it was only more evidence of the old world falling away. The sky itself might as well have fallen with that plane.

The plane crashed because something has happened. I'd seen it in the faces of the smiling jumpers, heard it in the trashman's broken voice. I'd heard it in the sounds and saw it in the wave.

I didn't jog toward the site. I crossed the street.

I had to see her face. Her mouth.

I stopped in the middle of the Flemings' yard. Closer now, I could see Mrs. Fleming had fallen awkwardly, which meant suddenly, as the inside of one arm faced the sky as it should not. I couldn't yet see her face, only the tangle of her graying henna hair.

She and Mom did neighborly duties for each other like collecting mail and newspapers during vacations. They swapped baked goods around Christmas and she always seemed to know what was going on with me and Johnny, waving as she made her way to her car, yelling across the street in a real voice, not a fake singsong, asking how we were, how's such and such going. Yesterday she was carrying groceries in—the hatchback of her aging wagon open, an old Subaru replete with political stickers (strident, baffling, some in Spanish)—and she yelled across the street at me that she was going to be watching the Macy's parade, we all will. *Todos nosotros.* I had to get close, to turn her over.

So, I blocked it all out, her voice, her friendly waving, who I thought she was, and summoned strength and focus like I did in band. I marched over to her and, steeling myself, moved the hair back and turned her over in one fluid motion.

Her jaw hinged open.

I was here rather than watching the plane burn to confirm it: her mouth brimmed thick with white webbing-like material I'd seen on the trashman. The texture mucoid yet dry, like no substance I'd seen. It had a translucence, a sheen to it. Her eyes open, her mouth stuffed with this cottony webby yet shiny . . .

I stand bolt upright, aghast, my hand to my mouth like I didn't want it to leap into me though I knew it didn't leap, move from person to person like a virus, bacteria, a gas. It came from inside. Something already planted.

An interloper, a freeloader. It's there from the inception, at the conception. Always been there.

It's there as mitosis splits us, as cells amass in the womb, latent for eons, but now it's come out at the beckoning of the dawnsounds. Starshine-white. Crystalline shards, like some malignantly alive cotton candy issuing from the throat. I can say that with some assurance now, but even then at that moment I sensed—it came from, if not far far away…a long time ago.

Though at the time I didn't stand there to ponder it—doing that at night when I can't sleep, listening for them.

"Don't do that! Don't you touch her!" a voice bellowed from the cracked door. Half of Mr. Fleming's face, a frantic eye. He jerked his hand at me once like shooing a fly. "You get away!" His voice feral.

"Mr. Fleming! Do you know what's going on?" My voice ricocheted and didn't sound like mine with that hysterical break in it. I took a step toward him.

He closed the door more, leaving only inches through which to yell. "You stay back! I've got my gun here." He tipped the barrel he gripped with his fist into view. "Loaded."

"I'm not . . ." I remember I didn't know what to say. I felt accused and didn't understand. I backed up a step and put my hands up in a defensive posture.

"You're not what, son? Responsible? Jesus Holy Christ." I'll never forget that because it confused me then as it confuses me now. Though now, I must admit, I do see maybe what he meant.

"Honestly, I just got home to pick up Johnny. I don't know what's happening."

His eyes scanned down to his wife. He stopped blinking and stared as renewed shock poured over him. His face was ashen and slicked with sweat. I waited for him to cry out. He looked back up at me. "I took today off. Woke up later than usual. Becky'd gone off to work. Then the exploding texts… then the TV…then I got my gun. Then I looked out the window." He nodded down like at a struck animal on the highway. "Saw her."

"I haven't seen TV yet. The radio's not been specific."

Mr. Fleming looked above my head at the smoke from the plane, rubbed his nose with his hand. He still wouldn't open the door. "Yeah. I'd say that's the gist of it. Nonspecific. Lacking in specificity." He chuckled.

Amidst the chaos of downed-plane-nearby and dead-woman-on-the-walkway, that Mr. Fleming said this calmed me a smidge because that's something he would say.

Martin didn't much like Mr. Fleming—so I did, by default. I'm sure Mr. Fleming never knew nor cared. Martin didn't think twice about announcing this dislike to us. Often he stood at the window, curtain parted with one hand, coffee in the other, watching his neighbor doing something as benign as mowing the grass, saying *what's that asshole up to now?* Martin didn't like him for the same stupid reasons people forever haven't liked each other. He assumed the other guy thought he was special and resented him for it. What made Martin think Mr. Fleming think he was so special, what made him think he was so *goddammed smart*, was that Professor Fleming taught at UT. Sociology, long-tenured, PhD. He tended his raised vegetable gardens with a big floppy hat Martin thought was *just precious*. A real homophobe, straight out of central casting. I mean, Mr. Fleming had been married for decades, had kids on both coasts. Sometimes the news interviewed Mr. Fleming as an expert on all things anomie—social media, texting while driving, little girls dressed like hookers, the starvation death cult they discovered out near Marfa last year calling themselves Breatharians.

So, when Mr. Fleming said "lacking in specificity," for a moment, we were talking like neighbors again. He the professor, me the befuddled kid.

"What?! What is this?" I demanded.

"TV's not happening anymore. It's happening that fast."

"What is?"

"I'd tell you if I knew. But don't touch her. Leave her alone, okay? I think the best thing you can do right now is go home and shut yourself in."

"How long has she been like that? Did you call nine one one? What were they saying on TV?" I was whining now, desperate to know anything.

He looked down at his wife and frowned, a commonplace frown you'd issue if your raked pile of leaves had been scattered by wind. I didn't understand it then. Now I do: he frowned at his wife's corpse because the sadness had become so absolute that his spirit was unable to do anything else. "Just all camera phone stuff. I didn't see any on-camera live footage. That's how fast."

"Footage of what?"

He paused. The constant faraway car and home alarms. "Listen, Kevin, I'm sorry but I need to close the door." He coughed. The look on the sliver of his face said pain and panic. He swallowed hard and looked back down at Mrs. Fleming. His chin quivered. His hand shook as with elderly palsy as he raised it to clutch his throat.

"Please. If whatever this is happens as fast as you say—" and I'm nearly crying now. I wanted to blurt out my guesses in staccato to him. Oh, I wanted, still want, to name this, put it in an airtight bottle, label it, put it on a shelf of logic.

"It is happening fast." The sound of a skidding car, a dull crunch-thud streets away. "Something black and awful. Nothing we've ever been prepared for or would have ever been able to prepare for. We couldn't have known this was a possibility." He coughed into his fist. "Something's happened, something's taken ahold now. It's just...death. I think it's extinction time, Kevin. I really do. But hell if I know what's causing it." He looked guiltily away. Something clouded his mind. "It's over. It's just...over."

This coming from a professor of sociology, it sounds official, confirmed. And in my heart I know he's right. But what about me? Am I going to die today?

I try but fail to not glance down at Mrs. Fleming's stuffed maw, her purpling skin. Swallowing hard, I say, "So it's happening that fast. I may not ever see anything about it because TV's out." I looked at him, beseeching. "I need to know. What did you see?"

He opened the door an inch more. "Only an hour or so. Total chaos on screen, at the newsrooms. Because they're not just reporting it. They're affected, too." I remember the wind dying down and hearing the roar and crackle of the plane wreck. "The first images were of whales on beaches. Lined up like rows of batteries, bleeding from the ears. Beaches in Mexico, Nicaragua, England, South Africa, India, Australia, Japan. Massachusetts. Down here at Matagorda Bay. CNN's running raw footage. Hardly any commentary. One woman, not even in makeup, a runner, an intern, was trying to report but she didn't stay on camera long. Shaking shots of people running nowhere. Staggering and grabbing their throats. And then scenes and scenes of people jumping from buildings and bridges. You don't even know what cities. There's no scrolling chyrons. They're not jumping from flames like on Nine Eleven. They're just jumping. People blowing their heads off with guns."

He looks down at his shotgun, back at me. "Anchorpersons only said 'we're bringing you this raw footage' and 'we're waiting for a message from the president.' Things like that. A static shot of the White House press room waiting for him. Minutes later the signal just dropped out. And then—"

"Professor Fleming, what'll we do—?"

"Go back to your house."

"Where's the military? The safe places? The contingency plans?" Panicked breathing.

"The military is made up of people. It's flesh. All that might means nothing in the face of this."

"This?"

"Go back to your house."

"But after that. What am I supposed to do?"

He closed his eyes and said calmly, "Go back to your house."

"You're a professor of...you know people. What is this? I have to know. A virus? A military thing gone wrong?"

"The world choking...and worldwide mass suicide at dawn, Kevin? I cannot conceive of a virus, bacterium, a gas..." He cackled with fright and wild hilarity. "It can't even be star monsters, or creatures wandering in from those other dimensions! *Those* maybe we could fight."

I didn't want to say it but I did. "End times? Biblical, Mayans, whatever?" A pause. "This white stuff?" As I waited for his answer, I viewed in my mind's eye the wave rolling up the river, heard the massive dawnsounds before that, the smiling faces under wind-whipped hair. The dark smiling teeth of my summerdreams.

He put a fist to his mouth and stifled another cough, his cheeks billowing out. "Heh. Pick a book. Pick a chart. Pick a pundit, a preacher, a Petri dish."

"But—"

"Does it really matter? It's over."

I stood there looking at him, felt his resignation. He sighed and didn't look at me anymore. He shook his head as if it was all just a damn shame. Glanced at his dead wife, then looked into the loom of his house like someone else was there. I could just hear him mumble into the room, "I dunno. I dunno. All ruined now. All done." He fell to a knee with a heavy thud, coughed haggardly, and closed the door.

I heard the dead bolt snap into place.

I expected to hear the shotgun.

But he was still there, behind the door, and I heard him whisper, "It needs you to need it."

I DIDN'T BOTHER TO GO in and help Mr. Fleming any more than I did scoop up that little girl on the Hancock Bridge. Sure, he'd locked me out, told me to go home, but I could've found my way in. But why? I knew: futility. I had to find my little brother, my friends.

WALKING BACK OVER, I TRIED calling my dad in Charlotte. He'd moved there just before I entered third grade. I saw him twice a year, talked to him maybe once a month. I don't even really want to talk about him much. He gave up on me, so I'll not give him much time here. He's got wavy brown hair, brown eyes, olive skin, thin, could eat anything he wanted and did without fattening up. Mom says I'm his twin, that I could pass for his very young brother. Apparently my dad, Nicholas March, was a looker, so I got from my mom, but that confuses me because I don't consider myself one. A looker. I think he just got bored with Mom. She aged, got matronly and provincial, he didn't. Simple as that. Though we kids never really know, do we? Gotta wait until we're adults, parents ourselves before we start seeing the world through their eyes. Guess I'll never know what happened. Like it matters.

Anyway, he strayed all the way to North Carolina. Now he lives with a twenty-nine-year-old woman (Mom calls her a girl) named Beth. She's nice. I'd even say "go Nick" if he wasn't my dad. I'm not into that being-friends-with-your-parents thing. Some of my friends' parents try to act all cool with us, like hang out with us and relate, and it's just an insult. One good thing about Dad: even though we didn't see each other much, when I went out to see him or he came to see me, he didn't try to be my buddy. He refused to be Good Time Dad. He tried to be a father. Stern and instructive, but not mean. That's what it felt like, anyway. I guess it doesn't make sense for me to say he gave up on me and then saying he tried to be a father. Like trying to make sense makes sense.

I pulled out my phone and called him, but nothing happened. I tried Martin's cell phone. Same thing. Texting. Anybody. Nothing goes through. The last ones I had were those two from Bastian and Kodie. When I couldn't reach anybody, couldn't get online, when no apps worked, nothing, I said, "Shit," and looked straight up at the sky.

I TRIED TO GET RECEPTION through the antenna on the old set in my parents' room. All snow except for one Spanish language news channel. It didn't come in clearly but I could hear voices and see some shadowy picture with heavy zigzags through it.

Some newsroom somewhere actually had a camera pointing at a newsperson. This man spoke Spanish which I took at school but he spoke so fast and the reception kept fuzzing so I couldn't begin to understand. He kept looking off camera and the camera kept moving. Once, the man got up from his chair and ran around behind the camera and you could hear him talking, consoling the cameraman who obviously faltered. The newsman gasped and called out, "*Antonio, Oh Antonio.*" The camera steadied.

"*Cerca cerca cerca,*" he muttered.

Back at the desk, he tried to compose himself. The reception cleared and steadied. He wiped sopping sweat from his brow with his hand. He said, "*Dios mio, es el final de nosotros.*" He crossed himself twice and kissed his knuckle and repeated "*El final el final,*" shaking his head. The guy sat alone in the studio. He lifted his head to a loud noise. "*Jesus Christo…El final*"— he coughed and grabbed his throat and got that look on his face. Pain and panic. "*Señoras y señores…me despido de ustedes.*" He got up and shambled off camera.

I left the TV on in case while I packed a backpack.

I got Martin's pistol and bullets from the closet. Though he did have a safe he kept it in sometimes, he didn't always. Martin had it stuffed in the back of his bottom drawer with his rattier T-shirts. While not exactly your rootin' tootin' NRA type, he did take his gun ownership seriously. He'd taken me and Johnny to the shooting range once and gave us the talk about how dangerous they are and how to use it and basically here it is, pop off a few rounds but then stay the hell away from it. Checking a box Mom had drawn for him. Same with the safe.

I dunno. Maybe I'm too hard on Martin.

I tell you, I'd give anything to see him now.

I held it heavy in my hand and stared at it.

I found Martin's nylon holster, strapped it on my shoulder and around my waist. It felt weird tucking the gun into its place. But I have to say, in sliding the loaded gun snug into its place not far from my beating heart, with all the horror happening and what I knew I'd come across out there, I felt so free right at that moment. Everything erased. Instead of total fear, right then I felt incredible hope. The guilt that came sidling along with that feeling I quashed by putting my hand on the gun butt just below my left armpit and looking out of Mom's bedroom window. Freedom. Newness. Not now, but soon. A fresh start.

Though I had survival to worry about, I had no other worries. Those everyday burdens lifted away from my head, my shoulders, and most of all my heart, the constant compression there unwrapped. The elation I felt forced a laugh from me. One big burst—*ha!*

My laughter came from the open-ended feeling before me, not from anything being funny. Shock and disbelief reigned. My parents were surely dead. The world, the human one at least, had broken apart. All in one morning, planes fell from the sky, billions of people leaped from high places, died of some fungal crystal coming in a slow upchuck.

I'd not been able to slow down enough to really think, to miss anyone. It's just been reaction, stimulus-response, fight and flight. Mostly flight. Running for your own life has left little room for mourning.

THE DOLLAR TREE IS IN a tiny strip mall on Burnet less than a mile away. The two stoplights on the way blink red. At first glance, nothing looks wrong except there's no traffic, kind of like how there's none on a 105 degree day on an August Sunday afternoon, nothing but spectral heat vapors rising from asphalt.

Way up on Burnet, a car rolls toward me. I sat at the blinking stop sign and watch the big older boxy Buick or Caddy. It looked like a drifting boat as it angled across the road going the wrong way against traffic, if there had been any. It runs up over the curb, hits the Hat Creek sign, and stops.

Nobody gets out. I remember thinking it's a rather benign apocalypse, all things considered. It's not just in T. S. Eliot's poem. This, in fact, *is* the way the world ends: not with a bang, but a whimper.

Then I think of the lipsticked smile, the little girl's vacant eyes. I think of the sound the nurse made when she hit.

Ends not with a bang nor a whimper, but a *whuh!*

I turned my head and saw a man dressed in dark clothing lying in the parking lot of the CVS. I stepped on the gas and turned sharply into the strip mall anchored by the Dollar Tree. I had expected to see bodies everywhere. I guess the dying went to someplace private to do it—that is, if they're not leaping from high places (with smiles on their faces)—like a sick dog will go off by itself to a secreted place to die. An atavism, something to be done alone.

You don't come into the world with anyone. I mean, sure, you're with your mother, but you didn't leap into life holding someone's hand, and you won't jump out of it holding anyone's, either.

I wish the experiences of birth and death were reversed. I wish we were more cognizant of being born. We get the full knowledge of our dying, unless it's so sudden that we can't, if we're struck by lightning or something. Another one of God's lovely mysteries at which we're to shrug our shoulders and utter *well, it's his will, not for me to wonder why.*

What. A bunch. Of crap.

Mr. Fleming had locked his door on me. Although I didn't hear the shotgun go off—for all I know it did while I watched the Univision guy say his last words before going off air—I know he went back in there to die alone. Muttering to the nobodies there in the living room.

Did Mom wander off to do the same? Felt the choking coming on and something within her told her to walk out of the house. Or...did she . . .? Oh, I don't want to think about that.

That first body, the body of a stranger in a parking lot, ratified and compounded the fear. Afraid of the unfolding circumstances, afraid that I wouldn't be mature enough, that I'd just crater with fear and ineptitude.

Kodie.

She texted me to meet her here. I work with her at the Dollar Tree. Doesn't matter what she's wearing, whether it's her standard black skinny jeans or her baggy Army-Navy store fatigues and Black Jack boots fully laced up to go with, or those same boots with a skirt, any skirt, well, let's just say I don't always ask debit or credit or say have a nice day because I am staring. The girl adheres in every way to the Euclidian Golden Ratio. And I don't just mean physically. She's in community college (studying to be a teacher or social worker) and likes Emily Brönte. A lot.

I'm not much on classics. She says I'm missing something and I say I doubt it. Customers watch warily as if a fight brews between us. When I tell her she's a pseudo-intellectual poser while we're restocking, she says the term pseudo-intellectual is used by pseudo-intellectuals.

"Why here?" I wonder out loud as I pull in to the lot in front of the DT's banks of glass. Here comes Kodie striding to the front door which is flanked by huge draping plastic jack-o'-lanterns with leering faces she and I hung up in the windows the last day of September. Her hair's dyed black but you can see the brown tint in sunlight. Half her head's shaved almost to the skin, the half that faces me when we work registers. Her sharp jawline and full lips really jump out in relief against the wall of hair hanging down the other side. A small nose ring graces a nostril.

Through the glass I see her cruising through the registers. She's carrying a baseball bat at its fat middle with one hand. She's stuffing something else in a deep pocket of her military cutoffs. She unlocks the door with her master key and smashes down on the door's crash bar. The sun reflects sharp on the glass. By the time I've closed the car door, she's on me. She hugs me so tight it hurts a little.

"You're okay?" She looks me up and down.

"Yeah. I'm okay, I think. Seeing you helps."

I squeeze back and lift her off her feet. When I do, first she kisses the side of my face then puts her mouth to my ear and with slow hot cinnamon breath whispers, "How's Johnny?"

I put her down and really notice her red eyes and a face that has been wiped several times over. "Gone. Not at home."

"Oh, God, Kevin." She stands with wide eyes, holding her elbows with her hands, smacking her cinnamon gum. "I don't know what to do."

"I don't either. Couldn't stay at the house." I couldn't tell her the reason was because I feared my neighbor across the street just might come calling with his shotgun.

Something was wary in the way she asked about Johnny. It let me know I wasn't crazy. Besides Kodie, a dying Mr. Fleming, the floundering trashman, the jumpers, the SUVs and flying cop cars, I haven't seen an adult. Not alive, anyway.

Was Kodie an adult? Nineteen. Old enough for war and voting. Probably not old enough to rent a car, but a motel room, sure. Those were legalities, business policies. The answer is: being an adult depends on the person. There's no bright line one crosses.

"Me neither." She spread her arms out, exasperated. "What the fuck!" She dervished round and round like the hills were alive, which was creepy because all you could hear were her boots scuffing the pavement.

Here we were on Burnet Road in the middle of greater Austin and I heard nothing but her boots echoing off the building. Glancing at the leering jack-o'-lanterns, I sensed my neck hair standing up and felt a chill.

I tried to shake it off. "I know, I know. Crazy. I don't . . ." I just wasn't able to articulate anything for the shock.

Kodie stopped twirling. In the silence of the strip mall parking lot, the fear came and I knew I had to keep it at bay or else I'd just drive home a capering mess and curl up on the floor. I couldn't do that, especially for Johnny. I had to find him.

Kodie tried to lighten things. "You know what I keep thinking of?" she asked with a nauseated chuckle. "How last week nobody had been in for an hour or so and you said it felt like the end of the world?"

I did remember. And we both had laughed and said that'd be cool. We can live free, no mindless job, no parents, no societal structure, total autonomy. We could feed ourselves from Whole Foods until the power goes, then we could shuttle food and refrigerate it at Barton Springs pool—assuming no roving gangs of the apocalypse, no sprinting zombies. Garden of Eden—*Here. Here's a cool apple for you, Kodie.* I'd pull one from out of the clever containing device I'd constructed in the spring-fed pool. And there would be no huge snake looming in the hoary live oak up the slope from the springs, its dark and bent malignancy reflected in the pool's calm—hissing, waiting, assessing the sin—and there would be no judgment. And Kodie would take a bite and juice would run down her chin and she'd smile. Her teeth glistening with juice, we'd both smile.

"Yeah, I remember. Freedom and all that."

"Yeah . . ."

"This ain't it."

"No."

"Do you know anything?" I asked her. "Woke up, got out of bed, dragged a comb across my head, and then.... " I snapped my finger.

"I was lying awake in bed, the sun up, when I heard alarms, sirens."

"Yeah, me too." I wasn't yet ready to tell her what I'd heard at dawn. I wondered if she'd heard the dawnsounds too and felt the same way. Because they are the sounds of insanity that if you admitted to hearing in the old world, you'd be told to get help, and if you refused, you'd be involuntarily committed.

But isn't that what those sounds asked of me? Committal? Involuntary... mandatory?

Kodie examined my face as if she knew the thing I hid. I broke up the momentary impasse with, "Your folks?"

"They weren't home. Car gone. I dunno. I tried calling and texting them. They have one car and ride-share to work usually. Early for them to be gone. Maybe…." She got lost in thought for a moment but shook it off. "Yours?"

"Same…but my mom's car is still there, her keys and phone by the door. Her hairdryer was on the floor but plugged in."

"Oh, God."

"Should we go try to find them?" We looked at each other. "Don't we know what we'll find?"

Kodie nodded, looked down, sniffed. Her chin muscle quivered. She looked up at me with moist eyes and nodded and said, "Yeah, we do," with mucosal thickness. "I've got to try to find them, though. I can't just…"

"I don't want that to be my last memory of them."

Silence.

Reality drilling down, striking rabbit terror which now bubbled up.

I prattled on like a soap opera matriarch glossing over profound familial injury. "Yeah. And that plane? You hear that? Crashed right behind our house. I watched it float right over."

"Man…"

"You see any media at all? I missed everything. Everything went down before…well, I did see this one guy on Univision. But that ended quickly."

"So…you don't know." Kodie said, not asked. She looked away in thought.

"Know? I know nothing. What is this?"

"Well, I don't know *that*, but for a little while on cable news they were showing camera phone footage. All over the world, Europe and Africa. Eastern seaboard, then Texas. Kevin, people were—"

"Yeah. My neighbor told me." I paused, inhaled. "I've seen that myself." Exhaled.

"You mean you saw people…?" Kodie lowered her voice and finished her question. "You mean you saw people…killing themselves?"

I nodded in eyes-closed solemnity.

"Where?" she whispered, loud and breathy.

I tossed my head in the direction. "Hancock Bridge over MoPac. You know, with the pedestrian sidewalk, that fence?" I put my palms together and made a discrete diving motion.

Kodie put her hand to her mouth and her eyes welled. "Into traff—" she stopped herself. Down to a clipped whisper now. "*Traffic?*"

This had to be a dream. Sure it was. I'd awaken and this would all seem a bizarro dream. I'm dreaming the world is ending because I've been kicked off the band squad and I'm stressing about the SAT and I'm stirring all that together with an increase in pot smoking and insomnia. Of course. I'd laugh and I'd tell Bass, "Dude, there were these fubar whalesounds at dawn, people foaming at the mouth and dying in their yards, people killing themselves with grins on their faces..."

Kodie paced back and forth in a five-step rhythm. When she pivoted away on the second pass, I noticed it. There, behind her on the parking lot cement, set so haphazardly that it said to me that this was no longer a parking lot but simply a surface on the earth.

They had been building out the strip mall to include a five-story apartment-condo. Lots of stone and brick and wood stacked around at the staging area there at the back of the lot. What I saw was made of some of the broken bricks and rocks, this little rounded pile, about two, three feet high, seven feet long. I hadn't seen it when I first pulled up I was so focused on Kodie.

My stomach went out on me, and my bowel did this shimmy-shift. Seeing it, I immediately looked over my shoulder at the CVS across the intersection, at the parking lot, where that dead guy was.

A neat pile of stones there now.

Wouldn't we have heard the stones clacking in all this quiet? That pile made me think about all the bodies.

All the bodies.

Kodie yanked me from my reverie. "You okay?"

"Yeah. I'm fine." Kodie saw my face and mouthed, *What?*

She already knows. Or intuits.

I asked her, "You? How do you feel?"

"I'm okay I think. It's all happened so fast. Seems like it would've hit me by now, you know? If it's infectious, or a gas, it's everywhere. I'm not feeling any different, physically that is."

Over her shoulder I saw Mi Victoria, the Mexican bakery where Johnny and I always got breakfast tacos. Mi Victoria likely had a cook in the kitchen dead on the floor from either choking on whatever-it-is or sticking his head in the deep fat fryer like he's bobbing for apples, that smile seared into his face. Mi Victoria wasn't cranking out egg and chorizos for the construction crews gentrifying the Burnet Corridor.

My head hurt right then. As it hurt in the summerdreams.

My face must have gone ashen because Kodie asked me in a panic if I was okay again, stepping to me and grabbing my wrist.

What disease *chokes you on glistening webby crystals? Quickly chokes you, like volcanic lava overflowing, too late to stop it once the seal brakes, and, oh, God, what* disease *makes you gladly commit violent sudden suicide?* "I'm fine, I'm fine," I said, straining to keep the reticent shake out of my voice. Reticent shake being another way of saying terror.

"You see that?" I lifted my arm and extended it slowly, my index finger rising to meet its target. Kodie turned around.

She froze, put a flat hand across her brow, a salute to block the sun.

"What is that?"

"Don't know."

"Was it there before?" Kodie asked.

"Don't think so."

What had she seen before she got here? Why was the door to the store locked when I pulled up? And why was she holding a baseball bat? Dollar Tree only sold Whiffle sets.

We heard a low boom far away which took our glances from each other and up to the middle sky. The sound seemed to have come from as far away as Camp Mabry off of MoPac a couple of miles west.

It sounded like a shotgun blast, or even something bigger. After September 11, 2001, Camp Mabry wasn't as open to the public anymore. I have no clue what weapons they have there. A mortar round? We didn't even ask each other if we heard it. It made our time in the parking lot feel like it needed to end, that lingering anywhere wouldn't do.

Kodie looked at me in agreement with what she saw on my face—the sense that we were exposed.

"How'd that…? How did we not…?" mused Kodie, her fright blooming. It felt claustrophobic even in this open, bright parking lot under that blue sky.

"Look." I pointed at the CVS.

She saw the pile now. "Kevin?"

"You didn't see it?" I asked.

"No. I've been at the back of the store."

"There was a man's body over there in that parking lot when I drove by. Now, as you can see, there's a pile of rocks."

Kodie crossed her arms, shot her hip, and furrowed her brow. She'd have looked cute as hell if I wasn't feeling ill with dread. Woo takes a distant back seat when the world's ending and you've got a gun strapped to your ribs.

We only did it the once. Rain slipping down her window, pattering the roof. Her folks were home but she lives in one of those garage apartments like you see all over Hyde Park. She closed her eyes and her lids fluttered. For me, much in life doesn't match the hype but that did and now I just think about Kodie all the time.

Kodie looked over at the nearest pile and kept her attention there. I stepped over to her and put my arm around her. "What are you thinking?"

She didn't answer. Kodie took a few steps toward the pile, hesitated, retreated back the same number of steps, keeping her eyes trained on it.

Kodie, detached, questioning her own sanity, "What's this covering bodies with rocks?"

She turned to the big jack-o'-lantern's grim rictus in the Dollar Tree's window, its brows screwed down in a scowl. Some things you can't continue to question, even when you want to. Some things just…*are the way they are.*

A memory of Johnny during one of his sleepwalks into my room interjected. "They're going to be waiting at the shore." He had flipped on the lights. He wore burnt orange Texas Longhorn PJs. I squinted. He didn't. "You think I want this? I don't," he'd said, more awake then. He burst out a single sob, swallowed it back and said, "It's not a task I want, Kevin, you have to know."

We stood stock-still. My throat and ears full and hot. I sniffed hard and spat far, shuffled my feet to keep from getting woozy. Kodie squinted in the sun glinting off the store's metallic sign. With one eye closed against the glare, she said, with maximum cool, "We need to get out of here."

I nodded.

Walking briskly to me, taking my elbow, she said, "We need information. We need to figure out what's going on. We need to try to find others."

"Food in the store," I said. We headed toward the door, agreeing that we needed to get inside and think, get this spooky exposed feeling off of us.

We had walked into the shadow of the store when we heard a man's voice behind us. "Hey! Stop!" The man in the big car that had struck the Hat Creek sign listed across Burnet, ran a tire up onto the curb, and came to a stop. His passenger window down, tinny music just discernable, his arm outstretched, fingers splayed like he's drowning.

Which he was. Drowning on pearlescent crystalline stuff that looks like home insulation. It sparkled like fake snow through its sheen. I found myself glued to the cement. Kodie too.

"Help!" the man croaked. The whine of the old car's door hinge. The radio jingle wafting across the lot to our ears, an Andrews Sister-like take on what to do when you need a sub sandwich. He had difficulty keeping the door open. He kept kicking it and it kept bouncing back and slamming closed. The jingle as background to his exit fit.

Under her breath, Kodie said, "Let's hold here for a sec. See if we can help him."

I didn't respond, fixated on the man.

The man made his way around the front of the car, bumping his hip, his face locked onto ours even as he stumbled over the curb. Choking noises came from him, sputtered and popped.

"Help," he scratched out. He lurched with one hand to his throat, one hand reaching out. You'd have thought the streets would be filled with such people, the near-dead stragglers choking and crying for help. Thing was, he's the only person up and down Burnet.

"I'm going," and I started jogging to the guy. I'm not sure why I headed for him. I couldn't watch from afar. It may be my last chance to see it, I'd thought. Turns out, I was right.

I reached him as he fell to his knees and grabbed his throat with both hands now. His sweaty face turned magenta. His eyes bulged. Something popped. The noise cracked loudly enough to make me take a step back, like you would when a firework's fuse has burned down but hasn't gone off.

And that's when the white cottony substance reared from his mouth, stopping at his lips. A ring of blood at the lips. Reminded me of the time Martin had me fill a few small holes in the wood around the house with that spray foam that puffs up and quickly hardens. On his knees, still just able to whistle in air, he looked like he'd just sprayed whipped cream into his mouth and was tasting it full and sweet before swallowing, that fun moment of being gluttonous and gross. I imagined him swallowing and wiping his mouth with his sleeve and exclaiming, 'You try!' The substance didn't smell as it effervesced from the man's throat. Coming from where? The stomach, the lungs? It was less bilious than airy. It seemed from those fractal bronchi, deep down beyond the microscope's vision.

He shook his head back and forth and gagged, drool slinging, looking like a diseased farm animal in its last throes in the shadow of a barn, not here in the parking lot of a Dollar Tree in the up-and-coming Burnet Corridor (Martin calls it BuRo, like SoHo), his eyes not really looking at me anymore. He reached into his back pocket, yanked out his wallet, and with shaking fingers marbling from oxygen lack, he tugged out a photograph.

Kodie joined me, bumping me aside. "How can we help? Tell us how!"

His eyes wild, his pallor hectic, scarlet lips working around the full mouth and spreading teeth, he managed to force out in a wheeze, "Pluh... eeshe!"

She took the picture and wallet from him as he collapsed to his hands and knees. He shook his head back and forth with rigor now. I looked over her shoulder. The wallet photo depicted a little girl with a natural smile posing with her chin on her fist, her elbow propped on a mound of blue cloth drawing out her crystal eyes.

"Your daughter?" I spoke loudly to him with a hint of disbelief, his daughter's beauty belying his homeliness. In my shock, I regarded this man as a specimen, not as a human to whom I could provide succor. Plus, I didn't want to get within arm's length of him. Arm's lurch.

But Kodie did.

His face to the cement, I could see he nodded. She squatted down. I followed her lead. He managed to lift his head, his face meeting ours. "She's here?" I took the wallet and flipped the flap up, showing the license through its window to him. His eyes swirled and rolled in their sockets and he coughed a cough that had nowhere to go, making his back recoil up into a hump where it stayed. He fell over. Upside down to us now, he pointed to the items in my hand, what was left of his life, and then his face froze and his arm fell.

We stared. Kodie, somehow burying her emotion, asked rhetorically if not clinically, "What is this in his mouth?" I shook my head. I couldn't tell her I thought that some transmission issuing from a black zone between distant stars called forth a process by which from deep in the lungs arose an ancient death mold.

"Wants us to find his daughter." I handed the picture back to Kodie. She inspected it, turned it over.

"Rebecca."

"How old you think?" I asked.

"Five, six. Her cheeks still have that rounded baby fat look to them."

The man's open car door still chimed and from the radio blared an ad that required the trumpeting of the University of Texas fight song behind what sounded like ex-football Coach Mack Brown's nasally voice.

The man's throat looked solid now, the stuff looking as though it had hardened, forming a cylinder from mouth through the throat and down into his body cavity. You could hear a cracking sound, like ice solidifying, or bones splintering. His face had swollen in the minute we'd been standing here, the substance still expanding and hardening.

"We need to at least try," she said. I thought of the little girl I'd left amid bus fumes. "Maybe she's there."

I looked at the license. "I know this street."

"I do too," she said. "It's near your house."

I inhaled a deep breath and felt the gun resist against my ribs. "My car."

"She's probably all alone. She could hurt herself."

We didn't go into the store. With this man dead before us, the notion of hunger didn't exist.

"Where'd you get the bat?" We drove in my car to the address on the guy's license. Lawrence Shields. DOB: May 16, 1969. DOD: minutes ago.

"Under my bed." Kodie eyed the streaks of plane crash smoke in the sky.

"You looked pretty tough walking through the store with that bat. All one-woman wrecking crew."

"Look at you." She pulled back my shirt to display the gun. Her smile waned from her eyes before it did her mouth. "You have bullets for that?"

I nodded. "Need to probably get more though." I banged my palm heel on the steering wheel. "I mean, can you believe this? My biggest worry, what? Two, three hours ago, was telling Martin about band and pot. Now I'm thinking I'm not nearly armed enough to drive through town. Funny, when the world was full of people I didn't even think about such a thing. Now that there's nobody left—"

"We don't know that."

"C'mon. You saw TV. You saw that guy just now." I flicked the driver's license against the wheel like a playing card.

"We don't know that for sure. It's a big world. Maybe there are big bands of people who went underground, were out on a remote island."

"This isn't a virus, not a chemical."

"How do you know?"

"I don't. Not for certain."

"Then why do you—?"

"Because it's pointless to think it's going to be okay. Having hope right now doesn't help us. We've got to survive and that's it. And we for sure don't need to fight about it."

Kodie crossed her arms over her chest in what would have been a huff in the old world. Now, driving through our neighborhood to check on some little girl we didn't know, it wasn't a huff. It was just an end to a discussion that served no purpose.

Reasons didn't matter. We were still here and the world howled with wind and emptiness. Trees bent over our car in the gusts and yellow live oak leaves shimmered down around us in a butterfly swarm. We drove through them at a funereal pace. I looked ahead at this October scene and wondered if there was anything more haunted than an empty backstreet without sidewalks, showering leaves, gutters packing with autumn's debris. Kodie asked, "Why are you driving so slowly?"

We left the Dollar Tree in a hurry but now, as we approached, my legs got heavy and my head swam. I remember time and space warping out of tune in those moments.

"I don't know. I feel like we're about to see something that's going to make all that's changed change just as radically again. I'm in no hurry to see it."

I thought about the long walk down the aisle to view my grandmother's body lying in an open coffin in front of the offertory. This was last year. I felt like a child of single-digit age, scared and unsure, the dreamlike quality of the moment dizzying.

Me and Ma Maw—Lucille to the world, my mom's mother—we were close. She'd lived in Round Rock, so I saw her a lot. She liked me to serenade her with my trombone, especially when I played The Saints. Boy, I could play that song. But she may have liked my stories and poems even more. Other than Mr. E, she's the only one I ever read them to. When I did, she'd say "oh"—and her eyes would be moist, her nose reddening and sniffling.

I never had the chance to read *The Late Bloomers*[6] to her, though. The one that wrote itself. Kind of like this, but that was, um, fiction. Glad I didn't write it before she was gone, actually. This was a story I wrote this past summer, a story based on vivid, recurring dreams of a dry June. We'll get to that.

Anyway, Martin, never deigning to get out of the car, would drop me off at Grandma Lucille's house and she'd cook for me. We'd watch TV and laugh and she'd always tell me how strong a person I was and that I'd be okay even though that man (referring to my father) wasn't there for me. Seeing her shrunken body lying on that puffed satin, her face darkened and turning inward, the brittle fingers of her hands clasped on her chest, I was so stunned and sick that I couldn't move. Mom had to urge me away with a gentle tug on my elbow.

That feeling came again under the faux butterflies of autumn. The street darkened with the shade of overhanging trees, forming a tunnel.

But for the passive act of driving, I couldn't move.

I was locked inside myself. Kodie touched my hand, like my mother did my elbow at the casket, and said under her breath, "I know."

---

6 A copy of this document is attached as Exhibit E

"You feel it too?" I managed to get out.

She nodded and gulped. "I feel sick. Here we are being pulled to this one little girl just because we randomly saw her dad die."

"Random. I wonder."

She let go of my hand and took one of those deep cleansing breaths one takes when they're next to speak to a large crowd. In my peripheral vision I saw that her hand shook before she swooped it through her hair.

"Tell me we should just turn around?" I asked when we pulled up to the house matching the address, my brakes whining. "Please?"

The house recessed back into a lot dark with shade. Pecans moldered in the yard, on the sidewalk and the metal roof.

I turned off the engine and we sat. The quiet growing around us felt alive and stifling. It forced me out of the car for breath.

Kodie got out and closed her door softly using two hands like she probably did as a high schooler when she got home post-curfew after mugging down with some dude. A twinge of jealousy came with that thought. Just a twinge, because as we walked toward the house, we heard voices. Kodie and I looked at each other with wide eyes. She accidentally popped a pecan under her boot. The small firework sound of it startled us.

The voices stopped. We froze. I felt watched.

So quiet. I almost preferred seeing the Hollywood zombie horde come tear-assing around the corner in high dudgeon at the sound of that crushed pecan. At least that was something we could see. We could run, repel them, something. But this quiet creep, this world devoid and howling.

Not knowing is the worst of fears.

It was then that I felt I was part of an unspooling narrative, one over which I had no control. The world had taken a strange turn on its axis and we'd become game pieces on a board.

The voices started up again and they sounded in unison, like a classroom of pupils reciting a lesson, repeating it. We tiptoed around the mines of blackened nuts along the sidewalk.

I clenched Kodie's hand for us to stop. I whispered into her ear, "Why'd you get that bat from under your bed?"

She carefully stepped to me and whispered, "These kids up the street I babysit, brother Eric and sister Sarah Jane, seven and five. They were standing in my yard looking in at me through the window. As I startled awake and sat up in bed this morning, they just stood out there still as statues, watching me, still wearing their pajamas."

Though we hadn't taken a step, the voices came louder. Something repeated.

Something chanted.

We peered through the windows. Nobody in the front room. I went to the door and opened it. Kodie had me by the hand. Their voices were many and metronomic. We made our way through the house, trying to land our footfalls in a heel-toe that would've been quiet but for the groan of the wooden floors.

We got to the hall leading to a back bedroom. The door stood open. A single bed sat shoved in the corner. One of the two screened windows was open a foot.

In the middle of the room in a perfect circle sat ten, twelve children, crisscross applesauce, knee to knee, boys and girls.

And now they all turned their heads to us in unison and now we could hear what they were saying. I felt my heart lose its rhythm and my face flush with the effort of getting it back. What they said in synchronicity was, *"They leap from high places with smiles on their faces."*

They locked their eyes onto ours and their moving mouths and jaws articulated it succinctly—*they leap from high places with smiles on their faces,* their tongues flittering and tripping on milk teeth soon to fall out of their heads.

I had heard these words before. In a summerdream? Graffiti? It was engrafted into my mind, but I couldn't place it.

They recited this several more times as we stood there unmoving. I was hardly aware of Kodie though she gripped my hand. Then they stopped and that new-world silence descended. The girl matching the photograph stood up. Rebecca's eyes didn't blink. They shone like blue moons. She wore a red knee-length dress tied around her middle with a wide band of white. She was peppermint with enormous icy-blue eyes and she asked coy and sweet, "Did you see my daddy?" A prideful raise of her chin.

Kodie and I nodded.

"He told you to come find me?"

We nodded. "He asked," I croaked, "he asked us to."

The little girl shook her head several times. Her hair fanned out and the curls in it rolled. "Well, you're tooooo late." It was an adorable laugh line from a sitcom, the baby of the family showing some sass. The laugh track should have boomed here. But nobody moved beyond the autonomic movement of diaphragms, an eye blink here and there. Each little face held the grimness of the cancer ward. The light from between dancing tree limbs moved on their faces. A pecan knocked on the roof and rolled.

Kodie tried getting on their level. She put her hands on her knees and bent forward, curled the hair of the long side around her ear. "Why are we too late?"

There was a beat of pause, then the children boomed, "*THEY LEAP FROM HIGH PLACES WITH SMILES ON THEIR FACES!*" as if such was self-evident. Their brows furrowed, their cheeks flushed. I thought I heard a guttural roil in their throats. If their ears could've flattened, they would have. In nature, you know when you're not wanted.

I actually felt my eyes dilate with fear. I don't know how Kodie was being so cool. The agitation in the air, their fear transforming into animosity, was palpable. My mind did the dirty math: twelve little kids, two late teens. They could take us. Yes they could, especially if the not-so-little boy next to me turned his head, clutched my calf, leaned forward and bit into my leg. And then if another one were to dash behind to shut the door…a death room. No one would hear us scream.

But it wasn't their number that bothered me. Not quantity, but quality. Their being was one of menace and strength, their might together exponentially greater than the mere sum of them.

I took a step back, away from the potential biter and into the doorframe. Just in case.

Kodie, hands on knees, ignored their awful chant and waited for Rebecca to answer. She possessed the patience of the sole schoolmarm, unflappable and resolute. "We know it's scary, what's happening. But if we all calm down and work together, it won't be so scary."

Rebecca looked at Kodie like an adult does a politician smiling at you with his hand out, like, *Okay, I'll play along, I like you, you like me, yes yes,* you'll *change things.* Rebecca's maybe six years old, and this is the look she gives. "Tell me, Rebecca, why do you say we're too late? We've found you. It isn't too late."

The room became so still it stiffened. The air itself attained a new property, went from gas to a semisolid, encasing us.

"But it is," said Rebecca. Her normal little girl's voice now. A voice that admitted that she was scared.

"No, Rebecca, it isn't. We can help."

"It is," she whined and stamped her Mary Janed foot once on the wood floor. She looked down at the floor at her feet like she was sorry. "It is."

The little boy right below me shot a glance inside my open shirt, fixed on the gun, then snapped to my face.

Then Rebecca said, "Too late for you."

Behind me, Johnny's voice. "Hey, Kev."

Surprised, not hearing him walking through the house, I spun around.

"It's only me, brother. No other," Johnny said in that dreamy voice.

"Johnny! Oh, thank God!" Just as I stepped toward him, several small hands pushed me into Johnny. I tripped over his leg into the hall and fell hard. The gun clattered to the wood floor and spun. The door slammed closed. I scrambled up.

Johnny now held Martin's gun flat in his palms and regarded it like it were a nonfunctional object. "What are you doing here?"[7] His eyes wide as saucers.

"J, careful with that. Give it to me."

He took a step back and turned the gun away from me, hunching a shoulder like he would after dinner shielding me from his dessert. "Hold on," he said.

I stood up and looked cross at him. "Johnny, give it back to me now. I mean it. If you don't, when we find Martin I'm going to tell him."

"Don't lie to me."

"I'm not lying."

---

[7] I didn't know what I was doing there, let alone what Kevin was doing. I have no memory of what happened the morning of. Seeing Kevin while holding my dad's glock in Rebecca's hallway is my first new-world memory. The sudden clarity, brightness, loudness of things stunned me. It was as if a thick wad of cotton had been extracted from my mind.

Through the door, "—Rebecca? What's wrong?" Kodie's concerned voice.

"My head hurts," I heard Rebecca whine.

The knob wouldn't turn. "Kodie, unlock the door."

"Rebecca? Boys and girls, can you help me? Rebecca's not feeling well."

Johnny. "You are too lying."

"C'mon. Give it to me."

"No."

"I'm your big brother and I'm telling you give it to me."

"—Kevin?" Kodie's voice from right behind the door. I could see the shadow of her boots in the inch beneath it.

"You okay? What's going on?"

"Kevin. Hurry."

"What? What is it? Can you not unlock the door? Johnny's out here in the hall and he's got my gun and he won't give it back."

"Kevin. I need you." Kodie's voice shook now. "The door won't open," she whispered. The knob toggled back and forth in slow, halting turns. I visualized her back to the door and her turning the knob awkwardly behind her. No sudden moves. If she faced the door and frantically turned and tugged, they'd pounce like vipers.

I tried it again. It wouldn't move. I laid a half-assed shoulder into it. Nothing.

The children muttered together, in unison, low-toned words I couldn't make out.

"Kevin...?" Kodie asked with a suggestion of mounting panic. "Jesus, Kevin, help me. Rebecca's...I don't know. She's... oh, now they're all holding their heads..."

Then I see Johnny holding the gun by the handle, finger on the trigger. He's examining it, rubbing the barrel with a finger. He doesn't have it pointed at me. He's transfixed, caressing it, lost in its potential.

I take two quick steps to him, grab his wrist holding the gun, and point it away.

"Ow . . ." he says. I twist his arm. "Ow, ow, ow. Okay."

"Take your finger off."

As soon as he removed it, I yanked it from him, flipped the safety back on and shoved it in the holster. Then in my rage I backhanded him across the face and he fell into the wall. He whimpered as I connected with his cheek. He put his palm there.

"You goddamn listen to me, Johnny. Enough of this shit. Got it?" I tried to mask the fear in my voice with anger but couldn't get the tremble out of it.

He slid his hand from his face, leaving a rake of red marks, and smirked. "Got it. *Dick.*"

My open hand flew out and popped him again. This time he cried out and it echoed loud in the small hallway. "No. That's not the answer I need from you. Got it, I said." My hand stinging, my stance wide, exhaling in nostril flares.

I just found him and the first thing I do is hit him. Twice.

Slumped against the wall with a tear line etching his face, he nodded with contrition. He slid down the wall and sat on the floor, head bent between parted knees, his hands clasped behind his neck.

From right behind the door, Kodie screamed.

"Get away from the door!" I bellowed.

I considered using the gun on the door but dismissed that idea as too dangerous. With fear came fight; with that, anger and strength. The door gave to my leg and foot, the jam splintering.

The advancing children stopped midstride. They'd been coming for Kodie, all but Rebecca who lay on the floor on her back with her arms crossed on her chest and her eyes closed. They looked ready for me to scold them. Then their myriad eyes set on mine, flat and unchanging, eyes of one entity, an enormous insect with dripping tips of poison on a lancing tail hidden behind its bulk.

I glanced past them at Rebecca and saw her belly swell and recede. Kodie quickly stepped beside me and seized my arm. I remember feeling her nails pressing into my skin, my heart beating there in the little grooves she made.

The door hung open and swayed a bit on its hinges as the doors of older houses do, the wind moving through the house.

"You okay?" I asked Kodie as we both tried to win the staring contest with the roomful of children. She nodded in my peripheral vision, gripped my arm that much tighter. Then, like spooked deer at the hissed signal they give, the children flew into motion. Around us they bolted, ran off like water down a sloped plane and laughing in the oblivious tones of recess. They thundered through the house, the floor shimmying on its piers and beams, and they were gone.

And Johnny with them.

I ran through the house to the front door. They'd disappeared like sugar dissipates into hot water.

Crestfallen then, sighing in the doorway, I didn't know how I was to find him.

From the back of the house, Kodie said, "They were coming for me, Kevin." I jogged back to the bedroom. "Jesus, the loathing in their eyes."

"She's asleep?" I ask, motioning to Rebecca.

Kodie shrugged. "She was standing there seizing. Hands to her sides in fists. Her eyes rolled back in her head. I thought she might swallow her tongue."

"What did the other kids do?"

"Held their heads. If I'd pushed through them and bent down to help her, I think they would've pounced. That's when I called for you."

Rebecca's abdomen swelled and deflated slow and smooth. I felt her neck for her pulse, lifted an eyelid. Like I'd know what to look for.

IF THINGS WEREN'T THE WAY they were, we'd've called her parents, we'd've taken her to the hospital.

There'd be nothing but horror at the hospital. I refused to go to public buildings, to engage in apocalypse tourism. To see people in hardening scrums soon to fall into a putrid slush.

We knew our parents were dead. Tracking them down to regard their corpses? To what end, closure? Seeing Grandma Lucille in a puffy casket was horror enough. I couldn't take a more macabre version of closure. We needed to survive, not mourn remains we'd never find anyway. This is what I argued to Kodie.

But she wasn't having it. "I can't *not* try." Rebecca's head lolled in her lap in the back seat. Kodie gave me a piercing look in the rearview. "I'll retrace their steps to work, I'll …I dunno. I'll go without you."

"It's dangerous to separate."

"I don't care."

I sighed and didn't speak until completing a turn. "Okay. You're right. Let's get some supplies first?" She looked at me again in the mirror and assented with a single nod.

Despite all, the basic drives still moved us. We were getting hungry, and not far off was the prospect of night. The hunger wasn't that common noon-hour hunger, but deep bodily hunger borne of lack. The energy we'd expended in all this shock had us tapped.

I fiddled with the radio. No jingles, no music, certainly no news. A lament of static was all.

I drove us to the HEB grocery store on streets engrained in my psyche but which now seemed foreign. Beyond the flick of a flag, a traffic light changing, a plastic bag rolling like a tumbleweed, only out of the corners of my eyes did I see movement. Dashing like cast-upon fish.

I flashed to me and my friends as sixth graders throwing water balloons at cars, ducking and hiding, running like hell and laughing until breathless, especially as the victim gave chase. We hid on our bellies under cars and barely breathed.

These grown-ups, gone forever now, who half-heartedly searched for us, couldn't remember why they once did these things. They yelled and shook their fists in tirades against youth itself.

I swerved with unease around more piles of rocks on Lamar Boulevard and in parking lots. The piles like anthills pulsing up from the ground owing to the swelling pressures of spring rains. We all saw them but said nothing. The fear was there, but also: What was there to say about something you cannot yet understand? We listened to the urgency of static and were afraid of what we saw and what we couldn't yet see. That was all.

That was how it felt the day of—stunned by silence, numbed by static, confounded by piles of stones, bewitched by twitches in the periphery.

OH, MAN I DID NOT want to go in. No shambling remainders weaved in parking lots. Inside, however…This HEB opened early, so I figured we were due for some bodies.

Afraid as I was right then, I knew I'd have to buck up if I was going to make it and that I had to make it because I had work to do beyond survival. There was something more for me. Something important. I had begun to feel as if I'd been uniquely spared. It just *felt* that way. The way you feel love—you can't explain its exact origins, you just feel it.

I'd been feeling it, this weirdness, since the summerdreams of June. You know when you have an intense dream and you wake up and the residue of the dream sticks to you for a while? It's still there in the shower, at breakfast, on the ride to school? And if it's really strong, maybe even it lasts until lunch? You can't shake it. It's like déjà vu. A brain cloud. Something. But then it lifts. It always lifts.

But this never lifted.

I had the dreams. The residue didn't lift. It clung and grew. I thought I was going crazy. I really did. Not a tweakable disorder but like psychotic, I was going over the hills and far away. Hell, maybe I have. Maybe I'm in a sanitarium right now like Holden Caulfield and in time I'll come out of it. T'was all a bad dream.

It didn't lift. I wrote the story *The Late Bloomers* to try to get it to lift. With the dawnsounds, it grew like mold, enshrouded me.

The chrysalis dream. The dream of the dream of sleep. The mouth containing the dark smiling teeth curling up at the corners segues between dream scenes. The non-voice issuing from it sounding like glass.

It grew more intense on the drive down the lane to Rebecca's house, and now in the parking lot of the HEB.

It's even more profound now as I talk to you as I float. Those dark smiling teeth, the sound of hardening glass.

We parked in front. In the old world, if you did this, you'd be assaulted by honks and within seconds a security guard on a golf cart with a swirling yellow light would arrive.

Little liberties like this were no consolation. All this freedom, what amounted to a new set of rules we didn't yet understand, they just made me feel sick for what was gone. Parking here to go in the store and take things unquestioned just reminded me that I loved my mom and that she was dead, and that the whole world was this big dead altered thing.

I turned off the ignition and braced for that quiet to settle like a cloak of volcanic ash. The sky remained cobalt. I hated it too, its mocking emptiness, the void it prefigured.

Kodie still held Rebecca in the back seat, stroking her hair now, providing her that succor I couldn't to her father. I had just gaped at him. God, what a galling sonofabitch I am for standing there with my idiot mouth open, hanging fire. How callow.

I wondered then: Would I do the same for Kodie if it struck her? It's wishful thinking, but maybe she's like me. Maybe we're goddamned Adam and Eve starting this thing all over again, starting it right.

Now, that's a thought.

Kodie stayed with rosy-cheeked Rebecca in the car, nodding for me to go ahead.

"You sure?"

"As long as she's here, I'm okay, I think. If things get weird, I'll honk."

"You won't leave her and come in with me?"

She lifted her bat from the floor of the car and smiled. "One-woman wrecking crew."

THE AUTOMATIC DOORS WHICH WERE never closed for the all-day traffic were closed now. The door sensed me and slid open. Cool air and the smell of vegetation hit me, as did the Muzak. And I thought Jesus, as soon as I can I'm going to play some real music. Nothing but ad jingles all morning, and now Muzak.

Nothing on the floor, nothing in disarray. The lights were on, the iced rows remained so. Not a puddle or drip. This HEB isn't like conventional Midwest grocery stores. This is the upmarket HEB, Central Market. Mom liked to shop here. Martin did not. Too expensive and full of trendy people who made him itch—forty-year-olds in skinny jeans and Ray Bans pushing $2,000 baby strollers branded in umlauted Helvetica. It's a labyrinth, forcing you through the whole store's maze so that you'll buy more.

Pushing a grocery cart, I bypassed the massive vegetable displays at which Mom would always stop and make us fan out with veggie lists. In the fruit section I picked up a bunch of bananas and dutifully made for the scale so as to weigh it for the price sticker. I put it on the scale then glanced back at the code on the display. I started keying in the SKU number and stopped mid-type as it dawned on me that my weighing and typing was pointless. I smiled, but…free stuff was no world's end perk. This wasn't a party. Still isn't.

Floating and terrified, that's me. That's us, right, Maggie? You terrified? You were on the ride home, weren't you? Sorry for that, girl. Okay? I'm sorry. I'm tousling her scruff. She looks over her shoulder, her face drenched in sun and blinks her eyes dolorously at me. Apology accepted.

I started grabbing. My mind thought in survival terms now. What I needed and how long things might last. Who knew how long we'd have power. I had no idea what went on at the power plants, water management facilities, what to do, how to maintain anything. I didn't even know where the power facilities were. Internet, gone. The smartphones which had dumbed us down (*it's all up in the cloud!*) didn't work. And if we got a phone book and a paper map and we found the power station, we'd pull a lever and blow ourselves up.

I panicked a little at these accumulating thoughts. Feeling very claustrophobic in this wide-open, not-so-brave new world.

Fresh things first. That's a good call. Get a bunch of fruit and vegetables. Meats. I talked to myself. "If we need to, we can use the fridges next door." I thought of what we might find in other houses. All the other houses.

"Why not just leave it here, then? If the power goes out, it goes out everywhere."

I had a discussion with myself. Like a madman.

"Sure. But it'll be close. And maybe we can get gas-powered generators going. Besides," and I stopped talking, tried to organize my thoughts.

"Besides...what?" I stood in the aisle, my mind toggling.

"Others may be out there and others may come and take more than their share. We need to get what we can when we can."

My stomach moaned long and demanding. It echoed. I let out an airy laugh through my nose.

Johnny's voice: "Your stomach sounds like an old Slavic woman trying to get out of bed." He stepped out in front of me from the side aisle. I audibly gulped.

It's a couple of miles from Rebecca's, at least. How in the hell...?

We stood at an impasse—trust, for the moment, gone.

"Why'd you run off with them?"

"Did I...?"

"I didn't bring you here, Johnny."

"I'm sorry. I'm so confused." His tone was flat.

"Will you stay with me? Help me?"

He looked over his shoulder. Held his head. Stepped to me and hugged me.

He slipped to his knees, grabbed my legs, and I rubbed his hair. We remained there for a few moments, him quietly sobbing, my flight-or-fight impulses receded. Sobbing and Muzak.

He peered up, his chin quivering. "We're still going to be okay, right? You and me?"

I couldn't say anything else but, "Yeah, J. We'll be okay." He stood up. "We just have to find out what's what out there, wrap our heads around it, and come up with a plan."

He just blinked at me. "I don't understand."

"I don't either."

"Why is this happening, Kevin?"

"I don't know. I don't think there's a reason. I don't think reason has anything to do with it. It just is."

"What is?" His eyes red, his nose wet.

"I think . . ." and I struggled with saying this because it sounded so final. "I think it's the end of the world, J. As we've known it, anyway."

I could see in Johnny's face that he wondered why I was here, why Kodie. He stared at me, blinkless. Looking into his face, I envisioned that wave fetching upriver.

He fell out of his trance when I spoke again. "I think, at least for tonight, as long as we have power, we need to keep food close to us at home."

"We staying there?"

"Why fly off half-cocked until we know more? We should, at least for tonight, until things settle and we can think." Johnny furrowed his brow, pursed his lips and nodded.

Now I took him in. He wore army pants I'd gotten him at the Army Surplus for his birthday and a Run DMC T-shirt from the Fun Fun Fun Fest we went to together, just us. My band friends had become real douches by then, about the time I started hanging out with Bass. We ditched them and watched the music together without the head-up-your-ass selfie-posting and tiny talk that goes on.

I heard a bang, maybe a wooden pallet, back at the loading area. Johnny and I looked at each other, arms full of fruit. We quietly put them in the basket. Just around the corner stood the stainless steel doors with rubber trim leading to the cold storage rooms and the loading area behind the building. That's where the sound came from.

"Hello?" I called out. We listened to dead air. "Hello?" Louder this time, taking a step forward. In the resounding quiet, I felt the prickles of panic. "Real quick, let's go back and see if the girls are all right," I whispered to Johnny. We loped back to the front. Johnny fell behind. Kodie saw me and I flashed a questioning thumbs-up. She nodded to me with a surprised look on her face, a smile even—*what?* I shook my head, mouthed *nothing.*

No time to dwell, I turned and redirected Johnny back past the imported oddities, the dewy organic delicacies. When we got to our cart, something felt wrong, like the air had just been displaced and we were arriving in the wake of its disturbance. Up ahead I saw the stainless steel doors swaying.

"Look." Johnny pointed to the cart. Still attached to a banana bunch lay exposed the meaty inside of one having been peeled, and a bite taken. The white inside a red apple framed by teeth marks.

Among the oranges sat a brown, fist-sized stone. I stared at it vacantly. My mind capered in a corner of my skull somewhere. Johnny dug it out and held it in one hand, feeling its weight. Once I blinked out of my stare, I asked rhetorically, "What in the hell?"

To lighten the mood, Johnny took the stone and placed it on the SKU scale. The digital numbers blurred to a stop at a little over a pound and a half. He dialed in a number he saw in front of him, the Vidalia onions, and out came the barcoded sticker. He tore it out and pressed it onto the smooth stone, put it in a plastic bag, spun the bag so it twisted up a straight line to be tied and knotted.

"Nice work." I patted the gun at my ribs. "C'mon."

Johnny knew where. With a set look on his face, he started walking ahead of me carrying the stone by the baggie knot between curled knuckles, the stone swinging idly. I whispered to him to hold up. He lagged, I caught up. We went straight for the metal doors and stood before them, nodded to each other once like in the movies, and I kicked them open, gun drawn.

We stepped through into the storage room the size of a squat gymnasium. Boxes and pallets and cool fecund air drifted in from far continents. Nobody there. Then came the echoing laughter through the catacombs of boxes and stacked pallets. Johnny snapped, "Hey, would you guys please stop it?" As if he knew them, a fidelity in his voice. "Why don't you come out if you're so smart? Come on out." Johnny's voice had command in it that I'd never heard him use before. They had numbers so they assumed strength within themselves. But the quiet that followed said they weren't so confident and had nothing to gain by confrontation. Then, the air no longer held that pregnancy. I was sure they were gone. Johnny stood there stunned as if having been assailed by knowledge.

"We should go," he said, looking into the gloom.

"Why?"

"We just need to go. Now."

"Johnny, they're gone. They're just kids."

He turned his head slowly to me, up to meet my face. "Okay." His voice told me he wasn't convinced but that he'd follow my lead anyway.

He flung the rock by the baggie knot down the corridor of boxes and pallets. It landed with a crack on the cement and rested there in the murk. We both looked at it as we might bait tossed into calm water we knew teemed under the surface.

A car horn blared. Its bursts came uneven. Not a car alarm. We realized the coordinates: outside, out front, our car.

As we ran, I thought I heard a rush of feet in the store running with us, in other parts of the store, as if we were in a footrace to get there. It could have been blood moving through my ears, my breath tearing through my throat hot with panic.

I was way ahead of Johnny when I got to the door to find my car not surrounded by people with mouthfuls of crystal-spit, but dogs. About ten of them. They were in a group and all wore collars. Domesticated dogs on a grand lark. A mélange of labs and shepherds and pit mixes, save for one little lap dog with long, well-coifed hair. When I bounded out the door, they spazzed and scattered with their tails tucked. They regrouped out in the parking lot and looked at us. The coifed dog yapped. The rest deferred to it, seeming content to let it do the talking.

I went to the car. "What happened? Why'd you honk?"

"The dogs," Kodie said, still leaning over the front seat. She got out, again holding her bat at its middle with one hand. "Dammit, that scared me."

"They're just lost, running around. You scared of dogs?"

Johnny's slapping footsteps came to a halt behind me. Kodie's head snapped to him.

"No. No, I . . ." Eyes on Johnny, then me, drawing the connection. "I love dogs, grew up with them..."

"So?"

"So. That," she pointed to them. The dogs mingled, panted and watched us discuss them. "*That* is a pack. A pack of dogs is different. Packs...of anything are dangerous. Of anything." *Do you follow my meaning?* her look said.

"Packs of gum aren't," I said.

"Shut up," she said as she stepped up and hugged me, looking at Johnny over my shoulder. "I freaked. Sorry. They came careening around that end of the strip straight at me. That's what was so weird. Just straight as an arrow."

"Did they Cujo the car?" I thought of the little dog in the car in front of the coffee shop, its gnashing and spittle on the glass.

"They got to the car and then kind of sniffed around. One of them went up to the store door and when it slid open it jumped back. I honked to get rid of them, not to call you. Sorry."

"We're jumpy," I said. "All nerves, fight or flight. And hungry. Bad combo."

I understood her. And it was more than just being jumpy. It's different now, I thought. Everything takes on a different cast, because the context is radically different. Common things, things we used to associate with good feelings, can seem a threat—children grouped in a room like in any preschool; dogs running with happy tongues flapping—and all the fears we used to experience have been replaced with the terror of the mundane, the things we took for granted, the not-scary things, like one's brother coming up behind you.

There are no more serial killers or fatal car crashes to fear, and any virus moving between people has its work cut out for it now. But there's the wind, the children, tall empty buildings with elevators cruising up and down empty. And the night. That primordial fear embedded in the DNA. The great world will spin and the dark would come soon enough.

"This is your brother?" Kodie asked. "Johnny, is it?" she asked, looking at him and trying to smile.

"Yeah. And he's going to stay with us now, aren't you?" I lifted my eyebrows at him. He nodded sheepishly and waved at Kodie.

Trying to cheer her up, I said, "Hey, let's go back in and shop. Get some beers? One of those little kegs?"

"You think it's wise to be boozing it up tonight?"

"Beer's not booze. How can it hurt? It'll just be us."

"And Johnny."

"And Johnny."

Kodie said, "And everyone still alive out there, with no police, no army."

"You know there's nobody," I said.

"We don't know this. Let's go with what we know which is we need to get food, drop it off at your place, and then figure out a way to contact people. Get a CB radio. Go to a radio station and figure out how to broadcast. Something. We need to drive around to see what's what. We need to try to make contact. We're alive, so there must be others. We're just really spread apart."

"All right." I agreed we had to try to establish contact. I couldn't yet say out loud that reconstructing the old world would be futile. The dark smiling teeth of my summerdreams had such power over me. Whatever they communicated, I believed, though I didn't want to.

"What we need to do is settle down," I continued, "get back and take a breath, eat and think. Let the shock wear off a little. I'm not sure time is of the essence here. What we don't want to do is make a false move out of panic."

Kodie nodded at this. "You're right."

I continued, "Now...I hate to say this, but we do need to get weapons after we get the food here. We can go right up here to McBride's." Kodie's one of the most peaceful and kind people I'd ever known, but she nodded at the concept of acquiring weapons. I wondered if McBride's had already been raided and stripped bare. I hoped that it had been because that would be evidence of life, of a will to survive existing in others.

The dogs still hung out, looking at us look at them. The fear of the pack lingered in Kodie's eyes.

"Hey, Johnny, see if can you get those dogs to take off. They're bugging Kodie."

Pleased to be of use, Johnny started walking in the direction of the dogs. The sitting dogs stood. All watched him with their ears perked, frozen, and they stayed that way until Johnny had claimed half the distance to them and put his hands up in the air like a monster coming to get them. He lifted his hands and he roared and they ducked and bolted across Lamar, which on any other day would have plowed them all to pieces. They sprinted down the street toward Medical Parkway. I could still see them as they veered left like track dogs, heads bobbing, neck and neck toward the hospital.

There were bodies at McBride's Guns. My guess is that when the smartphones resting on nightstands in pitch-black rooms concussed with texts and calls, lots of people ran down to the gun store to stock up, and then whatever was to befall them—the white stuff, suicide—befell them.

These piles over the bodies, these cairns, were the same shape and size as the others we'd seen. Just enough stone and debris to cover the corpse, forming a pyramidal shape. Johnny walked up to the suicide. I could tell he wanted to remove a rock to see, but he thought better of it. They had come, they had piled on the stones but didn't take the gun away, just an artifact of the old world to be left alone.

Inside was different. Ron, by the name tag, lay on his back between displays, the white hardened into something that looked like crystal. If it wasn't issuing from a man's throat, and if Ron didn't have his eyes locked on the ceiling as if his doom resided there, I'd even say it was beautiful, something you'd see behind glass in a dark room with a single spot on it. We found four more, all men. Over in knives, one had knocked over a display and a few switchblades had sprung open upon impact. He had died of the white. So had another, also an employee, lying behind the long counter with racks of guns lining the wall. Bullets were all around him on the floor and up on the glass counter.

Another guy sat slumped over, his head on the meat of his outstretched arm, his back against the industrial shelving. The halo of splatter on the boxes next to him spoke plainly, as did the Browning .22 on the floor a few feet from him.

You drew one or the other. One was the pitiless choking. The other, overjoyed suicide—the lipsticked nurse on the pedestrian bridge, the bald guy in his yard with his waving. No stones covered the bodies in here.

Then I got it: *in* here. The bodies weren't covered indoors. Why only cover the ones outdoors? I had to get out of there; the tang of blood in the air. I took long fast steps past Kodie and Johnny and made straight for the door.

Kodie called after me. I put my hand up in the air. I just need a minute.

I shoved open the glass door and the electronic chime bonged. I sidestepped the cairn in front of it, noticing for the first time the blue leather purse next to it.

Whatever this was, maybe it was stalking me now, I'd thought. It's taken me longer than the rest, but maybe that's because of my late blooming. Just a delay. Now it's here, come for me.

My heart thudded at my temples and in my throat so hard that I thought for a moment I might pass out. I thought of the suicides I'd witnessed. Just before they did it, they were ecstatic to be doing it. The rapturous look to them.

What calmed me down: I didn't have that.

Impulsively, I went over to the pile covering a suicide and I tossed off a couple of the rocks. An act of taboo desecration. They were watching from the thickets that ran along Shoal Creek. A multitude of eyes blinking at me behind the wall of green.

I yelled out toward the green, "We should be piling them in truck beds, burning them in pits! Not covering them up like cat turds in a litter box!" I stood up. "Come out!" I waited. "Come out, come out, wherever you are! Olly-olly oxen free goddammit!" I collapsed to my knees next to the cairn and peered down into the space in it I'd created. Through the stones I could see skin, the crew neck collar of a T-shirt. Couldn't see the face, and that was probably for the best, given the large kidney-shaped puddle of blood hardening as it continued to swell over the macadam, screening the sky's racing clouds.

That moment seemed to freeze for an elastic amount of time. My head buzzed.

I go back in and we load up with grim resolve like out of an eighties revenge movie montage: crossbows, shotguns, pistols, civilian-grade assault rifles.

I forced the trunk closed and we all got back into the car now stuffed with a small war's worth of groceries and gear.

"Gotta figure out how to use this thing," I said, holding up a small black graphite crossbow.

"Who you plan on shooting?" Kodie sat in the back, Rebecca's head returned to her lap.

"Well, like you said, packs are dangerous." We drove.

Kodie said, "God, imagine…imagine the rebound of fish in the oceans and rivers, the pollution in the air and water receding, the earth basically healing itself."

"Ah, cataclysm as environmental correction."

"Just saying."

"We've definitely peed in our own soup. The whole planet, though? It was here long before we arrived and will go on even after the sun burns out, a cold, indifferent rock, her scarred ocean beds smiling like Buddha."

"That's uplifting."

"Doesn't seem like a day for optimism."

All the windows down, the hair on all of our heads, Rebecca's too, lifting and flowing. Johnny rested an arm on the door, sunning his elbow. He leaned his forehead out to let the wind rush his face, eyes closed. Bliss in that face.

Not the bliss of the ignorant. No.

"And what, oh wise one, do you think about all this?" She waved her hand out the window as if she were a real estate agent displaying the available world to me. I felt a missing-Martin pang. "What does an organism do when it becomes infected with, oh, let's say a bacteria that just grows and grows?"

I wasn't taking the bait. I shrugged, looked out my window at the blurring green as we headed back north to the house.

"It defends itself," she answered herself. "Sometime during the industrial revolution, the earth realized that it had been infected."

Not wanting to get into it, I said, "It doesn't matter does it? Besides, okay, to your point, the earth doesn't have standards. It doesn't feel. The earth is an ever-morphing system. It adapts to the new thing." I looked at the rearview. Kodie cupped Rebecca's face with her hand. "I'm sorry."

"Nothing to apologize for," she said under her breath, shaking her head with small swivels.

"It's going to be okay, Kodie." I kept trying to get her to glance up at the mirror with my overt head jerks. But she didn't.

"You don't believe that, do you?" she asked, still not looking up. "That it's going to be okay."

Johnny emerged from his reverie and looked at me, restating her question with his face.

Too much time went by. I demurred, "The world always looks bad when you're hungry and tired."

"No disrespect, Kev, but the world looks pretty bad. I don't think some sandwiches and a nap are going to change that."

"Thank you, Johnny. Thank you for your perspective."

"You're quite welcome."

We held it in for a few seconds, but, thank God, that made us all bust out laughing.

I WAS AMAZED THAT THERE weren't fires burning out of control in the city, that nobody dropped a cigarette as they got the feeling, left a gas pump open and flowing. The skyline revealed no smoke save for an upward trickle coming from what I knew had to be the plane crash. Early afternoon now and the wave has hit and gone and now it's just quiet as hell. That's it. The world set to stun.

Somehow the charge in the air told me things were beginning, not ending.

Johnny asked, "Shouldn't we…? Maybe there's people downtown—"

I slammed on the brakes. "Oh, man! Bass!" Then I floored it.

"Bass?" Kodie asked.

BASS AND I TRIED TO grow a small patch of weed together just to see if we could, behind the equipment shed at the elementary school. If some maintenance guy whacks it down, so what, it's a weed.

Bastian's a varsity football benchwarming linebacker doing his time. Bastian puts on the pads, hits people at practice, but he's never started a game. He's on the team out of familial expectation, he tells me, and because it's good for college applications. Holds water with some colleges and with Daddy's sphere of influence when it's time for internships. It's a club badge, Bastian would say, as he did just last week as we sat in his beater Bronco and smoked from our first homemade bag listening to his Heartless Bastards on repeat. The smoke tasted like burnt lawn clippings and stung more than usual and it didn't get us but slightly lit which was okay with me. I don't like getting *stoned* stoned. An awful feeling.

How, you may ask, do a jock and a band geek become friends? Isn't this against the rules? True, cross-pollinations like ours are rare. I guess it's more Bastian being Bastian than me making some great leap across the social divide in a moment of altruism.

Social strata and rules between jocks and band, cheerleaders and punk rock girls? Man, all that's just…gone.

Bastian's a big guy, more lank than thick. He says that he's strong of haunch. This is Texas football, remember. Big public school. Even the benchers are monsters. He could break me over his knee on a cold day.

We'd been good friends at school for a year now. We didn't hang much outside of school except as smoking buddies. Not until recently, that is. I think his friends had been giving him guff about hanging out with me, too.

My friends—and here's the thing, and I wish the world was still functioning as this bit of insight might matter—they were the same way. I got tired of their assumptions that guys like Bass were mindless brutes. I wasn't angry about it because I think it's natural to defend oneself. High school, like nature, is red in tooth and claw. What I'm saying is Bass and I became tight this fall because we weren't interested in remaining in our guarded worlds.

"Bastian. My friend Bastian from school. He texted me about the same time you did. Said to meet him. Aw, dammit. Hope he's okay." I pounded the steering wheel.

"Do I know him?" Johnny asked.

"Huh-uh." My eyes scanned the road for issues as I hit sixty, took the curve around Burnet as it veers toward Hancock.

A pile of stones in each of the parking lots of the Pint House Pizza, the Noble Sandwich. Johnny's eyes toggled on them as we blew past.

Kodie gripped the door with her hand. Neither fussed me about the speed. The speed notwithstanding, I still saw movement, forms sliding into the city's slots.

Why didn't they come out with their arms waving asking for help?

We do this avoidance dance and don't know why.

They're the watchers. I'm the wonderer.

I took a sharp turn at Hancock and gunned it. "Hey, easy there, Ricky Bobby," Kodie said.

Johnny couldn't contain his smile. He liked the speed and the idea that the rules were now as out the window as his face thrust out into the sun and wind. "Shake and bake!" he yelled at the Yarborough Library. The eerie echoes coming off those walls made my guts turn.

"Meet where?" asked Kodie over the engine roar and tire squeal.

"Terrapin Station."

"What's that?"

"The graveyard up here."

"You've got to be kidding."

I shook my head.

"Why do you all call it that?"

"Just a dopey reference to a band we both loathe, the Grateful Dead."

"I'm not following."

"I don't like them either," offered Johnny. "Jam bands, ugh. I'd like to kick that Bob Weir in the balls."

I slowed down a little as we crossed Shoal Creek. "We," I paused and looked at Johnny. He's witnessing the world end and saw a man with his head blown off in the back of a gun store, so I knew my prudence was wasted. "It's where we grow pot."

"Oh, now I get it. Pot, the Dead, cemetery. Sure. Clever. Your little pothead code," Kodie said with no opinion or judgment attached to it whatsoever.

"Pot?" Johnny asked.

The stock points representing whatever reverence Johnny had of me, if there was any left after I hit him in Rebecca's hallway, went down a few ticks then. God, he looked disappointed.

We arrived at the entrance of the cemetery. "J, it's hard to explain."

BEFORE I CONTINUE—I KNOW THIS isn't proper memoir form, nor is it particularly good narrative development to just kill the momentum by doing this, but, lest you forget, dear reader, I'm doing this on the fly and borrowed time.

So, in case something happens before I finish, I want to insert a couple of poems. One from memory I'd written last year. I gave it to Mr. E. It wasn't assigned. On the extra-credit essay I wrote on *Lord of the Flies* over the summer, he'd written below the A+ affixed with a red smiley face, *What else you got?*

Mr. E's my teacher and my advisor. He said he made them make him my advisor. We've been hanging out a lot this fall. Go ahead, use the word mentor. Go ahead, use the words father figure, *in loco parentis.* Martin sure isn't one.

That's not true, Martin. I'm sorry.

Anyway, here's one that I'm making up now. Been experiencing these images.

I call it *Milkteeth.*

pretending it drips
from their soft milk teeth
they've all still got
so proud to still have them

those pristine pearly birthrights
rooted in malleable razor rows
suckle at the lips of wounds
gashed into their effigies

one at a time
each takes his drink

the reward a small stone
from which night's cold has leached
drawn away by coastal morning sun

when they're done
they look up and smile at everyone
laughter riots from their throng
like satisfied birds about to depart
in one massive uplift

an exodus that would eclipse the sun
long enough for me to get away
under its saw-toothed dark[8]

And here's the one I gave Mr. English in his office after he'd asked what else I got. I stood there and watched him read it, his lips moving. No title:

she emerges from those ozone fields
full of requisite thoughts coursing bodywide
not mattering if yesterday was
tomorrow's repeat or if
now is a lot like then[9]

It isn't my favorite, but it's the one that popped in. I guess it's because of Kodie—the emerging she and fields. Okay. So, yay, those stunning beauts are on record. I've got lots more doodling epigrams like that, but need to keep things going here. The rest of them are in a spiral notebook in my desk drawer right below the SAT preps.

I remember two of Mr. E's comments about it, after he lifted his eyebrows and blew out his cheeks. One comment was: "You know who e.e. cummings is." I nodded, ashamed. He said, "Hey, it's okay. Standing on the shoulders of giants is okay. That's how the giants learned their way—"

---

8 Included in *With Smiles On Their Faces: The Collected Poems of Kevin March*, attached hereto as Exhibit D.
9 *Ibid.*

I interrupted, "Hey, that rhymes."

His other comment was: "Why did you say *mattering* when *caring* makes more literal sense?" I remember him trying to hide the expectation on his face by taking a long sip of coffee from his Styrofoam cup. When I said I didn't know, it just felt right, he nodded and wiped his mouth down with his palm and said, "Good answer. Anytime you want to share your work with me, let me know, okay?"

I stupidly asked him if it was good.

He said, "What's great is that you said it felt right. Going on feeling rather than propriety, that's when you leap off the giant's shoulders. That's when you soar."

This whole thing here, telling this story, kayaking to the Matagorda— I'm taking Mr. E's advice: I'm going on feeling.

OKAY, BACK TO THE ACTION.

Remember how earlier in the day I was coming back from the bridge— the bus, jumpers—and passed the Montessori school and the cemetery was across from it? Well, we're back there now. Not in time, but in place.

Memorial Park Cemetery is where the writer James Michener is buried. I haven't read him but Mom has his books *Texas* and *Tales of the South Pacific* on the shelf at home. Big doorstop hardbacks. Mr. English said I should apply to the Michener School at UT someday for my writing and that he could help me when the time came.

The cemetery is actually a city park. Once you get past the initial creep of being among almost twenty thousand corpses just six feet below you everywhere you look for eighty acres, it's a peaceful place to bike through on its winding, tree-lined, curbless roads. Before I got my car, and often since, when the homestead was bringing me down, i.e., Martin and/or Mom riding my ass about something about as consequential as a mouse fart, I started coming through here so often that when Bass and I were driving around looking for a place to toke one evening, I suggested we should pull in here.

Problem was, we didn't think to commit the closing time to memory so there we were parked in his old Bronco at the back of the cemetery on the gravel shoulder under a huge oak tree and smoke's building up in the cab like Cheech and frigging Chong and up behind us rolls the sexton's black pickup. It's custom, all matte black, full-tint windows, hubcaps, everything. I notice it in the mirror as Bass is pulling on his quartz-cut pipe he got down at some booth on First Thursday on South Congress next to the drum circle and the Keep Austin Weird T-shirt vendor. I'm basically frozen looking in the rearview mirror like Death itself has crept up on us, scythe gripped in his boney hands.

Bass was about to roll down a window to blow out but I said no, don't do that, the dude's behind us and he says what dude and I said the cemetery dude the black Mad Max behind us and Bass coughed out his smoke while simultaneously uttering shit, sounding like sh-*cough* it-*cough*.

I snapped off the music. All to be heard was the fulsome chug of the sexton's black nightmare. The truck flared his brights once. We're expecting the guy to narc on us but instead all we saw were his hands hovering outside his window, one hand pointing to his watch. We were out of there idiot-giggling and the guy didn't follow us out or anything.

He had to have known. Probably deals with weird stuff like that all the time. Like, I'm always seeing this same guy walking through there, some dad-looking dude who's either reading a book while walking or listening to the radio and talking to himself. He's harmless, but I've also noticed a homeless guy smoking a pipe pulling his things behind him like he's rolling through Heathrow.

I swear, I'm not one of these goth kids. I dunno. It's more of a peaceful place than most parks full of nannies and moms and squealing kids and put-out dads with their hands on their hips, like, *can we go home now, dear, the game's on*, some huge Hispanic family having a picnic and cumbia's slave shuffle blasting. It's quiet, green, and nobody here expects anything of you.

As we were turning off Hancock to the entrance, I stopped and craned my head around and saw a cairn in the Montessori parking lot right next to that Volvo I'd seen with the arm hanging out the window. The Volvo's door was open.

Mad Max's window was down. In the driver-side mirror I could just see the sexton's ear and jawline.

We drew alongside the truck. The guy's eyes were open, white crystal effluvium protruding from his mouth looking like a crude spearhead.

Kodie uttered something under her breath and looked away. Johnny and I looked at the guy, his hatchet-faced gaze. He looked shocked to be sitting there with this stuff choking out of him, his wide eyes having the look of marble.

I accelerated forward. Kodie asked, "Why here?"

"You mean why'd we pick this place, me and Bass?"

"Yeah," answered Johnny. Kodie nodded in the rearview.

"I ride my bike through here a lot and—"

"Wait wait wait. You ride your bike through this graveyard?" Most girls would probably put on a face of disgust, but not Kodie Lagenkamp. She let uncork a knowing smile when she heard this and then said, "That's fubar, Kevin." Our eyes met in the rearview. I'd found a girl who not only wasn't repulsed by the fact that I often rode my bike through a cemetery but who found it understandable and endearing.

"I do. Well, I did before I got these here sweet wheels." I didn't want to lose that fascinated look on her face so I added, "But I still do. Once a week at least." I spoke the truth. Kodie shook her head looking down with that blushy smile still on her face. "Why, what? What's so funny?" We were in high flirt now.

As the world fell apart around us and we entered a cemetery to check on a friend I had no way of knowing was still here while a little girl we don't know lies on Kodie's lap in a coma, we were in high flirt. I mean, if this doesn't tell you how powerful the need for the species to continue is, I'm not sure what will.

I'm thinking about the species's survival now as I sit here in my kayak, the current taking me. Life will go on. It will survive despite this.

"It's not *funny*."

"Well, what?"

She kept shaking her head and stroke-combing the towhead in her lap. I toggled my eyes between the narrow cemetery road and her face in the mirror. "I do the same thing. I did the same thing. Did. Do."

"Ride your bike through here? I've never seen you."

"No. I go for long walks and lately I'll turn into this little place over in Hyde Park, behind the church. There's maybe twenty or thirty gravestones back there, old ones. Very secluded. More gothic than this. I'll sit and eat a sack lunch there sometimes, feeling morbid at first but then somehow I feel okay among them. The sun will break through the branches and come around the church wall and warm my face and I feel okay. It's comforting, not scary."

My eye caught on a grave decorated for Halloween with a softball-sized pumpkin and Dia de los Muertos sugar skull swarmed by flies. She continued. "What are the odds that two people, you and me, would both do something so rare like that and end up in such close proximity to each other?"

I found myself slowing down as she spoke and then I was at a stop, looking at her in the mirror. "Long odds, I'd say," and in my mind's eye, Grandma Lucille closed her eyes and nodded.

"Yeah," she said all forlorn. We had made this connection, but now there was a cast of melancholy to her, her *yeah* distant and fraught. "Long odds."

Rolling under the canopy of oaks and ash, cedar elms and pecans, the lack of that whisper-roar that always came off MoPac, which bordered the west side of the cemetery, struck me hard. I'd rather hear sirens, bomb concussions, even distant screams rather than this harrowing silence.

Right now in my ears sounds the hurry and rumble of this swollen river. But I know just beyond it: silence, stillness.

Up on MoPac you could see cars pulled over to the side. I wanted to see more chaos, more wreckage, something that told me we put up a fight. The end of the world can't be this orderly, this benign. Not this whimper, everything just winding down to a nullity.

Quiet welled such that it threatened to breach my sanity's threshold, so I had to keep talking. "We'd been here before in Bass's car. And then late one night, the Fourth of July actually, we jumped the fence, smoked some, and planted what was left. The plants have grown since."

I thought I knew where Bass wanted to meet. But that's not where he was. The small wood lining the back northeast corner of the cemetery is Terrapin Station. However, as I crested a small hill, turning right, and passing Michener's grave, up ahead, under the tree where we usually parked his Bronco, sat Bass wearing our blue-on-white Paladins football helmet.

He had to have seen us coming the whole time because the view down the hill to the road is clear almost all the way to the front of the park. Yet he wasn't standing up and waving. He just sat there and I thought the worst.

"Is that him?" Johnny asked, concerned.

"That's him." I honked the horn. The sound brought good cheer to the scene. He looked up and waved but stayed sitting. Closer now and I saw where his other hand was and the smoke rolling out from behind the face mask. I was dismayed at first but then I thought of those guys in Vietnam getting stoned before going on patrols. How to cope.

Bass stood as we pulled up, holding the pipe down to his leg, smoke filaments stretching up from the bowl. First thing he says with that radio-DJ deep voice of his: "Hey, want a binger?" like we'd just shown up at a house party and he's bored in the back room with his weed and remote control. The guy's a young Howard Stern with less hair and wearing a helmet.

Kodie laugh-snorted. He stood and again extended his arm out in offer. I threw the car into park and jumped out. "Bass, Jesus. You've been here since you texted?"

He shrugged and nodded, the unstrapped helmet jostling his skull. He relaxed his arm. "Mostly."

"You okay?" I asked. He acted strange. "Why here? Why'd you'd want to meet here?"

He peered at me through the face mask. "Not here. Down there at Terrapin. Where we always meet. I dunno, man. First thing I thought of. Felt safe, I guess? Our secret place. Didn't think kids would follow me in here." He turned his head one way, then the other, searching. "I was right."

"Your folks?" I asked. "You know for sure? I mean, we don't, me and J. Not…for sure." I glanced up at Johnny sitting in the car. He stared with a set jaw over at the church playground on the opposite side of the cemetery.

"Yeah," Bass muttered and sniffed, his voice full and wet. A step closer and I could see he'd been crying. "Yeah, man. They, uh, they…" His skinny frame shook and his shoulders rolled with racked sobs. We took a step to each other then. He dropped the pipe in the gravel and we hugged, my ear meeting his sternum. I let emotion fill my throat for the first time but fought it off, swallowed hard.

I attempted humor as we peeled off each other. "What's with the helmet?" He picked up the pipe, crushed the carbon on the gravel under his huge Converse toe. "That our stuff you're smoking?"

He nodded.

"Any good?" The stuff I'd smoked that morning was sour old shake.

"S'okay," he shrugged. He pointed his chin across the grounds. "Little bastards were throwing shit at me. Sticks and rocks."

"Where? Who was?"

"Dunno, little kids. That's why I came here. They were doing it as I was driving around earlier to see what was going on. They came at me from out of nowhere near Butler Park as I cruised down Barton Springs. I hightailed it here and texted you. I sat for a while, then got freaked and impatient so went to check on the plants and there some more were, throwing stuff at me." Now I saw the back end of his Bronco way back there just inside the tree line bordering that edge of Terrapin Station. "They won't come in here, though. I was all like come on, come get some, and was backing up waiting for them to rush me. They didn't. I've been seeing them here and there around the parameter." Bass jutted out his hand holding the pipe and pointed. "There! There's one of those little turds."

I followed his gesture and saw a boy in a red shirt and jeans walking by the chain-link fence at the church parking lot about seventy-five yards away. The boy stopped and looked at us looking at him but he didn't look unnerved in the slightest. He didn't look at us; he marked us. He kept walking along the fence line and then veered off into the daycare playground, where deeper within the swings were alternating back and forth, two other kids on them kicking their legs out for height and speed. The boy in the red shirt walked over to them. The swingers both dragged their feet to stop and they stood up to look at us. The boy in the red shirt pointed at us. Then they all turned and walked out of sight around the other side of the church.

Did these kids who were all alone now try to reach out to us for help? No.

Did they so much as wave at us, the only older people they've seen all morning? No.

Did this fact scare us? Yes. It did me, and I could see in Kodie's face and Bass's that it scared them too.

Bass said, "I notice you don't want to go try and talk to them. No more than I do. You know what's up. They throw stuff at you?" When I gave no immediate answer, Bass searched my eyes. "You've seen something, haven't you?"

"I've, we've, seen quite a bit this morning. And not one adult."

"What'd you see?"

I paused to think of a way to describe my trepidation. "We went to this house to see if we could help this dying man's daughter. Just over there in my neighborhood. About ten of them, sitting in a back room, chanting. Then they locked Kodie in with them after shoving me out. I had to bust down the door."

"No way. See, that's what I'm saying. What's going on, man? I'm losing it. You seem all calm. If you all hadn't shown up, I swear…I don't know. I would've stayed here all day. I was too scared to even go back and get the Bronco with them just over the fence running through the woods there." He put his hand on my shoulder. "Hey, come with me? Let's get my car."

I waved to Johnny and Kodie to stay here for a sec and we headed out. Bass kept his helmet on.

"Who's the chick?" he asked.

"We work together at the DT. You know."

"Oh yeeaah. *Kodie*. That makes sense." He spun as he walked to look at her in my car, turned back. "She's what, how old?"

"Nineteen."

"Well. She's the oldest live person I've heard of or seen."

"You didn't see your folks . . ."

He shook his head. "Found them." He said this in a curt whisper and I remember it making my neck skin gooseflesh. Though I had become fast friends with Bass—you could say he was my best friend—and I didn't yet know all his mannerisms and ways, this sounded to me like he was lying. I didn't want to push.

"Sorry."

"S'okay." Bass sighed and restarted. "So, you're almost eighteen, she's nineteen. I'm seventeen. I've seen no teenagers. I mean *nobody*. And I drove around before coming here, like I said. Nobody. Open car doors and piles of rocks. I'm afraid to even go over to the school."

"I doubt anyone even made it to school." I wonder if you did, Mr. E. I know you went in early to work on your book. Are you there now?

"How are we the only ones, then? Two teens close to you are the only ones alive in Austin? What the hell?"

It took Bass's stoned logic for me to see it. His point was well taken. Me and my two closest friends going into the dawn of this day are the only older people we've seen. Isn't that way too bizarre a coincidence?

I know what Grandma Lucille would've said—there are no coincidences. She had told me that only once.

She dropped that on me one night in early June. I had been practicing The Saints, you know—*oh when the saints, come marching in*. Been practicing it a lot. I could play it real well right from the start. My 'bone's slide hitting those slots spot on, my lips and cheeks finding their proper pressures. The Saints.

Okay, it's more than that. I'd heard its faraway echoed strains at the edges of my summerdreams. And Johnny hummed it when he sleepwalked into my room. Sometimes I heard him humming it at the dreams' peripheries themselves. I'd wake up with a start, feeling his presence in my room but he wasn't there, the pain in my head above my right eye quickly subsiding.

Grandma Lucille hadn't been feeling well, so I went over to her house for dinner, trombone in hand, on the promise of her gumbo. The woman could make it, having grown up in way southeast Texas, a tiny Gulf border town north of Port Arthur. Her gumbo? Meal of the gods when coupled with homemade hushpuppies and followed by her pecan pie.

When we were finished eating—me having had thirds and slopped up every last dollop of roux with the puppies—but before we settled in to watch *Mystery!* on PBS with our pie plates heaped, she asked me to play something. She knew we'd already started rehearsing for the next football season and probably expected to hear me play something from that. But for no reason at all, other than I'd been rehearsing it all day and that it had burrowed into my mind like an earworm, I ripped into this sublime jazzy version of The Saints, trying to ape the way I'd heard Trombone Shorty do it at a Tulane commencement I'd seen on YouTube.

Oh—how her eyes lit up. She clapped with her hands barely touching to the beat of the song and she swayed in her chair and when I came around to

those refrains her eyes closed and then came that beatific smile of hers, the
thing I maybe loved about her most, her eyebrows lifting convex, searching
for that highest note just before I hit it.

When I was finished, she sighed and said that was her favorite song and
asked did I know that? I shook my head and said no, that I'd just picked it up
the other day and couldn't get it out of my head. Wasn't that a coincidence,
I'd asked her. She shook her head and said stonily, "No, sweetie. No. There
are no coincidences."

Four days after that, she had a stroke. She died a week later.

Days after that, Grandma Lucille's beatific smile morphed into the
dark smiling teeth within the recesses in my mind and thus began the
summerdreams. I'd go to bed after the rising shrieks of new cicadas lulled
for the night, and those dreams came—night after night, the same thing.
And in the background, a muted soundtrack—The Saints.

At her funeral I played The Saints. Not a dry eye in the church. I barely
got through it, my emotion catching in the instrument, but I plowed on
with verve determined to see it through as if Grandma were sitting next
to me, lightly touching her fingertips in a silent clap to the beat. I played it
in a standard way, leaning toward a dirge, keeping the second line version
between me and her.

I FELT SAFE WITH BASS walking next to me across the sloping field of what
would have been an expanded cemetery even though he was wearing his
football helmet and was stoned to the bejesus. Bass was security in bulk, an
entire head taller than me with gladiatorial shoulders and calves.

"I have no idea," I'd answered to his *what the hell?* I still don't, not really.

The distance was much farther than I remembered. We walked an
incline and then sloped to the treeline. Johnny and Kodie would be out of
sight.

"Really a dumbass thing to do, smoking. Okay, I need to sober up." He
clapped his hands together hard once and then rubbed them, getting down
to business. As if in pregame psych ritual, he smacked his palms on the sides
of his helmet and huffed and puffed. Not that he ever played beyond kick
coverage when the Paladins had some team so by the throat that the scrubs
got in. "So, what we know is: one, everybody who's hit puberty but me and

you and Kodie look to be dead. I mean…the whole world??" Bass wasn't the only one to talk glibly. We all did at times. Subconscious comic relief.

He continued, "Do you think it's possible it's just the US? Maybe once we get communication going—"

"No," I said, my tone flat and certain. "Did you see TV at all? I didn't really."

"A bit just before I took off exploring. Net, everything crashed quick. Then I came here. All I saw was cable news running raw footage. People on their knees in the New York subway, choking."

I didn't even want to get into what Professor Fleming had told me. "It's worldwide. It's…just got to be. It's too…"

"What?"

"How can…? You saw how people died?"

Bass drew in a measured breath. "Saw my folks. Watched them."

Our banter quit. We stopped walking. "But you just said—"

"I know. I don't know why I said I *found* them."

"Sorry. I'm so sorry. You don't have to tell me."

"No. We've got to fetter this out. What we know because that's all we have. No matrix in the sky is going to tell us anything."

I nodded, tight-lipped, already a frocked member of the choir to which he preached. We walked and talked. Bass said, "We've gone soft. That's what my dad used to say. I used to think he was just a crank talking about self-reliance, the grid going down one day. He wasn't a shelter-digging survivalist, but he was definitely sympathetic—the economy collapsing, and with it society; sun flares knocking out the world's power; some super-flu or whatever. Bet none of them saw this coming. How could you?"

"No kidding. I still can't believe I'm awake. That you and I walk through a graveyard talking about what happened to the world. Still in shock I guess." I'd say this is still true. Nothing's worn off, just grown more profound.

"Tell me about it. I'm the stoned one wearing the helmet. Ever seen a more textbook specimen of shell shock?"

"PTSD."

"Yeah, that."

We shuffled a few more steps. I checked back over my shoulder, my car still in view. Residual morning dew collected flecks of new mown grass on our shoes and made their smoother parts glisten.

Bass readied himself. "Okay." He straightened up and took in a deep breath and blew it out. "My parents both died within minutes of each other. They...suffocated...God, I don't even know. I couldn't help them." We heard a low faraway boom and lifted our heads to it but kept walking. "Both of them still in their sleepwear, they said they didn't feel well, were going to call in to work sick. At first I thought it was kind of funny, the two of them such a pair. I put them in bed but within minutes they grew restless. They couldn't lie still and then very quickly came the wheezing which became too much. The panic in their eyes. Oh, God, Kevin. It was... I cannot believe it. I just can't."

We walked in silence for twenty yards or so. After sniffing, sighing, and clearing his throat, he continued. "They tried to hug each other and be together, and to be with me, because they knew something was very wrong, but their struggle was too much and they ended up going outside, separately, Dad to the backyard and Mom to the front. Like, they *had* to go outside.

"My mom staggered into the middle of the yard when she collapsed to her knees and that's when I ran out to her. She was on her hands and knees with her face to the ground. I thought she was going to vomit but it was a long thirty seconds or so of this crackling...wheezing...like I've never heard. I mean, Kev, she had bad chronic asthma, my mom, and I've spent many a day with her feeding her hot drinks to try to keep the breathing passages open, to keep her afloat until the prednisone I shot into her hip kicked in. I've seen her turn blue and heard her make deathly rasps before, but this...this was, ah, Jesus."

I thought, *lacking in specificity.*

"It gripped her so fast she couldn't even say goodbye to me. I was crouching down to talk to her and she was just shaking her head wildly... shit, Kev."

I patted him on the back as he wept. He yanked off the helmet by the face mask and threw it ahead of him. It clacked and rolled to a stop. We walked down to it and he took a knee like you see them do, gripping the face mask and leaning on the helmet. I got up on my tiptoes to look over the incline to the car. I saw their two heads inside.

Still kneeling and looking off into the middle distance, Bass, stone-faced now, not stoned, said, "She grabbed my leg and held on as she struggled for breath. She fell over onto her side. I wonder if she thought it was just another asthma attack. Her eyes found mine, and we just looked at each other as I screamed out at her. And then the life left her eyes."

I glanced at the church playground swings swaying empty.

"Then I saw it."

"What?" I asked. That low boom-bang again, like someone throwing something heavy into a dumpster.

"The white stuff. It stopped at her lips. In the minute I sat there it seemed to harden. Made ugly splitting noises like when you step on thin ice." He shifted his weight on the helmet. "I carried her into the house and then ran to my dad on the deck on his back. Same thing. Eyes open, that white hard foamy...*glittery*...stuff filled his throat and mouth. He died alone." Bass looked at me and towered over me and asked me like I knew something, nostrils flaring, caging his rage. "What is it, Kevin? You tell me what that is, what does that. To the whole fucking world!"

He calmed. We walked. "Got a crossbow and a pony keg in the trunk of my car."

"No shit?"

"No shit."

"Well now. It is Friday afternoon, after all." We sniggered and watched ahead, veering away from an outlying crop of new headstones which had jumped the road onto this new acreage. We neared the treeline and the Bronco. The church's playground was clear to us now, but empty. That one swing swaying in the breeze. The breeze made me remember the plane crash and I looked over that way and saw thin smoke.

"Man, right about now, if this day was what it was supposed to be... Well, I take that back. This is clearly what it is *supposed* to be. You know what I mean? Tell me to shut up, I'm high."

"Shut up. You're high."

"Thank you. Now, if this was the homecoming football game day it says it is on my phone." He pulled it out, scrolled the screen with this thumb, turned the screen to my face as proof. "See? Says Homecoming vs CP, right? We'd be getting out of class early and the teacher would be all sulky about it because us jocks get to leave and there's nothing they can say about it, and we'd be going to the locker room for a team meeting before going off to our absurdly early dinner at Luby's."

"Hold on," I said. "Let me see that thing. Thought I saw something."

"What?"

"Give it." I thought I'd seen the phone's reception bars moving and those buffering turning circles. If those things are moving, maybe the net or cell towers were working. On mine, on Kodie's, all day they've been dead since I got their texts.

He gave it to me. Looking at it again, I see it must have been a trick of my vision, my eyes wanting to see movement. I tapped and scrolled but nothing moved. Glowing hockey pucks at this point. Pointless plastic and gla—But then something did move, in the reflection off the phone's glass. Bass couldn't see it as the screen was titled away from him. I saw it though. Just as I'd seen its shadow in that first dream in June, just as I'd seen its shadow riding along that wave rolling upriver like an arrow pointing the way.

Winged thing. A long thin tail, something from the fantasy pulps lining my wall. Or Dante.

I startled and swung my face to the sky behind us to try to see it.

"What?" Bass asked, facing me, his back turned to the woods.

"Nothing." My mind scrambled for an answer. "Thought I saw...your buffering symbol swirling."

"The way you jumped." He shifted his weight and cocked his helmet. "You toke up?"

Apocalyptic paranoia brought on by skunk weed. That's all . . .

"I did just a little at dawn. Like, one hit. Then things went to shit."

But then I did see movement. In the trees.

As I slowly handed him back his phone, my stricken face to the woods, Bass whipped around. "What? You see them?"

Bass didn't see me nod.

"How many?"

My voice low and sure. "Looked like one kid—"

—Hey! Hey you guys come here!

A boy's voice coming from the woods, an echo tailing it. We jogged toward the voice, both of us understanding the voice to be earnest. My heart swelled and thumped high in my barren throat. I forgot all about Kodie and Johnny. When we got to the Bronco, it was dinged and webbed cracks spread across the windshield and windows facing the woods.

You'd think weeks of lifting your knees high while playing a trombone would benefit one's cardio fitness, but you'd be wrong. Out of breath, I asked Bass, "You go chasing one of those nasty fall hailstorms again?" I put my hands on my knees and scanned the woods.

"Nope," answered Bass who wasn't winded in the slightest. Though hanging onto the edge of the game roster by his fingernails, he had done the two-a-days, the man-killers. His head panned back and forth along the wall of green.

Not even birds scratched out their call-and-response language of warnings. That intense and intentional quiet thickened.

It's not just the quiet attendant to an ended world. It's a quiet of being watched, being tracked. A quiet that wicks into your marrow's sponge.

Feeling it too, Bass pulled his keys out of his pocket and made toward the Bronco with long strides and tossed the helmet through the open back seat window. "Screw this. Let's get out of here."

"Hold on."

There.

Down low in the green I saw the flash of his spectacles and I could make out a face in the ivy and wild shrubs that fortified the tree line. The boy knelt on both knees and he pushed his face through the foliage like he emerged from another dimension, a turtle forcing its head from its carapace.

"Hey," I whispered loudly to the boy. He hid from the others. From his face, he held a secret.

The boy waved us over while looking over his shoulder. When he turned back to us, the dread in his face made me stutter-step.

We knelt down to his level.

"I'm not supposed to do this," he whispered, his lips sticking, his throat clicking with fear. Though I saw his eyelashes flapping, I couldn't see his left eye through the webbed lens of his wire-rims. "They'll be here quick."

"Not supposed to do what?" I asked him.

He padded the air downward with his palm as if to quell my volume. He looked over one shoulder, then the other. The boy and Bass met eyes, and by the transmission between them, Bass knew to watch behind the boy for others.

"Who are you? What's going on?" I asked in a clipped whisper.

Clear-eyed and with a response that seemed readymade, he whispered, "There's no time. They'll be here. I'm Simon. I know what's going to happen next. And I think it concerns you." He pointed at me.

Simon looked to be maybe eleven, his ginger bangs sweat-plastered to his forehead, his freckles popping through his ruddy cheeks. I was so stunned at the surreality of a little boy from the green telling me this I could hardly think and certainly couldn't talk. Simon seemed to intuit this and he nodded his head with understanding.

"Here." Simon produced from behind him a plastic bag with something in it and tossed it to me.

I picked up the bag, felt the weight of it, holding it between knuckles by its knot. I recognized it to be a grocery bag, one of those you put your fruit or vegetables in before weighing, just like one from Central Market. I lifted it up thinking the kid had offered me some food. I lifted it up to get a look at it. My stomach freefell.

This Simon kid said, "Don't let your brother go. Keep him with you." And he looked dead level at me, tight-lipped and blinkless. I dove into his eyes but couldn't wrap my mind around why it mattered that I keep Johnny with me.

"What's this about Johnny? How do you even have this?" I lifted the bag and noticed the SKU price sticker on it. Vidalia Onion, $1.49.

Through the opaque plastic swaying before my eyes hung a stone. The stone Johnny had bagged and thrown down the corridor of pallets.

He shook his head, not able to answer my barrage. "You know, when those sounds happened," he said. He looked down at the ground, ashamed almost. "I saw this. Dreamed it, I mean. Now. Even this conversation we're having, me explaining this to you. Me tossing you that bag." His face churned into a howling sadness I'll never forget. "The feeling I had was that this is the end."

"We can see that," said Bass who still hunted motion beyond us with his eyes. "Yeah. Ending. Okay. So?"

"But it's the beginning, too."

"Beginning of what?" I asked.

"Whatever comes after this. I don't know." He shrugged. "I'm just a kid." His face changed, like he heard something.

"You see anything, Bass?"

"Huh-uh."

Simon turned back to me and locked onto my face again. "I just know it's the beginning. But the end has to come first, and it's not quite over yet. There are a few things that have to happen...I saw an ocean. Then a beach, and then . . ."

"When? What did you see?" Did we see the same things when we dreamed, this kid and I?

"I don't want to say." He shook his head and burst out a single cry and immediately sucked it up so that his throat got caught up in itself and he choked for a second. "No. I don't believe it." He shook his head hard, trying to loose whatever was lodged there.

Oh—he gave me the most pitiable look. His chin muscle quaked. Almost pouting, talking more to himself than us, he said, "Not everything I dreamed has happened. Maybe it's not true." Satisfied with that logic, he continued to me, "But one thing I know is true because I've been around them, all the kids. They're scared like you wouldn't believe. Not just because all their moms and dads are gone but because...well . . ."

"What?" Bass asked, still looking into the woods.

"They think there's a beast out... there." He motioned his hand out and up.

"A beast," I deadpanned.

He nodded and sniffed. "That it needs to be satisfied. Or else it will come for them. This is what the real end is. Satisfying it." In half a day, all innocence had left this boy's eyes. I couldn't muster a response. The hard look in his eyes stopped me cold. I knew it to be all the truth I required.

"Satisfying?" Bass asked.

"Feeding. The kids think it needs to be fed. They think it will eat them all up if it's not."

My mind flashed on the great shadowed thing. I asked, "But what—?"

And then they started coming. We could hear them flooding the woods. He hissed at us, "Go!"

We locked eyes for one shared heartbeat.

My eyes pleaded that he come with us. He shook his head with resignation.

Then me and Bass were in the Bronco and peeling out in reverse and then bounding over the cemetery dale, swerving around headstones.

I put my head out the window and craned my neck to see the tree line. Though the Bronco's motor roared, I heard screaming in the woods.

I remember snapping back inside, shoving my back straight against the seat and closing my eyes tight and not opening them again until we stopped. My mouth grew salty with nausea and Simon's scream wouldn't stop echoing between my temples. Bass concentrated on driving but he'd heard it too.

We pulled up to my car. Inside sat Johnny and Kodie. Rebecca hadn't moved.

"Meet us at my house." I jumped out and slammed the door.

"What happened to his car?" Kodie asked.

"Hailstorm," I said.

"Nuh-uh," Johnny said, incredulous.

"What the man said."

"But you don't believe that, right?" Johnny asked. Kodie knew I lied, felt the gravity of why I did, and, like Bass, said nothing. "Kevin, it hasn't rained in weeks. We didn't get hail last spring."

"It doesn't matter," I said as I turned the ignition key. Johnny looked past me into the faraway woods. From the corner of my eye I saw that he waved his hand reluctantly at whomever he saw there, and then quickly tucked it away. I didn't ask.

We did a lot of that in those opening hours. We saw but didn't say anything because we didn't want to know yet what we knew we would soon enough.

The traffic light was changing as we pulled out. "Look, still got power," Johnny said.

I heard him but didn't listen, for Simon's disembodied face was still screaming in my head.

THE FIRST THING WE ALL wanted to do was eat. We locked the doors and looked at the weapons lying about the living room like Christmas morning gifts from a very different kind of Santa. Safety and sanity returned with all of this.

Safety in numbers, in being indoors, in at least wrapping our collective heads around what has happened.

We pointed and grunted, guzzled straight from large containers, lines of liquid rolling down chins. The microwave thrummed.

Our minds reengaged. It occurred to all of us with our stuffed mouths that we were trapped in this new world we didn't choose. A type of rebirth had occurred, one we hadn't sought, as we are forced out from the womb by cosmic fiat.

The children had been reborn too, but they probably weren't examining the hows and whys like us. An old-world philosopher had said an unexamined life wasn't worth living. What a bunch of crap.

We sat at the dining room table in front of the big picture window to the backyard. An old playscape Johnny didn't use anymore rusted in the gloom. We kept glancing up at it. The swings swayed and the rust made the chains sing and we thought of children, the ones we used to be and all of them out there now. Those untold millions who didn't seem to have any need for our help. That they were hostile to our remaining. We stayed quiet on that topic.

But about other things, I couldn't stay quiet. "Okay. I've got to air this," I said. "Before we can plan our next steps, I think we need to come to a consensus—"

"What's a consensus?" asked Johnny.

"When everybody agrees," answered Kodie, leaning into Johnny.

I nodded. "Right."

"Agree to what?"

"I'm getting to that." I hadn't yet told Kodie what Simon had said to me. As the others put away groceries, I'd taken the bag with the stone in it and tossed it in the trash.

"We need to agree on something important. It's about you, Johnny."

Kodie's pupils dilated to their blue retinal edges. She conferred with her plate, looked back up at me, bated.

"Me?"

Bass reached into a flaming bag of corn chips and answered Johnny with a crunch.

"When Bass and I went to get his Bronco, we talked to a kid."

"A kid came into the cemetery?" he asked.

"He stuck his head through the brush at the edge of it." This set Johnny on the defensive. "Why do you ask that? I mean, you're a kid, and you were in the cemetery just fine."

Johnny responded with, "But I was with you all. It was okay."

Bass, Kodie, and I looked at each other with the shot eyebrows that come with a break in the case. What we were all thinking: there were these rules he intuitively knew. What we were all asking ourselves: had they been downloaded into him at dawn?

I just came out and asked, "Johnny, are there important things you think you want to tell me but don't know if you should? Maybe you think I'll be mad?"

He nodded. His eyes welled. Johnny sighed and said, "Tell me what you were going to tell me first. What about this kid?"

"The boy's name was Simon. He told me to keep you with me."

Bass and Kodie deferred to the brothers here, each of them being an only child. Bass crunched.

"But why? You weren't going to leave me, were you?"

"Of course not."

"So why does this kid who doesn't know us say this?"

"I was hoping maybe you'd tell me."

"How can I?"

"I think you know things. Things you want to tell me."

He looked at his lap, ashamed. "I don't."

"But you just nodded that you did, just now."

"I don't understand what's happening. I'm scared, Kev."

In my head I'm yelling at him, *Why don't you tell me the truth?*

"My head hurts," Johnny mumbled.

Why'd you let them push me out of that room?

I asked, "Do you know Simon?"

He shook his head and grimaced.

"You don't know a redheaded kid named Simon? Not at school, not from the neighborhood?"

He shook his head the same way while on his face was a mask of solemn duty which said: deny deny deny.

Kodie used her teacher's voice. "Do you remember this morning?"

"Sort of, yeah." Johnny swigged his soda and placed it on the table with a tinny bang.[10]

We just looked at him.

"Not really." Johnny was still too young to lie well.

She continued. "Do you know what's with the piles of rocks—"

"—Stones," corrected Johnny.

"Excuse me?"

"Say it." Johnny's face fell into a baleful smirk.

"Say what, Johnny?" Kodie asked.

"Stones. Say it."

"Why is that so important to you?"

"It's just more…correct."

"It's more correct? Why does that matter, Johnny? See what I'm getting at?" asked Kodie.

"No, I don't."

"Now you're being rude, J. Stop it," I said. Johnny looked up me, snapped out of his malevolence. "She's just trying to help."

He dropped his chin a bit. He looked back at Kodie but without the nasty look. "Sorry, Kodie. I…I don't know why. I don't. It doesn't matter. You're right."

"But…you felt compelled to say it, didn't you? I guess that's what I'm asking. Do you know why that is?"

He shook his head, drank, set the can down quietly this time.

I piled on. "Sleepwalking this summer, you said to me, and I do not paraphrase, 'it's not a task I want, Kevin, you have to know.' You remember *that*?"

He started to get upset. "Can we please stop? My head really hurts." He rubbed his temples.

---

10 I was confused and scared here, beyond all understanding.

Kodie sat back up straight, sighed deeply. "Sure, it's okay. I just want you to know that you can tell us anything. You don't have to be afraid to tell us anything you want."

"We need your help," I said.

Bass looked at Johnny and worked his jaw around his food.

Johnny slumped in his chair and nodded but evaded our eyes by looking out the window. We'd all scooted our chairs away and were starting to clean up. I'd gone into the laundry room off the kitchen to tap the pony keg when Johnny muttered from his chair, "There's more smoke." We all gathered behind Johnny and looked up at the twilit sky above the backyard oaks.

KODIE WAS RELUCTANT ABOUT LEAVING Rebecca sleeping in Johnny's room with her shoes off and tucked under a blanket, her diaphragm sine-waving. I locked the doors and set the house alarm. If it went off, we'd hear it, even down in the creek.

The smoke our beacon, we walked to see the wreck. This stretch of neighborhood looked as it would on any other night. Most porch lights were still on, as well as many interior lamps, enough to maintain the appearance of a normal evening in central Austin in October. Sodium-arc streetlamps kicked on as if heralding our progress. Everywhere in evidence was that ancient harvest time screw-you to winter's deathly approach: Styrofoam graveyards, some with boney arms piercing the earth's surface, cottony spider webs spanning entire front porches, pumpkins waiting on steps to be carved and lit. Johnny pointed out, "Look, the Millers' pumpkins. They always do great carvings." We didn't comment on his upbeat observation which so looked forward to the night when the neighborhood took on a *Saturday Evening Post* cast with the trick-or-treater traffic, some spaz-dad's machined fog caught in the live oaks, billowing costumes in the dark, flickering ochre of the jack-o'-lanterns, the squeals of delight and laughter.

No cars, nobody took their evening walks under the canopy of trees. You could feel the death settling in. Other than Mrs. Fleming across the street from us, there weren't any piles. The roaring quietude. The big fear residing inside it. Not with a bang but a *whuh!*

We ran over to a house with a front room filled with spectral flicker and looked through the front window, hoping that maybe we've been wrong in our assumptions, that maybe someone alive sat inside watching a news broadcast from a surviving corner of the planet.

Bass rang the doorbell repeatedly and we cupped our hands around our eyes to see in the front window. Looping in its DVD start menu was *The Wizard of Oz.*

As we heard Judy Garland singing that heartbreaking *why oh why can't I?* I noticed the woman in the chair. I couldn't gauge her age. Maybe fifty. We jostled each other to see her better. Bass continued jamming down on the doorbell. The violin interlude of *Rainbow* went on and then Kodie pulled away from the window and gulped and pulled Johnny by the elbow back with her.

I felt like I peered into a scene in an unvisited corner of Madame Tussaud's Wax Museum. The large kitchen knife buried to the handle just under the woman's sternum and the hardened black that had poured forth to collect in a pool on her lap. Only the TV light on her. If she had been smiling at Dorothy's Technicolor world, the smile no longer graced her face. Her eyes were open but the lids drooped like a zenned-out Buddha and her hands still had a loose grip on the armrests like she'd just come to a stop after riding a roller coaster.

We didn't want to go exploring old-world buildings anymore if we didn't have to. We knew what we'd find.

THOUGH THE FUEL HAD BURNED off by now, it did seem to be smoking more. The trees all around looked like they had burned but the fire hadn't spread. The rain earlier in the week defanged the roaring tinderbox established in August. One of the wings looked to have decapitated a house backing up to the creek. Only a rill of water ran under the plane through the creek bed. The fuselage acted as a slanted bridge of sorts. The windows were all burned out. The thing was so big as we neared that we feared getting much closer. You could smell fuel. You could smell cooked flesh and smoke. With small switches in the breeze, on top of everything, you could smell that port-o-potty sanitizing smell that had leaked from the flying toilets.

Our curiosity forced us down the embankment and into the creek. We'd jumped across a yard-wide run of water and stood on a limestone island strewn with faded aluminum cans. We could see coyotes on the other side of the plane standing in the creek looking at us, their eyes flashing yellow in firelight.

Bass roared and thrust his hands into the air. The coyotes didn't bolt. The alpha considered Bass and then calmly turned and walked away back up the creek. The others followed him into the tunnel of gathering dark, disappearing behind the fireglow.

We drew closer. The plane looked like a giant black alighted insect. Only in a few places did the silver of the fuselage show through the black matte carbon patina.

"The pilot tried to avoid as many houses as possible," Bass said

"Looks like he did a pretty good job, all things considered," Kodie said.

"But where are the bodies?" asked Johnny.

"Burnt up," I said. "Look." I pointed at the fuselage. Evening light hung in there though we spun toward night with increasing speed. You could just make out the charred humanoid figures sitting in their seats. I thought of the choking pilot trying to call out May Day to the tower but nothing coming out of his mouth but whistling. His eyes wide. His neck veins standing up. I thought of the air traffic controllers fallen out of their chairs. I thought of the world coming to an end while I toked up above it all because I was all sad about my little life. Idiot.

"What's that fire over there?" asked Kodie. "Looks relatively new."

"Probably debris caught from spilt fuel or something," said Bass.

"I don't think so," I said. "That fire was set."

"What makes you think that?"

"Looks like a pile of luggage."

Bass and Kodie squinted. None of us dared walk any closer to this colossus.

Johnny held up binoculars he'd grabbed from our cache of gear on the living room floor. "Here, Kevin, you look." He said this like he couldn't bear to see it confirmed.

The fire did eat away at luggage and it was clear that it had been gathered then set afire. The flames were too far away from the plane to make sense, too new and blazing. This is the added smoke we saw from the window.

The binoculars still to my eyes, I whispered, "Why?"

Johnny sighed and said, "To make us come check."

"To draw us out here," Kodie said.

Bass pointed along the top of the embankment.

All along both sides of the embankment, set against the dusky sky, were the silhouettes. They stood equidistant from each other, still and soundless as statues.

Johnny stood up on his toes, leaned into me and whispered, "They want me to go with them."

"You're not going anywhere," I said. I put my hand into my shirt, scratched out a single beat of ripping Velcro, and unsheathed Martin's Glock 9.

"That's loaded?" Bass asked out of the side of his mouth.

"Oh, yeah." I pulled back on the slide. The sound ricocheted nicely throughout the creek bed.

"Okay, good. I thought I was the only one." Bass pulled a handgun from his waistband and held it down to his side.

Kodie unsheathed a bowie knife I didn't know she had. Flames danced on its blade.

"Okay, listen up," I spoke loudly up the embankment, my voice echoing and carrying to the other side.

Kodie interjected. "We'd like to help you boys and girls. We are not going to hurt you and we know you're not going to hurt us. We can all help each other, okay? But right now we need to get back home and you all need to clear out and go back to your homes or someplace safe."

"You can come with us if you want to. Tomorrow's a new day. Okay?"

Dark invaded everything now, in just those last seconds, as my last *okay* echoed and washed out. The fire up ahead blinded us to everything beyond it. There could've been five hundred coyotes and an army of kids behind that fire. "We are all scared, all right? We know. But let's help each other," Kodie demanded. I looked up at one side of the embankment, then the other, staring into the voids of their faces.

All stood in silent standoff for maybe ten seconds. Then I muttered under my breath, "Okay, fine," and popped off three shots into the air and they scattered. You barely heard their scuffling.

I got the sickening feeling they possessed feral patience that belied their momentary fear of gunfire. Time is something they had. You felt they owned time. This was only the first night on the day of. They'd be less skittish soon, like those coyotes.

We made our way back up the switchbacked embankment, a switchback created by generations of neighborhood kids.

Though I didn't say so to anyone else, I still felt uneasy. It felt too easy, their sudden scatter. Less a reaction to the violent noise than a signal.

I had my gun drawn moving up that embankment in the lead like some sort of half-assed hero. A pot-smoking high school trombone player. Then, halfway out of the creek, we heard the home alarm blare high and urgent in repeated bursts.

We ran. Dark now. They'd busted the sodium-arc lamps. The glass sparkled on the street. Only the porch lights and whiteout TVs pressed back the dark enough. The alarm grew louder as we drew closer. At the house I jumbled the keys from my pocket with one hand, the other holding the gun, and keyed the door. I ran to the back of the hall and entered in the code.

The abrupt quiet was as starling as the alarm's onset. The others had gone into Johnny's room and when I skidded into the doorway, there Rebecca was, sitting in bed, crying as Kodie held her. The sliding windows were large and tall along the bedside. One was broken. Glass arrayed in a puzzle on the bed and floor. At my feet, a stone.

Through her sobs, Rebecca managed to say, "…tried to get in."

"We know. We're sorry we left you alone," said Kodie.

"It tried to get in!"

Johnny spoke up. "What do you mean 'it'?"

Rebecca shoved her face into Kodie's shoulder. Her voice muffled and wet, she said, "You know what it is, Johnny March. Don't act like you don't."

"SCREW IT," SAID BASS. I was with him on that, joining him in the laundry room. He sat on top of the washer, me on the dryer and below us the keg in a full red ice chest. We drank Warsteiner from Martin's best frozen beer mugs and after a minute of downing and burping, I uttered my profound retort.

"Yeah, screw it." I hopped down, the shift in me causing the release of a massive belch landing on the burp scale somewhere between old gaseous lion and horny walrus. It echoed in the room's tight confines.

"Nice."

I took the gun out and put it on the kitchen counter and leaned against the door jam. We both wanted to stay in this tiny room, a respite from all that space and quiet. "Man...so tired. Aren't you?" He nodded with the mug at his lips.

"This will help," I said as I bent down and refilled. I got back on the dryer and stared forward just as he did, jaw jutted out, eyes lidded. We looked like a couple of defeated caged monkeys wary of too many sugared children. But it had been a day of defeat, the longest day of all. I didn't want to think anymore, and put the mug to my lips, closed my eyes, tipped it up, and began to chug.

"Can you believe this?" Bass asked, beer-wet lips shining.

I chugged. His question felt rhetorical. When I finished, I wiped my mouth with my arm and belch-said, "No. The very definition of surreal."

Bass nodded.

"*Sur* is French for 'on.'"

"So, on real," Bass said.

"On real."

"We in danger? Tonight, I mean," Bass asked, bent over at the tap.

"Don't think so. Just kids and they're scared too. Nighttime. They're not—"

"They came here and broke that window."

"True. We weren't here. I don't think they're coming back."

"There's an arsenal in the living room," Bass said.

Two mugs down and now I was feeling it in my legs and throat, a flushness behind the ears. "C'mon. Let's do what we said we would. Drink this here beer, try and relax for a bit."

"Until you guys drove up...I was gone, really losing it."

Quiet. Stifled belches.

"Kevin," Bass said. "Why won't they come to us?"

I shook my head. "I don't—"

He jumped off the washer. "Why are they *against* us? You'd think they'd need us—"

"I wish I kn—"

"—come running to us crying and tugging on us." Bass exhaled an exasperated *pshhh*. "I do not get this. It scares the hell out of me, Kev."

I held up my mug to the flyspecked light and looked through the blond bubbles with one eye and redirected the conversation to the more hail-fellow. "You know, beer's a good thing. A good good thing. I am so glad that I insisted on grabbing this bad boy from the store," I said, kicking the cooler with my toe. "Did you know that in medieval times, Renaissance, when potable water was hard to come by, they drank beer for breakfast? Those beautiful churches all over Europe? Monks built those. Trappists, they made beer, man. They were drinking beer and building churches. Think about that."

Bass chugged a bit, bent at the knees, giving it a little body English. "Yeah. And the Rastafarians. They prayed using weed. God gave it to them so they could know him." *Burp.*

"I mean, wine's the blood of Christ for chrissake. Turning all that water into wine." I hopped down.

We both nodded at the concepts we'd just unveiled upon human discourse for the first time and in the fog of a beer buzz coming on, we stood there quiet for a moment and thought of the monks and the Rastas and God, the water and the wine and the weed and the expanses of stained glass set into all those churches' frames.

"Speaking of," Bass said. He looked at me and smiled.

"No, man. Not in the mood."

"Not saying that. Left it under the tree. Pipe too. Crap." He patted himself down to make sure. "No. Music is what I mean."

"Yes, good call. All day there's nothing but ad jingles and dead air. I'm not wanting to watch a DVD or even read. No playing Monopoly, Cards Against...Humanity. I don't think I can for a while, you know?"

"Yeah. Same way. Institutions, days of the week, none of it makes sense. A whole new framework built."

"You sure you're still not a little high?" I kidded and smiled.

"No, man. You know what I'm saying, right? It's like BC, AD, and now, whatever this is."

"I think we get to name it." I stared into the floor, shook my head clear. "But we're not going to think about it tonight, right?"

"Music. Music I can do. In fact, if I don't hear some music in the next minute I'm going to freak out. I've never in my life found it more necessary."

"Any requests?"

"You know, I could listen to anything right now. Anything."

"I've got some killer Dead bootlegs, man, where I keep my weed, man, in that ornate wooden box with the etched mandala under my bed, man."

"Okay. Shut up. Not anything. Not the Dead. Of all days. Let's not play the Grateful damned *Dead* today."

"Just kidding. Man."

Me and Bass raced to my room. Kodie jerked up and squinted at us. "What? What's happening?" She looked down at Rebecca, the child who apparently just couldn't get enough sleep. Badness teemed off her skin like heat. "I must've…What time is it?"

"Bob Marley time," announced Bass.

"Quarter past beer."

"You guys are *drinking*," Kodie said in this fantastic mock-disappointed mom voice.

"You are correct," I said, taking my phone from my desk and holding it up. "Damn thing's still good for something." I remember not even wanting to search the phone for clues about the outside world. I didn't care about vigilance, survival, the connectivity that could maintain it. Didn't care about people on the other end of the world who had figured out how to avoid the rolling death. The beer had claimed me into its short-lived euphoria, and I just didn't care.

Because I knew that there wasn't anything to look for anyway.

I wanted music. I wanted to live and to dance right then, not think about all tomorrow's maybes. That's all I've ever done, plan for tomorrow. Practice SATs, practice for Macy's, preparing for this, getting ready for that, forever rehearsing some life to be fully lived in that mystical more perfect future.

The old world's future was gone. I will never sit for the SAT. There will never again be a Macy's Thanksgiving Day Parade. There may never be parades again, with their pomp and symbols reflecting the past, foretelling a future, children's lost balloons floating into specks in the sky. On the night of the day of, with a belly full of beer, I got to understanding that zen idea of living in the present. Because that's really all there is.

Right. Now.

Martin was none too pleased when he knew I'd been messing with his stereo. God, he was such a dick! I touch his stuff and he freaks.

Though later I would feel bad about feeling so good playing Martin's stereo with impunity, it did feel good. We needed to feel good.

Kodie closed the door on Rebecca and got a mug of beer. Johnny didn't want to commit to bed after what had happened and had stretched out on the loveseat in what Mom called the reading nook of the dining room and was now asleep, looking like the cherubic little kid he was.

THE BASS SHOOK OUR BOWELS, thrummed in our chests, competed with our heartbeats. Bob Marley never sounded so full and glorious. Martin's great speakers stood tall on the wood floor. The sound fanned out along the polished grain. Now rain had moved in with the night, the clouds blooming up from the Gulf. We danced to all The Wailers I had on my phone for long stretches without talking.

Kodie had thrown her boots off as she let a third mug's foam settle while Bob's "I Shot the Sheriff" started up. She started in on this solipsistic dance, one where she closed her eyes and got lost in the music and spun slow with her arms twisted above her head, the knowing hip-sway and knee bends. It's the dance of the nymph, and when you see it you understand how men's ships let themselves be wrecked to wrack and ruin at the falling notes of the siren's song.

She was lost in her dance and me and Bass stopped whatever it was we thought passed for dancing and watched her.

And in Bass's eyes I saw what I hoped I wouldn't see. He watched and bit his lip as Kodie dipped her hips, as Kodie twisted and flowed.

She was showing off, proving so when she opened her dolorous avid blue eyes and smiled at us without a hint of self-consciousness, her cheeks flushed with the arousal that comes when all eyes are on you.

I stepped up to her and moved with her and she slid and bent into my movements, rendering them less awkward.

Bass went for his beer. Kodie and I danced to the thumping reggae and for the first time I felt myself grow jealous because I knew Kodie was watching Bass move across the room when I'm the one right here dancing with her. I lamely thought about something Martin used to say about loyalty—*dance with the one that brung you.* Like this was a date we were on, like she owed me. Absurd.

I watched her eyes watching him, watched her flick her hair back with a snap of the neck, and knew the math was wrong now. Our ratio summoned up an SAT practice test word problem: When it's the end of the world and you're pretty sure you're the last near-adults on Earth, what happens when there's one pony keg of Warsteiner, one girl, and two guys with her?

Fill in the appropriate bubble with your No. 2 pencil. And though this is multiple choice, don't forget to show your work.

A MOUTH TWITCHED AND SPREAD open into a broad smile of dark shining teeth.

I sat straight up in bed. My eyes shot back and forth in their sockets searching the moonlit room. Kodie lay beside me undisturbed, fully clothed as I. The alcohol trying to drag me back down but adrenaline overrode it.

I whispered to Kodie, "You hear that?" Her breathing remained the same.

The clock's digital green said three thirty. I sat there in a beer sweat, breathing shallow breaths, not sure what made my body go on alert when my mind had yet no notion.

Understanding came when I heard the distant light rumble. The Gulf rain clouds had met with a trough of cooler air from the north and the collision made thunder.

I lay back down slowly so as not to bother Kodie.

I don't remember when I grew tired of the music and dancing. I don't remember coming to bed at all, but here she was and all felt okay, cozy even, with the sound being diagnosed as thunder. The day after the day of was still hours away.

I turned onto my side to watch Kodie sleep for a minute, her silhouette silvery against the moon-cast window, and then put my arm over her and closed my eyes.

IT'S ONLY ME, BROTHER. NO OTHER.

Johnny's voice.

The thunder still sounded and soothed me and sleep snatched me down. Just before I succumbed, my drifting brain mined the subconscious and put together facts reminding me that thunder comes, crescendos, and then trails off.

This rumbling wasn't trailing off. A low note came along on top of it. It built, its source coming closer.

My eyes flew open. I knew this sound but my mind couldn't yet identify it because it was a sound so part of the fabric of my everyday life. Now that the new world had torn through that fabric, this noise stood out.

Kodie propped herself up on her elbows. "What are you doing?"

I stood in the middle of my room with my arms out and palms flared, listening. "Sshhh. You hear that rumbling?"

Kodie looked at the ceiling. "Thunder?"

"That's what I thought. MoPac."

"There're no cars, Kevin." She started to lie back down, but then she shot up. "Ohhh, the *train*. Now I hear it."

"Right. But…who's driving it?"

"Maybe it's been running all day. Maybe the engineer wasn't able to stop it before he—"

"Sounds like it's rolling really slow. You think it's pulling anything hazardous? I've been hearing that thing all my life. Never paid it any attention." My mind reeled at the insanity of a runaway ghost train coming our way.

"I don't know. Maybe. At some point it'll come to a stop."

"I think I should go see what's what. Just in case there's an adult running it."

"You don't think kids can run a train, do you?"

I stood there swaying in that space between drunk and hungover. How often we'd have to question things. Nothing would be assumed for a long time. Just how much we had ahead of us made the SATs and college and career and that life track in the urban information age seem petty and small. The learning curve ramping onto this new life felt too steep.

"I'm going to drive over to the tracks and see. I'm sure Johnny would want to see this." Was this what being a dad felt like? That's a parent's inclination, to consider including the child in an activity for the sake of pedagogy.

How *quick* nature is. The roles it assigns when change comes, how nature doesn't consider it to be change. Change is just…something else. I thought how nature isn't conscious. It just is. Understanding? That's man's angst. Well, it was. Was it mine? Did I burn to understand what had happened?

Then, I did. But now, no. I just want to live. And the only way to do that is to connect with them.

JOHNNY'S ROOM STOOD EMPTY AND cool for the hole in the glass. The plastic trash bag Bass and I had taped over it billowed inside and sucked back out, a palpitating sac belonging to a breathing thing.

Mom and Martin's pitch-dark room smelled of stale, sweet breath. I turned on the bathroom light so as to awaken Bastian. Then I remembered Johnny had passed out in the reading nook.

No Rebecca in the bedrooms. I walked with alacrity to the main part of the house and started flipping on lights. The living room was empty, as was the nook.

No Rebecca, no Johnny.

I hadn't put on the alarm. I dashed to the front door. The bolt was in place.

The back door off the dining room was bolted as well. I jogged to the laundry room, stepped down into the mud room. That door was cracked an inch.

The kids were outside.

Johnny was more than just outside. He was gone.

KODIE BEGGED ME NOT TO go, said that it served no purpose chasing it.

When I told her Johnny and Rebecca weren't here, she put her fingers to her lips. I told her Johnny once mentioned he thought hopping a train would be cool. Apparently, Martin did it once when he was young. Great parenting, planting that idea into your son's head.

One sleepwalking night, Johnny's in my room, standing in the dark, the train trundling. "Hear that, Kev? That's the future. Close, close, close."

Johnny was among the networks of the new world's children who didn't want us here, who have come to believe so by intuition afforded them when those sounds boomed over the world that dawn. It's their world now. We're the remnants, the revenants of the old world.

The Train Chasers. The Late Bloomers.

They wait.

They've got time.

Is sublime patience the reason why they don't just amass around us and kill us? Why don't a few of the older ones come find us with the guns of their fathers in their hands and just take us out?

Are we misunderstanding them? I asked myself.

Why didn't they? Because they didn't need to. Because, as the phrase goes, they have all the time in the world. They own time. They can remake it and reshape it and mark it however they want.

They're afraid and confused. I think they are between worlds, being tugged between antipodes.

It became clear to me then: They don't just attack us wholesale, assuming they want us gone, because that would be the way of the old world, to confront and eliminate your enemies with weapons, with machines. They probably don't see us as enemies in the literal sense.

Things are the way they are.

I thought about what that Simon kid had said, and then shuddered as if a blast of cold air had riffled up my shirt and grabbed my heart—*Keep Johnny with you.*

I know the trilling screams I heard as Bass and I drove off were his. That terrified little boy was willing tell me that. That and something else he couldn't let loose from his mouth. I saw his flushed face again, the freckles popping from his high cheeks, peering through the green, and I saw the bag with the rock as I lifted it up.

I ran out the side door, flung open the trash can in which I'd tossed it.

The rock was gone.

A KNIGHT ERRANT, I SPED off after a runaway train hoping my brother rode it. It had stopped raining and the air and the road smelled anew. Not a full day later and the *air*…my God. Soon that freshness would turn into a worldwide deathreek.

The train headed south. Johnny riding it… I don't know what I was thinking. I guess that's why I'm telling you, dear reader. Trying to figure out what I was thinking, hindsight offering a bit of perspective if not clarity.

Three tire-screaming turns later, without hardly touching the brakes, and I sped along the MoPac expressway through the pools of the arc lights at four in the morning, the new dawn not yet fathomed. Hundreds of cars sat on the shoulders. Some had veered and come to a stop at the median along which the train tracks ran. All of the doors to those cars had been flung open, their occupants gone.

Where were they? No stone cairns, no bodies. Just empty cars up and down MoPac, doors open, blinkers punctuating the dark.

The long freight train flagged aimless. It might quit right here. My speedometer clocked me at seven once I cruised alongside. At this crawl and by the lights I was able to make out some of the graffiti, glorious confections of color, shape, and menace.

It's not like I really chased Johnny. But I did give desperate panting chase like a dog without a clue what to do now that I'd caught it. I just needed to come see it, I think, a relic of the old world, like me, something, anything, still rolling along out of the past. I felt a stupid kinship to this train.

Following the train as it eased toward the downtown skyline, all my windows down, leaning out and listening to the mechanical clack and moan. I found myself waving at the engine though I saw nobody in the window. These things ran on autopilot, I guess. Inertia on display, a body in motion. Would it exhaust its fuel before plowing through the terminus end-rails? Nobody'd be hurt. No property would be damaged, no insurance claims filed. It would be of no more consequence than a wave crashing upon a beach. Just another old-world mover ceasing to.

How many still moved across the globe without engineers, without captains, full of dead passengers, running off rails and piling on top of themselves, cartwheeling over and over, massive cargo ships running the China to Los Angeles route tipping over in rough seas, all that cargo slipping off into the ocean, others plowing into ports, icebergs, undrawn bridges?

The dark teeth part of me smiled, the one that's close, close, close—
Bring it all down. Be finished with it.

Where did that sentiment come from? Often enough during those first
days I remember this nihilism flashing through me like a flicking shadow,
a hot wave.

I thought of stopping, running up alongside and jumping onto one of
the ladders, lope along the top like a hero with perma-stubble to the front
where I would slip feet-first into the engineer's car, shove the corpse aside,
slam down the accelerator, and plow onward into this odd future. I sped
up to get way ahead of it so I could time it, got out of the car, jumped the
guardrail and scrambled up the berm, slipping in the loose rock up to the
track. I stood on the track with my feet spread shoulder-width apart on a
tarry tie and watched it come. Austin's skyline loomed half lit-up behind
me. The tie shuddered beneath my feet. My molars clacked.

It rolled toward me, a hundred yards away now.

I closed my eyes and in my mind saw the nose of this massive metal
engine lifting me up and then me being ground under it. When I heard my
own screaming underneath the wheels, saw my body pummeled, I chased
away the thought.

At least I was still chasing away the thoughts.

The white stuff hadn't come for me, and I knew it wouldn't. But was I
getting a slow drip of the other? I felt like I was going crazy right then. My
mind splitting. Look at me, I thought, standing on a train track in the dark,
a dawdling train coming toward me, and I'm debating with myself whether
I should stay.

Is this what all the other late bloomers were doing? Fighting it off, going
mad in the process?

Was there anybody else besides us? Actuarial logic said there had to
be. Beyond that though, I *knew* there were. I had never felt, intuited things
so deeply and assuredly. I knew things now. Just knew them. I know them.

When I opened my eyes again, I knew the late bloomers left wouldn't be
for long if we didn't get together very soon.

The train was only fifty yards from me now. I waved my hands above
my head in big sweeping SOS. arcs. It came on slow and implacable and
pointless.

Just as it reached me, I stepped off and moved my arm in the way of a suave matador allowing the crazed bull to bellow by, bowing to it as it passed. The train rolled by an arm's length away. My hair moved in its wake. I looked straight at it in a blur for a minute but the squeals of metal on metal became too much.

From the car I saw the graffitied phrase scroll by over and over: *A Pox on Yo Lips.*

Apocalypse. The white stuff. My eyes followed the last tag for as long as I could still read it. When my eyes jumped back, directly in front me, in the flashing interstices between train cars, it stood looking at me. I knew what it was. I saw its wings folded to its ribs, its snaky tail coiled around its talons.

I did not blink. I did not breathe.

My view of it was indistinct as an image through a zoetrope. It looked at me as I looked at it.

The train rolled past. That I no longer saw it standing there wasn't a surprise. I leaned on the hood of my car and for the first time really cried.

ON THE SHORT DRIVE BACK to the house I wondered if we, Kodie and I—her and I alone—could rebuild. Could we do it right? Had Bass messed up that simple equation?

I turned on the radio and listened to a couple of looping ad jingles. Yesterday I found them annoying, dismaying, then macabre. Today, like the train, I'd rather listen to them more than just about anything. I could picture all the people involved and, though I didn't know them, I missed them terribly. I can see them in the studio standing around a boom microphone, all with headphones on, singing the inane lyrics they held in their hands but getting into it because it's work and work is good.

Working is living.

I saw the advertising people in their urbane outfits playing it for the client in some swank glassed room and they all nodded to it until they cut it off and then, after the moment of uneasy quiet, the smiles started and handshaking and backslapping wouldn't stop and then a few of them would go out to happy hour pleased with their work that day and a woman and a man would kiss in the car on the way home and remark to each other how they felt like teenagers and that each always had liked the other but was afraid to say anything.

Daybreak and there's no low roar of a city waking up.

NOBODY WAITED ON THE PORCH. The front door stood inches ajar. I pushed it open. Bass's snores filled the back half the house. A swing in the backyard set swayed. I stood at the picture window and saw Kodie come back to it from behind the stand-alone garage. I watched her rock back and forth on the swing. She sensed I watched her and looked up. I went out to see her.

"Did you catch it?" she asked, the subtext clear: *Did you find Johnny?* She coughed into her fist, looked at her hand, then tucked it under her knee.

I shook my head and eased into a swing. We listened to birds call and respond in the oaks above. "I stood on the tracks. For a sec, I wanted it to hit me and would've let it if it'd come faster. I chickened out and stepped off just before it got to me."

"That's not chickening out. C'mon, we've got to keep trying. Once Bass gets up, we should talk, plan." She coughed a little more, which then bloomed into a productive hacking.

"You okay?"

She coughed like a goose. She put her hand up to say wait a minute. When she was finished, she glanced at a shaded spot behind the garage where she had been when I first saw her out here. I followed her glance. In the still summer-green St. Augustine, I saw spots of red.

"Is that from you?" I asked her. "Kodie?" Dumbstruck. "Is it...?"

"I feel hot to you?" She leaned over in her swing and I felt her head.

"Yeah. Let's go inside and take your temperature."

"No. Let's just sit here for a minute. Please. The birds." She scanned the canopy and inhaled the fresh air. Grackles chivvied above us, not caring at all about our predicaments. A smile lifted her mouth's corners. "Where do you think they are?"

"Johnny and Rebecca?" After a long exhalation and running my hands through my hair, I said, "I feel like they're all together somewhere. Maybe in the city, but I feel like they'd be heading somewhere else, away." In my mind's lidless eye, from the boulder atop Mount Bonnell, I saw the river flowing to the Gulf.

"You feel that?"

"Don't you feel something?"

"A broad question given the last twenty-four hours." She coughed. "About them? The children?"

I nodded.

"Yeah, I feel it," she said, "but I don't know what it is I'm feeling."

"They're gathering. Waiting. They're not part of the old world. That's why they'll be leaving the cities. I'd say I'm having visions about it but that's…seeing them all together out in an open field." Lidless eye: On the beach. Rows of fires. Piles of stones.

She stood up, excited though stifling another cough. "Not dreaming, but in, like, little flashes. When I think of the children, that's what I see. Tens of thousands, like you'd see at a music festival or something."

I think not of sunny Austin City Limits but of a Las Vegas night, broken windows on the thirty-second floor, automatic rifle fire.

"Yep, me too." I start swinging, almost like I'm dismissing the coincidence. I wasn't seeing flashes, though. I was seeing, had been since midsummer, entire scenes. Had heard their hummed polyphonic songs.

"Aren't you at all interested in why we're both…or how?"

"Of course, I'm interested, but what to do about it?" I swung higher and higher, looked up into the umbrellas of oaks and knew I was right. "I just don't know what knowing it gets us."

"It's going to be important to you. And our common vision lends to that knowledge."

I swung and didn't say anything. She looked at the speckles of blood on her hand. She smeared it into her other hand. At the apex of my swings behind her, I could see that her shoulders were lifting and shaking as she began to cry.

I drag-stopped. "Come on. Let's go in and take your temp."

Kodie's temperature measured 102. She lay prone on the couch in the living room, her forearm resting on her forehead, her eyes closed.

"Shit," she said.

No, that's good, I thought. Fever means the body fights something from with*out*, that invaded and spreads.

Bass made coffee, moving about shirtless in the kitchen. He sniffed a lot, rubbed his palms under his armpits and massaged his pecs in a vain way he would do even if alone. "Warsteiner," he said with morning-after vocal fry.

I sat at the long white subway-tiled kitchen bar, waiting on the coffee.

"What's wrong with her?" Bass asked me, keeping his voice low.

"Why don't you ask her?" I gave him a look which said, *I saw you eyeing her last night.*

He coughed into a fist. "Because she looks like she doesn't feel like talking."

"Got a fever. Been coughing up blood."

"Blood?"

"Bass, when you saw your folks…Sorry, man, I've got to ask this. Was there any?"

The coffeemaker hissed. "Blood. Cracking lips, but not from the throat. The whole thing seemed very dry. If that makes sense." He looked off into the corner of the kitchen, his arms crossed and his palms under his armpits. It was that same glazed stare seen in the faces in the photographs of soldiers from the front staring off for a thousand yards. This all happened only twenty-four hours ago yet it seemed ages.

After several minutes of silence as Bass and I drank our coffee, prefaced by a deep sigh which triggered a coughing jag, Kodie said, "I don't know what to do." Her forearm still rested over her eyes.

Nobody said anything for a minute or so, which, following that question, was a long time indeed.

"What do we do?" she asked. "This malaise. Shouldn't we be freaking out?"

I said, "Maybe our survival demands that we don't do that. We're in shock, like when you break a bone and it doesn't hurt so bad at first. If we were to drive around all half-cocked, it'd be dangerous. Maybe this mellowness, not panicking, is part of it." My pontificating felt as strange as my defense of this course of inaction.

Bass grabbed his wadded dark green T-shirt from the counter, pulled it on, and asked, "What do you want to do about Johnny, Kevin? I'm up for whatever you want to do about it. If you want to go try to find him, I'm with you."

Heavy, helpless sigh from me. "I mean, where would we start? Johnny's with all the others. He came back before. But that Simon kid, though, what he said."

"The boy you talked to at the cemetery? What'd he say? You didn't tell me." Kodie started to sit up but didn't.

"He said to keep Johnny with us. Like it mattered in some big way. And he said that the kids were really scared. They think there's some monster—"

"—Beast," reminded Bass, his lips to his mug so that the word came out muffled, steamed and amplified.

"—beast, out there that needs to be fed or it will get them. Feeding this beast is what will bring on what he called the beginning."

Kodie sat up. She took the thermometer from the coffee table and stuck it under her tongue, clicking it against her teeth. We waited for the beeper to go off. "There. It's going down. I took something before you got home. I feel better."

"You took something?" I asked

"In your cabinet. Ibuprofen." Why hadn't she mentioned it?

"I think we need to go find where they all are," Bass said. "Johnny'll be with them. There's a hundred thousand kids out there in this city that we can't see or communicate with. That's the first step."

"All right," I said, up for anybody else to take the lead. My four a.m. train-chasing fatigue burrowed into my bones. "Let's get a ham radio somewhere. Maybe, just maybe, there's somebody out there." We all nodded.

"Walkie talkies," Kodie said. We all nodded.

"Don't cost nothin'," Bass said.

"Sounds like the beginnings of a plan are forming here. The malaise lifts," I said, smiling. "Kodie, you up for this?"

"I have a choice? I mean, we shouldn't go out alone or be left alone and we need to make some moves now. Before long the power's going to go. Yeah, I'll be okay."

The rumbling motor and rattling exhaust echoed between my street's halt houses. "We could just go get another car. A brand-new truck or something," Bass said.

"An urban assault vehicle."

"There you go. Like a Suburban. No, a Hummer."

"Hummer. Yes."

"How Green Zone of you," said Kodie from the back seat, still offering her old-world protests.

"Let's go find out where these kids are first," Bass said.

"Where to? I mean, where in the hell do we start?" I asked.

"Let's cruise around, see what we can see."

"I know it sounds silly, but it's kids we're talking about, right? So, the schools, the malls."

Bass demurred. "Huh-uh. Zilker. Butler."

Kodie chimed in. "What we were talking about earlier, Kevin. That's where I think I've been seeing them. Down by the river."

I nodded and looked back at her. "Yeah. And if you're a kid, would you want to go back to school if nobody made you?"

"Hold on," Bass said. He put the Bronco into park and chugged in the middle of the street. "You've been *seeing* them? What are you guys talking about?"

Kodie and I sat in silence, each waiting for the other to say.

"Okay. Don't answer me." He started to put the truck in gear.

"Poor Bastian," Kodie mocked. The flirty way she said it stung. "Tell you what. When we're all done, we'll go get you a nice new Humvee with a machine gun turret on top. That make it all better?"

Bass nodded childishly, bowed his head but lifted his beseeching eyes to her. "And ice cweam?"

"And ice cweam," I said, stepping on Kodie's next line to quash their rapport.

"Guys, shut up," Kodie said. She toggled her eyes in her head. "I know you don't care, Kevin, and I understand, but I've got to try to find my folks. I can't just not try."

Bass nodded. "Let me know where you want to start."

"My house," she said. "Hyde Park."

We started to roll when I noticed the door cracked at the Fleming's house. The door swung back and forth, an inch out, an inch in. "Hold on a sec," I said, "I gotta see something real quick."

"Real quick," admonished Bass.

I hopped out of the truck and jogged over to the Flemings' house, stepping around the cairn of stones covering Becky Fleming. I noticed the smell, the rank and the sweet marking the decay. Approaching the door, the smell shifted, then grew.

"There's no reason in the world why I've got to go in here," I told myself just before I pushed open the door with my toe. "Yet here I am," I said with my hand over my nose and mouth. The sound the door made creaking open came from somebody pressing play on a spooky sounds CD from the ninety-nine-cent post-Halloween cutout bin. I stepped in, left the door open behind me. I looked back at Bass and Kodie. They faced each other talking, and though distant and obscured, I could make out their bodily attitudes and I burned. They seemed to be arguing.

In the back part of the house, I heard tinny music Mr. Fleming had left on. Leaves had blown in. They scratched underfoot. I walked through the stillness, the wood floors similar to ours creaking under my footfalls. Tiptoed down the gloom of the hallway as if I were sneaking up. The smell intensified. The blinds and curtains of the house were still drawn as they would be at early morning, so by the time I reached the hallway to the bedrooms, I had to flip on the light. The wash of light bared out everything true and awful though I looked only at a plain hallway. Pictures on the wall.

Traipsing through someone else's house felt wrong and my anxiety at what I would find made me queasy. Though the house was musty and smelling of death, I also felt a current of air running over my skin. Thinking I felt movement in the house, a presence, I drew my gun, held it to my side. I crept down the short hall and my flesh bubbled up over my arms and hands. One hand covering nose and mouth, one holding the glock.

I pushed open the door to the back bedroom. The clock radio played big band. There lay Mr. Fleming, under a partially opened window, dressed in a navy suit and blue tie, polished brown shoes. Last night's rain had blown in, leaving his hair and jacket wet. The curtains waved.

I stood in the doorway and observed the room for a moment, trying to discern what happened in here other than that Mr. Fleming had died. On his desk was a yellow legal pad, a few pages rolled and tucked back under it, a pen laying on top at an angle that seemed purposeful, resting as it did at a perfect diagonal with the paper's corners. Something ordered in the chaos, to be noticed. Similarly, Mr. Fleming's shotgun was at the foot of the bed in a way that made me sure it had been set there carefully. A laying down of arms. Compared to all the others I'd seen, this scene of death seemed to be mindful, staged, Mr. Fleming accepting and ready to go, though I wondered about the window being half open and him right below it. Had he tried to climb out?

Then there was the other thing that made this scene different though my mind hadn't grasped it when I first came in. He clutched a folded piece of yellow legal pad paper and held it to his chest.

I knelt down and took it from his stiff hand, tearing a swatch off which remained between curled fingers. His face pallid, his eyes looked past me at the ceiling, the inside of his mouth glimmering white, morning light gilding it. His eyes held the yet unnamed combined color of gray and yellow, streaked across with red oxbows exclaiming the brutality of last breaths.

I holstered the glock, clicked off the clock radio, and unfolded the paper to the writing inside. I lifted my T-shirt up over my nose.

Outside, the Bronco's muffler blatted. Bass honked twice and I heard him yell out to hurry up.

I turned the paper[11] around, sat on the edge of the bed, felt the butt of the shotgun at my hip. Mr. Fleming's script looked harried, the letters jagged, the lines slanted.

KEVIN—JUST AS MY TIME COMES UPON ME, I SOMEHOW KNOW YOU WILL SURVIVE AND HOPE YOU FIND THIS. IN FACT, I KNOW YOU WILL, BECAUSE OF THE DREAMS ABOUT YOU AND THE YOUNG WOMAN I'VE BEEN HAVING THIS SUMMER. DREAMS THAT WERE MORE THAN DREAMS. IN THIS KNOWING ABOUT YOU, I'VE ALSO SEEN THE DARK SMILING TEETH, WHICH I KNOW YOU'VE SEEN TOO, THUS I KNOW THAT YOU'LL NOT BE STAYING HERE FOR LONG, SO, WHEN YOU CAN, BEFORE YOU GO, WILL YOU PLEASE BURY MY WIFE AND MYSELF AT MEMORIAL PARK?

I wondered if Bass wanted to bury his folks. Should I waste time trying to find Mom and Martin?

11 A copy of this document is attached as Exhibit B

I KNOW IT'S A LOT TO ASK. WE HAVE PURCHASED (NOT THAT THE QUAINT CONCEPT OF "PURCHASING" MATTERS MUCH NOW) TWO PLOTS IN THE NEW SECTION BY THE FAR EAST LONG ROAD. THERE IS A SHORT YOUNG HEDGE THAT RUNS BORDERING THE SOUTH OF IT. THE NEAREST GRAVE IS MILLER TO THE NORTH AND PARISH TO THE SOUTH AND SALAZAR TO THE EAST. WE PICKED THAT SPOT TOGETHER, BUT ANYWHERE IN THE SHADE OF THAT LITTLE WOOD WOULD BE MUCH APPRECIATED. I'M NOT SO CONCERNED ABOUT ME, BUT I CANNOT BEAR KNOWING SHE'S OUT IN THE OPEN LIKE THAT.

She's not in the open, I thought. She's under a pile of rocks.

I'm sorry, *stones.*

THIS THAT'S KILLED US? YOU'RE ASKING ME, WITH OBSEQUIOUS GENUFLECTION AT THE DOORSTEP OF THE LEARNED PROFESSOR? MY BEST GUESS IS…EVOLUTION IS TOO SLOW. NEAR-EXTINCTION IS FAST. WE'RE THE KEYSTONE SPECIES. WE'VE NOT BEEN HERE LONG, GEOLOGICALLY SPEAKING, BUT WE'VE DONE A LOT OF—SOME WOULD SAY DAMAGE. I DON'T SEE IT THAT WAY. I DON'T THINK THE EARTH DOES EITHER. I THINK WE'VE MERELY PUSHED NATURE INTO A CORNER. SHE'S PUSHED BACK HERE AND THERE, WITH AIDS, WITH STRAINS LIKE SARS, EBOLA, WITH MELTING ICECAPS. BUT NOW I THINK NATURE HAS GIVEN US A HARD SHOVE.

WHAT'S DONE THE SHOVING? SOMETHING LODGED DEEP IN OUR DNA CODE, HIDING, WAITING FOR THE TRIGGERING MOMENT, WAITING STILL AND QUIET AND PATIENT AS A SNAKE EYEING THE FLITTING MOUSE. IT'S BEEN WAITING THERE ALL ALONG, HIDDEN ON THE DARK SIDE OF THE HELIX.

I WAS TOO OVERCOME WHEN YOU WERE AT MY DOOR, BUT I DID WANT TO TELL YOU THAT AT A LITTLE AFTER DAWN—HOUSE AND CAR ALARMS STARTING TO GO OFF, THE VARIOUS CITY EMERGENCY VEHICLES SIRENS BLARING IN THE FAR DISTANCE— I LOOKED OUT THE WINDOW TO SEE THE JENKINS KIDS, THREE HOUSES DOWN FROM YOU, AND THE WALSH KIDS WHO LIVE AROUND THE BLOCK, ALL MEET IN FRONT OF THE JENKINS' HOUSE. THEY DIDN'T TALK. THAT HALF BLIND DANNY JENKINS KID PULLED THOSE COKE-BOTTLE EYEGLASSES OFF HIS FACE AND DROPPED THEM TO THE PAVEMENT. THEY SILENTLY TURNED AND WALKED DOWN THE STREET. THE CHILDREN OF THIS WORLD NOW? THE ONES YOU'VE GOT TO SOMEHOW CONTEND WITH

AND LEAD? CHANGED, AND CHANGING. QUICKLY. DRONES, LACKING FREE
WILL, LIVING IN VAST WORLDWIDE COLONIES.

IT'S JUST A GUESS, BUT I'M AFRAID THAT'S ALL I'VE GOT TO GIVE.

"Lacking in specificity," I mouthed to myself in a wet whisper. A dry
hank of Mr. Fleming's bangs lifted in the rising wind coming through the
window.

WE SURE WERE LOOKING FORWARD TO WATCHING YOU PLAY AT THE
MACY'S THANKSGIVING DAY PARADE. DON'T STOP PLAYING. THE WORLD
WILL STILL NEED ITS MUSIC...AND ITS STORYTELLERS, ITS POETS (YES, WE
ALL KNOW ABOUT YOUR WRITING; YOUR MOTHER WAS SO PROUD).

GODSPEED, KEVIN. IT'S YOUR WORLD NOW~

KENNETH FLEMING

I SLUMPED, ROUNDED MY SHOULDERS, and sighed. I reread the last lines
again about what the world will still need and doubted very much that I
should be the one to provide it, that I was worthy of such a thing. The part
about my mom being proud made me erupt in wracking sobs which I tried
not let consume me but when I did that it got worse. I tried to hold it in and
to suck it up.

Sucking it up, the smell of death in the room drew farther back and up
into my deep sinuses, and its pungency stung. I smelled the death of this
room and knew that the woman who carried me, gave birth to me, cared for
me, sang me to sleep, loved me only for who I was and nothing more—she
lay smelling somewhere too and it was almost more than I could stand.

Despair kept worming its way into me. The will to survive couldn't
plane the sharp edges of mourning. If I were to find myself alone in this, the
fear would drown me just as sure as the white stuff.

I noticed at the bottom of the note, right above where the paper had
been torn, a solitary *PS.* It hung there. He had torn off what came after.

I went to the desk and picked up the yellow legal pad and swung over
the page tucked behind. The name WARREN JESPERS PHD UT appeared at
the top, but had been crossed out. A false start. A change of mind.

I pulled out the wicker waste basket from under the desk. In it was
a neon-green Pearl-Snap beer can, an empty box of shotgun shells, and a

wadded ball of yellow paper. I snatched it out like it was Wonka's golden ticket.

The top of the first page was torn at the angle matching the note I'd just read. There was a second page as well.[12]

KEVIN, I'M RELUCTANT TO ADD THIS, BUT I THINK I SHOULD. I HAD A COLLEAGUE, MY GOOD FRIEND REALLY, AT THE UNIVERSITY, WARREN JESPERS, WHO HAD STOPPED TEACHING PRE-MED BIOLOGY TO WORK IN PURE RESEARCH WITH UT'S RATHER HUSH-HUSH GENOME PROJECT. IT WAS HIS PROJECT. WARREN WAS BRILLIANT, TENURED, AND TOO OLD BUT REFUSED TO RETIRE. THE BOARD OF REGENTS WANTED HIM TO DO HIS THING FAR AWAY FROM THE SPOTLIGHT. THEY HAD HIM AT THIS LITTLE-KNOWN ANNEX OFF MEDICAL PARKWAY IN A BUILDING THAT COULDN'T BE ANY MORE NONDESCRIPT. HE HAD A SINGLE ASSISTANT, MY WIFE.

The other thing she did besides tutor Spanish.

BECKY CAME HOME LAST MONTH ASHEN-FACED, ASKING ME TO HELP WARREN BECAUSE HE WOULDN'T LEAVE THE BUILDING, HE WAS OBSESSED. SHE'D BEEN BRINGING HIM FOOD AND CHANGES OF CLOTHES FOR A MONTH. THIS SOUNDS LIKE A MAD SCIENTIST SCENARIO, BUT IN THIS CASE, HIS MADNESS WASN'T DUE TO SOME NEFARIOUS THING HE WAS BUILDING BUT RATHER WHAT HE'D DISCOVERED. TO SIMPLIFY: HE DISCOVERED AN ELEMENT IN A GENE WHICH CONTROLS OUR PRODUCTION OF AN ENZYME CALLED MONOAMINE OXIDASE A (MAOA). IN LAY TERMS, THIS IS THE EVIL GENE, THE MAKINGS OF PSYCHOPATHS. THIS, COMBINED WITH A GENETIC KINK IN SEROTONIN RECYCLING…MAKES MONSTERS. HIS THEORY WAS THAT NATURE—THE GENE—ALONE MADE EVIL MEN AND THAT NURTURE IS NOT A FACTOR AT ALL, THAT THE IDEA OF NURTURE HAVING SIGNIFICANT INFLUENCE JUST MADE US FEEL BETTER. HE HAD ISOLATED THIS GENE, WROTE A PAPER WHICH WAS PEER REVIEWED, BUT NOT WELL. AS IS THE FATE OF MOST VISIONARIES, NOBODY TOOK HIM SERIOUSLY, SO THEY SHUFFLED HIM OFF TO THAT OUTPOST ON MEDICAL PARKWAY TO KEEP HIM QUIET. THEY PATTED HIM ON THE HEAD AND TOLD HIM TO GO PLAY. OVER THERE. WAY OVER THERE. BUT THIS ALONE ISN'T WHAT HAD HIM OBSESSED. ONCE ENSCONCED AT HIS LAB ON MEDICAL, JUST DOWN THE STREET FROM

12 A copy of this document is attached as Exhibit B.1

THAT PUB TRANSPLANTED FROM STRATFORD-UPON-AVON, HE FOUND SOMETHING ELSE, SOMETHING THAT HE HADN'T TOLD ANYBODY, NOT EVEN BECKY. HE ASKED ME TO MEET HIM AT THAT PUB, THE DRAUGHT HOUSE, JUST LAST WEEK. HIS FACE WAS ASHEN, TOO. WE SIPPED OUR PINTS IN THE BEER GARDEN. IT GREW DARK. HE WAS STALLING. WHEN THE GROUP OF HIPSTERS NEXT TO US GOT UP TO LEAVE, HE IMMEDIATELY LEANED ACROSS THE TABLE, KNOCKING OVER HIS EMPTY GLASS. THIS IS WHAT HE SAID: "KEN, I'M PRETTY SURE WE'RE ALL GOING TO DIE." HIS GLASS ROLLED AND FELL TO A CRASH ON THE CEMENT. I BLINKED AT HIM AND AGREED, *YES, WE ALL DO.* HE PROCEEDED TO TELL ME THAT LINKED TO THE MAOA GENE WAS SOMETHING ELSE, AND FOR THE LAST MONTH THAT SOMETHING ELSE HAD HIM WORKING NONSTOP.

OUR CIRCADIAN RHYTHM, OUR BIO TIME CLOCK, IT'S LIKE A MINOR SWITCH AT WORK, HE EXPLAINED. IT'S IN OUR GENES AND IT REGULATES WHEN WE GET UP AND WHEN WE SLEEP, AMONG OTHER THINGS. WARREN TOLD ME HE'D FOUND A MAJOR SWITCH AND THAT THIS SWITCH REGULATED WHEN WE DIE; NOT JUST WE AS INDIVIDUALS, BUT AS A SPECIES. "THIS THING (HIS WORD) HIDES IN PLAIN SIGHT LIKE DARK MATTER IN SPACE. IT'S THERE, IT'S SO EVERYTHING, SO EVERYWHERE THAT WE GENETICISTS DON'T THINK TO SEE IT. WE DON'T KNOW IT'S THERE, LIKE A FISH DOESN'T KNOW IT'S IN WATER. GENETIC SCIENCE WILL CHANGE," HE SAID. "IT HAS TO. THEY'LL THINK I'M CRAZY, BUT I'VE GOT TO GET THE WORD OUT ON THIS. MAYBE WE CAN REVERSE THIS DOOMSDAY GENE'S MECHANISM," HE'D SAID. HE NEEDED ME TO HELP HIM BECAUSE HE WAS SICK WITH A GLIOBLASTOMA IN HIS HEAD. TICKING. HIS SWITCH WAS ABOUT TO FLIP. AND NOBODY WOULD BELIEVE HIM. I'M MORE CREDIBLE, APPARENTLY. I'M ON TV ALL THE TIME. SCREENS IMBUE CREDIBILITY IN OUR WORLD.

WHEN I SAW MASSES OF PEOPLE ALL OVER THE WORLD CLUTCHING THEIR THROATS ON TV THIS MORNING, I KNEW WARREN'S WARNING HAD MERIT.

THAT'S THE OBJECTIVE, SCIENTIFIC ASPECT OF THIS STORY. WHAT WORRIES ME KEVIN, WHAT WORRIES ALL MEN AND WOMEN OF SCIENCE, IS THE UNKNOWN. IN THE OLD DAYS, THE UNKNOWN WAS ASCRIBED SUPERNATURAL PROPERTIES. THE UNKNOWN HERE IS: WHAT TRIGGERED THIS LATENT, DOOMSDAY GENE TO GO INTO EFFECT AROUND THE PLANET

SIMULTANEOUSLY THIS MORNING? AND DID IT HEAR ME AND WARREN TALKING OVER OUR PINTS? DID IT BECOME CONCERNED THAT WE HUMANS HAD STUMBLED ONTO SOMETHING WE SHOULDN'T HAVE AND DECIDE TO SPEED THINGS UP BEFORE WE COULD UNDERSTAND AND SOLVE?

AS WARREN WARNED, THIS SOUNDS CRAZY.

THEY THOUGHT COPERNICUS AND GALILEO WERE HERETICAL CRAZIES.

IF SOMEONE JUST TOLD YOU ABOUT THE HOLOCAUST, WOULDN'T YOU THINK THAT CRAZY? YET, IT HAPPENED. IF SOMEONE JUST TOLD YOU ABOUT 9/11? CRAZY. YET ...

BEFORE HE TURNED AND WALKED BACK TOWARD THE LAB I'D GLANCED DOWN AT WARREN'S CREDIT CARD RECEIPT. HE'D WRITTEN BELOW HIS SIGNATURE *IT NEEDS YOU TO NEED IT.* AS HE WAS WALKING AWAY I HELD THE RECEIPT UP AND YELLED AT HIM, "HEY, WHAT'S THIS ABOUT?" HE TURNED, PUT HIS HANDS UP IN SURRENDER AND YELLED BACK, STILL WALKING BACKWARD, SMILING IN APOLOGY— "YOU'VE GOT THE CONCH, KEN."

HE TURNED ON HIS HEEL, SHOVED HIS HANDS INTO HIS POCKETS, AND WALKED INTO THE DARK.

IT FELT LIKE I HAD the conch now, and it was heavy, and I didn't know what to do with it.

It needs you to need it.

Why had Fleming repeated that, whispered that to me from behind his locked door?

Professor, why did you tear that part out and throw it away?

I think maybe I knew why, but there was nothing I could do about it now. Too late. Like Rebecca said.

Bass honked, and I'm glad he did. I stuffed the papers in my pocket and ran out of the house.

As I approached the Bronco, Bass rolled forward, playing with me, making me run and catch up. Kodie laughed, slapped him on the shoulder and told him to stop. As I reached for the door, he lurched, the muffler popping. I said, "Dammit, please stop," laughing a little, savoring the camaraderie. I thought I could be happy if he just kept doing this, teasing me, and me and Kodie laughing and Bass smiling, the reek of death drifting out of my clothes, my hair, me chasing them forever and laughing.

"What was in there?" Kodie asked. We were taking turns without stopping at intersections, our bodies leaning and recoiling back, tires screeching.

"My neighbor," I mumbled. "Bass. It's not a race," I said, a little annoyed with his speed. He slowed a little but didn't look both ways when we approached the usually busy street, the border to my tucked-away neighborhood. Yesterday we felt uncomfortable, obeyed traffic laws, but just a day later and we're covering these streets like it's our own personal racetrack. The rule of law was falling away.

KODIE'S NEIGHBORHOOD WAS JUST TWO miles away. Negotiating a couple of roundabouts, we came to the house, a small wooden gray ranch style with white trim which filled the tiny lot. Tall Chinese elms flanked each side and overhung the house. Though she had said her parents weren't there this morning, that their car was gone, she wanted to start here anyway. Then I knew why.

"Oh shit oh shit oh shit." She leaned her forehead against the back of the front seat.

"What?"

"The car is *there.*"

"I thought you said—"

"I did," she sighed. "But sometimes they get up early and go to Hyde Park Gym."

"On Guadalupe with the veiny curling arm sticking out of the wall?" asked Bass.

Kodie nodded. "After trying here, going there was going to be my next guess."

"But they came back," I said.

"They go real early." She sniffed and wiped her nose. "They're so cute how they work out together. Mom's the one who hauls Dad out of bed at five." She laughed once and knuckled away a tear. We sat in silence. The old truck's metal ticked as it cooled. Kodie stared at the back of the seat trying to find something there that would give her permission to get out of the car. Suddenly, she grabbed her bat, flung the door open, and marched toward her house.

"You want me to come with you?" I asked. She spun around while walking, grim-faced, shook her head, spun back. When Kodie got to the small front porch, she stopped on the first of three cement stairs. She lifted her forearm over her face.

The smell.

Her parents.

She bent over in despair. I wasn't sure she was going to be able to do it. She stood up and waved me over.

"You okay?" I asked at her side. She gripped my hand and we opened the unlocked door. They wore workout clothes. The part of her dad's T-shirt I could see read *Gazelle Foundation Run for*. They were both on the floor right in the living room as we walked in, her mom on top of her dad like the final scene of Romeo and Juliet. The smell was overpowering. I coughed and turned away. There were flies. Kodie knelt down to shoo them away and touched them each on the cheek, bawling in hysterical grief. Their mouths were full of white. I sat down beside her and rubbed her back as she wept. There were no words. She uttered *oh* amid her cries and touched them. The flies were insistent. I'm not sure how long we sat there like that.

BASS'S BRONCO CHUGGED. KODIE SAT vacant in the back.

Bass asked, "Kev? You want to go try to find your par—"

"No." I looked at Kodie's garage door like it held a secret. I remembered what I had stuffed in my pocket. Just as I had it unfolded, Kodie snatched it from me and began scanning. "Hey, Bass, let's go to the Draught House."

"The movie theater? Which one?"

"No, not the Draft House theater. The Draught House pub on Medical."

Kodie was reading and reading and nodding faster and faster. "Yeah, let's start there. We can find the lab from there."

"Lab. It'd be great if you'd fill me in as I Uber you two to your destination."

ON THE WAY I TOLD Bass what Professor Fleming had said to me on his doorstep and read the letter's postscript, looking up, eyeing for Johnny every other sentence.

Bass flicked his eyes to us in the rearview. "A scientist thinks he found something important. It's not like we can continue his research or use his work. Basically, Kevin, so what?"

"Let's just go see, okay?"

"Yeah, let's go see," said Kodie. Her tone: something there worth knowing.

Kodie had read the entire letter. The first part about Fleming's feeling about me. She put the pages on my lap and patted them, turned her head to me and shot an eyebrow, nodding to the pages. She didn't want to discuss it in full here.

We pulled into the Draught House parking lot. There was a cairn in the beer garden. "Okay, which way?" asked Bass.

"Fleming said the lab was nearby, a nondescript building," I said, swiveling my head up and down the street.

"*And walked into the dark*," Kodie recited from the letter. She pointed. "There's a streetlamp. So, he walked the other way."

Bass drove out of the lot in that direction and within seconds lifted the index finger of his driving hand. "I'd say this right here is a pretty damned nondescript building." He turned in without our assent.

The building was beige, squat, without signage, without windows, and set farther back off the street than the rest at an angle.

"Gotta be," I said. Kodie held up her hand in high five. I matched my palm to hers, marveling at her positivity after what she'd just witnessed.

We were parked at the side of the building in front of a metal door. It was locked, so we went around the front and tried its glass doors.

Open. Slight sweet-sour death reek.

Beyond the tiled foyer, lights in the hallway to the left flicked and buzzed. As we went deeper into the building, the smell gathered, thickened. We made a turn and saw that at the end of the thinly carpeted hall was an open door to a dark room.

We lifted our shirts to cover our noses and mouths. Peering in, coughing and waving and blinking our way through the smell, we see that it's a hybrid office and meeting room with a big stainless conference table stacked with neat piles of papers weighted down by brown riven stones, manila folders, and books. I flip another switch on the wall by the door and another set of lights pop on and it is then that we see the man at the desk with his back to us at the back of the long room. We take in this tableau.

Even as death worked its putrefaction upon his body now losing its rigor, Doctor Warren Jespers's jowly cheeks were still soap-burnished and ruddy. He looked almost comfortable in his desk chair. His eyes, however, were wide and livid with shock as they fixed upon the massive whiteboard on the wall in front of his desk where it was written in large letters at the top *it needs you to need it*. Below that, linking it with a squiggled arrow, this man of hard science had written *Matthew 16:23*.

The walls are bare save for a gilt-framed sepia photo of a young woman holding a baby which hung anachronistically small next to the huge whiteboard. Over the woman's shoulder in the distance is the UT clock tower. I thought of the seven plunging suicides from that tower, that one's name was Moment and she had taken off her shoes before she jumped.

His computer's flat screen is frozen. The connection has long since been lost but the last image Jespers was looking at is of a similar scene: a man at a desk, dead. This man is slumped onto the desk. His face cannot be seen. At the corner of the screen is an instant message window. Faucheux, Guillaume. Doctorat, UPMC. En Génétique. Away 17 mins. 2 Participants. In the dialogue box, the French doctor had written simply: *Mort. Près près près.* In Jespers's box below it at 7:31 a.m. CST: *What's happening??? Are you ok??*

Kodie and Bass fan out. On Jespers's desk is a thick printout. Inspecting it, I realize it's the peer-reviewed paper Fleming had referenced replete with his acid marginalia in red pen. Wadded balls of it riddle the floor.

The ten-by-twelve whiteboard is full of equations and notes and flowcharts. Kodie air-traces them with her finger, whispering to herself as she reads. At the bottom corner she stops. She reads out loud, "Kevin March? Cody? (ask Becky)."

"Ho-ly *fuck*," Bass whisper-mused as he jogged around the desk to join Kodie and tap the board at my name.

"Indeed," I said.

"Huh. Cody. Me?"

Bass and I shrug-nod.

"I don't know this man," I said. "This was Fleming's friend."

"Maybe he told him about you," Kodie said.

I had the letter with me and shuffled through it. "Maybe, but there's no mention of you in Fleming's let…no, wait, he says here *you and the young woman*. Could be you. But how does he," I gestured to Jespers, "know of you? Your name?"

Bass cleared his throat. "Clearly, Fleming and Jespers have been discussing you two. Why, though?"

I handed him Fleming's letter. "Read the first part."

Bass reads quickly and drops his hands with the papers to his thighs in exasperation. "Dreaming about you? You've *got* to clue me in."

"But he knows my name. Fleming just says the young woman," said Kodie.

"I think it has to do with this business here." Bass read: "'The unknown here is: What triggered this latent, doomsday gene to go into effect around the planet simultaneously this morning? And did it hear me and Warren talking over our pints? Did it become concerned that we humans had stumbled onto something we shouldn't have?'" Bass looked at us, gobsmacked. "You guys. Fleming's dreaming about you two. They knew you were important in regards to this, to this *it* he talks about here. Fleming lives across the street. You and Kodie are a thing. I'm here. Connected. But wh—"

"Why?" Kodie asked.

I walked over the conference table and picked up a copy of *Lord of the Flies*. "We've got the conch," I mumbled.

Kodie and Bass came to the table. There was a tall stack of subscribed-to *Scientific American*s. And there were other books, heavier research and science texts with dense and arcane titles, but also, mixed in with them, a Bible, various translations of *Lord of the Flies*. Kodie held *El Señor de las Moscas*. Bass thumbed *Sa Majesté des Mouches*. *The Heart of Darkness*, *Wisconsin Death Trip*, Camus's *The Plague*, O'Nan's novel about a diphtheria epidemic, *A Prayer for the Dying*, wherein Jespers had dog-eared a page and underlined *she jerks as if pitching a fit, thrashes her head side to side… 'Jesus Jesus Jesus,' she moans. 'Jesus Jesus Jesus.'*

After a quiet time of perusing, Kodie shows me an underlined passage in her Spanish copy of *Lord of the Flies*, a passage: *cerca cerca cerca*, ending with *no vayas?* Without talking, I simply showed her the page I had my finger on, one Jespers had also underlined. It was the same passage in English. Now Bass holds up his French copy. Same highlighted passage.

"Yeah. That paper he tried to publish," I pointed to the floor, the desk. "A no go."

Kodie added, "He was still working on proof. And then, before he was able to…everybody died."

"I had written this weird story this summer. I *just* wrote an extra credit essay on this." I held up Golding's novel.

A beat of stillness and thought.

"I don't get it, but it's more than coincidence. I'm fucking spooked," Bass said as he begins to quickly unhook Jespers's desktop computer to take with us. I'm retrieving Jespers's paper from his desk, collecting and unwadding the pages from the floor.

Kodie says in dazed wonderment, "These men meant to lead us here so we'd know. They presaged this. Fleming wasn't ready to tell anyone yet because it sounds crazy. They want us to carry on with it somehow."

Just as I'd said, "Yeah, but what I can't figure out is why Fleming tore off and threw away this PS part, because it's got all the—" there was a loud boom at the metal door. Another. We went to it and as we unlocked it we heard shattering glass at the front. Kodie checked the metal side door while Bass and I ran to the front, me carrying Jespers's paper, Bass Jespers's computer.

Glass once in the doors was strewn all over the foyer. A couple of stones lay among the shards. Bass and I ran out the doors. "Johnny?!" I screamed at the empty street.

Kodie came around from the side of the building. "Nobody there."

"We gotta find these little shits," said Bass.

RADIOSHACK UP ON BURNET WOULD have a ham radio. None of us knew how to operate one but Bastian is one of those people who asks *how hard can it be?* when confronted with a novel task requiring an unlearned skill.

Kodie and Bass looked to me to do the breaking and entering. I wrapped my outer shirt around my right hand and punched in the door's glass. An alarm sounded and my pulse quickened. Bass noticed my hesitance. "Nobody's coming," he said. I kicked in the whole panel of glass and was able to crawl inside and open the door for them.

The RadioShack's hours, as stenciled on the glass next to the front door, were 10am-7pm. Nobody had opened the store yet when this all happened and, unlike McBride's Guns, nobody had come to stock up as things fell apart.

"Can we kill that alarm?" Kodie shouted, fingers pressed to one ear.

"I got it," Bass yelled over his shoulder.

"I'm going to get solar panels," Kodie said directly into my ear, and then we heard a slam and a bang and the alarm stopped. Talking normally, she said, "For when the grid goes down."

Bass came striding out from the back room comically wiping his hands together in a job-well-done manner. "There," he said, cruising past us.

Bass was already deep inside scoping the shelves, whittling down the location and the choices until we all gathered in front of the ones he stood looking at. Bass picked the most expensive radio off the shelf. Kodie and I simultaneously asked him if he knew anything about them.

"How hard can it be?" he asked. "Solar panels. Good thinking. Also going to need to get power generators and gas. Lowe's. But first, kids."

"But the Wal-Mart's got them low low prices," I said with a bubba drawl which in old-world mixed company might have offended.

They snickered and my mind flashed on the dark smiling teeth. My stomach roiled.

On our way out, I spied this[13] here Olympus digital voice recorder with intelligent functions, snatched it from the shelf like a kid shoplifting condoms. I also grabbed a pair of $1,000 binoculars.

WE BOBBED AND WOVE AROUND the few vehicles.

We drove fast with the windows down. We didn't talk, just looked with amazement out at our stilled city.

"There's just…nothing," Kodie finally said, more to herself than us. I figured that a day later we'd see some signs of infrastructure collapse, some evidence of things falling apart. But, still nothing. No smoke, no burned-out cars, no mounds of corpses in the streets. Not even flashing signal lights. They turned from green to yellow to red like the world went on, ghost cars

13 Sound of heavy thumping. KGM is tapping the device with which he makes this recording.

cruising through. There weren't even all that many mounds of stones. A few in parking lots here and there near all-night places, that's it.

I told Bass to go over to I-35. This stretch of one of the longest interstates in the country was the busiest so I thought (no, hoped) we'd see wreckage, jackknifed eighteen-wheelers, a city bus on its side, cars gutted, blackened and smoldering, hazard lights flashing. I still can't articulate why I was so panicked about not seeing any signs of panic. With panic comes haste and with haste comes waste and I saw none. Standing in the DT parking lot, we'd heard distant booms. Could've been faraway explosions, like what happened in West, Texas a few years ago. But other than that…the inexorable winding down of it is what scared me, the way everyone seemed to have simply succumbed to it. That whimpering way the world ended.

It had happened so quickly. Obvious now. It came over you and killed you quickly. The chokers and suicides out in the open were quickly covered with stones. Mr. Fleming, Rebecca's dad; these folks held out longer than most. It seems everyone died within minutes to an hour of dawn.

Did the rest of the as-of-yet-unaffected world know what was happening on the other side of the planet and just think, Oh, *shit*? What did they do as dawn rolled its way to them? Did they all hear those sounds? Did it go down that way? I. Don't. Know.

You reading this, you probably do.

Just knowing that in house after house after house, apartment, condo, and dorm, places of business open early, there's a succumbed corpse once belonging to a terrified human being not knowing what was happening. Just…oh. In each and every there was a Mr. Fleming with a suit on; a woman in her favorite chair with a knife in her gut; parents, like Bastian's, like Kodie's, lying at the front curb and on the backyard deck, on top of each other.

Mom had wandered off. Bass's parents had tried to. Mr. Fleming's open window. An overwhelming need to get out? Trying to go somewhere. All the cars we've seen on the roadsides are empty. Save for the sexton at Memorial Park, not a single car has had a corpse in it. All keys in the ignition, most doors open, door chimes binging away.

EVERYTHING HAD SETTLED NOW. The sky wasn't yesterday's cobalt and the blustery winds were gone. The sky was low, morning-gray and flickering electric as we headed back out of downtown and up I-35. My eye snagged on a huge blow-up jack-o'-lantern affixed to the top of a strip mall.

On I-35 we saw eighteen-wheelers stopped at the side of the road every fifty yards or so. We stopped at the first three we came to and checked the cabs. Empty. We stood on the shoulder of a flyover looking down at east Austin. No stone piles anywhere on 35 and none could be seen down on the streets below except for the couple I saw in a Fiesta grocery store parking lot.

"What the hell, Kev? Where did the truckers go? All the drivers?"

"Truckers've got CBs. Maybe they communicated and went somewhere? No idea." Specious reasoning. Bass didn't follow up. Most of our initial questions were rhetorical, WTF? questions.

Went somewhere. That took root in my head. I closed my eyes and my eyelids fluttered. I heard Bass ask if I was okay and though I nodded, what I saw behind my eyes were the dark smiling teeth. Smiling as if pleased that I'd figured something out.

Went somewhere . . .

I opened my eyes and swayed a bit. "Another vision?" Bass asked with true concern and reverence in his voice. He took hold of my elbow to steady me.

I nodded. "It's so hard to describe. All I can say is that I know many are gathered somewhere."

In the distance was Mueller's Park and the bright red Thinkery Children's Museum. Doubt kids were there thinkering about the old world. "Kids lived," I mused. "What a 'kid' is we're not sure. Pre-puberty?"

Bass nodded. "Yet we're still here."

I pressed my lips together. I looked over his shoulder at the Bronco where Kodie sat in the front. She had put her head back and closed her eyes, clearly not feeling well. "Some adults killed themselves." In my head the bald man shoots himself in his kitchen, the little squares of windows lighting up in the dark, and the smiling nurse sits atop the fence looking down at me with that wild glamour in her eyes, nodding yes. "I do not get that, but it's a significant number. Most died like . . ."

"My folks," Bass said with a raised chin.

"Like them, and like the Flemings, the Lagenkamps. And Rebecca's dad. The trashman on my street. It was getting him. The people at McBride's. The white stuff. But, where are they?"

"It's not like we've gone house to house. Maybe they're all still inside."

"I'm not so sure."

"Why?" Bass asked.

"Your folks were clearly trying to leave."

"Yeah, but I think they were reacting to . . ." He caught the emotion in his throat and swallowed. "Going somewhere…That's not what I saw in their eyes. They were panicking, flailing." His eyes shined as he staunched tears.

"Okay. My mom walked off somewhere. Martin's car was gone. I didn't see a bunch of people walking this morning. But all these trucks and cars. Even this police car over here." I pointed down the freeway and squinted. "See? The driver door's open. Empty. These truckers, cops, shift workers, they were driving through the dawn when it happened. All of them, they pulled over, stopped, parked, got up, and walked away. Where? Why?"

I saw whales lined up on beaches. Fires at night. Dancing silhouettes.

I thought I was starting to understand why. "Like the world's whales, they beached themselves. They went somewhere to die."

Bass pursed his lips as he measured my conjecture. Mueller Lake winked as a flock of waterbirds took flight from its surface. "All right. So, do we go looking for the kids…or this place the dead went?"

"Kids," I said, my voice flat. "I'm not sure finding where a bunch of dead people are matters."

"I'm with you. We need to assess and the biggest assessment to make is to find out where the hell a hundred thousand kids are."

And that's when we heard the roaring.

IT CAME FROM THE DIRECTION of the river. We heard it three more times as we drove with windows down. Each time we heard it, we narrowed down its location. We'd angle in on the sound, disagree with each other, the noise repeated, more terrifying each time. The third time we heard it we knew it was the sound of thousands opening their throats, like what you'd hear in a stadium, a big play for the home team, the starting chords of a smash-hit song.

But it had a keening, unhinged pitch to it. Having heard nothing for a day and then to hear this, from a distance—I thought my nerves might melt down.

We heard it again driving up Barton Springs. We were so close now that Bass instinctually slowed down. The dreams and visions had hinted this was the place. The children of Austin had all gathered on the morning after at Butler Park.

BUTLER WAS THIS OPEN GREEN centerpiece to the several cultural structures near Lady Bird Lake. Next to it was the Palmer Arts Center and the Long Center. A place of picnics, running dogs and children, a night-lit fountain, ponds and walking paths and the river curving just beyond. The grand backdrop was the downtown skyline. An idyll. Of course they'd chosen it to be their place of reckoning.

We crept along, ready to bolt. I know it wasn't just me seeing the potential scene here as we got closer. They'd hear us, stop their noisemaking, turn and come for us as a horde. It wouldn't take long for their two hundred thousand hands to get at us through the webbed glass.

Yesterday they were disparate and coming together. Now that they were in a hive, their reaction to us might be different. Strength in numbers. Strength in groupthink. You mess with one bee, you might get stung. Go home, put some ice on it. You mess with a hive…

What, we were going to shoot at them, mow them down with the Bronco? Even if we did, there were too many.

Oh, that damned muffler's hacking, even at this nil speed, was too much. "Kill it, Bass," I said. "They're gonna hear us. If we want to see them in their natural state, we've got to walk."

Bass pulled into the Peter Pan Mini Golf at the corner and turned off the truck. We sat in the quiet for a moment, looking at the twelve-foot elfin Peter who, in front of the course's building, had taken a knee and gazed into the great beyond not unlike the Great Sphinx of Giza, only this Sphinx wore tights and had a droll smile that did nothing to settle our nerves.

Bass: "Okay, let's roll."

We exited the Bronco, each having the presence of mind not to slam the doors.

"Let's go over to that building next to the park there, you know?" I asked.

"Yeah, Dougherty Arts," said Kodie.

"Let's see if we can climb up and see what they're doing."

"What about Palmer?"

"You think we can slip past them on Barton Springs? It's wide open there. They'll all see us and then it's a footrace. And we'd be treed up there if they saw us. The school's better."

We stood at the bus stop across from the Peter Pan. I was scanning around while Bass talked and in my head I heard the MoPac train from last night. Chasing that train had been futile, I'd thought. But now I'm not so sure because the residue of its sound caused my eyes to fall upon the bridge stretching across Barton Springs Road just yards away.

Bass yammered next to me. I slapped him on the chest with the back of my hand—shut up for a sec, I'm thinking. I stared at the yellow sign which read *13ft-7in* posted on the bridge across which only trains crossed. This was where the MoPac—the Missouri Pacific Railroad—took a turn through downtown Austin before making its way south. It ran right past the park, and from memory I knew it did so under the cover of trees and vines. When the train passed through it was a haunting sound because you couldn't see it. You just hear it motoring through the trees, the high whine of stressed metal, the thunder of rolling weight. Like a monster in the trees.

A beast, maybe.

"I got it," I said, my knuckles still brushing Bass's T-shirt. "Look." I pointed up.

"Ah," Kodie said. "Nice. We can scramble up there and look down on them."

"Won't they see us?" Bass asked.

I shook my head. "Too many trash trees and ivy. We'll be able to see them but they won't see us. I got this, too." I held up my $1,000 tactical binoculars. "If there's a problem, we can scoot down and get to the Bronco."

Making sure to avoid the beds of spiky poison ivy, within minutes we made it to the top of the incline where the cement braced the receding bridgeworks. Just as we got to the top, the children roared. At what impulse, we hadn't a clue. We made our way along the track, walled-off by thick foliage.

Down below us about twenty feet, bivouacked into a spot below, a leaning tree was a miniature tent city established by some homeless. Across from this was the back of the Dougherty Arts Center which was covered in colorful graffiti. The one which caught my eye, however, was simply the word *scary*, rendered in black and lacking artfulness there in the middle of it all above a back door.

At the wall's corners I noticed two identical tags: *a pox on yo lips.*

A place we'd never have gone a day ago, this little world behind the wide one; the dead person in one of the derelict tents, the graffiti-caked back wall, the vines which draped a curtain between us and the park.

We saw a small break in the foliage thirty yards ahead. I walked a couple steps ahead. Kodie and Bass drifted behind me. I gave them the hand signal to get low as we walked. From tie to tie we strode like creeping ducks toward the clearing. Even through the scrim of vine leaves we could see the park's open stretches as we walked. At the front of the park stood Doug Sahm Hill, named after the sort-of-famous Austinite who had a couple of national rock 'n roll hits in the early sixties. You know, that tired Austin Hippie Hollow Armadillo World Headquarters cosmic cowboy crap we young millennials yawned at. A cement path encircling the hill from bottom to top led to a plaque bearing his name.

We arrived at the break in the foliage. I got low, raised my head above the trestle railing, and peered through the wedge in the green.

What I saw removed my ability to breathe for a moment.

Bass and Kodie came up behind me and I guess our three heads lined up must have looked like some scene out of *The Little Rascals*, wide-eyed kids peeping over a whitewashed fence.

The entire front half of the park was blanketed with kids. I mean, you couldn't see grass for a quarter-mile square. They weren't fidgeting or running around squealing, not even the toddlers. The seven-year-olds, the ten and twelve-year-olds, boys and girls, held the sated, silent infants. Not one cried.

Dear reader, the way they collectively…*were.*

Words fail.

Their physical attitudes were in no way old world. They stood and watched, every face locked on whatever it was. I couldn't quite see yet. Something on Doug Sahm Hill. While not rigid soldier-like attention, together they exhibited the quintessence of new world.

Something in them had clicked. Just as something had in the post-pubescent population of the planet—making them explode white from the inside, making them leap from high places into traffic…Something had clicked and they were changed. Though I couldn't see it in their eyes, and wouldn't yet for some time, I saw it in the way they moved, or didn't.

And something else. If all the adults had essentially exploded and died within hours of that dawn, then the opposite had occurred to the world's children. Something, a big bang, had imploded within them. The outward manifestation of this was their melding. They attained this…this synchronicity. What I mean is they physically moved together. And the way they did made you believe they thought together, too. Like a flock of birds moving in the air, or the way a school of fish suddenly turns and darts as one, responding to some collectively felt stimulus. With no outward communication, they move as one.

This crowd of children rippled. They moved in nauseating undulations. My mind flashed to that most rogue of waves rolling up Lake Austin.

Imagine "the wave" as we know it, like we see at ball games. It was instinctual, autonomic as if of one contiguous organism. One kid moved an elbow and the energy of that moved out in a fan, rippling the crowd like calm water struck by a stone. The energy of one movement dissipated but the next and multitudinous others were ongoing, surging, dying.

The infinite movement of an ocean.

A sight such as this was impossible. It made me cold.

Now I was sure that what had happened was more than an extinction event. It was a leap in evolution. A sea change you could say, to use Mr. Shakespeare's phrase. The species was different now. Plain as that. What that meant and where things would go, well, I still can't say, but as I float along talking into this thing to you, I feel they are watching me. Sensing me. Just as we three watched them from the tracks, they watch me from the banks of this river. I cannot see them, hear them. But when I'm floating and talking to you and Mags, I feel them. They send out their waves. I feel them in my head. A delightful throb and whisper and I'm rocked and benumbed in the womb of the world.

THEIR OCEAN ROCKED AS THEY watched the top of Doug Sahm Hill.

We were all bent over with our hands on our knees like we're about to do the hand jive, standing on a railroad track upon which no train would ever again roll. The day after, they were gathered and waiting for the beginning.

I shivered. My teeth clacked. I had to clinch them to make it stop.

Kodie touched me on my back with her spread palm, still warm with fever. "You okay?" she whispered.

I shook my head slowly. "Just...I don't know how to even...*look* at them."

In my periphery on either side of me, Bass and Kodie nodded sluggishly. Kodie uttered under her breath, "My God. What's happened to them?"

"Happy Halloween," whispered Bass. We stared, too scared to move. "What's happening?" he asked, more to himself than us.

We were a good seventy-five yards away from the crowd's edge. I wondered if they had already registered our presence. How could they not hear, feel, the Bronco's blatting muffler, my clacking teeth?

"No sudden moves. No sneezing, nothing," I said. "Let's go up a bit to see what's on that hill." We did the walk again, tie to tie, for about twenty ties, then resumed our hands-on-knees pose.

What we saw summoned no words from our lips. What came from my throat was an airy low hiss of disbelief.

Maybe a full minute later I whispered, "Jesus Christ," to myself.

"No pun intended," Kodie said.

On Doug Sahm Hill were three kids tied to posts. With my $1,000 binoculars I could see they were each bound at the wrists. The posts looked to be four-by-fours, set into what I didn't know. On top of the hill, not seen from this vantage, was a huge concrete map of Texas, its major cities and its rivers, Austin's location depicted with a star. Surrounding this map and all along the top of the summit of the hill in a ring were cement benches. Behind was the vista of downtown and the river.

I rolled my finger over the focus dial to crisp the image. The boy in the middle lifted his chin to face the multitude below him. His face held not fear but rather resignation, maybe even absolution.

The face belonged to Simon. I didn't recognize the other two boys. All their cheeks were wet from tears they no longer shed.

And I thought yesterday was as bad as it got.

My mind felt thrown down a corridor where at the end only madness and blood resides. My mouth watered and I found myself fighting throwing up. Though we were far away enough to need binoculars, the sound of my vomiting would attract attention. There's no way to vomit quietly. Maybe you can stifle a sneeze, snuff out a cough, but once the gates open on heaving, it's full, noisy committal.

I held the binoculars but my eyes were closed. I swallowed repeatedly like I've done many a time after losing at beer quarters. I got the salty spits and my stomach sent the signal for full throttle evac, but I tamped it enough to speak.

"Simon's in the middle," I'd said with pre-vomit slur, salinized spit flooding inside my cheeks. Bass slowly reached for the binoculars and I handed them over.

He looked at me then did a double-take. "You okay, dude? You're white."

Kodie touched my elbow. I won the battle with my stomach.

When Bass focused in, he said, "Holy. Shit," the words over-enunciated, the 't' made with the teeth and breath.

"It's like they're being punished. Up on a hill, like Calvary," whispered Kodie.

*This girl...*I thought then. *I love this girl. She has a shaved head and knows the New Testament.* Even in the midst of post-apocalyptic atrocity, puke wanting to geyser from my innards, I'm in love-lust. Indeed, the species shall survive. It's definitely a go.

"Cavalry?" Bass whispered. "Huh...what now about horses?" He said this absentmindedly, his eyes glued to the lenses, his knuckles white around the binoculars. He's having a hard time grasping what it is he is seeing. Their movements you want to say are wrong, profane. You want to look away. Your brain demands that it stop moving like that, yet...you can't stop staring. It sickened me. Kinda like being seasick.

Never asking for the binocs, Kodie seemed to know not to look directly at it for very long, like one knows not to look at the afternoon sun. Medusa. Your parents having sex.

I use levity to take the edge off now.

I tried to explain. "Calvary's where Jesus was—"

"—one day and they're already meting out justice," Kodie said. "Incredible."

"That boy in the middle, Simon, he talked to us. They didn't like that."

"Yeah, no shi—" Bass said. "Hey. I just thought of something." But he stopped talking, totally aghast.

I prodded, "Go on."

"Simon said something about a beast? I mean, is this punishment or doesn't this look like they're being offered up for sacrifice? They're tied up like Naomi Watts for Kong." Bass continued, scanning the crowd now. "A bunch of piles around. I mean, wow, a bunch."

"Stones?" I asked, hurting like hell for my little brother. He was out there, I'm sure. I almost yelled out for him right then.

"Yeah. Some of the little ones are picking them up and dropping them. Playing with them. Tossing them back and forth and smiling. Oh, wait, now. The crowd is..."

Moving. The whole mass of them moving in agitated waves I cannot even describe. But I guess the writer must try, right? So here: it surged forward and then back, over and again. It's the best metaphor I've got—it's waves. The whole thing is just fluid, not the movements flesh and bone on dry land are supposed to make. "They're not moving their feet. They're, like, bending at the waist. Their eyes are closed. Goddammit, Kevin, what the hell is this?"

"Are we dreaming?" Kodie's eyes looked straight at it, wild-eyed and entranced.

Humming, as from a hive, rose up from Butler Park, became a single thing, moving the air in currents. I grabbed the binoculars back. All of them, even the toddlers, the infants, eyes closed and humming the low vibraphonic bottom-register hum, *Ohm*—

Electricity in the air. Pure harmonics.

Kodie whispered, "It's like plainsong, but it's not even singing. It's . . ." She went walleyed and swiveled her head no in tiny arcs.

My mom used to get bad carsick sometimes. I never understood that. Now I did. The motion, the hum. I had to look away else I knew I'd puke. My head hurt too. Stabbing pain above my right eye. I bent over and put my hand over it. I stared down at the track with my left eye.

To the left in my periphery, I thought I saw movement up the track. *Johnny?* My heart rattled my ribs, making me even woozier. I looked down the track but didn't see anything.

The sound they made swirled and augmented so oddly that it compressed your head. Maybe I won't survive this after all, I thought. Maybe it just takes us late bloomers longer to die. My head pounded with my heart. I looked up at an awestruck Kodie, the rims of her nostrils ringed with dried blood. From earlier, I guessed. I could hear her wheeze over the hum.

Just when the children's noise reached an almost unbearable intensity, it leveled off to a mellifluous buzz. A wave moving over and away.

Through the binoculars I watched their movements. "They're all looking down now, searching for something. Why are they...are they uncovering bodies?" Like a flock, like a swarm, like a school.

"Hush. They'll hear us," Kodie said, but she said it as if she were aloft. An angel with belabored breath. "Ssshhh."

Fixed in her eyes existed this meditative focus so serene it frightened me. She looked at inward galaxies and time and into the mind of God.

I'm essentially having an aneurysm above my eye, Bass is wigging, and Kodie has slipped away from us and so what came to mind was an old song Martin used to play real loud when we'd drive out to his real estate buddy's hunting lease, the dawn gray and cold but he's amped from his stainless tumbler of coffee (a song I really liked, Martin's liking it notwithstanding): *There's something happening here, And what it is ain't exactly clear.*[14]

Danger. The feeling of danger flooded me when my mind played that song. The need to puke disappeared, the head pain melted and my heart found its rhythm, warm and bright in my chest with a job to do.

The song's lyric continued in my head—*stop children, what's that sound, everybody look what's going down*, and with it I felt their eyes on me.

14 "For What It's Worth" by Buffalo Springfield (1967)

"Oh, crap, there's a couple little girls who see us. They're pointing," I said.

And then a hundred thousand little faces turned to us. Their heads snapped and locked in on us like radar dishes. Cold, inanimate.

We ice over. We don't breathe. I still held the binoculars to my face, elbows out, but I'm Tin Man stiff, knowing that the glare off the lenses, if moved, will not help our chances.

I'm thinking about the footrace to the Bronco. I'm thinking there's a few of the boy-soldiers of the group already peeling away from the back of the pack and heading in that direction. When I say a few, I guess I mean a hundred.

"We need to go," Bass whispered. The children looked at us in the huge mesmeric quiet. Kodie said, "If they wanted to do us harm, they would've attacked us already. They had their chances yesterday."

"Today's a new day," said Bass. Which was oh-so-true.

"They could've invaded like locust last night. I think they just want us to go. Not to—"

"See," I said. "They don't want us to see."

"Yeah," said Kodie with distance and wonder in her voice. The question floated through our collective heads: See *what*?

As I sit here, or I should say, float here, talking into this thing, I don't know what it is we saw that morning at Butler Park. I haven't seen them amass quite like that since. I'm sure they have, I just haven't seen it. Saw them at the pit, but that's different. Later.

I'm pretty sure when I get to where I'm going, I will see them amassed again. Maybe then I'll know why. I think I fear that most, seeing them like this again.

What did it do to Simon and the other two? What were they waiting on?

I think about that winged watching thing, its shadow moving over the house that morning. How it blocked out the sun for a second. I'll get to that later, too.

"Let's give these kids some privacy," said Bass in comic relief. "Get ready to run. As soon as we move they may come tearing after us." Think: the athletically gifted zombies trope, them tear-assing around the corner coming for us.

But I knew they wouldn't. Kodie didn't comment, confirming to me that she didn't think they would either. They just wanted us gone.

"Ready?" Bass said. "Okay, let's go. Go now." I lowered the binoculars and turned to him. He had taken a few steps down the ties. "Let's go," he whispered through gritted teeth, his tall frame hunched. "What're you doing?"

Kodie and I lifted our chins and gave the staring masses a last look.

We were making our way down the embankment to Barton Springs Road when we heard the roar come from the park that prickled the skin as it curdled the blood. We ran to the Bronco.

It came again and again as we ran, this hideous cresting surf-roar. Deep in the roar lived an inhuman screech. It hit the higher registers of our aural perception, pinged and tweaked them to the point that we flinched and clasped our hands to our ears, cowering as we sprinted across Barton Springs toward the big green elf.

They were still roaring as we shut the doors and rolled up the windows. The horrid noise muted, we looked at each other wide-eyed in the acknowledgement that it contained the sound of bloodlust.

KODIE HAD MANAGED TO KEEP her coughing in check on the track, but she began to cough now with the excitement and the running. Bass turned to look at her and I could see that he thought of his mother's demise yesterday. The struggle in her face.

"You okay?" I asked. The question came out lame. Of course she wasn't. She was older than me and Bass and now she struggled for air like the world's adults did.

She put her fist to her mouth and furrowed her brow and nodded she was okay, managing to mutter when she was done with the fit, "Yeah, just the running." She noticed me looking at her blood-specked fist. She tucked her hand away and looked out the window.

"Kodie," I whispered, "let me know what you want me to do. Okay?" She smiled and her eyes shone. A tear fell, then she coughed again. She took my hand and held it hard against her chest like a jewel she couldn't afford to lose.

"I will," she said, her voice a clipped-off wet whisper.

Bass didn't peel out. We sat in idle, our heads all turned to a pile of stones sitting right below the takeout window at the McDonald's next to Peter Pan Mini Golf. No car there.

Drawing your final breath on the oily tarmac of a McDonald's drive-thru, looking at a huge purple Grimace (A pained facial expression is a monster's name? And you sell food to kids with it?) and Mayor McCheese, the stench of hot reconstituted fat from the pickup window...This has got to be one of the worst places to exit this life. We stared as we passed. Just galling.

ROARING CHILDREN, A CAIRN AT a McDonald's drive-thru. The wincing smile frozen on Grimace's face as he waves his flipper, a smile which clearly says 'help me', Madness.

THE ROARING STOPS. IT LISTENS.

We're all listening, turning around in our seats to look to see if they're coming.

The seconds tick off and the swelling silence becomes unsettling. "Bass, go," I whisper. That damned muffler blats even in idle.

It's a reset. A do-over with the children while Grimace and a giant Peter Pan watch. The mass of children who move as an oil slick on troubled water. What had come that morning was not the destroying thing itself but rather the claxon call heralding the foaming white to bubble up. Triggering the fall, forcing smiling people to leap from high places.

I'm certain the children gathered as they did in Butler Park in every city and town the world over. They gathered in fields off the highway, or someplace behind the rows of tannin sorghum and tall fall corn in those places where we envision alienate crop circles. Back there, having their get-togethers like this, the roar not as loud but for the size of the crowd, but coming from the same impetus, and if you look real hard you can see how they move in synch just the same. Not a late bloomer among them.

Bass drove slowly and mused out loud, "I figure we're just below expiration, though I doubt age-in-years has anything to do with it."

"Three of us have already found each other within a day. You gotta figure there's more of us out there."

"I've been thinking. Let me ask you guys. Were you late bloomers? I mean, you know, relatively. Puberty wise," Kodie asked.

I nodded. So did Bass. We shot glances at each other.

Though I intuited it was, I nonetheless asked, "You think that's why we're still here?"

Bass shrugged and nodded. "If so, we'd've seen a lot more of us, but there's been nobody. Gotta be more than three in a city the size of Austin."

"We haven't been everywhere. We don't know yet," Kodie said.

"Would've run into them by now," deadpanned Bass. He scanned the road with his eyes with both hands on the wheel.

"Not necessarily," Kodie admonished. "They could be hiding. We haven't tackled this with any systematic—"

"—Okay. Yes. You may be right," Bass cut her off.

I continued to play golly-gee. Maybe it's because I didn't want them to think I knew something. The responsibility of that.

"It skipped over us somehow," I said.

Kodie inhaled and exhaled rapidly once. "Maybe it didn't skip us. Maybe it just takes us longer." The Bronco got real quiet. The muffler's blat and tire hum was all. I glanced at Kodie. She looked down at her hands, her face trying to conceal deathly fear. To hear herself voice it drove her eyes wild.

We drove slow now, crossing over Lady Bird Lake, and as we did it occurred to me that I'd never not seen a paddler down on the water until today.

I asked, almost rhetorically, "Why didn't they surround us, you think? They saw us."

Kodie curled a hair loop behind her ear. "I think it's...they're still just little kids, you know? They're scared. Our world, our lives have been turned upside down. Theirs has been turned inside out. They're clinging to each other. They're very much about safety in numbers. Rugged individualists they aren't." She looked out the window at a Lamar without traffic, its places of business and apartments tombs now. Staring, she said, "They fear."

"They are skittish. They haven't come near us. Not at the HEB, not at the cemetery. When we went to Rebecca's house, that was us going to them, surprising them a little I think," I said. But they knew. Bass turned in his seat a little to face me and Kodie. "You saw them all together just now. Whatever happened…that's the result. Kids acting as this one thing. No leadership structure. All stimulus-response, like a flock."

I turned my head as we passed by the bookstore Bookpeople and saw on the marquee that Sarah Bird was to be reading from her new one tonight, an Updikean comedy set at a Westlake dinner party on Halloween. In monotone I said, "Birds. Yeah," but I thought, *oceanic quicksilver.*

"A swarm. A hive," Kodie said, again looking down at her hands which now formed themselves into a rounded, hive-like shape.

Bass nodded his chin her direction. "Hives. Man, that's it. They've all gotten together into these mindless hives."

I said, "I wouldn't say mindless. Of one mind."

Bass equivocated. "But hives have queens. I'm not seeing any leaders."

I almost asked them right there if they'd seen the dark smiling teeth too.

"I felt kinda safe in the cemetery. Even though I was close to them. I didn't want to move. They stay in a group, but I've seen a few stragglers. Rogues. Not many. Boys, mostly. They don't venture far. I've seen them go off down the street and then come right back running. Eight, nine, ten-year-olds," said Bass.

"You say rogues, but I bet there's more to it than that. I bet those are the ones who act as hive police," I said.

"Bet those are the ones who busted up my car," Bass said.

And I thought, *and dragged off Simon and tied him up to a post atop Doug Sahm Hill.*

Nothing more to say for a few beats. In the old world, we couldn't take it, the building up of quiet like an explosive gas, and somebody would have to rush in to say something to fill the void. The old world abhorred a vacuum. Not anymore.

Bass said at the intersection at Twenty-Fourth, "God, there's just *nothing.*" He lightly thumped the steering wheel with the meat of his palm.

I kept thinking I should be despondently sad, and a part of me was, but for some reason the tears just hadn't come, at least not like the deluge I let go when Grandma Lucille died, like a damn breaking. You'd think I would've by then when I thought of Mom, Dad so far away, Martin, Johnny. My classmates, friends, bandmates, Mr. English. I saw their faces, flashes of them at least (amazing how quickly you start to forget even the most important faces in your life when they're not there to be seen anymore), but that profound mourning had yet to arise in me. Watching the train slide by did it to me, though, and Mr. Fleming's note. That's something, I guess.

Maybe I'm being strong for something bigger. I get that feeling now. After all, why am I paddling coastward, answering a summons I cannot begin to describe?

My aloneness is total. It's me and you, dear reader. And those who watch. I feel their eyes on me. It's my journey to make. What? a pilgrimage, a vision quest, a…hell, I don't know. Maybe I've tumbled full on into crazy. Me and Mags here. Ol' Mags the Killer. Aintcha, girl, huh? A goddam killa.

None of us asked why those kids were tied up on that hill, or what we thought happened to them. I waited for someone else to ask. Obviously, everyone else waited too. Didn't happen. Verboten topic among the late bloomers.

The silence peppered with muffler blats was short-lived. Bass muttered to fill the void, answered unasked questions. "They don't mill about. Total stillness, total discipline." I liked Bass for his talkativeness, his old-world want to fill the void.

"They didn't come anywhere near those train tracks. I don't think they trust technology, you know? The old ways of doing things? You'd think they'd be going bonkers, playing with everything, burning stuff, just going wild. Or at least wandering around lost and crying, looking for Mommy and Daddy, any adult. Pounding on the doors of the Palmer, something. But it's the opposite. They're so…contained."

Bass stepped on the gas and took a turn to the east. I assumed he was going to get on I-35 again. "Goddammit," he said to no prompt. Just pissed.

"Waiting us out," said Kodie.

I said, "If we insist, you know, assert ourselves as the elders and try to take charge, we'd be quickly dispatched out of pure fear. Like white blood cells taking out a pathogen."

"Fighting off infection," Kodie said. "We're the germs. Old-world cooties."

"I don't know, man. Fear? Those little bastards seem just plain mean to me," Bass said, stopping at the front of the Driskill Hotel on Sixth, throwing it into park but leaving the engine on. "Be right back." In our talking we hadn't noticed that Bass had backtracked to downtown.

"Wait, what? Where are you going, Bass?" Kodie asked out the window at him, worry in her voice.

He smirked. "I gotta go up and see about a ghost."

"Oh, stop it," I said. "We've got other things to do."

"You wouldn't understand," he said. "Be back in a sec."

Bass stopped on the steps fronting the hotel, an 1880s structure. I dunno architecture but it's terra-cotta-colored and textured, one of the nicest hotels in Austin and certainly the most famous. You could say it was stately.

Martin took us to the Driskill Grille once, for a steak dinner. He actually said that. *Let's all go out for a fancy steak dinner tonight.* He'd closed some deal and was feeling all magnanimous. A pretty great night, actually, near Christmas last, everything festooned and lit. Martin and Mom's faces flush with wine, the rims of the wineglasses sparkling, the civility of the table talk, the family's future seeming bright. Not that I had bad times—just first-world uptown teenage whiny sucky times, right?—but this was one of the good times. He insisted we all get steak and we did. He even let us have wine, and Mom said nothing about it. I'll hold on to that memory of Martin: his face flush and candlelit at his whoop-de-doo steak dinner at the Driskill Grille.

Austin lore, Driskill lore, says a ghost lives on the top floor. I knew that's what Bass was doing. Stoned in the dark spaces of Memorial Park, he'd get all mystic and delved into gothic what-ifs. He was superstitious too, or liked to pretend he was. We'd be standing too close to a grave and I'd be coughing up a lung due to some harsh smoke and he'd say, "Let's walk on. We need to let this guy sleep."

"Right now?" I whined.

"What, Kevin? What's the hurry?" Bass said, annoyed. "Seriously, take a breath."

I blinked hard at his logic, laying the smartassery on thick.

He exhaled loud. "Just…gimme this. A coupla minutes."

"She's just up there waiting on you. Today's the day."

"I've got a feeling. Given what's happened, I'd like to think there's lots of ghosts walking around. Whole damn planet's haunted now."

I hated to tell him that it already was haunted. Always was.

"We'll run into some on the way home. C'mon. Power grid's going to go anytime. We gotta—"

"We don't *gotta* do anything. Not anymore. We're the survivors," he pontificated, "and we don't got to do a damned thing." He stood astride the steps looking like a VIP telling off a hounding reporter. "Hell, I may sleep here tonight. Armed to the teeth, of course, and drunk on the Driskill's top-shelf hooch. Come up with me."

"No, man. I'm not into it. I want to get a plan going, get organized, then we can screw around."

"Jeez. I mean, Kevin, the world's already…It can't get worse."

"The hell it can't."

"We're still here. Let's live, dammit. You and your Warsteiner last night and now you're all taskmastering?"

I shook my head, a look of bewilderment, I'm sure, on my face.

He waved me off and went in. The smoked-glass doors to the Driskill swung open. I figured he'd come running right back out, his face white after seeing the concierge rotting on the lobby's marble floor before the doors even settled back into place. But he didn't.

When did bodies begin to smell? Mr. Fleming had within twenty-four hours. This became the topic while we waited on Bass. Kodie didn't answer. She went mute and I felt horrible for asking now.

"In a week and it'll be unmistakable," she said. "Do we pile and burn them? Bacteria and viruses will have nowhere else to go once they've burned through all the flesh. Rotting bodies don't cause disease in a population unless it gets into the water. We stay away from them, we should be okay." We knew we could never build enough pits to bury the world's bodies. The earth will just have to eat them all up and the dried bones will just have to sit there for time immemorial, or at least until the kids grew up some and decide they want to clean up the place.

But I was glad at least we were now firing off questions, brainstorming the new world. The stun was wearing off and now we needed to get with it. Bass didn't seem to think there was a clock ticking, but I knew there was.

I gritted my teeth with impatience now, my body's glands flaring and shoving its chemicals through my veins.

That was the old-world survivor in me competing with the part of me saying *screw it, why bother?* Roll with it, like the kids do. I think of my jazzier trombone pieces which makes me think of that saying heard around Mardi Gras—*laissez les bontemps roulez.* Let the good times roll.

There would be no more Mardi Gras. All the world's traditions, holidays moot. The Great Zamboni had come and all that scratched ice and those little piles of shavings and blood droplets gone, glazed over into a surface so mirror-like that yesterday's games are forgotten.

Martin had taken me to a bunch of Texas Stars hockey games. I feigned not wanting to go but I always relented. Looking back, I know that I desperately wanted Martin to take me. To cheer stupidly at the swirling red lights when a goal was scored and to pretend like we were father and son. Sometimes, in din of cheering and noise from the arena's speakers, I'd tear up wishing it was my real dad who took me to hockey games and high-fived me, our hands smacking in the cool air.

THE HOW AND THE WHY don't matter. Only survival matters. The kids, when they grow up, will have the burden of trying to figure it out. Then again, when I see them move and act as they do, I'm not sure they have any designs to do any such thing like figuring it out, trying to divine goddamned meaning all the time. Honestly, when I saw that wave moving up Lake Austin coming fast on the heel of those sounds, I wasn't surprised. It knew what it was. I couldn't put it into words, but I knew. I'd dreamed it. I'd written it in a story already. A version of it. The way it felt. Not the wave or the whalesounds, just the doom. Seeing it, my mind screamed, *there it is!*

I'm calm right now. Talking to you helps me. You're like my shrink, dear reader, my analyst nodding at my problems. As I talk this out, I feel warm and soothed like I'm floating in the womb of the world. I think I've said that before, *the womb of the world.* Of course, I am actually floating southbound on this turgid river.

Water. Womb. World. Whalesounds. Waves. Warm.

Not a whimper but a *whuh!*

WE MADE OUR WAY DOWN Sixth and zoomed up onto MoPac. No merging. It was all ours and its emptiness made my stomach sour.

"You see her, Bass?" I asked.

"Who?" Bass had spaced out a bit, snapped back. "Huh? Oh, uh, no. No suicide brides on the fifth floor."

I'll never forget the way he looked at me after he said that. It came out as such an obvious lie that I laughed out loud at him. When I saw his face, I stifled it. Though my heart raced with his look, keeping things light, I'd said, "Well, thanks for wasting our time."

The windows are down, for we are ever listening, and we're flying up MoPac and he turns and looks at me again, his face pallid and drawn, his eyes saucer-huge. It was enough to shut me up.

Such weirdness compounded here at the end of the world: My eyes whipping open this morning and then I'm chasing a train. Bass U-turning and running upstairs into an old hotel to see a ghost. Kodie and I compelled to go to Rebecca's house. Some random dying man's request. Now Johnny's gone. But for Rebecca, he'd probably still be with us.

What will be the repercussions of my compulsion to train-chase, Bass's attempted ghost-spotting, Kodie's need to stay with Rebecca, her siren's dance to *Legend: The Best of Bob Marley and the Wailers*?

We knew they were coming and we waited for them—the repercussions. That's all we could do.

BELABORING HOW THINGS LOOKED IN the days after, the bodies, the piles of stones here and there, the slow degradation of things—little things at first like the accumulation of trash and leaves in places where you'd normally not see it, at places of business, hospitals, and here, the Lowe's—gets monotonous so I won't bother with the apocalyptic tourism.

The corpses and the stink and the fear. It's all there, know that. That ever-increasing deathsmell hangs as omnipresent fog. The sweetness, the tang. So thick you almost think you can see the amalgamated fumes.

So there we were at the Lowe's up on Shoal Creek. Our talk and cries of shock and disgust at the sights echoed throughout the massive still building. Lowe's opened at 6:00 a.m., so folks had been here at daybreak. Employees and all those early-risen construction workers and painters in their speckled chinos. The handful of bodies were mostly chokers-of-the-white, but there were a couple of suicides (nail gun, saw).

We acquired two generators, an ass-load of batteries and flashlights and lanterns, a couple of those big portable space heaters (November cold after Halloween), and then we got gasoline in about fifty red plastic two-gallon containers. It took all afternoon. But we were doing something. Being proactive, Martin would say.

DOORS UNLOCKED, WE JUST WALKED into the Hummer dealer, found the drawer where they kept all the keys. No bodies and no piles.

Our shoes squeaked on the glossy cement showroom floor. We weren't agog or excited. Acquiring some material thing in the new world held no meaning. It was big, shiny, so what. Maybe we should just go take over one of the palace homes overlooking the lake. We talked about it. Maybe we would, some place that's all windows facing west and a wine cellar and beer fridge stocked to make Bacchus blush. Take over the W Hotel downtown, run amok, stay drunk. Maybe we would.

"There she is," Bass said with put-on drawling pride in his voice. The Hummer Bass chose was black on black, tinted windows, a tricked-out, violent rap video's ride. Bass hopped in. Over the harsh echo of the door slamming shut he put his wrist on the steering wheel, looked out the window and said, "Dig my ride, bitches?" I didn't answer. Kodie shook her head slowly, smirking at Bass.

We figured out how to roll up the front garage door. Before driving off, Bass stopped, powered down his window again, and threw me the Bronco keys. I bobbled and dropped them. As I bent over, he said, "It's yours, bud. But, I don't get it. Why don't you just take one of these? Get something else tomorrow? The next day. I mean, who cares?"

I shrugged.

"Maybe tomorrow."

I drove home in Bass's Bronco. He didn't even hang and wait for me. Kodie, clearly not feeling well, jumped in with him.

Maybe Bass was right: Who cares?

I FOLLOWED THEM FOR A bit, but turned off. Guess they didn't notice.

Driving alone in someone else's car, this muffler's death rattle caroming off every building back into my ears, I felt what it may be like for me sooner than I wanted to believe: Roaming these streets alone, hiding from the children as if they're killers, no girlfriend's hand to clutch, no little brother to hug, no compatriot in Bass. Nobody.

I had this impulse to drive away from everything fast but I jerked the wheel into the neighborhood where the elementary school where I used to play youth soccer was on a whim, to see if there were any kids milling around. Hoping there would be. Seeing anything like that, any humanness in them, confusion, fear, would have been better than to believe what we saw this morning at Butler Park.

I circled the grounds. They contained no life, no death, not a single stone cairn in the parking lots.

I wasn't a great soccer player when I was ten, but I was decent. I wasn't a thumbsucker and I tried hard. My coach liked that. This was when my dad was still around. He only came to about half the games. They were in the mornings on Saturdays and he and Mom seemed to always be at each other, if silently. But when he did come out, he got into it and cheered for me, saying nice job when it was over. He didn't say 'champ' or 'big guy' like the other cheese-ass dads.

But the cheese-ass dads came to every game and didn't move to North Carolina forever with some bitch named Beth. In retrospect, I'd've taken a 'way to go champ' any day. Go ahead, cheese-ass dad, tousle my hair and tell me 'we'll get 'em next time, big guy.'

I walked out onto a green field marked with faded lines for games that should have been played today and stood out among them. I paced a little and fought off despair. From my pocket I pulled out Mr. Fleming's yellow note and reread it.

I KNOW YOU WILL SURVIVE.... I KNOW THAT YOU'LL NOT BE STAYING HERE FOR LONG.... THE DARK SIDE OF THE HELIX...THE WORLD WILL STILL NEED ITS STORYTELLERS.... IT'S YOUR WORLD NOW.... STUMBLED ONTO SOMETHING WE SHOULDN'T HAVE?.... IT NEEDS YOU TO NEED IT....

When I drove over there I had considered just driving away, never to return. Overwhelmed with that feeling, by those dark smiling teeth. But the turn into this neighborhood, then these fields, changed that. I'm glad I had his letter on me. The gist of his note wasn't just 'please bury us' but 'keep going, you're the one who can't give up'.

LATE AFTERNOON WHEN I PULLED up to the Flemings' house. I opened the Bronco's tailgate and then went steaming in. The smell intensified on the way back to the bedroom, almost overwhelming now just hours later. The imminent rot of the world tormented me, how all was going to become a decomposing slush.

He leaned against the wall under the window, his jaw unhinged and frozen. I grabbed his feet and through his socks I felt cold hard flesh and I bellowed in gall.

The eyes show you things. The nose pronounces it with depth. But when you touch, you come to know certainty.

I wrapped my fingers around his ankles and pulled. His head thumped to the floor from the wall. I didn't look at his face as I dragged him through the house. There was no way I was going to get him up into the Bronco alone.

This made things real, the weight of the dead. The earth pulling the flesh back whence it came. His wet suit and hair left a trail on his wood floor. I kept saying *I'm sorry, Dr. Fleming, I'm so sorry*. On the porch I paused and looked across to see Bass and Kodie standing in my yard. They didn't offer help at first, just stared, not understanding what it was that had gotten into me.

They asked themselves, I knew: Why did it matter? Who cares? Not in a crass way, just matter-of-fact.

It mattered. Mr. Fleming's note said so and I believed him.

It matters. How we bury the dead, what we do from here. We can't just throw up our hands and give up. This has happened and yet we remain. We continue. You're here, dear reader, yes?

I dragged him farther and was almost crying with the effort and frustration, not understanding why he was so heavy, this slight, intellectual man.

Midway down the cement walk to the Bronco, Bass called out and they came jogging over.

They stood and stared at him, the abstraction becoming real. We'd seen bodies. Bass had watched his parents both die. Yet this stranger's corpse, that I was pulling it and wanting to bury it, came down on them. The fact that the old world had to be buried somehow. We couldn't just leave it to rot. But how? The children…they were changed, they wouldn't do it.

"Help me," I said through gritted teeth, pulling on him, putting my back into it. Bass took the feet. I went around and picked him up by the shoulders. His head lolled, his eyelids folded and I saw the death in them, the marbleized flesh of the man's cold eyeball. Kodie supported in the middle and we managed to lay him in the back of the Bronco.

"If we do this, what's to keep us from doing others?" asked Kodie. It was the first time I'd heard distance and coldness in her voice. "Where does it stop? My parents? Your parents, Bass? What about them?"

Bass looked at the street. "Yeah. Maybe later. Right now, I don't know if I can even…"

"I know. Me too. I'm sorry." Pause and quiet. The silence of the world. "But that's what I'm saying. We can't bury them all. And don't be melodramatic and tell me 'but, we've got to try, dammit.' I say no we do not." She sniffed and coughed. "When I go, I won't expect it of you."

We looked at her and froze, speechless.

"You're not going to die, Kodie, okay?" I said, still sucking a little wind.

"No time soon," said Bass with a wan smile.

Her eyes cutting to Bass, then me. "You're my guarantors, eh?" she said with a dangerous laugh. "Screw you guys. Don't soft-handle me. Don't pretend." She met and held each of our eyes on each word. "I'm. Dead. You're. Dead."

"Help me get Mrs. Fleming? Please?" I asked Kodie this directly.

"We haven't been spared!" she bawled. Her voice echoed. "We've been passed over, but it's…it's circling back to take us. You know it's true." She flapped her arms out and slapped her hands back onto her legs. "No. No, we haven't been spared. We are *not* the lucky ones. We are the ones who get to suffer the most, that's all. We get to watch it all crumble, think about it, feel it, mourn, then die."

Kodie refused to help more and walked back into my house. I heard her crying as she reached the porch. She closed the door and we began with Mrs. Fleming.

THIS WAS THE FIRST BODY I'd removed stones from, so its shock value was high though I tried hard to gird myself.

I started with the head. Bass picked off stones from her body and legs. Lifting that second rock, I saw her eye. It bored through me with a fear in it unlike her husband's. Once I cleared away the others from her face, the total expression wasn't fearful. It's just that her eyes were open.

"Want to close those?" Bass asked. "It's creeping me out."

Now I felt the prickles on my skin, thinking she could sit up any second, gawking at us like we're ghouls disturbing her place of rest. I saw that image in my head—Mrs. Fleming sitting up board-straight, her mud-caked, leafy hair sticking out in all directions, her greening skin loose and purple-veiny, then swiveling her head to me, blinking sluggishly one time and then letting loose a cry of the damned. A cry sounding just like the whalesounds at dawn on the day of.

Christ.

I made a V of my fingers and touched her eyelids. The chill of her flesh, cold as the stone I just pulled off her, ran through my fingertips and coursed all the way to a place behind my ear. The lids wouldn't go down. Kept flapping back up like cheap window shades. I tried several times, pushing down and then pulling with my fingers.

"No go," I said. "They won't move."

"Guess she's just going to have to watch us," said Bass. We didn't laugh at this but the attempt at humor made this bearable.

No go, I thought, harkening back to the title of the extra credit essay on *Lord of the Flies* written for you, Mr. E. The words came to mind and got applied to the stiffened status of Mrs. Fleming's eyelids. But there was more to those words; and the dark smiling teeth in my head—the ones spreading so wide within the mouth housing them that the glistening purple-black gums show too—and they say to me matter-of-factly: *things are what they are.* That quote, psionically-uttered by the head of a pig on a stick in the green island jungle as heard by the at-that-point disturbed character Simon—

Simon.

Christ.

Settle down, I thought. Lots of males named Simon in the world. You're losing it again, seeing patterns and coincidences that aren't there.

But Grandma Lucille said there were no coincidences.

Nausea flourished within and threatened to overtake me as I looked down at Mrs. Fleming. Her face seemed to say, too, that there weren't any coincidences, and that chaos and chance, like institutionalized gods, were conveniences we the living made up.

Mrs. Fleming's face saying: I knew, didn't I? The reason. That it was close, close, close.

I even heard her voice saying it to me—her voice coming in that neighborly tone of hers. From across the street while putting away groceries, just as she had the other day when she called out to me about the Macy's parade. That voice now reciting to me the exact epigraph to my essay in full, a quote culled from the heart of Golding's novel: *You knew, didn't you? I'm part of you? Close, close, close! I'm the reason why it's no go? Why things are what they are?*

I was nodding yes to her and she asked it again, louder. This time I saw her standing next to her politically stickered Subaru, hands on her hips, waving at me in a way eerily similar to the way of the bald man after the water rolled by his feet. *You knew didn't you?* Incredulity in her voice, almost shock. *Cerca, cerca, cerca.*

She was yelling it at me now, the tone this third time flatly accusatory: *You* knew, *didn't you!?* Her voice permeating the awful quiet, its waves funneling down into my mind's maw.

That third time, in my vision, she slammed her Subaru door, stood and looked at me, shaking her head in disapproval, as if what has happened was my fault.

Mr. E had commented on it, writing in the margin: *To choose this title for your essay and this quote to tie it together... Well done. You really saw what this book was about, didn't you?*

I damn near said yes out loud to her as if she had asked me, but kept it in. I was probably nodding yes. Bass asked if I was all right. I had stared at her face not believing, like the boy in the jungle had at the flyblown pig head with the lidded eyes of a Thai Buddha.

I was locked into her skyward gaze, thinking of the Simons, and the children staring at us with lapidary stillness so that we would go away, so that we wouldn't see what was to occur atop Doug Sahm Hill.

The next comment Mr. English had made at the top of the page was: *When are you going to let me submit that story of yours for you?* And so here's where it gets weird. It's something I haven't told you yet. I dunno, I just haven't wanted to yet. Besides, this is the proper place in the story to do it.

So, the other thing Mr. English had said to me in his office when I went to pick up the essay, which was really a ruse to hang out because he could've just left it in my cubby—with the door closed, which he never did, this stricken, beset look on his face—was that these sorts of stories are popular right now. That's not weird. What was weird was his tone which was low and careful like he was talking to a seething school-shooter holding Mommy's M-16 Bushwacker.

He had continued, "People in general are fearful of what's coming next. You can feel it in the air, Kevin. This apocalyptic vision of yours is not only well-written, sounding like something written by a seasoned writer, it's something people are actually going to want to read, maybe even talk about." A tight smile broke onto his face. "You could expand this and write a series of stories, which, if this quality were to be maintained…I wouldn't be surprised if it saw a little serialization. They could even end up being fixed up into a novel."

That's not so weird either. What's weird is the story's existence in context. The short story which I called *The Late Bloomers* is a story about the end of the world. Three thousand words. Not so weird. But in it—here's the thing—all the adults died leaving only the kids. What killed everyone was a virus like bird flu meets H1N1, and it took a while, more than a morning. But the story wasn't about the virus and how it all went down or anything like that. The story was a snapshot of the aftermath, how the humans—a specific group of people I placed in Phoenix, who were eighteen, nineteen, who were adults but they weren't—were dealing with it. The story ended elliptically but it seemed clear that the children and the late bloomers, the young adults who didn't die because they still had kid in them, were going to rebuild the world together. The late bloomers would take the lead because the world needed the kid in us to remake the world.

I didn't see it as good in the way Mr. English did. I mean, I was shooting for Carver realism and got this whacked-out end-of-days story. I guess that's what happens when you uncork your mind and let the subconscious roam about.

It's one story of several I'd shown him, but it was the one about which he gushed.

So, you get my queasiness now? I *just* wrote this story over the summer. I had given it to Mr. E in August. Right before my big pot bust was when he'd mentioned it to me. When I dropped by to pick up my *No Go* essay.

He was so keen on the story. The way he acted when talking to me about it, treating me like some sort of clairvoyant. He'd handed me the essay but held the story in his hands and he stabbed the paper with his index finger, saying, "There's something here." He gave me an accusatory look.

That's when he'd moved past me to close the door. When it closed, the room got cottony quiet. I realized just how stuffed with books his office was.

He sat on the edge of his desk and looked down at me. His eyes said sit. I sat.

I set my backpack in my lap as a buffer between me and him.

I wouldn't say he scared me then, but he wasn't the flip and comely rake of a teacher with bedhead hair, chunky glasses, and a half-sleeve of tats I was used to. Here sat a man with curiosity, wonder, and, I detected, fear in his eyes. The look in one's eyes you only see in dreams.

Like the one I'd had before I wrote that story. I popped up at 3:30 a.m. to write it.

I'd gotten to know Mr. English this fall, he being both my AP English teacher and my advisor. He'd requested that I be his advisee because he'd been on the Austin library's poetry contest judging panel last April—National Poetry Month—and he'd read the poem I'd entered. The poems were submitted anonymously. I thought it was just this tiny contest. Well, mine, a not-half-bad free verse thing called *My Unstrung Heart, Won't You Please Be Still?*, ended up winning in the high school category. It turned out to be not so tiny a contest. Mr. E read the poem aloud on the radio after Garrison Keillor had finished this especially glum delivery of a Galway

Kinnell poem, *The Silence of the World*, concluding his radio segment *The Writer's Almanac*.

Was Galway Kinnell one of my favorites? Yes, he was. You could even say he was my favorite. Was it neat-o that it was read right before mine, my poem rubbing elbows with his? You bet.

Given the tenor of this particular tale I'm telling you was the whole thing kissed by kismet in that now the aspect of this new world that makes my balls recede inside my body cavity is its silence and that Kinnell's poem, coming right after mine, had that as its subject matter, indeed, bore the very title? Uh-huh. Yep. You're catching on, dear reader.

Coincidences? Patterns? Early-onset schizophrenia? Psychosis? Grandma Lucille, what say you?

I know, I know.

So, anyway, you're sitting at the edge of your desk, Mr. E, staring me down like I'd done something wrong, holding my story, touching the pad of your index finger to it saying, 'there's something here.' You 'couldn't put your finger on' what it was, yet you kept putting your actual finger on it. Kept making little circles on it with your index finger like a conjurer. My eyes flicked to your desk's nameplate: Todd English, PhD (with such an education, why were you teaching high-school, Mr. E?), then to the framed black-and-white photograph of you and that smoking-hot wife of yours— Inga? Inger?—sitting on a boulder atop Mount Bonnell. My eyes stayed there. I hadn't noticed the picture before. I started to lift my hand to point at it when you said, "Yeah. That's new. We got engaged at that spot."

I kept staring at it, looking at the transect of lake way down below you, and the strip of lawn where the bald man had stood waving up at me with that sickening smile.

I looked at your wife's face. Intimidatingly beautiful with her square jaw, all blond Swedish model-looking. Real breasts, clearly. I couldn't help thinking of her swanning around your house in one of your T-shirts post-coitus sipping on a bottle of water imported from her native Nordic country. I knew you didn't have any kids. Fetching couple that you still were, I knew you'd probably be too old to conceive. You were the type who wanted kids. I knew it by the way you were, Mr. E. I thought maybe the pain and frustration I sensed in you wasn't because of the shelved novel but the baby who wouldn't come.

"Kevin? About this story. You said you'd had a dream?" you'd asked.

My eyes shifted from the photograph to your face. "Yes."

"If you don't mind my asking, what was the dream about? I'm not trying to analyze you or anything. I'm fascinated." Your finger still on the paper.

"Well, you were in it," I told you.

You sat up straight and cleared your throat. "Okay." You sat back on the edge of your desk and crossed one leg over the other, furrowed your brow and nodded.

"Not until the end though, and your appearance didn't connect to the rest. It was basically…what you and I are doing now. You, sitting on the edge of your desk looking as you do now, and me sitting here with my backpack in my lap."

You said, "hummm," and raised your index finger from the paper to your pursed lips.

"I don't remember many words passing between us. I remember you there and me here, and right now even I'm feeling…"

"Déjà vu?" you asked.

I nodded. "Still feeling it. See, I knew you were going to ask that."

The room. It was very still. Time slushed through my ears. Ticks of it rode molecules of my heart-beaten blood.

In the hall, lockers clacked shut, voices burst out into laughter. You looked startled by the world outside that door. You cleared your throat again. "That's really something, Kevin. I'm having the same feeling. And I had a dream, too, with you in it. Sitting there with your backpack in your lap." You nodded to me. "Just like that."

"Did you have a dream about the end of the world like in my story?"

You shook your head. "No. But this, yes." A beat of pause. "And now it's gone, that feeling."

"Yes," I'd said, relieved. The room opened and cleared. Like an eclipsing shadow lifting away with a flick.

You chuckled and shook your head clear. You sat in your chair and said, "Okay. Enough of that. Tell me about your dream and how it fueled this story of yours."

"It's a long time ago now, so the details aren't there, at least not many. But with dreams it's the ones that remain that are important, I guess, huh?"

"Could be. Again, I'm just an interested English teacher. If this is in any way uncomfortable…"

"No, no it's fine." I moved my eyes around in my head to remember and put the backpack on the floor. "I don't know what happened to the world. Just these few people like in the story. We're standing at some sort of overlook. Me, this dark-haired girl, and this other guy."

"Do you know them? Then, or still?"

"In real life? Yes, actually. This girl I work with at Dollar Tree and another student here."

You nod, your chin muscle flexing and tightening with thought.

"Below us is a mass of people. All these young kids. Thousands of them in a tight grouping. They're facing and cheering at something in front of them and we didn't know what it was. We knew we had to get closer to see but we didn't want the kids to see us. We were really frightened. I don't know why that is, but we were."

"So what happened? This isn't in your story. Do the things in the story occur in your dream?"

"Not really. The dream's residue gave me the feeling which led to the idea."

"In the dream did you go down to see what they were cheering about?"

"No, we didn't. We were too scared to move. Didn't want them to see us."

You formed a steeple with your fingers in front of your face. "How did you know it was the end of the world?"

"I just felt it was. We all did. It was just that scene. There wasn't any more to it."

"In the dream it happened in an arid place? You set the story in Phoenix."

I shook my head. "No, in the dream it was here in Austin, though I don't know where exactly. The location was ambiguous. Just this field. The story grew out of this feeling in the dream, a feeling of—" I struggled for the right word.

"I understand. You feel something powerful but nebulous and you write to bring it into some focus."

I shook my head. "—doom. That's what I felt. A horrible doom that made my heart race and my stomach sour."

"An apocalyptic vision will do that, I suppose. I'm sure it didn't feel good and I'm sorry you had such a, well, a nightmare. But it fed a story. Something good came out of it."

"But is it good?"

"Yeah, I think you've written a fine story here," you said, brushing it again. Very tactile with my story, Mr. E.

"No, I mean is that a good thing in general terms? To have a horrible dream and not being able to sleep and feeling forced to get something down on paper?"

"That's a hard question to answer. It's the essential art question, isn't it? Is the suffering one does, the privation experienced, worth the art it produces?"

I glanced at the wink of shine off Inga/Inger's aviator sunglasses and her geometric mandible making her look like an insect. "Must art be the result of suffering?"

"Not necessarily. But show me any work of art that isn't in some way tinged with bittersweetness, pain, the unknowable, existential ennui, our lives' ephemeral nature. I don't think you'll find one. Even humorous work is rooted in darkness, sometimes the most dark and fearful. My God, I mean listen to Richard Pryor or David Sedaris, Mel Brooks. Carlin, Bill Hicks. Robin Williams? I mean, *gah*—dark, despairing stuff under the ha-has." You traced the outside of the pages of my story with your index finger. I thought you might slice your finger pad open and bleed on it. It was profane, transgressive, what you were doing. Like, *who cares if I cut the shit out of my finger on this right now.* The way you stared at your sliding finger, meat along a blade . . .

I audibly gulped. "So, you're saying it is. Necessary. Suffering for art."

"What?" Startled. You put the pages on the desk. You winced and looked at your fingertip. "Oh, yeah. I think so." You swept your other hand through your hair. "Yeah, time and pressure makes diamonds from coal. Similarly, art is a by-product of life. We're a carbon life-form. Squeeze some of us just right and you get art." You chuckled through your nostrils.

As I say this to you, I think of Mom humming a Crosby, Stills, and Nash tune and singing the refrain while folding laundry dumped on the living room floor—*we are stardust, we are golden, we are sixty-billion-year-old carbon* . . .

Goddammit, dear reader, I miss her. I miss you, Mom.

"And then there you are at the end of the dream, sitting here talking about it, as we are now," I said.

You nod curtly once, re-erect your steeple of fingers, that one finger shying from the pressure. Then I saw a droplet of blood roll down your finger. You collapse the steeple and put the finger in your mouth. You wait. There's more, you know.

I said, "Then you saying to me what... you said."

The steeple was quickly back; collapsed, erected, collapsed like the eensy weensy spider dancing on a mirror. I wanted you to fill it in for me. "You know what you said in my dream, don't you, Mr. English?"

You didn't answer right away, and that's when my pulse *kerthumped* in a chaotic time signature.

You shook your head, cleared your throat with an air of annoyance, bored yourself up and donned a professional demeanor. "All I can say is what I said to you in *my* dreams. What I said was, sitting there at the end of my desk—you with the backpack—'they leap from high places with smiles on their faces.'"

To hear this dream-phrase uttered in the conscious world...I'm sure I looked at you hanging fire and pin-eyed.

"That line was in your story. Not in dialogue, as I recall. In a passage of narration." You perfunctorily shuffle my story pages as if seeking the phrase. "This is why I'm fascinated, Kevin." The look on your face didn't say fascination. It projected bald fear.

I hung my head and found myself muttering almost with shame, "You said it to me in my dream too."

I mean, Mr. E? The blood fell from your face. You struggled to keep your lips clamped together. You started to say something but your voice was a crack of air. You stood and smoothed out your shirt absentmindedly. "Stranger than fiction, huh Kevin?" Your look just totally haunted, eyes howling and dark against a blanched canvas.

You were out for the next week, nobody knew why, and then I didn't see you again until Coach Numbnuts brought me in. You sat behind your desk. The framed photo was gone. You pretended for Coach Numbnuts. I was any other punk on the wrong path.

Exiting your office and walking down the hall with the coach, I remember looking back at you. Your face fought itself. You attempted to give me the smile you'd wanted to give your unborn child, but your eyes failed you. Your mouth spread out in the mechanics of that smile, but the eyes didn't follow. They were hollow.

That was the last time we saw each other.

And now I think that fake smile is the dark, glistening one overfull with teeth.

Turning my head back down the hall, my eyes snagged on the wet new tag across lockers, *A Pox on Yo Lips*. Gravity still pulling down lines of the paint.

We'd shared portions of a dream. Grandma Lucille, I know what you'd say.

To share a dream like that…I'm with you. Can't believe that's coincidence. No such thing as luck.

How did you go, Mr. E? Did you walk out into the gray of that morning before the sky evolved that awful blue? Choke and fall in your bedroom, public radio pledge drive purr looping? You and that hot, barren wife of yours, are you lying in your house together now, she in your too-big T-shirt, you caught mid-shave and shirtless, the spumed white hardened? Or did you both get that holy-rolling look on your faces and then do it together in a gleeful improv suicide pact? Did you seek out a high place from which to leap? Or something more local and brutal?

The way you dragged your finger pad along the edge of my page.

Ah, hell.

"You okay, Kev?"

I plopped down to ward off vertigo. I breathed. Bass said, "It's going to be okay. It'll get better. The shock is wearing off, reality settling in. I figure we got to push through it or we'll never make it."

With his bottom lip pooched out, he bobbed his head to these general terms like one might a funeral litany.

We made quick work of it then, tossing the stones off of her—*clack! clack!*—lifting her stiff, heavy, bug-riddled body into the back bed of the Bronco next to her husband. Somehow, loading the Flemings into the Bronco made us feel like maybe the world could be cleaned up, if not literally every body interred, at least we could envision the old world coming back. We extrapolated from these moments the rebirth of the world as we knew it.

I got the shovel from the garage.

THE EARTH CAME UP EASILY in the place Mr. Fleming had described in his note. Two guys digging, our breath visible fog in the chilling evening, silence but for the sniffing and the breathing and the scratch of the shovel and the sound of loosed dirt landing in a pile.

We made one hole. It wasn't six feet, but deep enough. I got in the hole which came up to my waist and pulled them in. I hated to see how they lolled and flopped. Once they were both in, I situated them side by side and then we covered them without words, as this is the oldest of human tasks and no annotation was needed.

AT NIGHT IT BEGAN TO rain. The patter comforted us, this sound of the world still living. Kodie opened a window. When we finally got in bed together, I flipped on the recorder.

I erased our conversation, most of it being too far away to hear. She whispered and cried, said she felt she was dying. Her fever spiked again and I nursed her all night, barely slept. Her coughing became so intense that she couldn't stop for minutes at a time. We had to sit up. I brought her green tea nuked in the microwave. I thought of Bass's mom as I did it, how he used to do this when her asthma got bad. Kodie could hardly speak. The worst of it was just before dawn, when she said, "I take it back." She had grabbed my wrist hard and searched my eyes frantically, hers toggling back and forth between mine as mine did hers, neither of us able to alight on the other's gaze. "Will you do the same for me as you did for your neighbors?"

At dawn, the wheeze slackened. She slept propped up with her mouth agape. I let her sleep. After a night like that, she can do what she wants.

Though we have so much to do, all I want to do is take care of her, my Eve of the new world.

Though I erased this night's conversation,[15] I remember uttering, "please, God, don't let her die" at dawn. The agnostic in the foxhole didn't last long.

I'll say it again now, in case she's alive. *God? Please don't let Kodie die.*

There. A little supplication can't hurt.

Frankly, it's why I'm even doing this book. Because now I think God might really be there and that I'm meant to do this. If I feel I'm meant to do this, then there must be meaning.

For I was feeling stronger as all around me grew weak.

Obvious with Kodie, but I also saw it in the oncoming gauntness of Bastian's face. His shoulders slumped and he wheezed. They're winding down like windup toys having lost the kinetic energy twisted into them.

I'm being wound up. Stayed up with Kodie all night long and yet I feel no fatigue.

The death that has come comes slowly for us late bloomers. Just like in my story. There's still enough kid in us, ersatz Peter Pans, and the death is stymied, but would it be denied?

KODIE AND I HAD BEEN going down the street, house by house, breaking and entering, filling the bathtubs. Her breathing had cleared and she had energy for the task. Many of the doors we came to were unlocked, but a few times we busted in through a window.

Entering each was harrowing. The interiors mausoleum-still, the dim window-lit spaces. Kodie, ever hopeful, insisted on calling out *hello?* each time. Her call echoed through the halls and empty rooms.

It got to where we did two at a time, she in one, me in the other, filling. I filled the tubs in the houses that had corpses. I didn't linger around them much, tried to pretend they weren't there, whistling while I worked to keep the creep from settling on the back of my neck. Of course, the more you ignore, the more the feeling back-builds within and soon I was sensing

---

15 Somewhat incorrect. Everything was erased but those remembered, uttered words, the first words of this transcript.

movement in other rooms. Thought I'd heard a shuffling, a creek of wood, a groan. I'd turn off the water and stop whistling to listen.

Oh, the silence of the world sucks to behold, dear reader.

Each of the ten or so we saw died of the white save one. The ones that died of the white were all on the floor, usually near an unlatched door or open window. A kitchenette chair knocked over. Everyday things scattered on the floor—stacked mail, breakfast cereal, toothbrush and paste—from the last throes.

I took the houses with corpses. You knew from the porch. The one suicide was a block over from my house, a house smaller than ours and painted fire-engine red. On the entry wall hung a still spot-lit painting of a melodramatic Old West winter scene—two cowboys and a Native American guide bent against the wind on horseback, oceanic tundra all around. I got up close to it and saw that the paint had become alligatored on the canvas. I couldn't make out the signature at the corner. On the entry table were pictures of two men in various loving poses, wearing suits, tuxes, matching turtleneck sweaters. In one they held a small dog you knew was yappy as hell. The men were in their sixties, I'd guess. The house was in no disarray and the décor was contempo and clean if not breathtaking. That is, other than the cowboy painting from the mid-1800s. Seeing it spot-lit like in a gallery; that did take my breath. My mind vaulted to all the world's art, the museums which had become themselves still-lifes, white emergency lights pulsing in their corridors.

The guy I found was in the kitchen. Several drawers were open and a few implements strewn on the floor from his riffling. The man wore a robe but it was open and splayed under him. He lay nude and spread-eagled in his remodeled midcentury-modern kitchen, a cone of light from the stove focusing on the gash across his throat from ear to ear. The wound had blackened and puffed to something like a rotten eggplant, one made so deep that the blood had simply fallen out onto the floor. The entire kitchen was a kidney-shaped tarry sea stilled by air, gravity, and time. A huge and expensive Japanese kitchen knife was stuck in the middle of the blood, an artifact in amber. The smell and the sight made me catch puke in my mouth and my eyes water. I thought I was getting used to it, a blasé veteran. Not quite.

I suppose I'll always be shocked by death, the look of it on faces. Then all was still so…fresh, everything, even the outside air, smelling like a slaughterhouse town gone ripe.

I'd taken the painting off the wall and carried it with me under my arm from house to house, leaning it against porch steps next to uncarved pumpkins. Kodie didn't even question it.

It became rote work. We made entry, I'd clear the house to make sure it was safe, and then she'd flip on the lights and start filling. I'd check back, next two. As the tubs filled, my eyes would glaze over at the rushing water and I'd think about how it all used to be and how was it going to be. As the waterlines crawled skyward, I saw great dark stinking pits and they were filling with bodies.

Those visions felt like my summerdreams, which I sort of lied to Mr. E about. I lied in that I didn't tell him I was having them *every night*, the exact same one, only our clothing and the clouds changing, and every one had the MoPac train coming down the track we were on at the end, trapping us on the trestle. The kids would see us if we ran or jumped. We froze. Dream ended. My heart pounding as my eyes whipped open.

We made our way around the entire block, feeling good about our modest progress. We'd excitedly talked about the need for chlorine tabs to throw in the tubs. We'd need to hit the library and do book research on how to do this—how to do everything. In one house a bedside Bible caught my eye. I let the water fill the tub and flipped to the passage Jespers wrote on his whiteboard, Matthew 16:23—*Get behind Me, Satan! You are a stumbling block to Me. For you do not have in mind the things of God, but the things of men.*

It needs you to need it.

Seek you. Seek you.

The static and whine roared through the house. That sound and Bass's flat-toned imploring drew us into the room. We heard the buzz of static from the street. The front door was open and when we walked in we saw Bass standing in front of the rack of electronics he'd constructed. Top and center sat the ham radio. Bass bobbed his head.

He'd been busy. Before that, he'd set up the solar panels in an array on top of the detached garage to catch westering sun. I marveled.

Bass had connected it all to Martin's big speakers. He glanced back at us, lifting his eyebrows in acknowledgement. "Whole block's tubs are filled," I shouted, backhanding his shoulder. "Hey, kill that for a sec." He turned it down but the static was still there.

"So, this thing's going and I'm learning how to use it. Pretty simple, really. Just turn the dial slowly and look for open channels, listen for voices, keep calling out our existence. There's got to be another group like us out there banging away doing the same thing." Bass twisted the knob to a clear frequency, lifted the mike, and spoke. "Turn it to the US standard frequency here and…CQ CQ. *This is Bastian in Austin Texas USA calling CQ and waiting for a call…*"

"Seek you. You say seek you?" I asked.

"No. The letters. C and Q. Just the thing you say. Means we're calling any amateur radio station out there. There's all this protocol and codes in this guide that came with it," Bass held up the thick soft-backed book, "but it's meaningless now. You guys can do it, too, whenever. Just come over and grab the mike and push this here. I say we leave it open and ping away as often as we can."

The static compounded the emptiness, hissed how desperate our hope.

"Hey, it's Halloween," I said. Lifted chins and attempted smiles. This might be the first Halloween that truly scared us.

"I'm going as a ham radio operator," said Bass.

"I think Kevin and I already did our trick-or-treating," said Kodie.

I blurted in higher-octave *Peanuts*-speak, "I got a pack of gum!"

"I got a *rock*," Bass said like a deflated Charlie Brown. We laughed. Well, I only chuckled because when he said that, I thought of stone piles.

That image overwhelmed and so I blurted to dispel the feeling. "Do we hit the road and expose ourselves to God knows what, or stick here?" Silence. "Right now, I think we take safety where we can find it, and stick together. Agreed?"

"This radio's our hearth and fire. We stay here, I say, for now, for tonight at least," said Kodie.

"See any reason for us to be searching for some other place to stay? Any place safer?" I put air quotes around *safer*. "Before we set up any more stuff like this, let's be clear. I mean, we could go over to Camp Mabry and see what's what."

Kodie said, "Not tonight. Safety net's gone. No police, army, doctors, mommies and daddies. We can't go roaming around in the dark, not after Butler Park."

"No," Bass said. "I see no reason why we'd risk leaving what we know here. I've set all this up, you guys have made backup water available. I'll get the generators going."

"These first days are triage. Breathing room until..." I shrugged, motioned to the radio.

"Whatever we think of next," said Kodie.

"Whatever comes next," I said.

Kodie chortled. "I think we're good on weapons for now," she said, nodding at the arsenal against the wall. Bass and Kodie had moved the couch to another wall and arranged everything, the guns and ammo, so we could get to them quickly. We all turned to take in the impressive display.

"Should we go to someplace more fortified, a hotel or something? I dunno...." I said, still spitballing.

Bass answered, "Hate to say it. We'd be trapped up there, if, well, you know—"

"If the hundred thousand kids of Austin decided to turn on us? Is that what you're trying to say?" Kodie was kind of mad. "We need to stop tiptoeing on eggshells and talk plainly and honestly to each other or we're never going to make it." Oddly, she shot Bass a knowing look, which he returned. When I searched both their faces, they looked down.

And then Kodie wheezed, her first of the day I knew of. It crackled and whined. An uncomfortable static-filled quiet followed.

"I've loaded all these here," Bass said, waving his hand in game-show-display form. "I know guns. Fourteen different species of handguns here, all ready. Same with the twelve shotguns. Now, these automatics here, civilian-grade military assault rifles, your Bushmaster M-16s, these are all topped off. I can teach anyone to shoot who doesn't know how. We should all know how at least. Over here you've got your . . ." and as he continued with his proud inventory all I could think of was kids. Mowing down kids, sweating and sneering like Rambo. What else would we be shooting at?

When Bass was finished, I had to say it. "Let's not avoid the nine-hundred-pound pink gorilla riding the elephant in the room. Anyone here think there are adults alive? Show of hands."

Kodie raised her hand. "We don't know anything for sure." She punctuated this with a cough.

Me: "True. But, Occam's Razor. No military jets or tanks. There's nothing, right? We know this."

"Still. It's early. We don't know," she said.

"Can we agree they're dangerous? Are we willing to shoot to kill if it comes to that?"

Bass said, "If in mortal danger, we're going to protect ourselves as needs be. If a hoard of a ten thousand kids comes running down the street at us, I say we get out the M-16s and . . ."

"What, mow them down?" Kodie asked, slackjawed at Bass. More sarcasm than disdain.

Bass said, "If they're coming to kill us, then…yes."

"When I fired into the air the night of, they scattered," I said. "Probably all we'd need to do."

"They won't go into a cemetery for chrissakes," said Bass. "They're scared kids."

"But then why are we scared of them?" I asked. A measure of pause. "Because we are. It's the way they move, isn't it? What we saw. That was enough. Their roaring from two miles away. That hum."

Bass nodded his head with vigor. "Yes, definitely. They are changed. They're together and they don't seem to want our help."

We all stood in that circle in my living room and nodded to ourselves. Radio static. Kodie's sizzling lungs.

Bass turned to me and said, "Generators. I'll go, before it gets dark."

THE FIRST TRANSMISSION CAME IN at sunset.

We were playing coin poker on the living room floor while listening to my phone's music player on low volume so we could hear the ham. Not totally unserious about it, I had suggested strip poker. Kodie smirked.

"Two dudes, one girl. Right," she said. Her wheezing got worse with the dark and her fever returned, her face flush with it. While we were making our water rounds this afternoon, I had felt her forehead. It felt warm but I told her that I thought the fever was a good thing. I thought it meant she was simply old-world sick. She said she hoped so, adding that she'd had bronchitis before and this is how it felt. I thought, *bronchitis—three days ago we'd shrug and take the antibiotics or whatever. Without doctors, pharmacists…the flu, influenza, to use its deadlier-sounding real name, could kill us now. Sure, we could break into pharmacies, hospitals, pilfer medicines, but we wouldn't know what we're doing. We could kill ourselves taking these things. Shelf life, quantity, dosage, who knows?*

The adults knew. They left a gaping hole in the safety net. No, they'd taken the damn thing out from under us altogether.

Now children didn't dare cross into cemeteries. They threw rocks, covered bodies, clung together like atoms of water. Primordial fear. They left that for us too.

The precariousness of our lives now, the omnipresent dangers of the new world, started to flow through and fill the passages and chambers of my mind, threatening to overflow into a panic flood. Darkness itself was now fearsome, and it came again soon. I'd been marking the sun's scrape across the sky all day like prey dreading night-feeders.

When we heard the voice come over, we looked up from our cards and into each other's eyes with shock and threw down our cards. Bass had turned down the volume so we could hear the music over the static but now leaped from the floor to crank it up.

The voice sounded strong and articulate. A voice like ours, late-teens maybe, deep, male.

"*CQ CQ calling anybody. CQ CQ come back roger wilco shitfuck. Hello hello. CQ CQ this is Chris Washburn calling from near Medina, Texas. Awaiting any response. Hello! Goddammit, hello!*" Dogs barking in the background. Lots of dogs.

Bass grabbed the mike like Bono going into a chorus at Wembley. "Yeah, hey, hello hello! Bastian Calhoun in Austin, Texas! Hello!"

"Holy Christ!" The guy, Chris, yelled off mike: "Hey, I got someone!" Back on mike: "Yeah hey, Bastian in Austin. Wow. For godsakes stay on this frequency. In case we lose it, we're at the Utopia Ranch outside of Medina which is south of Kerrville, west of San Antonio about an hour. Holy shit man, I can't believe it. Over—"

"Chris, yeah, us too. There's three of us here, a couple miles north of the UT campus. How many of you are there? Over."

"Five, now. There were six yesterday." Pause. We didn't ask. "We're four girls, one guy, now. We're all high school seniors. Over."

"Same here, but two guys, one girl. You're all from Medina?"

"No. Hell no. We came together from San Antonio. We had to get out. The kids. Over."

"What happened? Why'd you have to leave? Over."

"We just got here today, this afternoon. The kids in San Antonio...I don't know how to say it. Well, let me ask. Any adults there at all? Anything coming together? Because in San Antonio there's nada. Nobody alive. We drove around and around looking for others for a solid day. No one. We'd keep trying, I guess, if it wasn't for the kids. Masses of them. They kept getting in the road, just standing there. It got to the point where they were blocking us at every turn. They didn't do anything, though, just got in the way. It became a maze and we finally made it out of the city with nothing. Kinky had this ham radio in here, so. And now we've found you guys. Over."

"Kinky? Over."

"Yeah. We're at Kinky Friedman's Utopia Dog Rescue Ranch. One of the girls here used to help out here summers and since they don't like dogs and it's really remote out here, we came here. Random really, but. Over."

We all looked at each other mouthing, *Kinky Friedman?*

"Wait, wait. They don't like dogs? The kids? And who in the hell is Kinky Friedman? Over."

"Kinky. Uh, ran for governor a few years ago. Musician, writer. I don't know much about him. He's, like, the only musical act to ever have its Austin City Limits taping fail to air. For naughtiness or something. In the seventies. Anyway, Kinky's not here. But, yeah, dogs' hackles go up when there's kids around. Bark like it's the Devil himself. They do not hang around. God, we feel sorry for the kids, but they're scary. It's like they know they're different now and can't help it. What is this that's happened? You guys have a frigging clue? Any media, Internet, phone working there? Ours all went out by I'd say nine that morning. Sorry, I have diarrhea of the mouth. Just so excited to be making contact. Over."

"Same here. No adults. No reception of any kind. Just looped radio ads and this ham radio. Over."

"Ha-ha yeah same in San An. The old world still shaking its moneymaker. Maybe the dead listen, head over to the great mall in the sky. Over."

Bass looked at us. We offered nothing but agape mouths among the scatter of cards. He stopped with the niceties and catch-up and issued an existential question meant to be practical. "So, what do we do now, Chris?"

Chris took it as practical. "We've been talking. Makes sense to us that we should get together with anyone we find. Out here would a good place to gather. Austin's probably not going much better than San Antonio kid-wise. Over."

"They're not doing much here other than amassing down by the river and roaring a lot. They are freaky, though, yeah, give you that. I think they're just all freaked out right now and if we just let things settle, maybe in time we can all work together. Over." Bass shrugged at us, like, *right*?

"You all clearly have not seen what we have. You wouldn't be saying that. Over."

"I take your word for it. We've seen…enough. They haven't done the roadblock thing to us. They've stayed away. They did surround us once when we went to go look at a plane crash, but that's it. Other than their Hitler-youth rallies that look like an ocean of waving wheat. Oh, and they threw stuff at my truck. Over."

"Yes! God, they move all weird. That alone. I mean, get the hell away from me, you know? Makes my skin crawl to see them do that. Not natural. Over."

"Yeah. Hey, keep this open. Don't leave. We need to talk, map you guys, etcetera. Okay. Hold on. Over."

"Gotcha. Sitting here, drinking a Lone Star, watching the dogs play, sun going down behind the hills there. Man…All good, Bastian, considering. The girls are cute. Lucked out. Over."

Bass took his finger off the transponder. I said, "In case we get cut off, tell them where we are, the address. And ask them if they're late bloomers."

They looked at me weird, but didn't question. Bass nodded and told Chris in Utopia where we were located. But he didn't ask.

"Got it. Happy Halloween. *Belch*. Over."

"Ask him, Bass."

Bass pushed the mike trigger, scooted up closer. "Hey, Chris? This may seem weird, but I've got a friend here wants me to ask you something. Over."

"*Belch*. Sure, shoot. Over."

"It's kind of personal, but I guess there's no use being all polite. So, here it is: Were you a late bloomer? Over."

Chris paused. The pause went on so long that I thought maybe we'd lost the connection. "Chris, you there? Over."

"Yeah, yeah. Sorry. I, uh, yeah, matter of fact I was. I was real self-conscious about it, too. I thought it was never going to happen. I remember thinking I was stuck in low gear, like I was really different. Being a teen's bad enough, but that made it really hard for me for a while."

Our heads nodded with grim understanding.

"But, then I bloomed with a vengeance, had a massive growth spurt and here I am, a non-virgin half-drunk monkey at world's end. Over."

I motioned to Bass to continue. He asked, "What about the others? Do you know? Over."

"Uhhh, can't say that I do. I think I know what you're getting at, though. Let me ask real quick. Don't hang up, okay? Over."

Chris came back breathless to the microphone. "CQ CQ you there Austin? Bastian? Over."

"Yeah, here. Over."

"Yeah, all admitted to reaching puberty later than most, as far as they knew. Late bloomers. Over."

Slowly panning his eyes across each of ours, Bass said into the mike with satisfaction, "Seems we have a pattern here, Chris. Over."

"Seems we do. And if that holds up, there are a lot of high school seniors out there running around like us trying to make contact."

Just as I thought I was understanding—that me and Kodie and Bass were the closest late bloomers to Fleming and, ergo, Jespers, that this is perhaps why we were still alive; to receive the message about Jespers's Gene, to bring this understanding into the new world—now here's this group of us in the hill country.

"So, do we go out there?" I asked the group. "Seems we're close to food and drugstores if we need them. Going out there, we'll be cut off. Away from kids, maybe, but cut off. The logistics of it."

"The way Chris is talking, it makes me think that the kids will be doing the same here soon. And if they're running them off that way by blocking their routes, it won't be long before they start figuring out how to use materials to do their bidding," Bass said.

What bidding? I thought but didn't broadcast. Kodie caught me looking inward. Our eyes met. She was thinking, asking herself, the same thing— *Bidden by...?*

"Maybe," said Kodie. "I'm not sure they plan on doing anything the old way. It's like they're starting from scratch. Like that's what all this is about. Evolution, Rapture, whatever you want to call it." She shrugged but had wide blinkless eyes.

Kodie had it pegged, articulated what we already knew.

"What I felt from them when I was locked in that room with them for that minute? That hostility? They seemed feral, cornered. I've never been so scared. My lizard brain got the adrenal-dopamine squirt. My skin prickled and my arm and leg hair stood up as if the room filled with static electricity."

"Yeah, I mean, think about it," said Bass. "They may be scared, but not too scared to stand in harm's way to block a moving car. The way they looked at us at Butler? Deathly. Like a snake rattling its tail at high pitch. I don't think they're scared when together like that."

"Point is, time's of the essence. I don't see peaceful coexistence happening with them, at least not for a while," I said.

"So, which? Tell Chris we're going to stay put for a while or go to them now?" Bass lifted the transponder.

And then, through the speakers attached to the ham radio, we heard the dogs of Utopia start to bark like mad. Chris had kept the line open, as if he wanted us to hear.

This went on for a minute. The next thing we heard was a whisper, sounding like Chris. "You all hear that in Austin? Get yourself a dog. I'm telling you. 'Cause they're here. I can't see anyone yet. It's dark."

I turned my head to the window to see the navy sky, knowing out there, away from vestigial city lights, with the hills and cliffs rising around the ranch, it would be darker.

"I don't think it's the meter reader or the FedEx guy the dogs are barking at."

After another half minute of louder barking came close, throaty whispers, the last we'd hear, lips touching the mike, the breath stressing its metal diaphragm: "Methinks it's trick-or-treaters."

CHRIS DIDN'T PICK UP AGAIN and navy evening turned to black night. Bass folded his hand and said *hold on*, he was going to go out to switch off the generators to test the grid. The lights and sound disappeared.

Me and Kodie giggled in the dark. I grabbed her hand and held it tight. Her wheeze sung its see-saw song. Her head was silhouetted against the picture window. I smiled to myself at her beauty, the shape of her head, her blinking lashes.

We heard Bass curse outside, but it was the humorous curse borne of frustration or clumsiness. We chuckled again, trying to allay the fear of sitting in the dark at the world's end on Halloween night having lost contact with Chris in Utopia.

Then, for the first time in two days while home, we heard a dog barking. We squeezed hands. Our neighbors didn't have dogs. This one sounded like it was around the block. It barked and barked.

There'd been no barking in the neighborhood when we filled the tubs. There was nobody for dogs to be barking at because there was nobody walking dogs, no invading servicemen. The dogs had been silent until now. Silent and very hungry.

Just as I had decided to get up to grab a flashlight, the lights flickered and the static pulsed once, twice. I froze, then all was back on. We heard Bass coming back in, laughing and snorting. He stopped as he rounded the bar to the living room.

"What's the cussing about?" I asked.

"Nothing," said Bass.

"What about this master electrician work you're doing, taking us off the grid, putting us back on? I wouldn't have a clue how to do that."

"Did I fail to mention that?" There was a hint of smarm in his voice.

"What's so funny?" I asked, a little perturbed.

"Nothing, nothing," Bass said with mock dismissiveness. "Really." He tried to make a serious face, but it held for only three seconds, then he snorted laughter through his nose. Then I smelled it.

"Ah. Terrapin Station. Didn't know you still had some," I said to Bass.

"A wee bit I found in the pocket of me coat. A little smoke for the hallowed eve," he said in a not-half-bad Irish accent. It lit up the room and we smiled at him. Life returned in these little moments and I could see how it would be possible to get it back someday. Humor and levity may be the most powerful forces on earth.

"Screw it," said Bass, clapping his hands once hard. "I'm going to carve a jack-o'-lantern. Okay with you?" he asked, looking at me. "Can I grab your pumpkin outside?" I said sure, buoyed by his bothering to ask me. After all, moms and dads brought home the pumpkins in October and sat them on the porches. My mom did. She always did, and it was Martin who carved. I'd usually help.

My throat got tight and I nodded after saying sure and Kodie gave my hand a sympathetic squeeze.

Bass sprang into action. Bass strode out the front door to get the pumpkin. He sat it on the floor by the ham and then called out a barrage of seek-yous. I felt useless so I got up to make myself available. Bass lifted his head and said, "You hang close to her. I'll do the Martha Stewart thing, and mind the ham." Bass had a talent for communicating in a way that was clear and forceful but never strident.

I helped Kodie up off the floor and we took to the couch. "Right about now I'd be watching a horror movie," Kodie sighed, staring at the flat-screen set within the hutch in the corner of the room behind Bass's set-up. "Watching Michael Myers rise up behind a blubbering Jamie Lee Curtis who you simply cannot believe is still standing there with her back to him. I mean, you stuck him in the eye with a hanger. Now, run, bitch!"

We chortled. She wheeze-laughed. Insane serial killers had become nostalgic. Bass was scooping pumpkin with his hands and slapping the wet seeds and stringy goop on a spread newspaper—*slap. slap.*

Kodie said, "I'm really wondering if we're not Jamie Lee, just sitting here. Maybe we should heed Chris in Utopia." She looked the window. "I think we should definitely go out there."

"I'm leaning that way. We need numbers. But, it's too late tonight. Let's go in the morning. Bass?"

Bass stopped carving, looked at all he'd set up, sighed, and nodded. "Yeah. We need to make a run for it and link up with those guys." He punched an eye hole through the pumpkin with the knife handle. "First light, let's start packing."

It was settled.

I took comfort in that and, for tonight, the existence of the arsenal in this room. I felt fortified, ready. I wanted to lighten things so I brought back the old world with Halloween. "I'd probably be taking Johnny around trick-or-treating. Last year, Bass and I were just getting to know each other and we hit the cemetery for the first time. Remember that, Bass? I took Johnny out for a while and then you and I jumped the fence and did our cemetery dance."

He bobbed his head, but was uninterested in reminiscing. Facing away from us, he hunkered and listened intently, called out into the present, "CQ CQ Chris you there? Anybody?"

slap. slap.

wheeze. wheeze.

(bark bark)

"Hello? Chris. Hello."

THE LIGHTS LOW IN THE house. We'd closed the blinds and curtains as if this were a normal Halloween night and we wanted to give the customary signal that we wouldn't suffer trick-or-treaters, we don't have any damned candy for you, go away.

Bass had set the jack-o'-lantern on the kitchen bar. I'm sure he meant it to be festive and comforting, but to me it was a reminder of what jack-o'-lanterns were all about which was to ward off the spirits of the damned come rap-rap-rapping on your door. Though the face wasn't scary per se—it was childlike with its rounded eyes and nose and convex eyebrows—it was mawkish and seemed to be laughing at us, in on a joke we weren't privy to, a joke that had real-life peril as a punch line, a byzantine joke that lost you in its labyrinth until it mattered, at the end, when you learned you were the brunt of it all along, its victim. Its ochre glow radiated, rendering incomplete shadows on the walls and ceilings.

"Cool, eh?" Bass had said when he first set it up. Kodie gave tepid applause through a stifled yawn. Kodie and I had started to doze, my eyes flying open when she coughed or when Bass spoke out into the abyss. My watch said eleven. Now Bass sat reading in a chair, I couldn't tell what, but it was obvious to me he hadn't been really reading but listening; to the night wind, to the gathered darkness, that dog barking. He went back to the ham. Bass had been at it for hours.

"I feel like if I don't keep trying, that's when I'll miss someone." I'd been asleep but his sonorous voice jerked me awake. I was still blinking my eyes and trying to figure out where I was, my life's context—couch, Kodie on me, her smell in my nose and lungs, family gone, world gone, night. "What if this is it? Chris in Utopia? I've heard nothing from anyone on this thing for hours."

Bass had placed the book he read facedown on an armrest. *Lord of the Flies*, my copy from my room where I kept it on a high shelf above my desk slotted in among many others, a decades-old forest-green cloth hardback. I could smell the decay in the yellowing pages from here.

When did he go in there? I'm confused in my sleepiness. I propped myself up on an elbow and looked at him. Bass said in a way-too-serene and measured voice, "Like Utopia Chris said. There are probably a bunch of people our age getting it together and doing just what I'm doing. It's just a matter of time."

I muttered with a tired croak in my voice, "Probably right." I tapped Kodie on her hot head. "You," I whispered to her, "pill time. Get that fever down." She got herself up, looked at each of us through eye slits, and waggled her arm goodnight, flopping her hand like it wasn't properly connected.

As she shuffled away, she turned her head to the jack-o'-lantern and started to say something to it, but demurred.

Bass seemed animated despite the hour and the day we'd had. He hopped back to the chair and lifted the book up again. His brow furrowed, eyes skirting along the lines. "I'm going to stay up. We need someone to stand watch. I'll start. I'll wake one of you guys up in a few hours. I'm into this book now. We were supposed to read this in, like, ninth grade? but I don't really remember it."

When he moved his elbow off the armrest, I noticed the pistol on the chair. He saw me looking at it and smiled. "Goodnight." Looked back at the book. "Progress today, eh?"

"Mmmm," I answered, too tired to care whether we had made progress or not and too tired to appreciate the need to stand watch. Such was the way of this new world. "Yeah. You got the conch tonight. Thanks."

He lifted an eyebrow at that, but kept reading.

KODIE'S WHEEZE WAS THERE, BUT muted, the war buglers of her sickness trailing off and though I was falling into the tumult of dreams, I clung to my belief that I was right about her, that her illness was just that: an old-world one that ignited, flared its orange spikes but now was snuffed.

This offered some comfort through the night in which I dreamt I was a chrysalis in a diaphanous sac through which you see my knees and elbows rolling and twisting in gestation's dull agony.

The chrysalis dreamed within the dream and it was this: Johnny standing in an open field wearing Man U's red home kit, shin guards, cinched cleats. His arms are outstretched and his chin is lifted with pride and his eyes are closed in basking. The children pool around him, hug him and jostle him, but he maintains his messianic stance.

I'm seeing this scene as a flying thing, hovering just above, then I swerve off through brightness and come upon maroon raw meat centered on a white plate on a pine table in the house with the winter cowboys. The meat starts to shudder and jump and maggots burst from the middle and spill out like white lava from the puckered flesh. In the background I hear frantic Spanish being spoken but I can't make it out. It's as though the disembodied Spanish speaker is calling a tight soccer match yet I know he's describing to an audience what I'm seeing.

I watch the maggots flow out, too many and too much for one piece of meat to hold. A magic clown car of maggots.

Again, I'm flying and now I'm whipping through the air high above Lake Austin. I'm darting down for the waving bald man. In the corners of my many eyes I see that wave coming. I skim the water. It's coming on my left and just when it gets to me, I lift myself over it and it moves past. I'm still looking at him, feeling it roll under me. But it's not just water. It entrains an unfathomable power with it. I feel heat come off it as it passes under me. The bald man is waving like a sugared-up kid. His smile is profane. I zoom to him and hover.

His face loses its smile. His waving hand falls to his side. His torso goes slack. His mouth drops open on a rusted hinge, and his eyes droop and I see red crescents under the corneas. Dark, viscous blood falls from his slackjawed mouth.

He produces a glock just like Martin's, the one I now have with me at all times, and puts it to his head and he fires and buckles to the ground. The lake water forced ashore by the wave comes up to his body and surrounds him once before receding, pulling a thin current of the man's blood away.

It is then I find myself standing in the man's yard. I turn to watch the wave seethe and hiss north.

I turn my head downriver and I feel profound doom and destiny.

There's an echo within the river canyon. The frantic Spanish—now I understand it to be coming from Bass's ham radio—has slowed to something the speaker wants me to understand. I shake my head, unable to. Then the voice says in heavily inflected English—*they cannot do it alone.* The voice lets me consider this. In my thoughts, I assent: I can help. *No, they need more than that, señor.*

THAT'S THE CHRYSALIS DREAM.

Now, Johnny stands over me and Kodie while we sleep. Dreaming? Unsure. Johnny says, "We do need you. I'm sorry I had to leave. You were learning to dream the dream of sleep and I couldn't disturb that. Because you'll need that, probably more than anything, the dream of sleep." In his pause he became more himself, my little brother. His shoulders relaxed, his tone his again. "There's no point in worrying, Kev. Okay? Trust me. No point. We'll see each other soon." And Johnny strikes that pose again, arms outstretched, palms up. His eyes and mouth become orbs of white light. My eye draws to his clenching right hand. He breaks from the pose, drops his arms, and immediately goes into a throwing motion, kicks out his leg and—

Shattering glass, together with whalescreams.

I see dawn and piles of stones on a beach.

I startled awake at that, *soon* tumbling in wet echoes.

I heard my name shouted. I heard pounding. I shook my skull side to side trying to rid it of the words, the screams, the dawn beach.

I sat up and there in my room I saw a head on a stick, the eyes Buddha-lidded, flies crawling and buzzing. I can't make out the face it's so covered. The buzzing pierces.

Truly awake, in my room. Kodie's deep asleep. I get up slowly so as not to rouse her. I check to see if Johnny is in his room, what I'd do every morning, but it's just Wayne on the wall doing his Christ pose in the gloom.

The world came back, the one I lived in now. It's dawn. Spanish comes over the ham radio in the living room.

Ciudad de Mexico—

Eeef anyone ees dere, pleeese—

I made my way to the front of the house expecting to see Bass hunched over the ham. Light from the front door windows filled the hall.

A late bloomer's voice: *Hello, hello, estamos aquí, is anyone there? Weee are de Ciudad de Mexico—*

I flick on the hall light switch. It does not come on. My footfalls quicken down the wooden floor of the short hall.

Los niños aquí, dios mio—

"Don't." Bass's sonorous voice, aggrieved and wracked, from the front room before I even get there. "Don't, Kevin."

I step through the doorway. Before I turn to him, I see Mom's car through the front door. It's riddled with dings, the glass starred in constellations.

There's a boy standing in the neighbor's yard beyond the back of the car looking straight at me, still as a rabbit, a sentinel spy. His hair is blond. It moves in the breeze. He's bigger, older, yet a boy.

Bass is naked. He holds the pistol. His face is red, his eyes are swollen from crying. He shivers blue-lipped, yet he's starting to smile. His face forces this smile upon itself. A mucosal laugh barks from his throat when his eyes shift to look at me, then he says as if answering, "I don't know I don't know I don't know I don't know." He shakes his head each time he says this and each time the smile seems to spread.

"Bass," I said. I didn't move. "C'mon, man."

"Don't."

"I won't, okay?" I stepped forward, my foot gingerly finding the floor as if it might contain a landmine.

"Don't!" Bass shoved the barrel under his chin, gouging his skin. He breathed quickly, his nostrils flaring.

"Jesus Christ."

"No."

"What do you mean, no?" But for my mouth, I didn't dare move. He held the gun to his neck like he was his own hostage.

"The opposite."

He shook his head, closed his eyes and gulped. The sheen of sweat of his neck shone in the light as he swallowed and spoke. He kept shaking his head in denial, sniffing, his lower lip quivering, the gun still very much there. "Close to sunup. I couldn't sleep, I was listening to the ham and then…"

"I'm not moving, Bass. Okay? Just…put it down? Please."

He lowered it from his throat, holding it flat and diagonal against his chest looking like a confederate soldier posing for a daguerreotype. He rocked back on his heels and leaned his shoulder blades against the wall.

"Why didn't you come tell us?"

"I kept calling for you!"

I'd heard noises, but they were interpolated into my nightmare.

Two boys now, towheads, their twitching thatches of hair all that move. They stand under the magnolia tree with their arms to their sides. One wears a green long-sleeve T-shirt, the other a grey hoodie.

"Who're the trick-or-treaters?"

Bass said, "Been there since right before…I…wasn't feeling…well. They show up. When I picked up the gun, they just stood there." He glanced at them and shivered. "I think they're waiting for me now."

Kodie stepped up behind me and coughed. "What's going on?"

"Don't," said Bass. He stood erect again, gun wavering between us and him.

Kodie peered around me, saw Bass. "Oh my God," she whispered. She seized my upper arm, her knuckles brushing my gun.

"No," said Bass. "Definitely not."

I asked, "Bass. What are you doing?"

"I don't know I don't know I don't know."

"Are you…do you want to…?"

He nodded vigorously. "Yes. I want to." He burst out a single wet cry.

"Can you tell me why?"

"Feels right. Feels…*good.*"

"Don't," I said.

"But it's coming on slow. The need. I'm so afraid. I don't really want to go, but—"

"We can help you," Kodie said from behind me.

He shook his head violently. "No. You can't. You should stay away. You should go away and just let me. Your being here makes it hurt more."

Kodie teared up and sniffed.

"That doesn't help," Bass said. "If you don't leave me alone…it seems so glorious. It'd be wrong to leave you here. To suffer in this…this cesspool of a world. It isn't ours anymore. They're just waiting us out." He nodded to the front.

Kodie got up on her toes and looked over my shoulder out the door. "It's just like what they did that morning at my house. Goddammit, can't they just leave us alone? Or…do…*something.*"

"You could come with me." He lowered the gun at us, then back to his chin. "Please stay away, Kevin. I'm not sure what's going to happen next, okay? I'm feeling very strange."

"Bass? Now don't get mad at me. I'm trying to help when I say this. Don't shoot, okay?"

He shot me a basilisk glance, started to nod.

"What if I give you something to make you sleep? Knock you out? We could figure out what to do."

"What could you *do*? Fix me? When I wake up, I'll be right back to feeling like this. Except you'll probably have me secured and then I'll just go crazy."

"You'll still be alive—"

"So? What's so great about that? Look around, Kodie. This is a nightmare. We're in hell. Why would I want to stay here? Why do you?" He pointed the gun at us again, his shoulders squared to us, chest heaving, nostrils flaring.

The sweat on his skin had become a full-body slick. I wondered how long he had been standing there, there within eyeshot of the boys outside. In my peripheral vision, I saw the boys drop down, out of sight. Not turn and walk away. Drop down.

Though frightened to have this gun pointed at me by my friend whose eyes held such terror and pain in them I cannot even begin to describe it, though to do so is the writer's want, I felt impervious—calm, even. If bullets came, they'd miss. But I knew they wouldn't come because I had an idea.

"You have to let me do this," said Bass. He sounded exhausted now. Ready.

"Okay."

"Please just go away and let me do this. Then it'll all be over."

"Okay. But can you go outside?"

Bastian's face fell downcast, turned confused.

It was working. I wanted to get him thinking about it, to derail him. Though the white stuff seemed to be unstoppable, I wasn't convinced the suicides were. It takes an intentional act to do it. I figured if I could disrupt Bass, get him thinking about something else, he could find a way to beat it back. I chose to act uncaring, resigned. I wasn't, but that was my gut instinct: throw him off by doing something counterintuitive.

Bass lowered the gun and placed it back flat on his chest. Thoughts whirring through his mind's infinite passages. I stood sick with fear, hoping that my friend in his last despairing moment wouldn't feel I'd abandoned him.

Kodie nudged me in the kidney. "Kevin, what are you saying?" I counted on Bass hearing her and me not answering. I stood more erect and took in a deep breath to punctuate the fact that I meant business. I mustered a look that said *go ahead, leave us, coward.*

On his face hung disbelief and hurt. As long as he felt something, he had a shot, as we all did, as long as we didn't go numb.

"Wait. What? You want me to go outside to…?"

"That's right. I can't stop you, but could you just step outside to do it?"

"I can't believe you."

"What can it possibly matter to you? You're leaving us behind. So what does it matter where you do it? It doesn't." Brief pause, pregnant as hell. "But if it *does* matter, then things matter to you, and if things matter to you, then life matters. Being alive matters."

Bastian held the gun in his hands like it was an alighted butterfly. He regarded it as an artifact of his past rather than a tool of his shortened future.

He considered. This is what mattered. With consideration, there is hope.

The three of us stood there breathing, our hearts beating, the moment turning back on itself over and over, not stretching forward into the next.

He dropped his hands to his sides and began crying. The gun was still tight in his grip and he beat it against his hip.

"Give it to me, Bastian. Okay? I'm going to step over there and you're going to give it to me, all right? Slowly."

As I took my first step toward him, the house went dark, as if the thickest of clouds swam before the sun. Eclipse dark. Just as quickly, that darkness lifted, and through the kitchen window I saw the massive shadow move along the garage, a neighbor's roof and then gone. There was this final flapping flick to it.

The house light again, Kodie screamed into my ear. Bass pivoted toward us, his eyes expanded and shining. He lifted the gun, aimed, and fired.

I had closed my eyes. It happened so quickly, the shadow, her scream, his turning to us, I didn't react. Maybe it's because I thought I knew the bullet would miss.

I heard glass shatter and felt a burst of air. When I opened my eyes, I saw a broken front door. Jagged shards of wood, glass daggers. On the porch lay a kid, clutching a sucking chest wound weltering through his fingers. He struggled and cried out, inhaled and exhaled rapidly for a few seconds, then went slack, the last movement belonging to his blue tennis shoes.

"Oh—" uttered Bass. Though he had just shot a little kid to death, it had kept him from doing it to himself. That he cared he'd done it ratified his will to live. He dropped the gun to the floor. "Goddammit. I…I just reacted. He just appeared. Looking in. I don't even know how to say what his face looked like. It was all…moving. His face wasn't still."

I snatched the gun from the floor and took a step away from him. "It's all right, Bass, okay?"

He blinked at me like someone awakening from a dream. Looked at Kodie, down at his nakedness. He immediately covered himself. He brought his knees together and hunkered. "Man...what the hell? What was I...?"

"You beat it, Bass," I said. "You beat back what millions upon millions couldn't." Like I thought I had beat it back at McBride's Guns. I think late bloomers have the ability to beat it all back. Adults didn't and got overwhelmed with it. All conjecture, of course.

"You did it. You saved me, Kevin." When he said that, I specifically remember a wave of electricity coursing through me, numbing my hair, tweaking my pinky toe.

I stammered, "I just reacted. I thought you were going to take us out. Are you...?"

"Okay?" he asked, a look of amazement on his face. "Yeah. I feel great. I mean, oh my God I feel like something's literally been lifted off of me, a weighty fog. I can't believe I was about to..." He shuddered.

I flicked the gun halfheartedly at him. "Can you maybe get away from the rest of the weapons there and put your clothes back on?"

"Sure." His voice trailed away as he stared at the kid on the porch. "But I don't know where they are just now."

"Let's go look," I said. "You don't mind if I keep this thing on you for a few minutes until I'm sure you're cool?"

"Whatever makes you feel better. But I swear," and he chuckled here, "I'm not ever going to get in that...*place* again. I can't explain it. It's gone, and it won't come back. Thanks to you."

I BELIEVED BASTIAN. MOUTHS MIGHT, but faces don't lie. He had defeated the feeling, whether it was with my help or not I'm not sure. The way he treated me thereafter, you'd've thought I'd taken the bullet myself and then risen three days later wearing a muslin robe and sandals.

I didn't have the heart to tell him that I gambled and won, that's all. Fifty-fifty shot. You can't tell someone that, shrug your shoulders and say yeah, well, I got lucky and so did you. Someone's very life is worth more than that, the result of a coin toss. You want to believe that, anyway.

His face and demeanor changed. He became the positive one. Convincing us things would get better.

Something strange happening. He had this, what was it? A reverence for me. I'd catch him looking at me all starry-eyed. He was agreeable to anything I said and very solicitous. If I was bending down to lift something, he'd say, *let me*. Sometimes he'd look at me with his lips parted and all walleyed staring, like a dog looks at you when you've got too much of a meat sandwich on your hands.

Maybe I did save him. It was lucky.

Grandma Lucille. Well, you know what she'd say about that. Instead of saying 'There are no coincidences, Kevin,' she'd just as likely say, 'There's no such thing as luck.' Same thing.

Whatever it was, there was a dead kid on our porch. The kid wouldn't be dead if I'd managed to get Bastian outside or if he'd just shot himself.

I think the kid was there to report on events. That one of the last of us was about to go. I think he was a messenger, an errand boy.

THE DEAD KID WASN'T ONE of the kids who were standing in the neighbor's yard. This boy had darker, shorter hair and he was younger. He's maybe eight, nine. I didn't know what to make of Bastian's claim that the kid's face wasn't still. His words. *In flux* he also said of the kid's face later, looking at me as we sat at the table eating cereal, looking at me in that…way.

Thing was, Kodie admitted the same thing later to me. That's what made her scream. Not just that he was there. His face.

Whoever the kid was, he was dead and he was lying on our porch through breakfast and no kids showed up to cover him with stones. Must've driven them nuts.

I wondered how long it would take them to arrive and push us out—like they did to the Utopia bunch in San Antonio—now that we'd killed one of them. Maybe because we did, they'd not be so kind as to just push us out. Maybe that's the incentive they needed, I thought. The fear grinding to a fever pitch among them. They'd come and overwhelm and destroy us. That seemed a stretch, and I knew nothing. Except that I felt their impatience.

LAST NIGHT WE WENT TO bed saying we were going to Utopia today. Given recent events, we'd decided to collect ourselves and gauge the kids' reaction. It was only a three-hour drive. We just needed to beat the dark.

Midmorning. The ham's static filled the house. Bass would look over his shoulder and smile at me. It was like a smile maybe I'd have given to you, Mr. English, if this hadn't all happened and you were there in the audience at some reading of mine in the far future. My discoverer and patron. A reverent and hopeful smile.

Kodie sat on the swing outside, idling side to side. Grackles wound themselves up above her. She didn't cough. She said she needed some other clothes. She'd been wearing the same thing for days now.

The thin hiss of static inside and that dog nearby barking. And barking.

I was angry at them for their fear of us, if that's what it was, for their coldness, their unspoken excommunication of us. Their staring, their stealth. I was angry at how different they were. A different species than us. A new branch on the taxonomy tree.

The power that caused it frightened me, yet also emboldened me, because for every action there must be a reaction. One force cannot exist without another acting upon it. We, the survivors, we're part of whatever it is that acts against this change. I can't and won't assign the words good and evil to them because those are old-world words. The forces simply are, one against, or maybe more accurately, one acting with, reacting to, defining another. Yin and yang.

Afternoon. Heavy rain. Rolling blackouts had started and the water pressure had lessened. We'd decided to keep trying Chris on the radio, pack properly and leave for Utopia in the morning. Before venturing out in the Hummer to get Kodie some clothes, we decided to go check the bathtubs in the nearby houses in case we found ourselves off-grid sooner than we thought.

The boy's body was gone from the porch. The dog had been barking and now I knew why. I imagined a small group of them, the ones assigned to watch us, a blur of silent little scavengers.

The rain pounded. We stayed together under two umbrellas. Me in the middle, Kodie and Bastian flanking me. Holding the umbrellas over me.

Before we got to the first house two doors down (Kodie and I skipped my neighbors' because I knew Anne and David, a young childless couple who had moved here from Washington DC, and I didn't have the chutzpah to see them just starting out), Bass asked me as we walked, "You know what that ghost said to me, Kevin?"

"Which one?" I keep seeing glimpses of kids but Kodie and Bass don't see them. Or they don't say anything. The kids show themselves to me. I'll look somewhere, deep into a backyard through a chain-link or open fence, and they'll step into my view as if to say *peekaboo, we see you.*

"Hah. Funny. You know, the lady of the Driskill."

"What'd she say? I thought you didn't see her." Humoring him.

"I did. And she saw me. I ran up the stairs to the top floor, came to the landing, stepped through the door at the end of the hall, and looked down it."

We stopped walking and stood in the middle of the street. Rain boomed on the umbrellas. "Let me guess," I said. "She came out because you were staring down the hall." I turned my head during Bass's dramatic pause and stared at the corner of a house far up ahead. A beat, two. Around came the little forehead, the little face, stern and doll-like, making sure to meet my eyes even from that distance, then ducked away.

We kept walking. "She appeared, dressed in a long beigey-gray thing. Turn of the century. Materialized at the end of the hall to where she looked almost solid. She was looking down, her hands motioning like she was about to key the door she stood in front of, and she said something to herself. I couldn't hear it, and as if I had said that, that I couldn't hear her, she turned her head to me. What she said was, 'He said he loved me.' It sounded like a real woman's voice. She sounded distressed, spurned, about to cry. 'He said he loved me. He said I was the only one for him. And *now* look. Look what's happened.' She turned to face me. She started to walk toward me. She shoved one sleeve midway up one arm, then the other. I thought maybe she was coming over to punch me out. Her dress swayed at her feet. Her head forward, jaw set, brow furrowed. The hall lights above her winking and strobing with her progress. She turned the insides of her arms to me. They had been deeply slashed from the meat of her palms up to her elbow."

"Were you not just terrified?" Kodie asked, taking him seriously, as we got to the first house and stood on the small porch. "How did you just stand there when you saw her coming?" I looked at her like she was mad yet loving her earnestness.

"Well, yeah. Scared the hell out of me. And this is the thing. I couldn't move. Overwhelmed. Like this morning until Kevin here saved me." He gripped my shoulder and squeezed. I grew anxious to get inside. Though I couldn't see them, I felt the kids gathering like Hitchcockean birds. "She got up close to me, about an arm's length, her face alabaster, her wounds deep maroon, but dry. She looked at me, searching my eyes, and said, 'If the world hurts so much, Bastian, why don't you just leave it?' I nodded my head at her stupidly, blinked at her. Then she repeated, 'He said he loved me. He said I was the only one for him. And *now* look. Look what's happened.' She said this the way my mom or a stern teacher would talk to me after I've misbehaved. Like it was my fault. She was cross with me, her eyebrows all downturned. She slipped an arm behind her. She brought it back around and displayed a straight razor. It gleamed and flashed in the light as she turned it. 'Why don't you just leave it? You can, you know.' I just ran."

We stood on the porch of this house out of the rain. I really did not believe him.

"Why did you even go in there in the first place?"

"We all know that story of the ghost. I always wanted to go check it out. When we drove by, I felt, I don't know, compelled, to stop and go up."

"So you could go up there so she could suggest that you kill yourself. Fantastic. That's great," Kodie said.

"You looked freaked, but you said you didn't see her. Why are you telling us this now?"

Bastian shrugged and smiled at me all beatific-like. "Dunno, man. It just seemed like the right time." And here that smile turned so big and bright that it frightened me. It wasn't the Suicide Smile. No. It was the I-Love-Kevin Smile, the Kevin's-My-Hero Smile. I've seen Bass's *muy stoned* smile but this was something else entirely. "I'm wondering now," said Bass, pontificating, his eyes looking at the sky, "if maybe all the suicides were urged to by a ghost, a voice. When I was naked in your living room with that gun to my throat, it was her voice I heard. Her saying, 'you can, you know.'"

"I don't..." His morning protestations replayed between my ears then—*I don't know I don't know I don't know.* I shook my head at him and opened the door. We stepped into water. I ran and slid through the house, the floor sopping. I peered around the bathroom door hoping that maybe we'd just screwed up and left the water running.

The tub was busted. The porcelain edge of the tub exposed to the room had been demolished. Big white chunks of tub lay on the floor in an inch of roaming water.

Kodie and Bass came in behind and said iterations of what the hell. "Let's check the others," I said. Kodie and Bass gave each other this big-eyed knowing look I couldn't decipher then and I was so freaked by the water issue that I didn't ask what their deal was.

We ran to the next house in the rain. I led. A dog up the street barked. Kodie and Bass lagged behind, whispering.

That's right, you guessed it, dear reader, same thing at the next one, though this time we saw the water on the porch having seeped under the front door. We checked the next several and each tub bore the same violent marks, each house a small flood.

The pattern was obvious. Panicked now, we jogged home and our thirst grew. A click formed in my throat.

I was the first one back to the house, dashing inside, hand on the kitchen faucet handle. Kodie and Bass came up behind me as I turned the knob. Air sighed through.

We still had a few cases of bottled water, but now the dynamics had shifted. They had made a direct, emphatic statement.

We don't want you to have water.

We don't want you here anymore.

I'm pissed now. Illogical. I'm loading up, scrambling around the house, packing more heat than made sense, striding out to the Hummer. "C'mon, Bass. Let's go be that beast they're so afraid of."

Kodie and Bass stood the porch. "Kevin, no. We agreed."

I stopped midway down the walk and turned to her holding an umbrella and a graphite crossbow. "Agreed to what? They're saying they want us dead. It's a formal unambiguous declaration."

"But this isn't what you do, Kevin," said Bastian.

"The hell you talking about?"

"There's something going on with you, Kev. I feel it, and I know Kodie does too." Those two looked at each other with conspiracy in their mien, exhaling and nodding like *well, we may as well tell him.* "And you do too."

"What?" I shifted my weight. "This isn't funny." My throat dry, voice cracking. But I knew what.

"I know you thought that we..." Bass checked back with Kodie. Her face said *go on*, but he stalled so she continued.

"We didn't get together that night when you fell asleep. We found ourselves talking about you. How best to keep you going and positive."

"You saved me, Kevin. You say you got lucky." He shook his head. There was that word *luck* again.

I looked at Kodie and she just nodded, sniffing her red nose. Though evening was hours away, the November air grew cold with the rain. The air soaked, the colors of the afternoon shades of gray. She shivered in her T-shirt. "I know it freaks you out, but, Kevin, whatever all this is that's happened...all I can say is, I," she glanced at Bass, "we know that there's something special in store for you."

I eyed them incredulously, one then the other. "What exactly do you mean?"

"If I knew exactly, I'd tell you. It's like...dreams, but it's a feeling. It's... You're the leader now. Not by default, but by choice. You've been chosen." Her body quivering, her face grave. "You think we come upon Jespers's discovery otherwise? But that's just part of it, it's more than that. It's—"

"Chosen." I tried to get them to fall apart laughing by staring off into the middle distance with a rigid jaw, chest thrust out, crossbow fist on my hip like a superhero atop a mountain. Their faces stayed rigid. "We've got things to do. The water's out, the grid's probably—"

"Not kidding," said Bass. "Do we look like we're kidding?" I looked long and hard at each of them. They didn't look like they were kidding.

Kodie shivered, from cold or illness or fear.

"Well, we need to pack up for Utopia if we're going to go."

She shook her head at me. "We can't leave here," she deadpanned. "They'll kill us out there. Now that we've killed one of them."

"Goddamned gremlins," Bass said under his breath. "At some point we are going to have to get more water."

"They're kids," I said.

"They're more than that and you know it. They're a swarm," said Kodie.

"Kevin," Bass said. "You're not getting it. Me and Kodie…we have to protect you now. We are both alive because of you. It's our duty."

"What?! *Duty*?" The weird feelings and dreams of doom and some important inscrutable role I was to have in it all I'd had since summer were coming true. Still, I wanted to delay, pretend it was, is, all a dream. So, backed into this corner, I got surly. "Assuming I saved you, Bass, which I do not, how did I save you, Kodie?"

Her retort came quick like she was ready to give it, a debating politician jumping on a question about a topic she's been dying to discuss. "I think I've had the white stuff, Kevin."

I stood immobilized. My jaw fell open.

"Now I don't. I've spent two nights with you at my side caring for me. It went away."

"Well, this is just horseshit," I said. "You were *sick* sick. What? You *felt* the white stuff?"

Kodie paused, then nodded. "You were gone, chasing the train. I was in bed and it…bubbled up my windpipe. Burpy. A slow creep, but it came. I was dreaming of drowning in green mossy dead water. Something swam, lurked in that water and was there with me." A roll of thunder with the rain now. "I felt it coming up. You drove up in the driveway. It receded."

"Psychosomatic. You are both full of it."

They both shook their heads with their eyes closed, solemn faces. Bass said, "Why would we make this up? What's to gain? We don't have time for games. You need to *know*, man. I mean, you think I'm particularly jazzed about it? In the parlance of our times: it is what it is." He lifted his arms and dropped them to his sides, exasperated. "I don't love it."

Good. A little levity at least. "You mean the parlance of those times a few days ago," I said.

Kodie continued. "I ran outside to the swings to collect myself. You saw the blood in the grass."

I stammer-asked, "Was it…from the…stomach or…lungs?"

"Lungs. Definitely."

"A trombone player in the high school band who just got busted with a baggie of weed in my locker. A leader of many."

Lifted eyebrows, nodding and shrugging.

"Leaders emerge from all sorts of backgrounds. They evolve into the role. One way or the other, they do rise. Gandhi was thrown off a train and got pissed." I don't remember which one said that. Something Kodie would say, though. I was so flummoxed with them standing there confirming my belief that I was meant for something that my memory isn't so good on who said what.

"You're crazy, both of you." Even though I knew they weren't. "Why'd you wait until now to tell me?"

Bass said, "We didn't think you'd believe us and—"

"I don't."

"—and now that they've backed us into this arid corner, now that we have to start taking chances, we had to tell you."

Kodie sighed. "I'm not saying you have all the answers. At some point, you're going to be important. To them and to us, too. In how we continue on. Right now you need to stay safe."

"We're going to run out of water fast. We can't just stay here," I said. "We have to risk to survive."

Bass said, "We have enough for now. In this rain, it'll be dark by seven. Too late, again. I'll get the power going with the generators, keep pinging Utopia."

"We're okay. Tomorrow." Kodie was cool. They'd formed a united front. Staying on message.

"C'mon, Kevin. We can't risk a rash move tonight."

"We said that last night."

"Well, things changed today. Bass, and the dead kid. The tubs. They're pushing us. Let's go on our own terms, calmly, with a plan."

Then it hit me. They got to them. The kids, the new world. Something's happened. A switch has been flipped. These two are not who they once were. Bodysnatched. When did this happen? How did I miss it? Have they been pretending all this time? Have they been with the kids all along?

Have I been blind? Paranoid as hell?

"Yes," says Kodie.

I jumped. It was as if Kodie had read my mind and answered my internal questions.

"Keeping you safe, 'let's not be rash'...I know it's hard to process. Me too. I couldn't believe it at first either. I mean, the morning of, the Osterman kids standing in my yard staring at me, and the first thing I thought of was you, to try to contact you so you'd meet me at the store. Only after I texted you did I wonder about my parents."

"Same here. I tried contacting you first thing, Kevin. Heard the sounds at dawn and watched TV for a few minutes, the whole time there's this overwhelming need to contact you. Couldn't call so I texted to meet at the station. Just after that, literally the second I pressed send, my parents . . ."

Bass, sounding exasperated with his perception of my being dense. "The Fleming/Jespers connection. You're the late bloomer across the street. We're your closest friends, also bloomers. It fits. Forget *chosen*, if you want, forget *special*. It just fits. The right person at the right time. Happened in the old world all the time."

The dog down the street started up again. We all looked up in that direction.

"So, if I drive off you'll...?"

Bass said, nodding with his eyes closed, "I'll stop you."

"I'm armed." I displayed two loaded handguns I wore, one being Martin's glock. I held up the crossbow, arched a brow.

"So am I." Bass cocked his head and smiled, took a pistol from his rear waistband all gangsta.

I looked at his gun. "I'm so needed in this new world, and you're to protect me or whatever, you'll shoot me if I were to run. That makes sense how?"

"When you look at it that way."

I feint toward the Hummer. "You'd, what? Shoot me in the leg?"

"Ah, an incapacitating flesh wound. Good idea."

"Yeah. Gandhi had a limp," Kodie added, needling. "Kevin, enough... okay? Listen." She took in a deep breath, held it, shot a glance at Bass. Exhaling, she said, "I've seen the dark smiling teeth, too. The night before it went down."

Bass raised his hand, sheepish and nodding. "Me too. That night. Didn't know what it was but knew it was something to do with you. Thought it a vivid nightmare."

I hadn't talked about that. Those were *my* dreams and visions, me and Professor Fleming. But I thought of the strange and scary conversation Mr. English and I had in his office. We'd shared dreams. Why I wouldn't I also with Kodie and Bass?

Their faces softened. They knew I believed them.

THEY HAD A POINT ABOUT not going across Texas right now, I'd even argued that last night, but now I felt like this was too much waiting, and if you're waiting, you're waiting for something to happen.

Kodie and Bass fell asleep. It was dusk and I snuck out, taking Martin's bolt cutters hanging from a peg board in the garage and went four doors down to get that dog. It was quiet for now. One of the neighbors on this street I didn't know at all. They had plastic playscapes for toddlers in their yard and sometimes I saw a woman, a nanny or a mom, I never knew which, sitting on the porch steps watching them play. She never waved when I rode by on my bike. She'd look up but never wave. I waved at first but, over time, stopped. You tire of waving at people who don't wave back.

I could've brought the dog through the house, I guess, but this was a house we'd skipped. I'd seen the woman who didn't ever wave lying on the floor through the window.

The dog was a mix, not big. Brown, maybe some lab in there, likely some pit, but some other breed too, keeping it smallish. When I first walked up to the gate, the dog came hauling up to the fence and barked. I could see its agitation through the slats. After a few seconds of that it whined with anxiety like it wanted to see me. When I pulled myself up to look over at it, it wagged its tail and twirled around in circles. God knew how hungry and frightened the thing must have been. "I'm getting you out, okay? Hold on." The dog sat at my voice, tail wiping the concrete, clearing away an arc of leaves.

I snapped off the fence lock with the bolt cutters. The dog nosed through the opening, shoving its way out as I unhinged it. It spazzed and ran around me, leaping, licking. I put my hands on it and it sat and I took a look at the dulled tag on the collar. Maggie. "Hey, Maggie. That you barking your ass off, Maggie? Yes, I know it was you." I talked baby-talk to her and she nuzzled my legs. I bent down and she leaned into my body and I held her. Her body shook.

Maggie followed me home. Kodie and Bass stood in the yard. They buried the worried looks on their faces as I approached once they saw Maggie running up to them.

We all went in and fed her people food. The dog ate in huge inhaling gulps and drank water from a mixing bowl for a minute straight, her metal tag clinking the bowl. Maggie replete and belching, Kodie and I sat at the kitchen counter bar and said nothing as the sun fell on All Saints Day. The Day of the Dead. We waited. Bass sat at the ham radio and listened like a SETI scientist listens to the cosmos, from time to time making calls out to the void. Loud, unnerving static assaulted our ears.

THE FEAR OF INERTIA FELL over me. Maggie stirred at our feet. The Utopia voices, the Mexico City voices, the last we'd heard, had long ago stopped coming over. We flipped on the TV, radio, phones and laptop just for grins, but of course browsers decried errors, mobile phones found no towers, landlines dead. The only life was from the radio, some nameless station with ads still looping, one for car insurance, one for fast food.

The Earth spun. We rode it.

LORD OF THE FLIES WAS still on the chair where Bass had left it. I stood at the huge front picture window watching the darkness, knowing I looked like a skewerable fish in a bowl to them, purposefully stood there as counterfeit sacrifice, in a dare—*c'mon*. An eldritch half-moon hung above gnarled live oaks. Celestial bodies shone bright without city light to blot them. In the window's reflection, I watched Kodie pick up the book, thumb it so that air lifted her bangs, close it. She pivoted to me, and I watched her reflection approach, felt the heat of her once she arrived beside me, smelled her hot cinnamon gum.

We looked at each other's figures in the window. Kodie slipped her hand into mine, then got on her toes so that her mouth hovered before my ear and she whispered through the ham's cosmos static, "We're still here."

MY LAST KISS WITH HER was before we fell asleep that night. Our teeth clicked as we pressed harder into each other, moving our heads back and forth, scoping and hoping for more, to get beyond the limitations of skin, muscle, bone, tongue. Trying to climb inside each other.

THE FIRST STONE COMES SOMETIME after midnight.

Having never reset it after turning on the generators at about five in the afternoon, the clock blinks 7:19 7:19 7:19. Kodie slumbers on her side, her back to me, her curves like a cello silhouetted against the window. The static's roaring in the front of the house. Bass listening for patterns in all that negative space. Beyond that, the low hum of the generators.

Maggie's bark somewhere inside the house makes me sit up. Kodie does too. We grip each other's forearms.

Before you realize the power's out, there's silence. All that booming static is gone. That drumming generator hum falls off. Even the dog goes quiet, her alarmist duties disrupted. The Utopia guy, Chris, had told us that dogs and the kids don't like each other. Maggie was here not only to let us know something wicked this way comes. Maybe she could thwart it.

Maggie resumes her baying. Moonbeams slant in and pool on the floor. Bass's footfalls thud down the hall. He jostles the locked knob. "Hey, guys! I think—" and that's when we hear the first crash of glass somewhere in the front of the house.

Maggie's barking augments to communicating more than *something's here*; it warns *stay away or I'll rip your lungs out*. She's in the room where the stone came through. Kodie says, "They're trying to get in."

I open the door to Bastian. "Let's get the guns," he says in a clipped whisper. I nod, but what I really want to do is find Maggie as she's the one on point. Bass jogs through the house ahead of me and starts grabbing weapons in the living room. I pick up Martin's glock from the nightstand.

"Stay here," I say. The hall brightens as Bass looks for things with his flashlight. I grab a flashlight from the line of them set on the entryway table, jog it back to Kodie and toss it on the bed. "Don't use it yet," I tell her.

"I'm *not* staying here."

We join Bass in the living room, his flashlight beaming around the floor on guns, boxes of bullets. "Turn it off," I tell him. "They're watching."

But for the moonlight, the room goes pitch dark. Maggie starts in again with volleys of barks, running from room to room now, her nails skidding and clicking on the wood floors. That's all we hear in the dark besides our breathing—Maggie's barks, growls and skittering, the pads of her feet trying to achieve purchase with each new directional change corresponding to their movements and smells. She's everywhere, playing whack-a-mole, going from window to window to door to door, making sure they know she's omnipresent and against the very idea of their encroachments.

This goes on for a long minute. Nobody says anything but Maggie who starts winding down, just growling and pacing. The dining room window is the one that's broken, a huge picture window, now with a grapefruit-sized hole in it, splinters radiating around it. High-quality double-paned tempered glass. Martin reminded us all of this often enough, especially when it iced once a year. Kodie, Bass, Maggie and I are all in the dining room looking at the hole, feeling the air. We smell smoke in that air.

I turned around and looked for the stone that must be on the floor right behind us. "Smoke?" Kodie asks, that bowie knife in hand.

"What's burning?" Bass whispers.

I find the stone. It's fist-sized, heavy, water-riven smooth. I hold it to my side. My throat constricts and dries.

It all happens so fast:

Maggie panting at our feet, we all stop scanning the windows to focus on the one with the hole in it, and the vaguest glow way in the distance. We look at it with idiot-moth reverence.

Maggie tears into shouting yowls, making us all jump, barking with such ferocity that her body crouches. She slides back with each bark.

In answer, we hear the children roar as one.

One booming burst that comes from all around us. How many of them, a thousand, more. No knowing.

All of us grab at each other's arms and shudder and crouch. Maggie rages at their movements in the dark. They roar again, higher in pitch, wet-sounding. You can hear the little children among them, screaming in perfect unison with the rest.

My blood zings through my arteries looking for some escape but there isn't one so the centripetal force of it makes me lightheaded and I feel that my throat might burst open in a gush.

Heavy thudding footfalls on the roof. A buzz-hum coming from outside. Maggie whines and shakes her head like it itches. I'm half blind with confusion and bloodrush. My breath seizes in hitches of panic.

A terse, louder roar precedes the hail that falls upon us.

Glass from every window in the house comes in at once. All we could do was duck. The drumming and pounding against the roof, the walls. It's not only the windows. The entire house is bombarded. A tornadic din grows.

Such chaos follows that I cannot tell you the exact order of what happens next. We're on the floor scrambling on broken glass but we don't know where to. We shout at each other but there's no hearing, no more than you could hear someone trying to tell you something amid a field of exploding landmines.

The world washed out. It broke apart all around me and I remember just waiting to be taken asunder too, in a way welcoming its inevitability because I didn't want to be a part of a world where this happened. I didn't want to save it, lead it, be in it. That's when I almost gave up, right there.

One of the drawbacks to the house, Martin told us every spring, is that there isn't a safe area to go to in case of a tornado. Best we could do was all get in the bathtub and pull a mattress over our heads. We actually drilled on this, Johnny thinking it was a riot, Mom thinking it was necessary, me thinking it was stupid because it's something Martin wanted to do. In general, if Martin was excited about it, I wasn't, no matter what it was. Typical shit-ass teenage step-kid. I miss him.

All we could do was stay down. Within seconds, Bass and Kodie are on top of me and covering me. Maggie barking. Interminable drumming and pounding. Goes on for so long that Kodie cries out, "Why won't they stop?" I try to budge them off but Bass is too strong. I was lying on my front, struggling with them. Bass keeps yelling through gritted teeth to stay down. Glass bits tear at my shoulders and kneecaps. Sandy shards abrade my cheek.

This shower of stone and glass. Unceasing waves. The house coming apart in places, the actual wood and sheetrock and insulation spraying out in puffs. The holes become spaces and the spaces allow more to come through with their vicious aim, to connect with us, our tissue bruising now, and I wonder how long it can last.

This is when all the fear and wonder of these days went from nebulous gas to bright star in my mind, under the siege of stones. That bright star winked and shined and its message was *they are trying to kill us.*

How many are out there and how many stones can there be? Did they carry them here or have they been stockpiling clandestinely all along, lying in these supplies for days unseen?

My God. It must be.

I hear Bass take one to his body and he says *oh.* We're covering our heads now. The barrage is so complete that we don't dare stand to run elsewhere. There's nowhere to run. It comes from all sides.

Maggie barks somewhere, whines in pain, continues.

Kodie covers my head with her body in fetal position and weeps. She's hit in the back a couple of times and she cries out like I've heard mothers cry out giving birth, a shocked, bewildered cry.

They cover me and take this. For *me.*

I don't understand it, yet I do.

I think of Mr. English, the thinking steeple he creates with his fingers, leaning back in his chair, looking at me in a manner both quizzical and fearful.

It's so loud, violent, and malevolent that I just want it to end, for all of us. *Enough,* is what my mind flashed. Over and over it flashed *enough of this, Johnny* and *let it end, Johnny.*

A lull. Bass off of me and standing, I could now see him, a man in full, teeth bared, seething, bloodied in the face, his clothes tattered, drips of blood falling from a fingertip. All of this as shown in moonlight. A comic book scene. My mind put him in a square on a page and above the square in a caption block it reads in that handwritten small-caps script, Bastian's Last Stand.

Fury fills his features. He looks out at the dark and says, "You're gonna make it, Kev." Outside, they roar in a burst. This time the roar is polyphonic, terrible, wholly belonging to the new world. I'd even say it's inhuman if I didn't know it was new-human.

Taking it as a battle cry, Bass jumps over us and dashes through the collapsed doorframe, yelling rebellious. Kodie and I turn away bracing against the next deluge and Bass voicing what it means to be pummeled. But all we hear are his footfalls on the wooden deck and then his yell falling into the distance like he's pitched himself into a ravine.

KODIE AND I LAY ON the floor. They were gone. You could feel that. Bass was gone, too. You could feel that.

Kodie and I pulled ourselves up. I kissed her and asked if she was okay. She sniffed and bobbed her head that she was but said she wasn't sure about her back. "I'll have some sexy yellow-and-purple bruises." Then she said, "He's gone, isn't he?"

"Yeah."

"It's you and me now."

I grabbed her hand. "Flashlights."

WE PICKED OUR WAY THROUGH stones in the dark, each one casting its own moonshadow on the floor. The windows gaped with treacherous blades of glass. We went out the hole in the dining room where the back door had been, stepping over the rent screen Bass had leapt through.

Middle-night still, the quiet immense. We aimed our beams around the yard, the trees, back at the house. The house looked shot-through. We searched the front and back yards. My beam fell on a large nest in the trees. A perch for them, I thought, a slapdash treehouse.

No Bass, no body, and no cairn either. We had to get out of the dark.

I heard Maggie whining somewhere outside. I called out to her which stopped her whining but she didn't come and I didn't want to wait.

THE COLD TOLD US THE house was no longer a house, but it took the predawn to show us. My home was bones now. The floor looked like the end zone of a landslide. Stones blanketed the wood. Drifts of them rose in the corners. You couldn't take a step for kicking one. We didn't touch them. The brown ones, the pumiced, the river rocks, the limestone, all the size throwable by small hands. The floor an anthology of earth tones now, Martin's proud pine gouged and hiding.

THE SKY STARTED TO COLOR. Kodie and I hunkered on my bed with our flashlights and waited for daylight before doing anything else. I had my high-powered beam pointed up so that the light radiated out on the remains of the ceiling. Kodie lay in my lap. I petted her forehead. What had been done to the walls and windows had not been done as much to the roof. Light rain came and with it wet breezes.

We shivered and listened to it come down so much louder now without windows and walls which looked like the cannon-shot hull of a wooden frigate. But we weren't sinking, not yet, and that was good. We'd survived a battle and had suffered a dire casualty in Bastian, but they'd failed. We were still here, hangers-on of the old world.

My mind raced with the rainsounds. At first light, what would we do? The shock of the night wore off and the future had to be considered again. There was a future to consider. There were moments last night when that didn't seem possible. That there still was a future buoyed me, as did Maggie trotting in all wet, panting like mad and shaking off all over my room. She jumped up onto the bed, peaceable thunder rolled in the firmament, and the three of us sat there and let sleep find us.

HER GROWL WOKE US.

My flashlight had fallen over. A white spot on the bed. Kodie lifted her head from my lap and I sat up from the headboard. Violet filled the skyward house holes. I had fallen asleep with my palm on Maggie, and now she bristled. "What?" I whispered to Maggie. The dog reflexively turned her head to look at me and then right back to the door to the hall. Morning brewed along the horizon, but the house was still dim, the wet air making it feel more like a cave we'd bivouacked in.

I grabbed the flashlight and aimed the beam at the door. The light caught the swirling mist in the air. Maggie stood up in the bed and perked her ears.

"Come on, let's go look," I said.

Kodie's voice creaked. "There's too many, Kevin. You know that." I spoke to her silhouette against the purple veined with tree branches. I couldn't see her eyes. Her head moved up and down. "Okay," she said, her throat halting and mucosal. "Okay."

I stood from the bed and took her hand. "C'mon, Maggie." Maggie padded in front of us.

We went down the hall a few steps, Kodie stooped and limping, clutching the knife. A stout breeze funneled through it, and in it Maggie found something. She barked and bolted. Our flashlights tried to find her but she was gone and outside before we knew it.

Then I heard it, sounding faraway.

Help.

A voice. Not far. Just outside.

Kevin, help me . . .

Bass's muffled, pained voice.

Maggie's bark said something's treed. Maybe Bass was up in that nest thing I saw. It's all my mind would consider, Bass hanging in some sort of cocoon.

"Bastian!" I yelled. We started to run. The rocks on the floor troubled us, our ankles straining, the flashlights shooting all over the house walls, the holes, the ceiling.

I make a struggling sound and Kodie, finding herself ahead of me a few steps, pauses to look back over her shoulder at me.

My beam finds the boy's face looming right behind her.

His face in the bright light has a ghastly pallor and red-rimmed eyes.

I try to keep my light on him. My throat freezes but my jaw starts to move and when Kodie asks what is it, I am finally able to yell out at her, "A boy! There's a boy! Right there!"

She turns. Her light finds him. Adds to my light. Kodie screams. He's an arm's length from her. She falls, drops her knife, starts to scramble backward over the stones. Her light fell off him, but mine's still on him and his face does something.

It moves, it blurs. A wave flashes through it, under his skin, muscle and bone.

That's when I feel small cold hands on my ankles. I'm yanked hard backwards with monstrous strength, falling on my front, bashing my face onto the stones covering the floor.

I fade, hearing Kodie. At first, though there was heady fear in it, the voice of the teacher she wanted to be said to them, "Now boys and girls, let's all calm down. Let's each take a turn, tell each other what we're feeling, okay?" They responded with shuffling, gathering quiet.

Fading more now, I hear her voice devolving from articulated speech into a repetition of a hysterical monotone that echoes through this house of holes, "No! No! No!"

I crane my neck up to follow my flashlight's beam which has fallen to the floor next to me but which still aims in the direction of her voice.

The last thing I see in the off-centered shaft of light is a group of children surrounding her with workman-like demeanor. They wear jeans and branded T-shirts and Velcroed sequined tennies, one-piece knit dresses, denim skirts and pigtails swirling.

They put their hands on her skin, run their grubby fingers through her hair.

One has her knife.

The last thing I hear is her silence.

BRIGHT DAY STREAMED THROUGH THE hole. I'd been looking at it there and again for the last several hours but my head wouldn't yet let me wake up. Finally I roused, my head aching, my jaw sore from how I landed. I worked it, rubbed my hand over it.

They'd pulled me back into my bedroom. The rain left and the smell of smoke had grown pungent. Maggie the dog lay beside me. First thing I did was feed her. She inhaled the bread and bananas, the first things I could find.

But for the dog's smacking: the stillness. The quiet. Just me now. A wet broken house full of rocks and distant smoke. I checked the fridge instinctively. The light out, cool but not cold. A cursory survey of the outside revealed destroyed generators, slashed tires on all the cars, even Mom's, save for Bastian's beater Bronco. They wanted to hear me coming. Fine. I could easily get another car, but fine. Whatever you guys want. I was pissed now.

I missed the water. I had cuts and stingers all over and wanted to wash them out, wash my face off at least, brush the suede off my teeth, slake a brutal thirst. I felt relief when I remembered the cases of bottled water we'd stored in the garage. When I checked, of course, they were smashed and spilled out. I found a couple bottles intact and chugged one down in seconds. I used the other to rinse my face off.

Back inside, I made my way through the rocks, kicking at some. They hit the walls, popped and echoed. I changed clothes and in Mom and Martin's bedroom I found the glock and holster and put them back on. My uniform.

As I walked out of the bedroom, my heart panged. There on the dresser by the door was *Lord of the Flies*, Kodie's pink gum in an imperfect ball stuck to the green cloth hardback cover. I picked it off and put it on my tongue. It took a few presses of my teeth to get it into chewing shape, but once it moistened it still tasted of hot cinnamon, of Kodie. Her hot laugh in my mouth.

I wanted to collapse with her gone, but I couldn't. Stony resilience bred within me.

The change of clothes felt so much better than I ever thought a change of clothes could. I collected the *Lord of the Flies*, a few guns and boxes of bullets, my $1,000 binoculars, and climbed into the only vehicle they'd left me.

Maggie came running out and I opened the door for her to hop in over my lap.

FOLLOWING THE SMOKE, SOUTH. No kids. In the blur of my motion I do notice that the few cairns looked disturbed. The bodies had been pulled out. I'm pushing the Bronco as fast as it will go without losing control. The muffler's blat in all this quiet heard for miles.

Ask me if I cared anymore.

NOW, HOWEVER—FLOATING ALONG HERE, I hear them in the trees. They fill my head with euphoric hum. It's a new-world serenade and its impact is physical. It makes me feel good. They know to do it when I'm feeling sad or tired or scared. Usually it's all three at once. It calms me. Like I'm at the dentist and the assistant has slipped the nitrous oxide tube into my nostrils. My head fills with sweetness. She asks in a mellifluous, warbled voice, *You feeling more relaxed now, Kevin? Good,* the light panels on the ceiling looking soft and I can only nod at her.

A lullaby is what it is. It feels so good that I don't care. Grows stronger as I float south. They're helping me. They're easing me down down down to the sea whence came the wave. And when they cut it off…I'm their junkie. More. I keep going in hopes of feeling it again.

I speak these hosannas when I'm feeling their song, as I do again now, which is why I click off.

Now: no song. When they cut it off, I come to my senses. Things clear, I've lost hours, but I've gone many miles. No portaging necessary for the flood.

Got to tell it faster now, as I'm getting closer.

How many more like me stood upon high watching them do this? Were there any? In over two days the ham found nobody else. Was there somebody in some field outside La Paz watching a similar scene? Some savannah on the outskirts of Nairobi? A chilly expanse near Winnipeg? If there are, the children aren't wanting us to get together. Seems they've moved on from the initial shock and crazy download they all got to burning.

The rising smoke my beacon, I finally arrived near its fire. Southbound MoPac ends and takes a hard right to the northwest. I stopped on the little rise of an overpass.

Unlike the other day at Butler Park when we approached slowly and quietly, this time I'd come roaring up, Bass's muffler heralding me. Maggie barking. When I got to the top of the overpass, I put the Bronco in park and let it chug. I get out and stand on the shuddering hood with my binoculars. To my right is the Circle C housing development. They're in the open space south of it. Moving as an entity. Their movements a sea. They hummed. This is what they do.

Beyond their mass, the fire.

I put the binoculars to my eyes.

One looks over her shoulder, then they all do, and the movement of their turning heads fans over the thousands of them looking like wind stirring a millpond.

They've dug a pit. Still expanding and deepening it, kids digging around its perimeter. Without binoculars they look like ants working their pile to some end they don't comprehend. The pit is aflame. In it I see mounds of corpses. The kids drag them. I see no vehicles. My mind staggers: How in the hell did they get all those corpses there?

I scanned around with the binoculars. In the trees surrounding the open area hung nests. Maybe I saw ten. They have rounded, basket-like bottoms made of branches, sticks, and vine. The watchers sat there, disconnected from the rest. All ages, the watchers.

I see nests here and there along the river. I've seen a head pop up a few times, a semicircle of dark against the sky, darting back down as soon as I notice.

These open spaces, these burning pits. I imagine this happening all over the world right at this moment. Out where the city melds into the pastoral there are children digging pits, dragging the corpses that had been under cairns. Rolling them in, watching them burn.

Will they next burn entire cities? Or will they simply acquit themselves of the metros to let them crumble and overgrow? Seems that's more their style.

It dawns on me for the first time that in looking at them, other than Rebecca, Simon, and Johnny, I've never seen or hear them speak. Not to each other, not to us. They hum and they roar.

ANY PITY I MAY HAVE had for them in the beginning was gone. I should've held no faith in reserve for them after seeing them in that room in Rebecca's house. They've killed my friends, taken or killed my love, Kodie. They've taken my brother away from me, demolished my house when all I'd tried to do was help them. I told them as much at the plane crash. Their shadowy ranks just stood there. And now they were probably burning Mom and Martin and Mr. E in that pit down there.

WHEN YOU STAND AT A busy anthill, the ants barely notice you. You have to kick the hill to get them to move.

I pull *Lord of the Flies* from my waistband, took out the glock and held them both high over my head in each hand. I fired into the air, screaming my throat raw, "Burn this too! Burn books with the dead. Go ahead! Be my fucking guest!" I threw it at them, smacking Kodie's gum as the book flew out from the overpass.

THROUGH THE BINOCULARS, FOCUSING IN on one little boy at the back of the mass, leaning against a shovel taller than he is. He's got it gripped in two fists in front of him, his forehead to it, eyes closed as if he's resting.

My stare bored into the back of his head. I whispered, "Turn. Look at me."

When he stood up straight as if something had stung him, his movement rippled out over the swarm. He turned slowly around and the ripples flared out. He faced me. The scene shook a little through the binoculars due to the distance. This kid with his cropped hair, gamer's body, and doughy face wearing an Under Armour tee ordering all to *Just Call Me Awesome*, he called me over with his arm. All around him did it. Beckoning me to come down. He lifted the shovel and held it up.

They wanted me to help them dig. Taunting me.

He smiled wide. They all did. All their smiling teeth.

I said, "No. I won't help you."

Then I heard a new noise from them.

Thousands, laughing.

WE'D LOST CONTACT WITH UTOPIA after Halloween night. If anybody there was still alive, maybe we could pull together others. If not, well, hell, I didn't know.

Using a map in Bass's glove box, I zigzag my way up to Route 290 west. The roads to Utopia are pretty much open. An hour from Austin the rain starts. It's comforting. The world goes on. Shooting through a rainy Hill Country of postcards now, the road cutting through them on Highway 16 heading south toward Medina from Kerrville. Maggie looks out the window, tired as I am.

Fredericksburg looked an Old West movie set. I expected a tumbleweed to roll in front of me. A few disturbed cairns. No askance vehicles. I did see a few more cairns on the way. Parking lots in Dripping Springs, Johnson City, Kerrville's outskirts, cutting down the Medina Highway. Each of them disturbed, its former resident dragged off to some fiery pit. I saw a few lines of smoke here and there, dousing in the rain, a big one all the way over in San Antonio.

Only a few times did errant cars force me off road. Once, my back tires spun in the mud off the shoulder. After I got unstuck, I closed my eyes in relief, finding myself whispering prayers, hoping they had influence and could shield me from a thousand incidents like this waiting for me.

As I approached the I-10 overpass, a long line of them stood up from what must have been crouched positions. Standing in their ranks, the children watched me pass under. I winced, expecting they'd throw rocks at the car. Maggie bellowed. In the rearview, another long line of them shot up to watch me go.

A murder of crows on a wire.

Angling deeper into the higher, remote Texas Hill Country. A deer leapt across the road, followed by a heard of them, hundreds. I got excited. Animals don't have to contend with our fences and deathly highways anymore. No kids, no piles for miles. The silences deepening and welling, but they are soothing silences, for they belong here. It's the silences of the cities that unmoor your soul.

The Utopia Animal Rescue Ranch was up ahead. Maggie sniffed at the air. The Bronco rollicked through the twists and turns through the steep hills and walls of cedar and oaks. I had to double back a couple of times, relying on Bass's notes from talking with Chris.

I pull in and immediately dozens of dogs come rushing up, their tails wagging like mad and jumping up. So glad to see me. Maggie jumped down and made friends. There was none of the usual initial break-in phase with the dogs where they fight a little, gnash teeth, establish pecking orders. I found myself laughing out loud at their glee to see us.

As excited as they were, they didn't seem as desperate as Maggie was when I let her out. She was ravenous, the ribs showing just above her abdomen. A few steady meals staved off her developing into an ectomorph, which is what I'd expected to find here. Not the case. They looked free and glad—you know a smiling dog when you see one—and they looked fed. Either they'd gotten into the food supply here, had been foraging or hunting, or somebody had been feeding them.

The rain had let up but the air was timorous. A bunch of dogs who hadn't managed to escape barked and wagged like mad in the big open-air pens. These were hungry and whining. The pens had wooden donor plaques hanging from them—*Don and Linda's Homestead*, etc. I let them out and the group of them gathered around me like I was the pied piper.

Around back behind the main house, which was constructed of beige stone, the wooden parts painted red, I found a Bobcat diesel four-by-four ATV. There was a well-used pickup and a recent model SUV. The SUV had bumper stickers on it indicating its San Antonio origin—one a euro-circled SA, another proclaiming a parent's child and money went to some private school. The truck had done the ranch work and the SUV had brought the refugees from San Antonio, whom we'd talked to on the ham. Place felt abandoned. No souls stirred here.

The air inside the main house wasn't as stale as expected, and certainly didn't contain the deathreek of the houses on my street. Fat flies buzzed.

No sign of the San Antonio late bloomers now but for a pillaged kitchen strewn with wrappers and empty containers and butter knives smeared with condiments and various open jars of peanut butter, a pyramid of empty Pabst Blue Ribbon tall boys against the wall stuck together with Crazy Glue as evidenced by the open tube stuck to the table, a condom unfurled on the bathroom floor like snake molting.

Flicking dead switches, tapping the various buttons which used to grant access, perform a service; the fridge water dispenser, the iPad lying on the kitchen counter next to the open mayonnaise jar with flies buzzing the rim. Maggie ghosted behind me, sniffing at yet another condom on the kitchen floor. I toed her nose away from it. The other couple of dogs who came in with us scavenged the pantry. I heard them in there knocking things over and munching. I came to a wood-paneled office with a desk and lamp and desk calendar blotter decorated with yellow sticky notes, and a dead computer screen. A cheery room with art done in clumpy paint on the walls and a wooden figure folk art thing with a cigar in its mouth leaning against a wall.

Here was the ham radio Chris had used. I picked up the microphone from the floor and placed it back on the table, pressed the power button. No juice. On top of the ham was a relic: a Polaroid camera. I pointed it down at Maggie, pressed the button, and heard that glorious old-world noise, smelled that chemical smell of quick film development. It came out the slot at me like a tongue, a critical missive inserting itself from the world of a few seconds ago.

That mechanical sound of the camera is how long each of the several whalesounds lasted. That's how quick the world changed.

A button pressed and here it came, no stopping it.

To hasten its development, I shook the Polaroid picture, and danced to that Outkast tune in my head. Maggie looked at me like I was out of my barking mind. I looked down at the picture. There she was, a perplexed and innocent dog face looking upward.

Where did they go, the bloomers who were here?

Where did everyone else go? Toward where the pits would be? Must be. Kids couldn't have moved them all there that fast. If they walked, how come I didn't see anybody as I drove home from Mount Bonnell?

Hold on, that isn't true, is it? I saw the garbage man, who had just abandoned his truck. He was walking south down my street. The man on my street in his robe. He stood out there, dumbfounded. I bet he was a walker too.[16]

But solving that little mystery is pointless. It's a footnote to this, a shoulder shrug.

"Get it through your head," I'd said, standing in Kinky's office. "They are all dead." Even the late bloomers now, these few days on. Kodie had been right. The late bloomers just got to see and suffer more.

There's no telltale kid-destruction here. I could've gone looking for them, these late bloomer wonderers, out there in the brush, risked hurting myself out there alone. But why? I need to stay alive and that's it. *Why* doesn't matter right now. Fleming/Jespers, or whatever the cause, could be tackled later. Much later.

On the desk calendar, fitting perfectly on the October 31 square, Polaroid pictures sit in a short neat stack. Portraits. Names written on the bottom in their respective scripts. There's the black Sharpie next to the stack. Twelve pictures of six people, four young women, two young men, all

---

16 While none of us remember these early days, we now know this is what happened to many people that morning.

ridiculously attractive. The portraits look like headshots of the cast of some Disney neon-drenched dubstep music video / porny spring break movie.

The first six photos in the stack are the portraits. Each of them has posed with the folk art wooden cigar chomping man standing here like he's a spring break buddy, Mr. Party, the older weirdo guy hanging around spring breakers and nobody knows who he is but the intoxication is so total that nobody asks or cares. Old-world cupidity and sex is in their eyes despite having fled out to this dog rescue ranch at the end of their world.

The next six are group shots, five people in each. They are petting the dogs out in the pens, sitting on chairs outside on the landing which gives a view to the thousand foot high hills. One guy carves a pumpkin in each of these, not looking up at the camera. No beer cans, not many smiles. One girl, Kimberly (cross-referencing the inscribed portraits), seems to really have it for one of the guys, a Lance—he of the backwards-set ball cap and throw-pillow pecs under Hollister tee—by her torchy glances at him in each. Lance, ever aware of the lens, smolders for it, for all the ladies out there, seeming to forget there's nobody left but them. Old habits die hard for smoldering dudes. I understood. Sure I did. Probably had his shirt off later, prancing around after a couple of brews.

And my nasty little brain uttered to nobody but me: *Will the world miss these people?*

This must have been Halloween day, the day the ham operator, Chris, made contact. The last one, a thirteenth photo I found off by itself on the desk, is a selfie, taken here in this room, his face washed out from the flash. Deep black doom in the eyes. A selfie because he's the last one.

He has written at the bottom—I'm certain it's Chris's script, from his other, happier headshot—the two short words I used as the clever title to my extra credit essay for Mr. E's English class.

Both end with an *O*.

You guessed it.

Mr. E's words, in his voice from his note at the top of the essay's title page, echo here: *You really saw this didn't you?*

Mrs. Fleming's shout from across the street echoes right after it: *You knew, didn't you?*

I put my hands flat on the desk at either side of the array, elbows locked, head thrust down, and I looked into each face, found the good in each, quickly came to know them as their mothers' children and that they all had the same secret, sane, and simple desires of the heart as I do.

Were the dogs heard on the ham just baying at the Halloween moon?

"Who knows?" I said to Maggie, who twisted an ear at me. "No shattered windows. Nothing like what those little shits did to us."

Through the window I see a vulture swoop down over the empty pen. No shadow followed it. Its flight embodied patience, a scanning glide, knowing there always would be plenty of death upon which to feast. I pick up and look at the developed Polaroid I'd just taken. My brow creases and my stomach clenches. I angle the photo to the window to see it better.

In the extreme top left corner of the photo, I see a foot. The toe of a small-sized tennis shoe.

My heart thuds against the roof of my mouth.

Prickles of gooseflesh shoot across my entire skin as fast as kid movements, a wave of it moving over me instantaneously.

Before I could turn around—"I knew you'd come."

The child's voice issued from the gloom. Maggie and I spun around. She growled deep and long and stayed put.

The kid emerged from the shadow behind the office door. He stepped out, holding his hands behind his back. I never sensed him. Maggie hadn't either. The *somehow* is what bothers me now. That boy had to have been standing there stone-still the entire time we perused the room. That Maggie didn't notice his presence still confounds me, confirming that he and they are of a thoroughly different kind.

The boy was maybe ten, and though younger than Johnny, he was taller, having brown straight hair that looked neat as if he'd just combed it. He wore the clothes of a young lad off to school, clothes maybe his mother had laid out for him after he'd fallen asleep on his bed populated with stuffed animals, something she didn't do much anymore because he was such a big boy now. His long-sleeved light blue oxford, which still held the shape ironed into it, was tucked into chinos a little big on him, his mother no doubt in the habit of buying her sprawling son's clothes two sizes ahead now that his spurts seemed unceasing. His tennies had seen some wear but no time out in this recent rain.

Though he had the voice of a normal child, there came a resonance with it, as if his voice were not simply on the cusp of acquiring preteen depth, but that it wanted to go straight to a young adult's. It had a disquieting flange vocal effect to it, as if two voices issued out at once but at a slight timing difference so that it twined around itself. Twined and swirled. It sounded… wet, and made me dizzy.

"Are you going to hurt me?" he asked. The layered voices entwining tighter. His voice made me want to scream.

I shook my head. "No," I said, clearing my voice. He blinked at me with inquisitive calm. Oh—he unnerved me.

Maggie, though rigid with fury, had no inclination to move. A standoff, us three.

The boy broke first, his hands relaxing at his sides, and as he stepped more into the light of the office, I noticed deep indentations on the bridge of his nose. Only then did it occur to me that not one kid I'd seen since the morning of, other than Simon, wore glasses. In looking at them through binoculars, something else had bugged me. That was it. No glasses. Mr. Fleming had mentioned this as well in his note.

The boy glanced down at Maggie. With effort, he lifted his chin and looked back at me. He hid his terror of her deep in his blue eyes. His nostrils flared, venting his pent fear.

"Your dog?" he asked, his voice normal now.

"Now she is. I saved her, brought her here with me."

"You came from one of the cities." Though I preferred this voice to the other, the result of his deception was coldness. I nodded.

Maggie stifled her growl. You felt the air move from her throat's oscillations. I know the kid felt it.

"How long have you been here?" I asked.

"I don't know."

"You don't know?"

"I don't remember."

"Where are you from?"

He shook his head. The dogs in the other part of the house made a scuffling noise and the boy shot his eyes in their direction. "You don't know where you came from, how you got here. Where are your parents?" Me, the interrogator.

"I don't know."

He said this honestly, not seeming to comprehend they were dead. His ironed shirt made me sad for him.

"Do you know what's happened? Out there?" I gestured to the window. "Do you even remember your parents?"

"I remember everything, but it seems so far away, a long time ago. Whenever I try to remember something, like my parents, or where I used to live, it's cloudy. It's muffled. As soon as I start thinking about back then, it feels like my head gets filled with cotton and it starts to hurt, so I quit trying." Cotton made me think of the white stuff. He started to cry, and when he did that, his voice went wet and flangey again and while I wanted to comfort him, what I really wanted was for his throat to quit making that noise.

"Hey, it's okay." I took a reluctant step forward. I put my hand on his shoulder. The moment my hand rested there, he stepped into me, put his nose to my collar bone and sobbed. That awful flange unabated closer to my ear now. "Hey, hey, hey it's going to be okay, all right? Settle down."

I glanced back at Maggie. She hadn't moved.

"Have you eaten anything?" I asked. He shook his head in my chest. "You hungry?" He nodded and stepped back.

"Very," he said, and I thought a smile was about to emerge from his face now red with crying.

"You couldn't make yourself a sandwich?"

His voice normalized again, he said, "I've been too afraid to even leave this room." Dog tussle noises within the house made him blink and wince.

"The dogs?"

"Not just them." He looked into the middle distance over my shoulder. "They know everything, feel all movement. They feel me and I feel them, no matter how far away, though it's less and less the farther you go."

"The farther you go from whom?"

"The kids I was born with."

"*Born* with?" Even Maggie perked an ear and tilted her head.

"Yes." Wetness to it—*yessss*. My mind reeled.

"You mean you've been hiding around here since…?"

He shrugged.

"Jesus . . ."

The boy looked at the floor, rubbed his nose with his palm, then back at me. "That's what one of the girls yelled when they grabbed her and dragged her out. 'Oh, Jesus .'"

"Who dragged her?"

"The ones I came with."

"You stayed behind?"

He nodded.

"Why?" I asked.

He shrugged.

"The dogs. What did they do?"

"They're why the kids couldn't stay."

I turned and grabbed the Polaroid selfie of Chris and showed it to him. "And him?"

He took in the photo, glanced back at me.

"What happened to him?"

"Walked out the door. I didn't follow."

WE WALKED INTO THE KITCHEN. The kid moved slowly as if every step registered somewhere creating a beacon on which to be honed in. The dogs inside left, shouldering through the screen door. I grabbed the one package of bread that had been twisted airtight, waved away flies, pulled open drawers for a knife. "What's your name?"

He sat down gingerly at the varnished knotty pine table in front of a large window looking out onto the pens. I pulled up the blinds quick and loud. He blinked and squinted. "Nate."

The dogs sat out there looking at us. They sat out there in the rain and made not a sound, yet all their faces were directed at us and all their ears were perked.

"Hi, Nate."

"Hi." I was starving too, so I quickly made up PB&Js with the J I'd pulled out of the fridge just holding on to the last of its cold. I popped open a couple of warm sodas and set them before us. We took big bites and ate in famished quiet for a minute. Then I repeated, "Do you know what happened?"

His cheeks full, he looked up at me and shook his head and I believed him. His eyes fell upon the gun at my ribs as I leaned over to take a last bite, my shirt falling open a bit. His eyes remained there even as I continued.

"Do you miss your parents?" I buttoned my shirt one more up the chain.

He swallowed and nodded. "When I think of them, my head gets cloggy and it hurts."

"Nate what?" I asked around smacks and strained gulps.

"Huhm?" Breadcrumbs on his face stood out in the shifting light. The rain plowed down now. Maggie sat patiently equidistant from us. Crust awaited. Nate tossed her one and she made it disappear in a snap. He smiled a mouth-full smile.

"What's your last name?"

He stopped chewing, toggled his eyes upward to recall it. "Dyer," he managed.

"Does it hurt even to remember that?"

"Sort of," in muffled chewing.

"I know it hurts, but can you try to remember some things if I ask you?"

He swallowed. "I can try," he said with a solemn look. He looked up from his crumbs and empty can. "Why do you need to know?"

"I'm lost. I need to find out what happened so I can go on. Figure out what to do next. But I need your help. You're all I've got."

He nodded and sat up straight, got a fixed look on his face and creased his forehead. "Okay, I'm ready."

"Don't hurt yourself," I said, trying to lighten the mood.

Failing. This Nate was not processing levity.

"Okay," I sighed deep and long, not sure I wanted to do this myself. "Do you remember the morning this all happened?"

He shook his head slowly with big innocent eyes.

I searched his face for duplicity, seeing nothing but the most scared and blameless waif's face, skin still dewy from his tears.

"Before I say…do you have any sisters or brothers?"

"No." He shook his head almost in shame.

"Okay, well, what happened is…"

He looked up at me, his face curious yet full of dread.

I told him.

He nodded like he knew, like I'd delivered a diagnosis confirming what in his heart he'd already known to be a lethal syndrome.

"How do you know for sure?" he asked in a cracked but normal kid's voice. It sounded the most normal yet, now that he was upset.

"Because I've seen. And because the world is quiet."

"Mommy and Daddy?"

I shook my head. "Nobody. Didn't the teenagers here tell you?"

He shook his head. "I hid from them. A large group of us came here. But the dogs were…they left. They took one of them, a girl. I stayed behind. The other teenagers left soon after."

"Do you know what happened?"

"No. I saw one girl walk away down the road there. She held her throat and cried."

Silence for a few moments. A spindle of drool fell from Maggie's jowl, her eyes fixed on our food.

"We've tried with the radio, we've driven through the city, I drove out here from Austin and saw nothing, we've—"

His brave face crumbled, his eyes filled with tears which spilled over his lids and rolled down to his chin where the drops collected weight and gravity.

He burst out in a cry, a single loud one that echoed in the great room. I got upset too. I sniffled and swallowed it back, cleared my throat. I gave him a moment. His head hung and his emotion now so overwhelmed him that he went silent and he looked at me with his mouth open in that hideous pained way people do when their throats can't even manage noise.

I don't think he had understood until just that moment. It had taken my presence to draw it out. Whatever happened to him, all of them, that morning, I don't believe allowed for understanding or pain or loss.

But here we were, these in-betweeners…falling through the fissure between the old and new world, feeling it all.

Nate sat in his chair and sobbed. Maggie waddled over, sensing the boy's fear of her had slackened, and licked the hand he'd let fall to his side when he put his head down on the table. He let her. She wagged her tail. He turned his head to the side, laying his cheek on the table. Then he raised his licked hand and pet her head, and she let him.

One down, my head said.

MAYBE I'M THE WARMTH THAT breaks their ice. Maybe they all just need a good cry, to remember, to have a dog lick their hands again. The clarity of it struck me then. It made sense: they didn't want to remember. It hurt too much. Their heads literally hurt. They didn't want to remember and whenever we older ones were around, it made them hurt, made them start to remember. Mommies, Daddies. Home.

The pain was too much, and they fought against it not knowing why. Of course. This is why they stayed away and threw rocks. Pure reaction to stimulus.

My job, I thought then, was to let them feel their pain, to remember. So that then we can all come together and rebuild.

I float along now, and as if they agree with my thoughts, ratifying them, they sing to me, but not in words.

Maggie licking Nate's hand was the first time I'd had any real hope since hearing those sounds the morning of.

MY WONDER GROWS MORE PROFOUND now as I get closer to the coast. I've plotted my course on a folded paper map I've sheathed in a Ziploc. This river, the flooded Colorado, has taken me through the south of Texas and now wants to deposit me at Matagorda Bay. It's up ahead, maybe another day's travel. I hope the travel remains smooth so I can keep telling you this story of my experiences during these first days. Once I get there, I'm not sure I'll be doing any more talking because I think I'm going to be very busy. From what Nate told me, which I'm getting to, I know I will be.

THERE'S NOT MUCH I WANT to say about the river, my trip down here. This isn't a story about that.

Besides doing this for you, Mr. E, and you, dear reader, and for myself, I am doing this for them, so that they have a record of what my first days were like and how I came down to help them. Down to the place whence it came—the sea. They want me to come down, but to come down slowly, a pilgrimage, and in so doing take the time to record my story for them, for you, for you are, after all, one of them, aren't you? You're a new-world kid.

Even though I don't feel the need to describe this trip, for nothing terribly eventful has happened, I do want you to know this: Maggie lies asleep in the front part of this tandem kayak. I'm sure she's tired of hearing me talk to myself. Know that when the rain comes, which it has every day, and it comes now even as I speak into this, these rainy times are my favorite times. I erect my umbrellas, one for me, one for my dog, I fasten them to the boat in the cup holders next to each seat. I keep paddling, steering really, this current carrying me down. I feel this story come out better and faster when it rains. I'm at ease when it rains. I've got my headset microphone on, the recorder in the Ziploc with the map, and I'm just yakking away.

It's raining right now, droplets hitting the water. You hear it? All those ripples moving out from each drop. Know this too: Though at one point during a rough patch of rapids yesterday I thought I might lose it over the side, I've still got my trombone.

And know that I don't believe in luck.

WE SAT AT THE LACQUERED dining table listening to rain that seemed mad at us. I told him everything that had happened to me from Mount Bonnell on, including the reason why I was up there in the first place, point by point as a witness to my own small history.

A rather cold synopsis, really. I didn't get into with him what I've gotten into with you, how I felt, how I feel, who I miss and how much. I didn't tell him about Mr. English, my summerdreams, my story *The Late Bloomers*, the extra-credit essay, none of that. Mostly because he's a little kid and wouldn't get it. But also because that other stuff is between you and me.

He had stopped crying and gone stone-faced as he listened. He got lost at times in the narrative, and whenever I broke that spell it put him in, his face tensed up from the slack wonder it had fallen into.

Because he looked exhausted and because it hurt his head to remember, I couldn't yet ask him what he knew.

EVENING CAME, THE RAIN CONTINUED but had lessened to a patter. I told him I was going out to feed the dogs. He nodded and said, "Kevin? I'm not like them, but I am…what I mean is they'll know I stayed behind. I'm like a piece broken off, and they'll…"

"What?" I let the screen door close, took a step back into the room. "They'll what, Nate?"

"They'll come back. They know you're here. They won't be coming for you when they come back. They'll be coming for me. But I don't want to go."

I patted my gun. "Between this gun and all these dogs, I think we'll be okay. I came out here to find those teens. But instead, I've found you and that's something. Hang tight with Maggie, okay? She likes you. We need these others, so I've got to go out here and feed them so they'll stay around. Understand?"

He blinked and put his hand down to Maggie for her to lick.

I FOUND THE DOG FOOD in aluminum trash cans up on a foot-high riser at the back of the carport. I filled several big pans for them. Making several trips like a harried waiter, I placed them down and each time the dogs waited until I had walked off before eating. When they did, they did so orderly and quietly, all standing around the bowls, heads down, no fussing or fighting.

When I came back in, I noticed how dark the room was now that the sun had gone down. It had descended faster than I expected here in the hills. The windows were purple and the trees and hills framed within them black silhouettes. I'm in a place I don't know. As small and simple as it is, once it's dark, it will become a cave of unknowns.

"Nate?" I called out.

I heard Maggie whine once, close in the room. "I'll get you yours in a minute, okay?" I said, more to make myself feel better in hearing the sound of my own voice, like whistling past a graveyard.

I called out to her. "Maggie?"

Lingering light allowed me to find Maggie sitting next to Nate who lay asleep on the couch in a part of the room where there was a flat screen and some magazines spread on a coffee table.

"There you are." Maggie stayed seated. "Nate," I whispered the first time. "Nate," I then said aloud. I shook his leg. "Nate," I said even louder, my voice banking off the vaulted ceiling and tiled floor. He didn't move. "Maggie, stay."

Pleased with myself with how quickly I found candles and lighter the owners had laid into the first kitchen drawer by the door, I sang a bit (that graveyard whistling instinct). *"Come on baby light my fire. Try and set the night on...fire . . ."*

The candlelight lent a gothic cast to my wandering. I needed a flashlight. Badly, particularly when lightning lit up the rooms, throwing unfamiliar objects into relief, gave each a shadow.

Standing in this hall holding this candle, the lightning flash afterburn leaving matters even darker, I was maybe the most scared I'd been yet, even with Nate asleep nearby.

I had to make noise to stave off the fear, so I made busy, opened cabinets and closets looking for a flashlight. Nothing in those cabinets except dead scorpions stuck to glue board traps.

In the walk-in pantry, spaghetti crisscrossed the floor like pick-up sticks among all manner of cereal the dogs failed to eat. Top shelf, there the several flashlights were with packs of batteries stacked next to them. I put four flashlights on the kitchen counter. I tested them, replaced batteries. I lit three more candles and placed them on the bar, on the dining table and one over near Maggie and Nate. Place looked like goddamned Dracula's castle now, less the cobwebs draping over staircases and the conspicuous lack of mirrors. It was indeed a dark and stormy night, dear reader. Candlelight, lightning flashes, hardened shadows, and, underneath, pulsing quiet.

And it would stay dark because, after all, were the strong, capable people at the power company working on it somewhere out there in the night, with gritted teeth and know-how? Nope.

Maggie sidled up to me and leaned against my leg when I sat down on the couch next to Nate. I tried to imagine his child terror but it wouldn't form in my heart because whenever empathy kindled, my mind heard their roars and his flange enmeshed within it.

He hadn't told me anything yet. He slept. I still didn't know where he came from or even how old he was.

Maggie jumped up onto the couch and curled up next to me. Watching Nate's diaphragm rise and fall, feeling the rocking of Maggie's panting next to me, I drifted to sleep.

THUNDER ROLLED DOWN FROM THE hills into my dream. I dreamed of Johnny and me playing soccer together under a low gray sky bringing rain, just knocking the ball back and forth. I wore new cleats. They felt good on my feet, all soft and formfitting. Johnny wore a red Man U jersey. When he turned with the ball, faking out a nonexistent opponent, I saw the name on the back of the jersey curl over his shoulders: Rooney. Johnny kicked the ball high and directly above him, as high as one of the trees lining the field's chain-link. He did this show-offy twirl, and when his back was to me again, I saw the name wasn't Rooney, but March, blazing white against that Old Trafford red. He trapped the ball to his feet like it was an egg, just taking it out of its sixty-foot drop and laying it gently at his feet. Johnny was a good player in the old world, but in the dream world, which felt part of the new world, he could do things with the ball that he never could have done in reality.

He passed it to me with crisp and assured pace. I swatted it back to him but not as well. He had to stretch to bring it in, and once he did, he dismissed me and started juggling. The ball a magnet to his feet, thighs and head, he moved it around his body and there was no chance it'd touch the ground. I watched rapt and proud.

In the sixty-foot trees behind me I heard *Kevin! Kevin, help me!*

I turned around quickly like someone had tapped me on the shoulder, my eyes scanning the trees. Johnny's ball-work staccatoed its leather-on-leather thumps behind me. A shape in the trees. I knew it to be a kid nest. This one had the look and shape of a brown felt bag. The bag bulged and rolled like a third trimester belly and from it the cries came more muffled now. *Ke-uhnn…Elllp eee.*

"Heads up," he said, and as I spun around I heard a thump unlike the others. I didn't see the ball but rather felt my head snap back and then my feet flying out from under me.

Johnny's shadow fell over me. I couldn't move yet, still stunned. I rubbed my right occipital bone. In my periphery, I saw the ball in the grass.

"Sorry about that," he said, stifling a laugh. "You okay, Kev?"

In my periphery, the ball was gone. I turned to look for it. Where it had been, a riven fist-sized stone.

He stood over me now, blocking much of the sky. He did Rooney's Christ pose. "Helluva shot, eh? One for the books," he said.

He puts his hands on his hips, looks down at me. "I'm your brother so I'm not scared of you, but the rest are. Scared of you yet needing you. When we're near you, we feel more our old selves. You'll be able to help us bridge the old world and the new. But right now is a time of change. We're not ready. And something..." Johnny's eyes hollow out, his face falls into a terror mask, but then snaps back bright like a struck match. He sighs one of those *oh-well, what're you gonna do?* sighs. "I can't talk about it."

I sat up on my elbows and squinted at him. My mouth felt stuffed with cotton.

Johnny looks at the sky and seems to draw from it. Then, the blue of the sky having transferred into his otherwise brown eyes, he lowers his head and stares into me. "You're it, my brother. You have been for a long time." He chuckles to himself, pops his cheek. "Don't know why it's a dork like you, but."

The muffled cries grow louder. Johnny looks in the direction from which they come, narrows his eyes to slits. "Don't listen to that, Kevin. They don't understand."

MAGGIE GROWLS. NATE'S TALKING. MY eyes fly open. Nate is sitting up, staring ahead unblinking, mumbling in his sleep. He doesn't react to the flashlight when I point it at his face, but his pupils contract to pinpricks and his speech clears. "You have to go, Kevin...you can only go one way....you already know. You must go alone." Then in a faraway disembodied flange voice he says, "*It's only me, brother. No other.*"

Those six words are said in Johnny's voice.

I detect that he's conflicted. He's breathing hard.

"Nate, wake up." Barely awake myself, I find it hard to separate Nate's words from Johnny's, the dream world from this one. They overlap and I am unsure. "Please, Nate, wake up and talk to me for real."

This kid sitting up and staring past the flashlight glare speaking in monotone had my pulse going, the reality of now thrumming through me.

I yelled at him. "Nate! Wake up!"

I beat on his legs with my open palm. He blinked, turned his face toward me. Growling from Maggie. Maggie leaning into me, ready to pounce.

Nate's face gathered up into a fearful shudder. He recoiled and pulled his legs away from me. "Oh, no! It's you!" His eyes grew wide and he shook his head with petulance like the child he was. "No. I don't want to. I don't want to."

"Don't want to what, Nate? C'mon, it's me. Kevin. You're okay. You're safe here."

"No, I'm not safe. Never safe." The voice wavered between old and new.

"That's not true. Don't you remember? We've been together all day today. I've told you all about me." I reached out to touch his shoulder. He jumped back onto his heels on the couch, his knees at his chin. Maggie startled but I made sure she stayed put with my other arm.

"Why did you come here?" he asked in a whisper.

"I told you."

"They'll find me!"

"Nate—"

"And I don't want to go back to them and I don't want to be with you because you make my head hurt. I just want to be left alone."

"Nate—"

His eyes shot back and forth and his breathing shallowed in rapid hitches. He huffed his breath and whimpered in abject pain, overwhelmed.

My presence confuses things for him.

"When they find me, they're going to..."

"What?" But I already knew. I flashed onto Simon's freckled face, fish-belly white, peering through the curtain of green.

"Because I'm not...I'm not...complete."

He looked up at me and his eyes implored that I believe him. I took the flashlight beam off his face, no longer interrogating him. "And they'll just kill you for it." I remember saying this without derision. I said it quietly, stating fact.

Though he did not respond, his face was grim.

THE NIGHT'S BLACK DIDN'T ALLOW me to see that puddles in the gravel quivered with droplets until I waved my beam out across the drive. Lifting the light up, I saw the dogs' eyes spark yellow. They sat still, watching, ears perked to our conversation. I lit new candles on the bar. Sleeping no longer occurred to us.

I sat and slumped back into the couch next to him. Nate sighed deeply, chin to his chest.

"You'll stay with me. Here. I like it here," I said.

"You can't protect me."

"Worked so far."

"They wait."

"For what?"

"For you."

"I'm not leaving."

"Yes you are."

"No I'm not."

"Yes you are."

"Forget it, Nate. We're staying here. We'll wait them out. Things'll settle. They'll stop being so scared and after a while we'll be able to make contact and work together." I embellish that line a bit, because right now, floating along, I feel this is true.

"No. You don't understand. They're not scared of anything anymore. Except you."

"Hush—"

"Haven't you ever needed something so badly that you were afraid of it?"

There's need and there's want. Wants came to mind. Publishing my first book, the bookstore letting me play my trombone at the first reading.

I thought of wanting to be with Kodie, watching her ring up customers, wanting to be with her. No, that felt more like a need.

I thought of Grandma Lucille with her eyes closed listening to me play, then eyes closed laying in her coffin. I thought of how badly I wanted the world to be different as I sat up on that boulder smoking...and then here came that single rolling wave...

It needs you to need it.

"Of course," I said.

"That's how we, they, feel. They need you but they're scared."

We sat there looking at each other in a bit of a standoff. The tension of the moment tormented Maggie and she jumped down and looked back and forth at both of us and whined. I found myself questioning this kid. He'd stayed behind, sure. But now I'm really wondering why. Is it even possible that they'd let him, that they'd not notice? Or did they leave him here to serve a purpose?

In the old world we'd call him a plant, a spy, or in this case, a double agent.

These thoughts bearing questions had no answers. If I asked him, I don't think he could give me a real answer if he wanted to.

"When you were talking in your sleep you said something to me. Do you remember what you said?"

"What did I say?"

"I'm asking you."

"Uh . . ."

I scrutinized his face. He seemed confused by my behavior.

"Um, I think I said, 'oh no it's you'?"

I shook my head. "Before that."

He shook his head back at me, shrugged. If he was lying to me, he was a thespian extraordinaire. If he was lying to me, it wasn't intentional.

"I don't remember saying anything before that. What was it?"

"It doesn't matter, okay?" I could see trying to remember pained him.

"Tell me."

"No, Nate."

"Why won't you tell me?"

"Because it doesn't matter and because I don't think it was you telling me. It wasn't you talking."

His shoulders hopped up and down as he immediately began crying. "I'm sorry. I'm sorry..."

"For what?"

"For what I told you. Whatever it was."

I slid over and hugged him. He hugged back hard and desperate. His mouth was to my ear and mine to his. "I won't ask you to remember, okay?"

His chin drilled into my neck as he nodded. He sniffed loudly in my ear and deep in his throat his little boy voice whined. He tried to contain it but he burst out in a hoarse cry.

"It's all right, Nate. I'm glad I came here. I'm glad I found you."

His chin dug in more, his grip on me tightened. His whispers came out wet, not in his new-world voice, but in his old-world mucosal little boy's voice, the voice he'd have used if talking to his daddy after he'd taken a nasty fall off his bicycle. I felt his breath there, and into the swirl of my ear he pleaded, "Please don't leave me. You can make my head hurt. I don't care. Just don't leave me here."

He clung and his body shook.

THE MORNING IS AN AMETHYST sky that melts away into blue by full dawn. November cold comes with it. Here in the hills, winter's prelude arrives early. Uncontrollably shivering on this couch, I understand what it means to need wood. The steel wood rack lining a wall of the carport stood empty save for maybe enough wood to burn through in one cold day. Today, the front and the rain having passed, was that cold day. Halloween's celebration of the harvest, of mocking the death promised by winter, was over. Now, the cold.

We could see our breath indoors. We'd need wood to keep warm and to cook, there being neither power nor gas. We'd need it for flickering comfort.

My old life had its fires and fireplaces, but those were always novel, weren't they? Winters in Austin got below freezing, sure, but we didn't really need a fire. It was extra. A blazing hearth in the room was for atmosphere, a First World aesthetic.

This morning is the first time I've ever felt the cold as a threat. It's a threat when you're not sure you can escape it, that it might seep into your bones and remain.

Cold had infiltrated my bones overnight. In the purple dawn, it wasn't leaving. Dawn light tickling my eyelids, stirring my circadian stores of serotonin, didn't wake me. Cold did the waking. My body announced via biological bullhorn: *wake up, you might die if you don't find warmth soon.*

Layering helps. In a hall closet next to the bathroom I found a skuzzy sweatshirt someone had clearly used for a smock while house painting, and an old peacoat that fit me well, that and a burnt-orange longhorned scarf and one of those hunting caps with woolen ear flaps. I pulled a smallish jean jacket from the closet and set it next to Nate along with another one of those caps that looked too big.

I covered him up with a blanket I'd found draped over an armrest. I let him sleep. He lay there with his breath pluming out into cartoon dialogue balloons. In each, his hold on me tight and bony: *just don't leave me here.*

In my ridiculous city-boy-playing-ranch-hand outfit, Maggie and I quietly exited through the screen door by the kitchen. I needed time away from him to think. Outside, crunching the gravel, keeping a lookout for roving dogs, I thought we could stay here, me and Nate. We could live out the winter here. An entire cold season really could change things.

Cold's what you apply to an injury, isn't it? Time heals.

Cold plus time . . .

What would the world full of children—those at latitudes farther away from the equator, that is—what would they do when the cold came upon them and there they are out in it? Would it change them? Would they, to survive, deign to use old-world warmth, occupy buildings, use machines?

Probably not, I thought. They'd go *old* old world and build big goddamned fires out in the open. Like they did the burial pits. The good thing was, they'd have to stay near them.

Maggie trotted next to me. I stopped in the middle of the gravel drive and did a three-sixty turn. What a beautiful place. I'd been to Durango, Colorado, and this place was the Texas version. No kidding. Yeah, I could live out the winter here. A good amount of food sat in the pantry. The fridge and freezer have salvageable items that I can keep cool at the stream

I crossed on my way in. And there! There's the huge chicken coop the size of a racquetball court. There they are, clucking and squawking around. The list of things to do in my mind populated fast. I loved the feeling of having things to do other than worry and be afraid, though that's always the bass line of life's song. The way it was in the old world, too, just a different set of them, a manufactured set. These were real because they pertained directly to survival—not acceptance, not ambition, not material attainment, not even getting laid—and because this was so, I felt a burgeoning wholesomeness springing from my feverish to-do list.

This is the utopia I'd hoped for. But I'd wanted it with Kodie. How I missed her now. She'd be so into this idea of staying here, just us, for the winter at least.

I let my finger fiddle with the glock trigger so as to push the thoughts of her away. A redheaded turkey vulture glided on a thermal at the mouth of the valley. I aimed and fired at it. The gun's report echoed and all went quiet. The bird didn't even so much as dip a wing in response.

The slight wind coming from behind brought me Nate's cry.

I jogged back and got within earshot, where we could see each other's faces.

"My truck's right there," I'd pointed to the side of the house. "What, you think I'd just walk away from you?"

He leaned over to see it around the corner. "Oh," he said. His head panned the scene from side to side as I walked up the incline to the wooden wraparound porch where he stood. "Where are the dogs?"

"Dunno. I'll rattle the feed bins. They'll come running, I'm sure."

He took a step back into the shadow of the porch. "Wait until I'm inside, okay?"

"Sure. Maggie's okay for you, right?"

He paused, nodded, slowly at first, then assertively, trying to please me by being brave. In that moment, Johnny's features overlay Nate's, making me pause my ascent. Maggie sat next to him, looked up at Nate, back at me. The dog knew we spoke of her; the dog knew I was experiencing powerful emotion, and that Nate's fear was not yet quelled just because I said it should be.

As I say this, dear reader, know that I am leaning forward to stroke my dog's sunbaked fur. The kayak shimmies as I do. She keeps her eyes closed, enjoys the sun, the water's rock, having felt me do this innumerable times on this river and knowing that when I do so that I always think how her coming into my life when it did was pure providence.

Now that my old world had been forever stripped away, I can say things like that because now I believe it. And I can also say this: that it's by providence that I'm doing this, telling you this story while heading toward the bay, for what else could it be?

"I've been thinking," I said to Nate.

"Uh huh." His response came out more circumspect than I thought possible for a ten-year-old. He pushed the too-big hunting cap up his forehead.

"I think we should stay here. For the winter."

"Really?" His brimming excitement let show through the old world.

"Yep. It's the best thing, I think."

"And after that?"

"After what?"

"Winter."

"Let's get there when we get there."

He nodded knowingly, brow furrowed—*yes, of course, when we get there.*

"You like coffee?"

Nate shook his head, his tongue jumping from his mouth in a grimace.

"I'll make a fire. Cold cereal is all we got right now. We're going to need to spend the morning collecting firewood. Then we can get eggs from the coop."

"Okay."

"But first, let me feed the dogs. We lose them, and the winter here isn't as attractive."

Nate turned on his heel and dashed inside. He stood at the tall single-paned glass door and watched me at an angle as I fed the dogs. The noises I made did indeed make them come, about thirty of them. "Can you feed her in here?" Nate yelled from the cracked door. Maggie sitting next to him, waiting, knowing.

THE CEREAL WE ATE HAD held its crunch and the fire I'd conjured filled the room with hope and warmth. Out the window, the sun was a white coin pinned above the ridge. I showed Nate the empty wood rack and said we'd need to go out and collect a bunch of deadfall. The dusty-webby storage room contained all manner of axes and saws, chained and toothed. Nate found clothes that fit better in the closet up in the loft above the great room he'd annexed. He'd claimed the loft with blunt territoriality, running up and down the flight of steps, fleet and noiseless on the jute carpet.

We set out to collect wood with a green wheelbarrow. Plenty of it in the immediate area but the real stuff we could see was beyond the tall industrial barbwire fence. An aluminum ranch ladder straddling the fence didn't help us wood-gathering-wise. I considered snapping the wire with one of the million sharp objects in the medieval oubliette of a storage room, but a part of me thought it best not to.

Then we saw why. Buffalo. Only twenty-five yards away on the other side of the fence, lying so still I had to blink to make sure. Two of them lying on the slanted meadow in the sun between cedar copses.

"A whole herd of them out there," Nate said. "Forgot to tell you that."

"Huh. Buffalo." I'd heard stories of people out in the boonies having panthers and ocelots and zebras. Never heard of buffalo out here. I muttered, "Well, should the fecal matter really strike against the rotating blades, we could hunt down one of these and eat for a month."

"What?"

"Oh, nothing. Just postulating."

"I don't know what that means either."

"That's a good thing."

The only animal I'd hunted was quail. A few times in high school, Johnny coming with us the second time just last winter, we'd driven out to a hunting lease in Hill Country, near Burnet. Martin and his real estate bud, Frank somebody. We'd go out in the blue dawn and drive many miles just to shoot quail. Sitting in the bed of a beater pickup, Frank's brown Labrador, Bevo, would flush them out from the brush under mesquites, coming back with pear cactus quills on his muzzle, then go retrieve them once they plummeted from the sky. I'm not a bad shot, truth be known, but I took no pride in it. I wasn't into hunting, not with Martin at least, not for, uh, sport. Starving to death? Totally could do it.

We decided to stay inside the fence wire for now and succeeded in finding enough wood in the immediate area to keep us warm for a while, thanks mostly to a keeled hackberry which I hacked at until noon. Nate got proficient with wheeling the wood to the porch though slowed by his need to look over his shoulders every few yards. When he dumped his loads at the entrance to the carport, he'd run back to be near me with that wheelbarrow swerving. I wondered how long his acute fear would last.

"This will do us for today, with some left for tomorrow, but we've got to make this a daily thing to keep up with so we can hopefully get ahead of the weather. Maybe tomorrow, we'll take that Bobcat farther away."

Nate nodded. We loaded the last of what I'd chopped into the wheelbarrow and made our way back to the house. Nate strode apace and close enough for us to bump. Halfway there, he hooked fingers into the pocket of my peacoat.

I KNOW I LOOKED LIKE Rocky Balboa, hunched over, chasing those chickens. Nate laughing at me. I finally grabbed one and held it to my body as it squawked and flapped. I petted it and it calmed. "Just seeing if I could do it," I said to the brown hen. "You keep laying eggs and it'll just be for sport."

Nate and I made our way around the coop, ducking under the corrugated roofs, filling our baskets with eggs.

We lined the eggs in rows on a towel on the kitchen counter. They needed to stay cool and I didn't want to get in and out of the fridge too much for fear of losing what little cold remained. The immediate need for warmth solved, the need to keep food cool and fresh now presented itself. Coolers tied with bungee or rope outside would work, though raccoons would solve those riddles.

The carport storage room with all the torture implements could act as a large fridge. I'd inventory and transfer salvageable fridge food into the storage room, including the daily eggs.

Somehow the water still ran and the toilet flushed. I guess the water came from a well. No idea how long that would last or what was involved in making sure it did. What did I know of such things? How many different ways could I make things substantially worse by monkeying with it?

Would this be my life? Was it just a matter of time until I boxed myself into a deathly situation? Maybe, but I felt we had the winter and the dogs, enough of a buffer. Maybe I could make contact with others, if they were out there, and maybe, just maybe, the kids would change.

Look at Nate. My presence has had a major impact on him. Couldn't the same be achieved with other kids? Occam's Razor says: of course. True or False SAT answer: True.

Let a long cold winter chill us all out. I smiled at that thought as I watched my fire dance upon the wood I'd collected. All I needed to do was keep things fresh, keep water available, and feed the dogs and chickens. At some point we'd need to drive into Medina to get more food and feed. Inherent risks there.

What I needed to do was be resourceful and live for today. Maybe that's all there is. This whole world of ours got too crowded and busy and mother nature just decided to hit the kill switch.

Did she use Jespers's Gene to do it? Were those old guys nuts? As time goes by, it seems so farfetched. But, then, look what's happened. Farfetched.

I don't know. Philosophy is so old world.

IT TOOK THREE DAYS FOR something resembling normality to set in. A rhythm, a beat structured the hours for the first time since the morning of. I sensed my shoulders relaxing from their residence near my ears in constant defensive mode. My hummings and whistlings flowed while I worked, and not just to quell fear. These songs I hum-whistled were original tunes from my subconscious which didn't want to recall and revamp old-world melodies and arrangements. I collected these tunes in my mind like eggs, like firewood, put them on a shelf for later. Then, in the evening by candlelight, I wrote them down in a notebook[17] I found in the office.

Before the morning of, my life was prosaic. Now it started taking on the more elegant and exalted forms of poetry, of music. Three nights in a row I've gone out into the dusk to flesh out these things I've heard in my head

---

17 This notebook of songs is on view at Records. Songbook rehearsal copies are available for checkout from Custodian.

all day. I use my lips and throat as a horn, missing my instrument terribly. When Nate and I go back to Austin in the spring, I thought, I'll retrieve it, bursting with a notebook full of songs to blow through it. Hope springs eternal.

COLD CAME AND LEVELED OFF in preparation for its full invasion. I couldn't wait for more cold. I thought of them out there in it, how it had to change them, break them into something approachable.

What we did in those first three days, we did together. Nate never wanted to be alone, and the things we did were simple. We got our bearings and readied for this newest of seasons. The simplicity of the days gave them rhythm, and with that, comfort.

Setting the pieces up on a large stump, I got good at splitting wood. Nate would smile when I got on a roll. The rhythm, the breathing, the cadences. I drank it up through my pores. It nourished me. Whenever I took a breather, I'd ask him if he wanted to try and he always paused, then shook his head.

MAYBE HIS HEAD HURT. I didn't ask him, but sometimes when leaning on his axe and staring off glassy-eyed into the sky I thought maybe it did. My earlier desire to know what he knew had evaporated. He didn't know anything anyway, not that he could relate. He had been part of the hive, and the hive thinks as one. Now that he'd broken off from it, or been exiled, I don't believe he had anything to tell me. He's excommunicated and thus incommunicado. What he said to me in his somnambulism was it. There were no such moments thereafter. It all seemed moot. Tabula rasa.

On the third day, Nate told me he could do the egg-gathering by himself now. He wanted to do it next time, first thing in the morning. Busy with my chicken chasing while hearing the *Rocky* theme in my head—*getting strong now!*—I grunted sure, go for it, you know where the baskets are.

IN THE AFTERNOONS WE SCOPED around the property's perimeter, going a little farther down the road toward the nearest ranch each day. We could've taken the Bobcat but Nate bristled at the idea of getting on it. He always gave the vehicles a wide berth whenever we stacked wood in the carport.

He clung to me when we got near them and he eyed them like they were sleeping creatures which would pounce if awakened.

That third afternoon, he didn't want to keep going but I told him we were fine. He asked if we'd see dead people and I said we might but that I'd go in ahead of him and let him know.

He tugs on my sleeve, telling me he wants to turn back. As much I want to find this other ranch, can sense that it will come into view around the bend of this hill, I'm feeling it too. A fearsome pre-dusk density filled the air. I nod, I'm okay with turning back.

"Sorry," he said, the shame in his voice a good thing. "Tomorrow we'll go all the way."

"Sure. No rush, though, okay? Baby steps. No shame in it."

He cracked a smile and I tousled his hair. We turned around.

Maggie had been right there with us, usually leading the way and checking back. "C'mon Maggie," I called out, my claps for her echoing off the limestone cliff walls. "Going back," I cried through cupped hands, opening and deepening my voice. We both did a three-sixty turn. No Maggie.

With as much buoyancy mixed with calm as I could muster, I said, "Huh. Well, she's off chasing something. She'll catch up." I think I even shrugged my shoulders like some fifties sitcom kid.

We began walking back. Our shoes crunched the trail which was mostly caliche, but in some places plates of limestone. Neither of us admitted that we didn't hear her run off, heard no paws scratching on the trail. Neither of us wanted to admit that we didn't see her dashing away. That neither of us wanted to discuss it made us walk faster.

Two vultures assuming their V-shapes made spiral sweeps down past the tree line horizon between us and the house. We had progressed a few hundred yards from the house this time, the farthest we'd been by a lot, and now the safety of a dwelling seemed far away and we felt exposed. The quiet, the distance from the house, and our nervous crunching feet got to me to the point where I wanted to draw the gun from my holster and walk with it, flick the safety off while pirouetting to see if we were being watched or followed.

Immense quiet does this to you. Even to you, dear reader, you there, sitting in a quiet place reading this. You feel it too. The quiet makes you uncomfortable. It makes you squirm. You have to look up to answer the questions all beings ask themselves all the time, consciously or not: Am I being watched, tracked, hunted? Even you, reading this, will now wonder and look about.

My watchful lieutenant of a dog had vanished. We were a good distance from anywhere. While we started this walk in the afternoon, I have to admit that I didn't check the time nor the sun's position in the sky and maybe we did depart from the house a bit later than before.

I didn't want to scare Nate by drawing the glock, so I didn't. I considered reaching in to pull loose the Velcro fastener, but I didn't do that either.

What I did was pick up the pace and start whistling. I whistled a variation of one of the many themes that had come into my head those days. In my head I heard my trombone.

Nate had to trot some to keep up. "Kevin. Wait for me."

I slowed just enough so he didn't have to trot. "You know this one?" I asked. I started whistling the tune from *Bridge Over the River Kwai*. On the second pass, he tried to pick up on it and he got it on the third. We whistled like that for a hundred yards, walking fast enough so that the whistling became a challenge of breath.

Nate put his hand on me, stopped whistling, and asked, "Are you scared?"

I stopped whistling. "Huh-uh," I lied, "just want to let Maggie know where we are."

"Well, I'm scared."

"Don't be."

"You've got a gun, right?"

"I do."

"You know how to use it?"

"Yeah." I started whistling again. Our pace had not slackened.

Winded, Nate asked, "You shot anything with it?"

"No, but I've been quail hunting with my stepdad. We used rifles."

Nate got real quiet. He put his palms over his ears and then rubbed his temples with his fingers. "My mom carried one in her purse." He blinked and jerked and stutter-stepped, as if he just heard it go off.

God, this is how his mom went. He was witness to it. "Hey. It's all right. Listen, don't try to remember right now, okay? Not right now." Our feet scuffed the path. Some bird of prey overflew.

He burst out in a throaty cry, wiped at his eyes, and held his head.

Nate's memories flooded him now. His face showed more panic than pain, his eyes wide and toggling back and forth at onrushing memory. I wanted to stop and hold him but we needed to keep walking. I called out loudly for Maggie, ripping the holster Velcro as I did. Then I whistled the theme to *The Andy Griffith Show*, my arm around Nate's shoulders.

So there we were at the end of the world, seeking out hope and a future, striding fast, me whistling, eyeing the birds, watching the open spaces, gun drawn and held down to my side, my other arm around a boy who's sobbing at the recall of his mother pulling a pistol from her purse and firing its bullet into her head—no doubt with a horrible crazy rictus on her face—and all along I'm deathly worried about Maggie, I'm deathly worried about what tomorrow brings. I'm deathly worried.

All our ersatz normalcy and rhythm dashed, once again we lived in the fearful moment. I knew this is how it would always be.

My whistles came back to us from the walls of the valley louder than they left.

ROARING FIRE INSIDE, SMALL FLAMES on the grill outside and I'm cooking eggs in an iron skillet. The sun plummets and it's cold enough that I'm seeing my breath. Nate looks down at me from the tall rectangular window of his loft.

I feel him up there. Watching me. I pretend to focus on the skillet, but in my peripheral vision, I see his forehead and palms are pressed to the glass. His stillness is palpable.

He'd gone mute since we'd returned. His eyes had retrograded on me, looking like they did when I first met him in the office holding that Polaroid in my hand.

After a few minutes of me pretending to not know he's up there staring down at me, the eggs I've stirred together popping into a scramble I'm sure will bring in the dogs (hoping to Christ it does), I attempt to nonchalantly look up over my shoulder and feign surprise to see him perched up there.

He's staring, his oceanic eyes wide. I force a smile. Because it's false, his face doesn't change. His gaze bores through me. I wave my spatula at him. He blinks the sea-stare from his eyes and tepidly waves back.

Then he suddenly pushes off from the window.

"I'm ready to talk now." I'd just looked back at my eggs and then Nate's voice was right there. Standing in the garage doorway, he'd materialized so suddenly that I jumped and spun around brandishing the egg-dripping spatula as a weapon.

This should be funny. We should both break down laughing to release the tension.

I don't like how he came down, so quiet and fast. As I recall this now, I think of him moving in a sickening new-world blur from his window and down the stairs.

I don't like the look in his eyes or on his face either. While he doesn't beam malevolence, I know within him a battle rages. The urges belonging to a scared kid of the old world named Nate versus implanted directives of the new.

"Talk about wh—?"

He cut me off. "When we first sat down the other day and you made me a peanut butter sandwich, you wanted me to tell you what I know." I could swear I heard a smidgen of that flange in his voice.

"You don't need to explain anything to me. I doubt there's anything you can tell me that would be worth your pain."

"But I want to."

"Do you think it's important?"

"I don't know."

"Is it hard for you?"

He paused and said, "Yes."

"Then I don't need to hear it right now."

"But—"

"I trust you, Nate." Oh—how his face fell when I used that word *trust*. He lowered his eyes to the cement. I continued. "I think you'd have told me already if there was something I needed to know. I know you wouldn't keep things from me that would hurt me."

His pause before responding signaled calculation. His eyes drifted back to mine. "No, I wouldn't do that."

"We have tons of time. Okay?"

"Okay." He slumped, plodded forward like any kid. "I thought you'd be mad at me."

"No. We're doing fine. One day at a time, all right?" I turned my back to him to evidence my trust.

It took a moment for him to speak. "I'll go out in the morning to get the eggs this time, okay? I know how now."

"You sure?"

"Yeah. The chickens like me. I want to."

"I'd feel better about it if Maggie went with you though, you know?"

"No, it's okay, really."

"Swear?" I turned back to the grill. I had to turn around and ask again. "Swear?"

"Swear."

It felt older brotherly. In his voice I could hear him wanting to please me. He wanted to do something on his own. He wanted to be an individual, and to stop being afraid. I thought it was a good idea. I'll admit that gaining an extra half hour of sleep did appeal to me.

Though early evening, eager stars had winked into position. I spoke over my shoulder, "Eggs are nearly done. If you'll go get some bread, I'll toast it here and we can have breakfast for dinner."

"Again?" he teased. Our thing.

"Again."

Cue television laugh track.

I HAD INCORPORATED THEIR YIPPING and sniping into a dream before awaking, one of those dreams of a nebulous world at your periphery— blinded to it, you keep turning, your mind, your psyche, whatever you are, you're spinning in a white void trying to connect.

The auditory connected because there was the yipping. A group of them, gathered outside. The feeling that they had returned woke me. Usually, I'd call up to Nate in his loft soon after I woke, but that morning I didn't because I needed to know whether I had dreamed these noises or they had issued from the conscious world.

I sat and listened, moved my eyes back and forth in my sockets.

There—the yipping . . .

Sounding victorious and celebratory. There was also anxiety in it— *wake up, come see.*

I'd washed my clothes last night in the kitchen sink. They hung from a line of cooking twine I'd stretched across the front of the fireplace. As I slipped them on, dry and warm, the noises outside amplified.

The dogs had returned. I mumbled a missive out to the God that let this all happen, "Please let Maggie be among them." I shrugged on my peacoat.

Beyond the ambit of the fire, I felt the morning cold before I reached the door. The storm door creaked. The dogs were gathered near the carport waiting to be fed. "Oh, so I guess you're done carousing and you're back to punch your meal ticket. What, hogs outrun you?"

Getting closer to them, I saw I was wrong. Each of their snouts, the fur on their chests, glistened red. A wave of revulsion moved through me. They froze as if gauging my reaction. I didn't see Maggie. "I see you had yourselves a hunting lark after all."

Their muzzles dribbled and dripped. Fresh kill. Standing among them now, they meandered all around me as if seeking praise, lifting their heads for my touch. Droplets of blood dotted my shoes. Some smeared on my hand-cleaned pants.

"*Ack!* Back! Back you fiends," I kidded. The dogs scattered a bit, giving me room with laughter in their eyes and grisly smiles on their faces. Each had a gout of blood on its snout like they'd dipped it up to their eyes in red oily paint. They seemed to revel in it. I'd not seen them so happy and satiated since coming here.

"I doubt you're hungry. Huh, you killers? Yeah, you guys are killers," I teased and reveled with them as I arranged their food pans, looking forward to reestablishing the routine again, that rhythm we needed after yesterday's scare. The coppery tang sluicing from their mouths intensified as they dug into their food with abandon. "Guess I'm wrong. Famished. Famished from the glory of the hunt. You killers you."

I turned around at movement I felt behind me. Up the path came Maggie in silhouette, the sky brassy with dawn breaking behind her through the crease in the valley. She sauntered toward me. I didn't like her deliberation—she had the uneasy gait of a rabid, untrusting canine gone fey—but I ignored it, squatted down and opened my arms to her. "Mags! Where the hell'd you go? You went poof on me. Worried us."

She didn't come running. She came more into focus and I saw that her muzzle shone bloodslicked as the rest.

And something else. The shine on her muzzle. I looked back at the group of dogs eating. I walked over to them. Having breached the horizon, the sun poured light on the dogs. Now I saw how slick and splotched their muzzles were. Along with the blood, flecks of eggshell clung to their yolky smiles.

The chickens' silence struck me as unusual for early morning. Dawn broke behind Maggie yet no rooster crowed.

Maggie stopped in front of me, her muzzle dripping of egg and blood viscous and vermillion. Unlike the others, Maggie didn't wag her tail and didn't seem to revel.

"Oh, man! Tell me you didn't get into the coop. Please tell me you didn't just slaughter the hens and scarf the eggs." Maggie averted her face from mine.

I strode through dewy grass to the coop, chuffing steam-breath into the air, yelling over my shoulder, the echoes highlighting my solitude, "Goddammit, you guys! This is our lifeline!" Maggie obsequiously loped behind.

When I got to the coop, I found it undisturbed. A couple of chickens came out of their holes and poked around. No blood, no signs of breaking and entering.

I circled the coop twice to make sure, thinking *no feathers on the ground, no feathers on their snouts...*

Maggie, tail tucked, scooted clear of me as I turned to run.

I didn't call out. I topped the single flight in three bounds. The mattress on the floor of the loft lay empty, the comforter folded back, the pillow still impressed with his head-shape.

Downstairs, and I see the egg basket is gone.

The dogs weren't disturbed as I tore out of the house. The storm door slapped the frame. I ran back to the coop. The chickens squawked and dashed back into their places when I barged in.

All the nests were empty.

My heart thudded between my ears and my stomach dropped.

He had wanted to do it himself. He didn't want to wake me.

FOR HOURS I YELLED OUT for him. I ran around the compound breathless and panicked.

Shadows thinned and slanted. I sat numb at the kitchen table and stared at its lacquered knots, black holes through which I tumbled.

I remember sitting there wishing I would cry. I just tumbled, I don't know for how long, the silence of the world beating at my ears.

THE DOGS LAY IN A tight pack in the sun. A cool wind blew over them. Their bellies engorged with new-world blood, they all slept save for Maggie who sat at the front of them with her ears up, waiting for me.

I hadn't made a fire. The room grew cold by noon. I tumbled.

I took the Bobcat around the property. About a quarter mile away in the other direction from the way we'd been walking—which means he must have been running from them because he wouldn't have gone that way otherwise, not without me—up near the mouth of the creek which dumped into a small lake on the property, I found his egg basket, bent and slimy, a spray of shells like spent firework paper, his too-big hunters cap in a wet wad, and the grass all around matted with blood gone brown.

I stood there in the cold looking at the scene, wondering where the carcass was, wondering about what he had seen the morning of, wondering how much horror can a little kid see and still live on, wondering what kind of foulness had descended on the world to allow a little boy to witness his smiling mother blowing her head off with the pistol she kept in her purse.

I stood there and the sadness never came to me. The anger came. It came as an entity and swirled inside me under my breastplate, rooted itself and made a home there. My eyes stung with rage, and though I yearned to, I couldn't scream out into the valley because it wasn't a valley. It was a void which would only throw my own voice back at me in mockery, the void knowing that's the most painful trick of all.

I searched all morning but never found him.

"How could you?" I asked Maggie as she recovered and reset herself in the seat.

The day shone bright but there was no hope in it as the Texas Hill Country scrolled past, its small burgs with no working stoplights blurred in the landscape. No distant smoke spires. They were done with that.

We drove fast down the middle of the roads and highways, the SUV straddling the dividing lines. Leaves, trash, and debris created a wake that swirled up behind us as we crashed through. The roads were no longer neat strips of access and egress. They rolled out before me cluttered and treacherous. The new world would cover them with organic matter until they were vague, ancient paths crossing the expanse.

But today I plowed through at high speed, my jaw set, my eyes level and hooded. Maggie sat in the passenger seat of the black Tahoe with the encircled SA sticker on the back bumper and panted, switching her eyes to me every time I spoke. Furious with her, every once in a while on the drive back to Austin, I tapped the brakes so she'd crash into the dash. Each time I did it, I yelled at her, my voice cracking, "How could you?"

I had dumped all the dog food out onto the garage floor cement, saying nothing to the dogs as they leapt around me like I was their piper. They didn't understand. While I was upset with them, I didn't berate them. What good would it do? They were only doing what came natural.

But I held on to my anger toward Maggie.

I didn't bother to wipe the scuzz from her snout. She licked at it enough so that by the time we hit Route 290, the red egg slime was gone, save for a smear of it on the dash where she'd face-planted. Her chest fur remained dyed red like she wore a scarlet letter of guilt. I wouldn't help with that. Let her smell it, let its reek remind her.

Goddammed dog.

"How could you, Maggie? You of all? That sweet scared little boy? Didn't you see he was different? How could you?" I tapped on the brakes and swerved. She tossed and plowed into the walls of the car.

But I knew how she could. Of course I did. As Kodie had said, packs of anything are dangerous. The pack, the hive, colony, marauding horde—they lose their individual minds, surrender it to the collective madness of the congregation and the riot.

Though I don't want to, I suppose it's nature's way. We humans tried to ignore that such was our nature, always hubristically seeing ourselves beyond nature's reproach.

The road makes you think. When you're done being pissed at your dog, you think the things that need resolving and somewhere between points A and B, resolutions are made.

I stared at the horizon. The wind busted on the windows. Tuning the radio wasn't worth it, its scanning roundelays yielding nothing but static. As much as I loathed the world's silence, I couldn't bring myself to rid it with music played with such verve before all this happened. I had tried to play CDs, what they had in the car. I couldn't take more than a few bars of LCD Soundsystem's dance punk, the chugging opening riff to that Toadies hit, the singer's vocal a vampiric dare—*make up your mind, decide to walk with me…*

I listened to the wind and road sounds and Maggie's nervous panting. She felt my wrath. Moreover, she sensed my fear.

"I'm sorry," I eventually said to her. She lifted her eyebrows my direction, then back to the road, doing her own resolving, her own remembering.

HOME WAS FULL OF HOLES but it's where my trombone's buried. Austin's where my mother lay down and died. If that isn't forever your home, then I don't know what is. Maybe home becomes the place where you have and raise your own children. I'd never know that kind of home, so, the soil of the city upon which my mother collapsed and died was home. It's where my friends died.

And, to be honest, it's where I knew they'd let me go. I had a feeling that if I veered off and went in any other direction, I'd be thwarted.

The pumps didn't work at a station I pulled into. I had to siphon gas out of a parked car using plastic tubing I'd found in the dark garage smelling of oil. No bodies, but when I opened the refrigerated units in the back I got a rush of warm rot in the face. I coughed and grabbed Gatorade and Cokes, some chips, and a whole display of beef jerky and ran out.

Maybe in Austin I could still find Johnny. That's really the only hope I had left. Maybe I could wrest Johnny from them and bring him back as I did Nate.

But if I did that, wouldn't the scavenging dogs—literally, figuratively—come to pull him apart too? Can I be so callous as to think otherwise? Maybe it wouldn't happen days later, a month, but they'd come for him—the vulnerable one separated from the rest.

When Nate crept past me, did he know he went out to collect his death with that basket? Or was he trying to show me, and himself, that he had changed, that he wasn't afraid to go alone? Did he think going out to collect eggs on his own at dawn was the threshold he had to breach to be old-world Nate again? Would his head not hurt when he tried to remember? Did he hope to convince the kids that they could do it, too?

Was it expiation? Self-sacrifice, throwing himself to the dogs to satiate the beast they feared?

Did the kids get into his head, force him into that vicious dawn? *Never mind the dogs, go outside with the egg basket.*

Maybe some are trying to break away, enduring the headache, looking for themselves again. Maybe Nate caught that wave. Maybe Johnny can.

It's the ones looking for their old selves again. They're the ones who need me. They're the ones who sing and guide me downriver now.

Johnny was my objective. I gripped the steering wheel and smiled at Maggie.

Here we came onto the iconic green road sign: *Austin City Limits.* The headlights were on by default due to the gray day. When the light filled the sign in a flash of white, that's when Nate's flanged screams filled my ears, his panicked eyes beseeching the dawn sky for solace through gnashing teeth and flying fur filled my eyes.

I SPIED A POLICE CAR on the shoulder of MoPac near the Windsor Road exit. Keys in the ignition. I wanted speed. I wanted search lights. Maggie hopped in. "K9 unit?" She wagged her tail. We were good again.

I flicked on the loud siren, ran it for a few cycles. Echoing, echoing. Maggie ducked at the noise. I kept the lights on as I cruised at cop speed, Barney Fife sniffing, wrist-driving. Emergency. Clear the area, everyone.

On the Congress Avenue bridge. A wintry front's wind spread and chased ripples across Lady Bird Lake.

Lamar's yellow lines blurred. In my fog and blear on this last stretch of road home, I realized they'd been trying to tell me since June that this moment came. Johnny, standing in my room, his eyes fixed in sleepwalk, mumbling—*coming...coming...close...close...close...*shifting his weight back and forth on his feet. Simon, his pale face in the green bordering Memorial Park Cemetery, had said the kids feared a beast.

From writing my essay I'd learned that "lord of the flies" translates in Hebrew to *Ba'alzevuv*.

In Greek...*Beelzebub*.

MY HOUSE LOOKED LIKE A shipwreck from the age of the Barbary pirates, cannon-shot and listing. The other houses looked as they always did. Now that the cold had come, the yards weren't weedy. It was possible to believe the neighborhood was simply experiencing a sleepy Sunday.

When we pulled up, cats flew from the holes and disappeared. In the middle of the street about four houses up stood a coyote frozen in mid-lope with its ears perked. It watched us get out of the car. I stood behind the open door and stared at it. It stared back at me like I was a dead man walking, then completed its unhurried crossing into a yard where I lost sight of it.

Exhausted. There's no hero in me.

From the street, I hear it. This flapping. We walk to the porch and I see paper under a stone sitting atop my trombone case in the entryway.

It's a foot-long receipt from the Dollar Tree dated September 24. It's folded in half. On one side is written a note[18] I've seen before:

512-455-4688 CALL ME TO DISCUSS ALL THINGS PSEUDO-INTELLECTUAL
—K

Kodie had left this note for me in my cubby in the storeroom on that day. I'd asked for her number several times. She'd been coy. But then on that day she gave it to me and I had called her and that night we went out

---

18 A copy of both sides of this document is attached as Exhibit C

to dinner. We got looped on free margaritas, the bartender dude giving me the stink eye the whole time because I think he was one of her wanna-bes but never-wases. Then we'd gone up to Ginny's Little Longhorn, this tiny, bar painted UT burnt orange with a Baptist church steeple on top. They wouldn't let us in so we hung out with the regulars in lawn chairs in the parking lot, the door open. We listened to a country band covering Beatles songs. She sat on my lap and we kissed and the regulars all said *awwww*.

I'd kept it folded in my desk drawer, thinking someday I'd show it to her when we were older and have a laugh. I turned it over.

In the same handwriting, but different ink, the text uneven and slanted, it read

KEVIN, COME DOWN

WE CAN START OVER

ADAM AND EVE JUST LIKE YOU SAID

—K

The euphoria I felt knowing she was alive was dampened by the weirdness. It doesn't sound like her. More like Nate's somnambulistic oratory, but with a pen.

I never told her about how I thought we could be like Adam and Eve. I'd only thought about it. I've only told you, dear reader.

MAYBE *INNATELY* IS FARFETCHED, BUT to describe how I knew where she was, that's the best word I can come up with. Although she could've given a specific location (*lacking in specificity*), she doesn't, or the kids don't want her to. My quest. Up to me.

I figured I didn't have much of a choice.

When she says "come down," in my mind's eye I'm looking south from atop Mount Bonnell on the morning of. That wave rolling. So calm in its progress. I know that's the direction I'm to go.

I remember thumbing Jespers's copy of *Heart of Darkness* in the stack under *Lord of the Flies*, Kurtz declaring, "*My Intended, my ivory, my station, my river, my—*"

The river. Kodie waits for me where the Colorado River unburdens itself into the Matagorda Bay. On a beach there, she will be waiting.

One look at that note and I knew this innately.

That and the beach at night, their bright fires.

MAGGIE AND I WALK THROUGH the house of holes and the rain pours through and cold drops strike my scalp. From under some rocks I manage to pull out Martin's big canvas bag he used on his outdoor buddy excursions—still smelling of funk and fish—dragged it to my bedroom, stuff it. So tired, I just want to curl up.

Curl up and die, my brain banged at me. Not my mind. This came from my reptilian midbrain. *Curl up now, Kev, and you will die.*

Then that brain of mine shoots me up with adrenaline. My pupils dilate with a snap. My hands shake.

I hesitated before the fridge. They'd smashed the shelves and everything had dropped and congealed at the bottom, the stench nipping my sinuses. I closed the door, and that's when I looked through the place where the kitchen window used to be.

There, on the cement, placed, no, *presented* in front of the bashed portable generators was my twelve-foot periwinkle blue tandem kayak, the oars lying neatly within the rear paddler's well. A floor display at REI.

The kayak had been stored in the standalone garage, suspended by ropes and pulleys attached to the crossbeams, a condo for wintering mice. They'd bashed everything else, yet here sat this cleaned-up kayak.

Take me.

"No no," I said chuckling. "No way. Not happening." I looked at Maggie. "We'll be taking the K9 unit."

Night was coming yet I knew I had to leave. I saw movement in the trees, scurrying silhouettes against the sky's violet crown.

I HAD WATER, FOOD, MY bag and my dog. I sat behind the wheel of an Austin Police car with a full tank of gas. A loaded policeman's shotgun stood near the gearshift and my glock was strapped snug at my side. I opened a crisp map of Texas, plotted my general course under the dome light, and pulled out. Highway 71 south. All the way to Matagorda Bay.

FULL DARK BY THE TIME I reached the letter avenues intersecting Forty-Fifth. I haven't driven alone in the dark since chasing the train. That had felt different. I still had friends waiting at home.

No streetlights, no ambient light from storefronts. Pitch dark. Not even a moon shone for the rain. I had my brights on. No oncoming traffic to blind. Deer and cats darted across. "Slow and steady, steady and slow, that's the way we always go," I said to Maggie over my shoulder in Goofy the Disney dog's voice. Her tail thumped and she put her snout on my shoulder. I smelled bad egg sulfur and Nate's blood.

The blood smell reminded me of feral kids. This was no river. When would the windshield turn into stars from thrown stones?

FORTY-FIFTH STREET CROSSES TRAIN TRACKS before the airport which takes you out southwest to Highway 71.

We rolled slowly like we're patrolling.

Maggie growled in my ear.

There.

They suddenly appeared in the headlights along the train tracks as if arising from the earth itself. They stood in rank after tight rank like a phalanx of Trojans. I stopped the car, flipped on the search light. I dragged the beam slowly along them, examined each face in the front row. Mannequins in the cold rain. Not a pair of eyeglasses rested on a nose. They blinked in dolorous synchronicity. They didn't utter a sound, didn't move. Though winter approached, they wore no coats. Some wore the pajamas they woke up in the morning of, some the filthy clothes of that morning, what they would've worn to kindergarten and elementary school. They quaked and stood stone-faced.

Despite my ire toward them, in that moment I found myself suddenly overwhelmed with the need to connect to them. I felt such pity for them. I craved the ability to expand my reach so that I could surround them with my arms and hold them tight and tell them we are all going to be okay like I had Johnny and Nate.

I know they did what they did mindlessly, without conscience. When an animal does something vile yet in its nature, you find it abhorrent, but you understand. You can forgive it. Although what Maggie and the Utopia dogs did was beyond abhorrent—the thought of him running from them in his panic with that basket of eggs, their baying and snarling and running him down and when he screamed they tore into him even more. But, ultimately, I could forgive them.

But these are human children. They've woken up to this new world and they haven't a clue what's happening. I can forgive them.

I put my lips to the loudspeaker handset. I pressed the button. "I forgive you." It came out loud and authoritative.

The rain came down harder and they shook more.

"Let me by, at least," I demanded.

They moved shoulder to shoulder in one quick motion. It was a bit more than that, dear reader. A bit more than shoulder to shoulder like the von Trapp children.

Their faces all morphed. A wave radiated through.

My heart beat in my ears.

I got out and stood behind the open car door holding the handset. "Why?" I called out to them in a plangent voice, almost begging. "Why won't you let me go?"

I flicked on the red-and-blue lights. Nothing. I blasted the siren. Nothing. Not a blink. Nothing but shivering bodies so tight they looked woven together.

I looked closer. I was the one blinking in the rain, in disbelief.

Maggie rumbled low from the back seat.

I got back in and put the car into drive and pulled up so that we were twenty feet from them. The headlights and emergency lights splashed all over them. Their eyelids flexed in the lights and rain. Drops sparked as they passed through the beams.

Their shivering became shaking. Then it became a fearsome quaking, set to explode.

Their flesh—at their bare places, elbows, knees, ears, and even cheeks. The skin started to…join.

The white stuff. A mesh of it flung out like webbing, conjoining them. Before my eyes, in seconds, that latticework thickened. They formed a human wall.

I put my shaking hand to my mouth. My body and mind thrummed with ancient terror.

All the noise in the world was the sound of rain hitting the pavement and car metal and Maggie's throat rumbling. In my rearview I saw the silhouette of her hackles rise. I felt my hair and skin rise and turn to gooseflesh.

The kids' skin morphed and connected. Ours rose and spiked.

Organisms displaying vital tropisms at a standoff.

In park, I revved the engine, let it fall off. I repeated this, the car lifting and surging, hoping to threaten them. Angry with them, I threw open the door, pulled out the glock, stood between car and door, and drew the gun down on them.

They stepped forward. I didn't move. They came at me, moving together. The lines of them extended beyond the road. They rose together out of the foliage and trees on both sides. Before they could surround the car, I jumped in and reversed with the pedal floored.

Fifty yards up the street from them, I spun the car around, stopped, and looked in my rearview. They, too, had stopped, and I could just see that they drew apart into individual beings again.

The rearview mirror shook with the police car's acceleration.

It stood behind the children.

Its spread wings spanned beyond the road.

I'M FLYING DOWN SOUTH ON Red River, trying to beat them over on to I-35. Up ahead looms UT's indoor athletic practice facility, which had been a huge white dome made of air-inflated fabric. The dome was gone; the thing looking like a collapsed cake.

I swung a hard left and there they were, spanned across Dean Keeton Street.

Back down Red River I flew, past the stadium, through MLK, assuming they'd have an established checkpoint there too. Past Brackenridge Hospital, through the Red River music district. I didn't want to cut over yet, didn't want to lose time against them.

There couldn't be enough of them to cut me off at every turn. At some point they'd get spread too thin. I get down to First Street going freeway speeds, catching air in this police cruiser more than once, Maggie hitting her head on the ceiling.

When they were all together like that, I knew I couldn't physically get through. I couldn't do it anyway, plow into them like that idiot at South by Southwest a few years ago, at Charlottesville. If I did, I'd take the first three rows of kids out, but they'd be all glued together like that and by sheer mass and size they'd stymie and surround me.

Then what? I didn't know.

I thought of Nate as the dogs surrounded to him. His cries echoing the cliffs.

The frontage road to I-35 becomes visible. I punch it. I'm getting through. I'm laughing with Maggie. We come over the rise doing eighty and I imagine thousands of children running to this spot realizing that they aren't going to make it and their collective panic rising into some frenzied quantum entity capable of doing things I can't conceive.

We take the rise. We catch air. My headlights skim the clouds. Rain drops little meteors. I'm flying.

The tires hit the pavement and there it is. A pile of everything they could get their little hands on, all smashed and swirled together forming a macabre mountain, a mockery of the old world. Reminded me of the pile of furniture in the bottlenecked street in *Les Misérables*, but this one was lined with corrugated metal and an actual stop sign they'd transplanted into the middle of it all. It was thick, it was tall, and it covered the access road and well beyond into the dark. Off-roading over the wet ground, down the slope, would be chancy at best.

The stop sign bore their handprints like paleo cave walls.

They'd done this everywhere, I knew. In every street out of the city there would be old-world heaps. Busy beavers while I was gone. Sure, I could try to blow them up with scavenged explosives (blowing my hands off and bleeding to death in the process) or plow through them with a vehicle from Camp Mabry. And let's say I could even start making headway through. They'd be waiting for me on the other side.

They'd act on fear. They'd just as soon jab me with pointed sticks like Jack's gang in *Lord of the Flies* than lift me on their shoulders, their hero.

They'd already destroyed anything I could've used to go around or get through. I'd find tires slashed, engine blocks smashed. I was still holding on to hope of some sort of control, a solution based in the old-world way of thinking, which is the only way I knew to think.

They were going to show me another way. It had to be their way.

They'd let me back in but now they wouldn't let me leave.

I heard them coming, a rumbling herd in the dark closing in. They sang-hummed. That flanged polyphonic nightmare-dream sick-sweet sound rode the air into my mind. They flew through the night, leaping and climbing over anything that got in their way. Night of the locusts.

THE SUITE AT THE W Hotel was heaven. The sheets, dry and crisp and smelling of industrial soap. There was the stink, to be sure, but once I climbed up to the tenth floor, the smell dissipated. I looked out over the black city. Not a single light, fire, nothing but abject darkness. The only light in this entire city was my flashlight flitting about the room.

I'm sure they all looked up at my window, the light swirling around inside.

MY ALARM DIDN'T GO OFF and it's SAT day. My alarm didn't go off and I'm in a New York hotel and the parade is over. Nobody came to wake me.

I was late. Kodie needed me and she was so very far away.

To get a better view, I had run up to the top of the hotel, wandered breathless toward the first open room door I saw. Outside the door stood a housekeeping cart, spray bottles hooked along the side.

The woman from housekeeping lay on the bathroom floor. I couldn't look long. Nature had carted away most of her flesh. It stunk, but not so bad as in the first days. Fat angry flies jumped from her to me. I ran out and slammed the door. The next open door was to a big suite, windows open to half the city.

They had done it. On every road out of town. Piles of stuff dammed up onramps, freeways, regular streets that led out of the city. From up here I saw the rough pattern of their blockades formed a huge circle. If I managed to get through or around, it'd be the wall of flesh again.

Lady Bird Lake, Lake Austin, thinning down into the Colorado River. The morning sun burnished it silver atop the blue and green.

The path of no resistance is the river.

An umbilicus to the womb of the world.

I LASHED THE BOAT SLAPDASH to the top of the police car, went inside, picked up my trombone case inside which, checking it a last time before departing, I found this recorder. I don't remember putting this in there (kids could've), but it was there and here we are, dear reader. It's you and me now.

I PUT IN AT THE Austin Rowing Center. The water from all the rains without river regulation had filled up the lake behind Tom Miller Dam. I could see water coming over the top of it. Water must have been spilling over Mansfield Dam up at Lake Travis to be filling up Lake Austin.

My eyes bulged at the sight of the water coming down. Not your docile blue-green urban waterway anymore. Foam eddied and swirled in angry chocolate water. Debris, limbs, and small trees floated by. Nature took things back. Soon these dams would break from the pressure. Clearly, the Longhorn downriver already had. The valley below Mount Bonnell must be a hundred feet higher now, all those palaces along the river under water. I just hoped the dams don't break when I'm on the water, or within a mile from shore for that matter.

If it didn't get too rough downriver, all this water ought to help me because I won't have to get out and portage the twelve-foot boat. All the places along the river I could rely on for food would be flooded out now.

PARKING ON VETERANS DRIVE, I dragged the boat across the crushed gravel hike and bike trail down to the rowing center which, with the heavy flow of water, was creaking and about to burst away from shore.

I had to make several trips to the car and back. I almost forgot my $1,000 binoculars. Maggie stayed on the wide wooden dock, watching me go back and forth. As I was coming back over the trail for the last time, I heard her barking.

Across the river they stood. A long line of them as far as I could see in either direction. I stood with my hands on my hips and scanned the line of them, a hundred yards away from me. Between us, this mad river.

Toddlers to tweens stood among the trees. They waited to see me disembark, for once on the river, on the river I would stay.

I stowed a gym bag of clothes, my trombone case, an umbrella, a pot, and a couple of long-necked utility lighters in the storage compartment behind me and stuffed as much junk food, beef jerky and apples as I could everywhere else.

I sat in the boat, held my oar across my lap. I had to coax Maggie but she stepped into the front well gingerly. Her legs shook.

I SHOVED OFF. IT FELT wondrous to be fully buoyant. There's nothing like that feeling, your body instantly recognizing the gestation sensation. The buoyancy forces you to take in and let out a huge, deep, cleansing breath. I felt a heavy pang of missing my father as I eased into the water's rhythms. I was a pretty skilled and experienced paddler for my age, having gone out a ton with my dad when I was young. My dad was a total kayaker. A solo, lone wolf kind of guy. When I regurgitated this phrasing I'd picked up from Dad's pontifications to my mom, she'd said, "Hah, he certainly was a lone wolf. That's for sure." I knew now she was talking about his affair. Affairs.

Since he moved away I'd paddled less. Not Martin's thing—such the man's man hunter of deer and fowl—and not soccer-Johnny's thing either. But I still managed to get out a few mornings a season, on Sundays usually. My church.

The kids have been snooping my head. They know this comforts me. Gives me time to recount all this to you, dear reader. They want me to do that. I get a powerful sense of that.

Hold on, dear rea...they're hummsing to me on that thought. So strong...guess I struck a nerve . . .

ONCE I GOT GOING, I knew I was too heavy. I couldn't control the boat well and the water was hectic, water like I'd never known, unbound, moving on its own. Too heavy, but I couldn't jettison the dog, nor the trombone, nor the food because it was all I had and this was hundreds of miles. I had four half-gallon bottles of water. I'd have to make it last. I was glad for the cooler weather.

THEY DIDN'T NEED TO BURN the old world down. Most of human population was near water. When the dams broke, when the Panama Canal went bust, the water would flow and change the coastlines. When earthquakes and hurricanes came, there'd be no cleanup. When the tsunamis moved in . . .

The world's nuclear reactors. When would they start melting down? Were they already? How was I supposed to save the world's children from these things? I didn't know, but once I was a mile downriver and things stabilized, I felt good, like all would be solvable. Traveling does this. Provides perspective. I've come to believe that the beginning can happen, as Simon said, and I am its catalyst. I may know nothing about how to run a world, engineering and science, but I believe I can lead them. Kodie and I can do it.

Much later, when the time is right, we can try to understand Dr. Jespers's theory. I locked his computer in the trunk of my police cruiser on Veteran's Drive.[19]

I AFFIXED THIS RECORDER TO my jacket, Mr. E. The river has been high and easy to navigate. Most of this trip has been a dream. I've been floating and my mind has too and when they sing, they pull me toward them. As I've said before, I've lost hours of time feeling their song.

I don't need to paddle much. The water's been moving with the upstream influx. All I've had to do is dip my paddles to steer. I try to stay near the banks but they've overflowed so much that at times I'm afraid of getting caught up in drowned trees or an eddy.

The morning of, the children got a download, and I think I did too. The code has been buried within me until now. Now, on this river, it's starting to boot me up into this new me.

I tell you this story when I'm on shore before sleep, after boiling water and feeding Maggie, but mostly when I'm in easygoing miles-long sections. Telling this story has helped me process it all. It has kept me company, kept me hopeful, and has enabled me to see the bigger picture. It has tracked my journey, my evolution from the sounds heard that dawn to now.

---

19 Dr. Warren Jespers's recovered 2018 Dell HPC (High Performance Computer) is in a secure location.

I feel as if I am actually communing with you. Talking to whoever may read this, in a future that is hopefully settled and sane, it makes me feel good when nothing else does. That's as best I can say it.

But, really, I pretend. I pretend to have a conversation with someone else. There's hope in the noises I make. Like whistling past a graveyard.

THE RIVER HAD ITS NOISES, moaned and whispered its way to the sea. Birds followed us overhead, their wingspan at full sail in these new winds.

"What do you think, killa? Should I begin way back in June when I was having those dreams while reading *Lord of the Flies*, writing *The Late Bloomers*, Johnny's sleepwalking?"

Mags looked back at me, these being the first words I'd uttered since we veered away from the rowing center's platform. The hinges holding the thing to the shore had screamed as we paddled clear. The shipwrecked kids in *Lord of the Flies* feared a beast. The naval officer says at the end, "Fun and games." Then the boys all cry, smudging their war paint. They are saved. The end.

Maybe I'm the naval officer. I come by boat. When I arrive, Kodie and I will convince them that there is nothing to fear. The world has changed, but this beast is just a residual nightmare representing all that fear that has come with such sudden, jarring change. Change is their beast. I'll help them.

I COULD TELL YOU ABOUT this float trip, but that's not what this story is about. And really, it's just a river swollen over pastoral Texas, trees and hills, a few towns. The water is so high now, the towns on the river flooded. The tops of trees, rooftops, commercial signage sticking up just above the surface looking like eerie buoys.

Cruising by the Hyatt Lost Pines resort hotel, I could see right into the rooms of the third floor, the top. The kayak brushed against the metal patio bars. Maggie's ears perked; she peered inside, too. Pillows floated. We'd gone there for a family trip about three years ago. Johnny and I played in the little water park. We had a good time, though I was always wary of looking like a tool in front the girls sunning themselves at the pool. Mom read a thick paperback (though she kept stashing it, I knew it was *Fifty Shades*). Martin would meet us for dinner each night all sunburned, beer-blitzed and talking loud with golfing buddies. She and Martin weren't talking much.

Paddling under Highway 71 and later I-10, I looked up and thought my head clearance was questionable. Dark and unnerving and full of echoes.

Maggie keeps watch at night. I catch her copping Zs during the day, standing there swaying with her eyes closed. Sometimes she just curls up in the front well.

I ration my jerky. I drink my boiled water. I'm so tired I'm in a daze. They help me. Their singing helps me. I don't see them, but they're out there. I wish they'd talk to me. I'll just keep talking to you.

I'LL SHARE A MEMORY. I haven't and won't go into a bunch of stuff from my life, mostly because it makes me too sad to think about. Though this is about my experience during these early days of the new world, here's one far-back memory I like to hold on to.

It's of me and Mom and Dad. This is when I'm young, like six, a couple of years before they got divorced and Dad moved across the country. I guess I hold on to this because it's the last time I can remember our threesome being happy together. Not saying there weren't other times, just saying this is the strong one that popped into my head. The ground in the front yard was hard underneath the blanket we'd put down. This was in the first house I ever lived in, the one I came home from the hospital to, on Waterston, not far from Town Lake, which is what it was called back then.

Fourth of July, evening. We awaited the fireworks display which would shoot over the lake. We could see the whole thing from our front yard. Dad had a radio out there with us and the classical station played the patriotic marches, but what I remember is the 1812 Overture. We had finished eating grilled hot dogs, potato salad, and apple pie and we were just waiting for darkness to come.

Dad and Mom lay on the blanket facing each other propped on their elbows. I was drinking a Coke in a tall beveled glass bottle. They drank from glass bottles too. The ground was too hard for me so I marched around, knees up, chin up, officious look on my face, hamming it up for my folks. They laughed so hard that Mom's forehead fell against Dad and she snorted. I just kept going and then they got up and fell in behind me. We marched all over the yard, then up the street still within earshot of the music, and back again.

It got dark and we'd forgotten ourselves. Then a big boom. We stood in the street in front of our house, and the thundering sound scared us and Dad picked me up, held Mom close. We looked up and there was the first firework, huge, in bloom and expanding. We could hear the faraway crowd cheering. Mom, Dad and me holding each other tight, the initial fear wearing off, standing in the street looking up.

Just as I finish having this memory, replaying it for you now…this is when I hear the children, thousands of them amassed in the dark, cheering, and it sounds so much like what my memory tells me I heard that July night eleven years ago that it makes me cry.

On the bank of this engorged river, it's finally hitting me.

There's a heaviness in my throat and in my chest and I know that this is what mourning feels like.

Maggie's tied to me with a leash. She comes over to me as I cry and leans into me.

They kept cheering and cheering in a mad loop. Finally, I had cried myself out and then they stopped. But there's no sleep.

Nope, I lie awake, talk to you, looking up at an array of stars like I've never seen, what the ancients saw when they looked up and now I understand the awe and fear they must have felt. With all of our lights and rationality, we humans lost our awe. At least the adults did.

As for the late bloomers like me, like Kodie, we're stuck in the middle. And in the middle in which I am now stuck I am feeling pretty damned awed.

I lie here under this incredible smear of starshine and want to be awed some more, but I keep thinking of the webbing jumping between them as they stood in front of the tracks.

Out there they anticipate my every breath. They breathe with me, a sighing sound that starts to merge with the sounds of the ocean in my mind.

I feel their need.

MAGGIE SMELLS IT FIRST. SHE'S been probing the air with her nose all morning, drawing in big drams of it. I know we're getting close. When under the hot light of a south Texas morning I see the first fronds of a palm tree poking above the water's surface and I smell the ocean's salt, my pulse speeds up and stays there.

THERE'S BEEN NOTHING SINCE CROSSING under Route 59. Not a town, not a landmark, nothing but treetops and the tops of a few sturdy windmills and far-off gas station signs. I must've skirted Bay City east of the river and another, Buckeye, which was just west of the river. Maybe those things sticking up earlier was Buckeye.

I'm just steering. This river swells and swells as it nears the bay. When Maggie first smelled the scent of the sea, she'd whined a little, looked back at me a lot. I think she smells the sea's vastness, the stink of what rots at the beach, and most of all—she smells them.

THE SMELL WAS TAMPED BY more light rain from the Gulf as I'd pulled off to camp for the night. I had to be pretty close to the Intracoastal Waterway which flowed laterally along the coast, located just south of the town of Matagorda.

Evening and now I'm hearing it. The thud and roar of the breakers. I needed sleep. Once I rounded the town of Matagorda, I'd have to paddle my way down through the brackish alluvium of the huge bay. This freaks me out because though I've always enjoyed kayaking, I've only paddled rivers and lakes. I don't care to be paddling out at sea.

I can fight my way up the Intercoastal Waterway a bit after the town of Matagorda, I can cruise down its southern leg to the peninsula without having to cross that bay where the Colorado dumps into the west bay. But with the river so high, I'll be paddling like a madman upstream for a mile, maybe more. If I can do it, it'll be a nice float down there, just a few miles. The Lower Colorado River Authority ran a nature park down at the beach. That's where I want to head.

After all, kids like parks.

DAWN. I DREAMT THE DREAM of sleep. Maggie stands on the riverbank facing the sea.

As we approach the new western edge of the town of Matagorda, I tell her, "We're going to have to hump it northeast. Ready for that?" I slalom between the roofs and telephone poles of Matagorda. I now paddle past the top of a sign with a pirate parrot with an eye patch and a mug of beer curled in its wing—*Matagordaville.*

FROM HERE, DEAR READER, I'M documenting as I go. This story writes itself now. It's crossed over into immediate reportage. No longer a memoir. Nope. Your intrepid reporter is finally at the place and time where the past and the future meet. Where the old world meets new world. Where the land meets sea. Still got this microphone clipped to my collar. Sorry if my speech is harder to hear and all that because I'll be moving and talking. Choppier, less prosaic. All happening in real time. I'll keep talking as things develop.

This is Kevin March, reporting. Back to you, Bob.

OKAY, NOW I'M AT THAT spot where if I go left, and it's wanting to pull me that way... hold on. Okay, I see the other route. Gotta paddle hard for a while. Please hold.[20]

OKAY—*WHEW!*—THE WATERWAYS MEET IN SOME places here where I know they're supposed to be separate. Looks like five hundred feet or so and I'll be out of the either/or zone.

Straightforward float now. On my left to the east are the tops of palm trees and among them rooftops of what must have been river-to-the-sea homes. More telephone poles lining the flooded road.

ALL ABRUPTLY ENDS AND NOW I cruise this channel. The sun rises ochre brass and carnation pink into a sky brushed with cloud wisps. I can't see it yet, but the sea is there ahead of me. I'm here.

Looking for a place to pull off and walk to the Matagorda peninsula's beach. It's part of the long barrier island stretching for miles on the Texas coast. Hopefully, that nature park is still there. I think most of the Colorado's floodwater veered off to the west. We'll see.

---

20 The sounds of heavy breathing and water splashing, presumably from paddling.

Man, it's beautiful out here, isn't it Mags? The only thing is the smell. Can't see them yet, all those whales that beached themselves the morning of.

THERE IT IS. LOOK AT that, Maggie! Gulf of Mexico.

Looks like a dredger there in the mouth got turned over. The beach here—on the east side of the river to my left, right before the long seawall creating the channel out to the mouth—the sand is white. Lumpy sand dunes with tufts of grasses. I can see some buildings to my left. Must be the nature park. All these beautiful white sandhill cranes standing around. Hundreds. Their heads moving down to the sand, back up to look at me.

RUNNING THIS KAYAK ONTO THIS beach before the seawall and I really do wonder if this has been a dream. It doesn't seem real. None of it has. Not since the moment I heard those sounds. Part of why I had to record this story. Just to try to make it real for myself. It's been like recording a dream I just had. Sometimes that was literally true, huh?

I wouldn't do it to you. Don't you hate that? When you've invested your finite life's time in a long book; or you've watched some movie and at the end *it was all just a dream*. *The Wizard of Oz* pulled it off, but other than that, it's like, what the hell, are you kidding me?

Not a dream. This happened.

So, what is this? What's happened to me, the human race? Dr. Jespers was on to something, and that something required the action of an intelligence we don't understand. Mr. Fleming took a stab. I lean their way. I haven't asked this so directly yet, and neither did my friends who were with me. We danced around it. Too big a question. You're not going to get any facile exposition here, dear reader, no end-of-tale Scooby-Doo explanatory rehash. Sorry. I just don't know what happened. *Yet.*

What will you make of it, I wonder? Will you liken it to Old Testament wrath, like Noah with his flood and couplings of kinds? A Rapture in which all adults are taken?

On the SAT it'd say or *D, None of the above.* Maybe that's what I choose as I find myself walking this half mile across white sand to the seawall, weaving between dunes with my dog, these grasses grazing my legs, carrying my trombone case, my $1,000 binoculars, and my boat bag with the dregs of jerky and sunflower seeds, Professor Fleming's letter, Dr. Jespers's paper, and Kodie's note.

IF I'M WRONG ABOUT EVERYTHING, if you've all survived this, and you've listened up to now—because I don't know what comes next—Mom, Dad, Martin, Mr. English…just know…I'm really glad I did this. It has kept me company, kept me whistling on this swollen river past all those graveyards.

I wish I could click my red sequined heels together three times, say there's no place like home, and wake up and it's game day and I've got some explaining to do but it'll all work out.

Once you dream the dream of sleep, you don't ever dream again, the dividing line between dream and reality erased. The line between the old world and new one gone.

My answer? Yep, it's D, None of the above.

So, there you have it. My first book. First draft. *Finito.*

As they say in ham radio-speak: Over and out.

I'M PINNING[21] THE MICROPHONE TO the inside of my shirt now, running the wire down under my clothes to the device in my back pocket. I want to keep telling you what's happening, but for obvious reasons I can't keep a running commentary of *everything*, nor can I reflect on it or fill out the full picture in the way, hopefully, I did earlier. I want you to hear it all. Listen to the constant ambient sounds of sea and gulls crying.[22] I'll be describing visuals to you mostly. And some of what I'm feeling. Deal? It's this or nothing, and, well, we've come this far. It'd feel wrong just cutting it off behind the seawall. After all, this is what we came for.

Waking life abuts dreaming life.

Okay. [sigh] Moving forward.

Whaddya say, Miss Maggie, shall we climb to the top of this wall to see what all the fuss is about?

Stepping nearer to the wall. Way beyond it I hear a thudding, the squeak and scream of stressed wet wood.

---

21 Close scratching and thumping noises.

22 There is a pause here. KGM wants us to listen.

IN THE SHADOW OF THE seawall now. I feel sick.

Though I haven't seen a kid for days and miles, now I hear them.

Oh—

Their song welcomes. You hear that?[23] One note. Beautiful. Layered harmonics, and though it comes from their throats and out their mouths, it is sourceless, endless, and without rhythm. They sing for my arrival. They rejoice!

Listen to that!

Climbing up the sandy slope to the top of the wall now. Scrambling on all fours. Would be easier without the trombone and binoculars.

I hope you can hear that. Beyond that low, constant sound of the breakers, the clatter of surf on hard pack, its hissing retreat—I hope you can hear it. Though they've sung and hummed their lullabies to me often on this trip, it's never been like this. This is…I don't know. Divine.

I STAND ATOP THE SEAWALL. I look down on the beach now [sounds of KGM's fast and heavy breathing].[24]

They fill the beach. All those little faces…facing me. Hundreds of thousands.

My eye is drawn out to the horizon. Blue and gray. Darker than sea and sky. There's something out there.

Way beyond the white line of breakers, something…I see a…Is that a deep-sea oil-drilling platform? Yeah. Gotta be. But what…*sits* on top of it? Can't be a helicopter. It's as big as the platform. The indistinct winged thing I think I've been seeing wasn't so big as to take up all the space on a drilling platform. But it's so far away. It heliographs fiercely whenever I try to look at it. I don't see it when I'm looking through the binoculars though. It's when I take them away and squint. That's when I see the shape.

Naked eye, there it is, shimmering, bouncing that sunlight at me. Through the binoculars, it's not there. Yet it is. That space is…full. It's opaque and it shimmers. I see the ocean through it.

23 There is a pause here. KGM wants us to listen. The sounds of singing and humming grow louder.

24 Ambient or non-vocal sounds as well as voice descriptions, e.g., whispering, shouting, will be inserted between brackets instead of footnoted for the remainder of the document as the sounds often directly impact, edify, and sometimes modify what is being said.

Don't have time to ponder this quirk of ocular physics because just as I'm noticing this thing out there, they sing louder with harmonics that want to split my head with euphoria. Listen to that! I feel a rising, blooming, bloodwarm…joy. This scene, the sea, the breeze, the scree of birds, the singing of multitudes of children, my feet rooted to the top of this seawall. It's glorious.

What must the children think of me talking to myself up here? They're used to it, I suppose. I've been talking to you for days. And if not you, this dog.

Maggie, you're trembling. It's okay. Oh-kay. I put my hand on her head. She's shaking. Poor girl. You stay with me. You'll be all right.

IT MOVES [WHISPERING]. ADJUSTS ITSELF, like it's just alighted there and now settles in for a long wait. It's miles out there. If I can make it out from here…How big is it?

The mass of children fills the beach out to the water and under the long jetty fishing pier that stretches out a couple hundred yards out into the surf. Matagorda barrier island splits just off to the west and I don't see them beyond that, but in the other direction, to the east, they fill the beach for as far as I can see. Among them are the whale carcasses. I don't know how many. By the holes among the kids, there's fifty, maybe more up the beach. With the binocs I can see a few of their rotting jaws agape.

There are a couple of whales floating and rolling with the surf near the beach, running up against the jetty pier's concrete columns. Big ones, black and gray. When they roll into the pier there's a thudding and a wet-wood squeak. Shark fins pop up all around them. I can see one thrashing and tugging with a mouthful, its eyes rolled back white. In the frenzy the water whitens and foams.

DEAR READER, GOTTA TELL YOU: there's fear in this much ecstasy. They fill me with it. Euphoria, intoxication like I can't explain. I want to laugh out loud, I brim so.

I feel the burden of their need. They need me. They hum now, low. Competes with the waves' roar and hiss, the pier's thud and squeak. They pull me.

I fall apart here…I can't explain. I just can't. What I'm seeing, hearing, feeling. When a writer can't do that, he puts his utensil aside and waits. Maybe he comes back and picks it up again. Maybe he doesn't because he just can't, and more, doesn't want to. The story finishes for him and it's then that it belongs to the world and to time.

The elation I feel is exquisite. I could die feeling this good.

ALAS, MAGS. A BEACH. WHERE we crawled from the smile. I mean slime. Heh. Feeling a little woozy. Sitting a seawall sit in the sun. Hey, alliteration. All litter rationed.

THAT THING JUST SITS OUT there. I know it moved. I saw it. Staring contest it wants? Fine.

THE KIDS MAKE ME FEEL welcome with their humsong, yet they won't approach. Like one wouldn't approach a powerful force, a hot electrical wire, or wild flames. The euphoria I feel juxtaposed to their wariness of me. Cognitive dissonance doesn't cut it as a description because it's beyond mere cognition.

THE SUN MARKS THE SKY's midpoint. Time I stand up. I'm standing to face them, reader. When I lock my knees, their singing stops. Maggie sits next to me. The euphoria lifts up and away, venting out through the top of my head so suddenly I think I might throw up.

I think of that lipsticked nurse and that little girl. How I threw up right there on the Hancock Bridge.

THUD. SQUEAK. HERE, LISTEN. [THUD-SQUEAK of whales hitting pier]

The thing perched on the drilling platform. Does machinery move and flinch like that? It's miles out there. It could be anyth—

—wait. Way out on the pier. The very end of it. I hear a voice! Solid, old-world weight and fricative. Not a nauseous song.

I'm wincing through the bright. She's walking, now running down the pier to shore.

Kodie.

I'M JOGGING ALONG THE TOP of the seawall. [breathless] Toward the dunes in front of the nature center. She's running parallel to me on the fishing pier which is about a hundred yards to my right heading inland. She's running and waving.

"Kevin!"

Is she glad or fearful? Seems like she's good. No kids running after her. C'mon, Maggie! Let's go see Kodie!

THE KIDS KNOW TO BACK up, give us room, we relics of the old world reconnecting. I'm on the beach in front of thousands and thousands of them. I feel the weight of their stares. Their faces contain ghosts of smiles. They all have the same look, measured in the same amount of ghost. I scan for Johnny. No eyeglasses on any of them. Not one.

Here she comes. Wearing new clothes, like a wispy sarong wrapped around her hips. Toga-like scarves and stuff on her torso. Barefoot. I'll shut up now.

KJL[25]: YOU CAME! YOU'RE ACTUALLY here! Oh my god. [the microphone pops and scrapes, sounds of deep long kissing]

KGM: When they took you, I thought you were—

KJL: Oh no! No no no! They've been good to me. They've bathed me, fed me, sang to me. They put me in…*this.*

KGM: You look good.

KJL: I feel fine. Unsure, but okay. I'm good, actually. Believe it or not. I've been in such a daze, though. How long has it been? What's this? [tapping sound]

KGM: What? Oh, yeah. On my way down here, hazy days, maybe a week? I've been recording what happened to us since the morning of. Like a woefully raw and unedited audiobook memoir.

KJL: Why?

KGM: You know I wanted to write. Dunno. For me. For us. So we don't forget. Make it a real book someday.

---

25 KJL is Kodie Janine Langenkamp

KJL: Hummm.

KGM: Because things are going to change.

KJL: Oh, I know.

KGM: This is a transition period. To remember these early days…You're nodding, smiling, blinking.

KJL: Yeah?

KGM: Sorry. Sometimes I may lean down into this mike and say something. I've been doing this for so long now, talking into this, to myself. This running commentary now…Maggie thinks I'm crazy.

KJL: Hi, Maggie. You kept her. All this time. Brought her with you all the way on the road. I can't believe it.

KGM: No. No no. The river. I kayaked down here from Lady Bird freaking Lake.

KJL: What?!

KGM: Yeah. They didn't tell you I was coming?

KJL: They don't talk, Kevin.

KGM: You wrote that note? How did—

KJL: What note?

KGM: Your handwriting. Look. [Velcro ripping, papers shuffling]

KJL: Um, yeah. My writing. I have no memory of that.

KGM: Is Johnny here?

KJL: Yeah. Out there on the pier with me.

KGM: Why were you all the way out there? *Johnny!*

KJL: They wanted me out there. I stopped asking why a long time ago. They take me wherever. I don't struggle. They're never mean. But they are rather insistent, just by their sheer numbers. Johnny says they won't be like this for much longer, things are about to change. Like you said, a transition period. Shaky and weird. [pause; beach sounds] Ah! You're here! But, wait. Hold on. You *kayaked*, with a dog, all the way from Austin?

KGM: Yes. Floated mostly. River's completely flooded. Nobody manning the damn systems upriver. Tons of rain, Austin, Utopia—

KJL: You were in Utopia?

KGM: I drove out there to see if maybe I could find those guys who contacted us on the radio.

KJL: Did you?

KGM: Nope. Nobody there.

KJL: What? What's wrong?

KGM: There was a kid there. Nate. They say anything to you?

KJL: Did Johnny say anything to me about a Nate? Huh-uh.

KGM: Look at that. Guess they're burning whales' blubber?[26]

KJL: Living on the fat-o'-the land.

KGM: They do this before?

KJL: Huh-uh.

KGM: How'd you stay warm?

KJL: Nature center.

KGM: They keep…guard?

KJL: Kind of. You know how they are. They don't do anything like it was done before. Whenever I'd stir in the night, get up to go to the bathroom—

KGM: The water works here?

KJL: Oh hell no. No. Out in the sand.

KGM: Oh.

KJL: Yeah. So, when I stir or start wandering around they just kind of show up. The numbers increase as needed. Reminds me very much of how ranch dogs herd. They just kind of…insinuate violence. They hardly ever touch me. Their numbers just increase as I get more and more agitated.

KJL: You try to run off?

---

26 Evening now, by the time stamp. It is believed they sit above the beach on the sea wall.

KJL: Oh yeah. I've tested them a few times. They won't let it happen. They surround, urge you back, create these corridors with their bodies. So quick, it's just…well, it's frightening. They seem so on edge. Jumpy. Especially in the last day or so. Guess you were getting close.

KGM: Fighting some internal conflict. Yeah. I got that from Nate's behavior.

KJL: Hmm.

KGM: Johnny, and that Simon kid on the day of, and then Nate in Utopia, they all said there was a beginning coming. I think you and I together, here, mark it, cause it.

KJL: They do seem docile now that you're here.

KGM: All the way down, every fifty yards. Those whale fires going on into the dark.

KJL: Hmmmm. Pretty.

KGM: But you're okay, right? No attacks of white stuff?

KJL: No more coughing either, huh-uh. In fact, after the shock of them taking me, and me losing some time there, I've been incredibly bored. The new world is boring. Watching them gather and hum and fish.

KGM: Fish?

KJL: Yeah. Oh man, you won't believe it. They've got it down. No tools, nets, boats.

KGM: Yeah?

KJL: Yeah. They go out in teams. They're good, I mean, like you wouldn't believe. One thing about these kids is that there's no hierarchy or leadership. But it's always a complete mix of older kids and younger. Little mentorships going on. I guess the older ones tend to be stronger and faster, but the little ones hold their own.

KGM: Speaking of little ones. I haven't seen babies. And I don't hear any crying.

KJL: Oh, they're there. Just they're out in the middle of them. How they protect them, I guess. I mean, Kevin, they're a new species, okay? I know we batted this around in Austin, but I've been with them for a while now and I'm telling you it's...you and I are...I don't even know. New rules, that's all I know.

KGM: Are you scared?

KJL: See, that's the thing. I've felt very...okay. Very pacified. It's like I've been euphoric, some times more than others. Usually at dawn it's most intense.

KGM: Me too. On the way down here they'd lay into me. Man, it's—

KJL: —ecstasy.

KGM: Yes.

KJL: Actually, your arrival today? I knew you were here not because I saw you. I felt you.

KGM: How?

KJL: I felt normal. Old world. Gravity and heaviness, at home in my own skin. I actually settled into myself, and I don't mean psychologically or emotionally. I mean I felt my bones tug, my pelvis and skull feel the weight again. I felt...tethered, like I wasn't about to lift off into the sky like those sparks out there, as I have for days and days.

KGM: You're pointing.

KJL: Huh?

KGM: I'm just telling the recorder here that you're pointing out at the beach fires.

KJL: Ah, right.

KGM: Now you're nodding. Nodding and pointing doesn't work. Say something so the court reporter can hear you.

KJL: Oh, sorry. Yes, your honor. [Kodie's voice loud and close to the microphone]

KGM: Actually, it's dear reader.

KJL: Huh?

KGM: Who I've been talking to.

KJL: That's cute. *Dear reader*. You're cute.

KGM: You're batting your eyes at me. You mock.

KJL: I'm a mystery wrapped in an enigma.

KGM: How'd you get down here?

KJL: I don't know.

KGM: Really. You remember nothing. What do you remember?

KJL: Flashlight beams crisscrossing over all those stones. Screaming "no".

KGM: That's when I went out. They tackled me. So much for nonviolence.

KJL: Really though, they haven't been. Not once since I've been with them.

KGM: But they won't let you leave.

KJL: True.

KGM: And how's that not violent? Kidnapped by kids.

KJL: You know what I mean. They haven't physically hurt me. Fed me. Kept me warm. Let me have the run of the nature center.

KJL: A cage at the zoo.

KJL: If you look at it that way.

KGM: I do.

KJL: Don't think I haven't thought that too. That's how I've felt at times. Serious case of Stockholm Syndrome has overtaken me. And the kid-ecstasy has certainly helped. [sounds of the ocean; whales rubbing against the pier; sounds of gulls crying]

KJL: Can you declare your love to me on that thing? Make an official record of it.

[sounds of the ocean; whales rubbing against the pier; sounds of gulls crying]

KGM: What's happened?

KJL: [pause] It's a reset, I think.

KGM: Clicking refresh.

KJL: Nature, God, she's hit the reset button on humans. The whales are collateral damage.

KGM: Jespers's Gene. Fleming's letter. I've been reading Jespers's paper. I can see why his peers didn't review it favorably.

KJL: Yeah. His lab-slash-lair certainly raised hair on my neck. To see our names on his whiteboard. Do you really think what he was doing in some way caused this?

KGM: My Grandma Lucille once told me there's no such thing as coincidence. In all the thinking, and talking, I've been doing on my way down here I've come to believe her. Best I can gather is Jespers was scratching the surface of something bigger than we can understand and that maybe it triggered the event that morning.

KJL: I don't think he was alone. There was that guy in France he was talking to.

KGM: I get the feeling a cabal of big-brained people like them were on to something.

KJL: If there were any scientists and theologians left, the debate would be raucous.

KGM: Yep.

KJL: Why did we make it? You're shrugging.

KGM: Look at those fires.

KJL: No, really.

KGM: We've got the conch. The keepers of the flame.

[sounds of the ocean; whales rubbing against the pier; sounds of gulls crying]

KJL: Something I haven't told you.

KGM: What.

KJL: I'm pregnant.

1 [sounds of the ocean; whales rubbing against the pier; sounds of gulls
2 crying]

3

4 KGM: [WHISPERING] WE HAVE TO try to escape.

   KJL: You insane? No way.

5 KGM: I still have my gun. And Maggie here.

6 KJL: I told you. I tried. It's impossible.

7

8 KGM: You were alone. Two of us can do it, I think.

9 KJL: How many bullets you have there? I mean…they need us, Kevin. I
10 don't think—

11 KGM: I thought that. They had me thinking that, coming down here. The
   dreams. You and Bass kept telling me I'm special. I think you've been given
12 a whole lot of Kool-Aid.

13

14 KJL: I'm sorry. What did you just say to me?

   KGM: Not your fault. I don't know. Maybe they want to keep us.
15

16 KJL: C'mon. *Keep* us? For what? I don't think their intentions are sinister. I
   really don't. I think they're very confused.
17

18 KGM: Yeah, but…it doesn't feel right. It never has. I've offered to help. We've
   offered. They don't take us up on it.
19

20 KJL: But I don't—

21 KGM: They're too different now. I think what we are is in the way. They've
22 been battling against something since day one. Now that I'm here, this
   doesn't feel *right*. I'm telling you.
23

24 KJL: Kevin, then why didn't they just destroy us when they had the chance?
   Why did they stop that night, kill Bastian, and leave us? Just us?
25

26 KGM: If I knew that…Maybe they want us to reproduce for them. Create an
   underclass, a slave race.

27

28 KJL: Oh, you're being silly.

   KGM: I'm not trying to be silly.

KJL: They brought me here, they brought you here, why separately, I don't know. Clearly they fear you, but respect you on another level. Otherwise they would have brought us together. Oh, this is such guesswork. I don't know.

KGM: Why bring us at all? Have you tried to talk to them about why?

KJL: Of course. I've asked and asked. They don't answer. I don't think they know.

KGM: I don't think so either.

[sounds of the ocean; whales rubbing against the pier; sounds of gulls crying]

KJL: I AM NOT DEFENDING them! I'm just not seeing the facts the same way you are. You haven't been here. You haven't seen.

KGM: They've been saving you. You're pregnant. I think they used you to lure me down here. These repeated dreams where I'm sleeping. They seem so real. I dream I'm sleeping in this chrysalis thing and I'm tossing and stretching. Gestating.

KJL: Yeah, and…honestly, Kevin.

KGM: What? You're looking at me with a *duh* face.

KJL: You've been having dreams of me being pregnant. A typical man, you're terrified of fatherhood. Hel-lo? Attention. Calling Dr. Freud. Dr. Sigmund Freud. Please pick up a white courtesy phone.

KGM: Heh. But, I was dreaming that even before we did it. Know what I think?

KJL: What?

KGM: I think they need to keep us alive and breeding so that when they get old enough they can crossbreed with our offspring and…it's like they're haploids and we're haploids. This beginning stuff.

KJL: You're guessing.

KGM: Of course I'm guessing. And you're not? You want to stick around and find out? What life will we have here?

KJL: At least we'll have one.

[sounds of the ocean; whales rubbing against the pier; sounds of gulls crying]

KGM: I've never said I'm sure. Not about anything. But, if they really needed saving, you'd think there'd be a sense of urgency. They'd ask.

KJL: Looks like they're celebrating down there. They're gonna pop the question tonight: *Sir...*

KGM: Of course, they're Dickensian street kids. *Pardon me, but suh...*

KJL: Right. Heh. *Suh, will you 'elp us?*

KGM: [laughing]

KJL: Why do you have to see this as bad? You've been advocating the theory that this is all evolution. An abrupt jump.

KGM: I never told you that.

KJL: You didn't?

KGM: No. I told this that. [thumping the microphone]

KJL: Huh. No, in the car you said...Oh, shit. Let's say they do need us to mix with them, to state it crudely.

KGM: No other way to state it. Let's not be politically correct here. Talk about old world.

KJL: So, let's just say. Why is that a bad thing? What are our choices?

KGM: I don't know. I've not known anything for sure since the day I was born.

KJL: Except that your mother loved you.

KGM: Okay. Sure.

KJL: And now you know that I do.

KGM: [pause] Back 'atcha, kid. I'm making pistol fingers and winking one eye.

KJL: Be serious for a moment.

KGM: Kodie, there are whales on fire up the beach and into the night more numerous than I can count. Hundreds of thousands, maybe a million, kids on the beach among them, surrounding us. It's serious.

KJL: Yes, but you're not.

KGM: That's because I'm scared. When I'm scared I get unserious. You need to know that about me if we're going to repopulate the earth.

KJL: So say it then.

[sounds of the ocean; whales rubbing against the pier; sounds of gulls crying]

KGM: I love you, Kodie. How would you ever not know that? [pause] You're smiling self-righteously.

KJL: I do. It's just nice to hear you say it. [sounds of the ocean; whales rubbing against the pier; sounds of gulls crying]

KGM: WE SIT ABOVE THEM on the seawall, watching the fires, the silhouettes of children moving around them, noiseless. A silent million children groping for something in the dark. Winter's come here to the beach and they are cold in the sand. She puts her head on my shoulder and we watch them move under a sky of stars and a moon so pure and bright that it makes a silver trail on the ocean leading to the shore and us. A pathway to the fathomless deep.

KJL: Wanted to be a writer, eh?

KGM: Still can be.

KJL: Who'll buy your books? Doubt they read much.

KGM: I will write for myself. The craft is its own reward.

KJL: Ah, the mythical artiste.

KGM: I will write love sonnets for you. Batting your eyes again.

KJL: I kid. I'd love to hear one of your sonnets.

KGM: In time, me lady. [sighs; pause] These kids are humorless. Boring. Ain't got no soul.

KJL: Ever heard of a collective soul?

KGM: One-hit wonders?

KJL: No dummy, the—

KGM: Yes yes. You're being pseudo-intellectual. You don't know crap about it. You're just dropping the concept on me you read online from clickbait.

KJL: You're totally right. *Cosmo Online. O Magazine.*

KGM: She wraps an arm around me.

KJL: [Snort]

KGM: She laughs.

KJL: Dear reader can hear that I'm laughing.

KGM: Oh. Right.

KJL: Speaking of souls. You remember when Bastian said he saw that ghost in the Driskill?

KGM: Yep.

KJL: Think he was lying?

KGM: Why would he?

KJL: So you believe he saw that woman ghost on the top floor.

KGM: Yes, I think he saw her.

KJL: So, you believe in ghosts.

KGM: Didn't say that.

KJL: You're saying you think he thinks he saw her.

KGM: Yeah, that's right.

KJL: But you don't really believe in the truth of the matter asserted.

KGM: Run that by me again.

KJL: Dad was a lawyer. Sorry. What Bass said she said to him is hearsay.

KGM: Right. I guess. You're losing me. I'm only a pseudo-intellectual. A little slow.

KJL: He claimed to have witnessed something. He told us about his experience. But you don't believe him.

KGM: I believe he saw it. But whether or not it was really there I don't know for sure, no.

KJL: You ever see George Washington?

KGM: No.

KJL: Um…you ever see gravity?

KGM: Uh, no.

KJL: But you believe George Washington lived and you believe gravity to be a real phenomenon.

KGM: Yes.

KJL: Why?

KGM: Because I read about them in books. Saw it on the TV.

[laughter; sounds like she slaps him on the arm]

KJL: Because someone told you. Right?

KGM: I get you.

[pause][sounds of the ocean; whales rubbing against the pier; sounds of gulls crying]

KGM: Why do you ask about that, though? Bastian's ghost.

KJL: Dunno. I've had a lot of time here to myself. It's just been rolling around in my mind. He was so certain. I believed him. I guess it's just kind of weird that you don't.

KGM: Didn't say that.

KJL: It's just…you. You don't believe *this*…

KGM: You're waving you're arms around above your head—

KJL: —Stop it. You don't believe that all that's happened is any more than some evolutionary-slash-extinction event. A natural occurrence.

KGM: Didn't say I don't believe. I'm not sure, okay? Jespers was a scientist. He discovered something, or thought he did, and he brought others in, but what happened *that* morning? I don't think he or any of them saw that coming.

[sounds of the ocean; whales rubbing against the pier; sounds of gulls crying]

KJL: The agnostic who peddles through graveyards. The agnostic paddling down a flooded river at the behest of nubile throngs.

KGM: Sticks and stones.

KJL: You're a mystic. That's what you are, Kevin March.

KGM: Oh, shush you.

KJL: I mean, they made you come here on a boat! [laughs] And you're like *oh, okay...*

KGM: You left me that note!

KJL: They made me, apparently. I don't recall, Senator. But I'm glad I did. I didn't tell you to come by boat.

KGM: They didn't give me a choice. You're saying there's a reason.

KJL: There has to be one. A vision quest. Preparing you. On a donkey from the desert.

KGM. Oh, c'mon.[27] There's no risen Lazarus here.

KJL: Not what Bass thought. He was a dead man.

KGM: But he wasn't. And neither were you.

KJL: Whatever you say. What you say and what you believe are different things. [sounds of the ocean; whales rubbing against the pier; sounds of gulls crying]

KGM: Kodie, look...I was trying to get out of Austin in a police car. They stopped me. Your note. Your handwriting. There's the kayak. No other way out. What was I to do?

---

27 It is interesting to note that KGM said exactly this was the reason he thought he went down the river on a boat, yet he won't admit such thoughts to KJL here.

KJL: Nuh-uh. You were driving around in a police car?

KGM: It's all on here. [tapping at microphone] Later, okay?

KJL: You honestly think there's no reason they stop you from going by car but then do nothing when you go by a kayak they obviously set out for you? That they're just scared and acting bizarre?

KGM: You tell me what it is when their freaking skin connects.

KJL: What? What do you mean their *skin connects*?

KGM: When I tried to drive out of Austin in my police car, over on Forty-Fifth and Airport, they huddled and drew together and as I rolled toward them the…white stuff jumped between them like webbing, started pulling them tighter. To form a wall.

KJL: Jesus.

KGM: Yeah, that's what I said. They really didn't want me leaving that way. I mean, I saw that[28] and I freaked out, threw it into reverse.

[sounds of the ocean; whales rubbing against the pier; sounds of gulls crying]

KGM: Cars, roads, all the old-world ways…they don't…I never told you this, but the morning of, I was sitting up at Mount Bonnell and I saw this wave come up the lake. Just this one rolling wave and it kept on going north, under the bridge. I know it came from here. I heard that awful sound, and then that wave came upriver.

KJL: But there's that dam there…[fingers snapping] what's it called, uh…

KGM: I know. This is what I'm saying. I was meant to see that wave from that vantage. I knew right then that I would go back down the river just as that wave came up. That I would come to meet whatever it was that made it come up. And that I'd do it alone.

KJL: You just admitted it. *Meant to see.* You're shrugging and looking down at your lap. You're nodding.

---

28 KGM doesn't mention the "winged thing" he saw to Kodie. See NDC-13 for more detail about Kevin's First Days Manifestations.

[sounds of the ocean; whales rubbing against the pier; sounds of gulls crying]

KJL: That's why they didn't bring us together. You had presaged this.

KGM: I'd dreamed it. Last summer.

KJL: Okay, you dreamed it.

KGM: Vaguely. Whenever I did, Johnny came into my room peeing down his leg, sleepwalking and mumbling.

KJL: Kevin. They key off you. If things don't go as you saw that it would, they can't let it happen.

KGM: Sounds pretty woo-woo.

KJL: Whales on fire? A million kids down there. Pretty woo-woo. [sounds of the ocean; whales rubbing against the pier; sounds of gulls crying]

KGM: So, there I am, on that boulder and I'm questioning things pretty mightily because I had just smoked a bowl, you know? Her comely silhouette nods in the dark against a thousand fires, the smell of charred whale flesh and burning blubber oil all around us. The constant ocean curling in, hissing, the gulls' laments, the boom and scrape of the dead behemoths against the pier reaching out into the dark sea.

KJL: Nice.

KGM: [laughter] I didn't know the world was ending, per se. I just knew something had changed, it was big, and that I'd be here at the river's end before too long. Then, I didn't even know the Colorado came here. I just knew I'd be going the other direction that wave came from. So here I am.

KJL: Prophetic mystical you. Graveyard cyclist, paddler of swollen unknown rivers.

[sounds of the ocean; whales rubbing against the pier; sounds of gulls crying]

KJL: It's like the earth was hit by something and the wave was the aftershock.

KGM: No asteroid, though.

KJL: No earthquakes, tsunamis. Killer virus. Lions tigers bears.

KGM: Just white stuff emitting from your lungs, cementing in your windpipe. Billions. Within an hour or so of dawn.

KJL: [long exhalation]

KGM: Lions tigers bears don't make you commit sui—

KJL: Let's not even...okay? That's one thing I've thought about a lot here in my museum home behind glass. I can't understand it. It makes me very very sad.

KGM: Okay. Me too.

[sounds of the ocean; whales rubbing against the pier; sounds of gulls crying]

KGM: Hell if they weren't adamant about me coming by river.

KJL: And you came. [sniffing]

KGM: I came for you. You're nodding. [KJL sniffing]

KJL: I left a note. [her voice breaking up with crying]

KGM: You did.

KJL: [through crying] Love you.

KGM: Love you. [KGM sniffing]

[long pause][sounds of the ocean; whales rubbing against the pier; sounds of gulls crying]

KGM: You cold?

KJL: A little.

KGM: Let's go up to the nature center. You can show me your digs.

KJL: Oh, they're impressive.

KGM: C'mon, Maggie. Bet you're hungry huh? Speaking of—

KJL: Oh, they always leave me something. I've eaten a whole lot of flame-broiled fish. And sometimes fruit. Good, too. They can cook, the mutes.

KGM: Fruit? Where they getting that?

KJL: Don't know. South Texas. Lots of agriculture down here.

KGM: It's November. There's nothing on trees right now. Harvests are way over.

KJL: Dunno.

KGM: What, they've raided grocery stores and farm storage? Not very new world of them.

KJL: Dunno.

KGM: How are they surviving? Where are they crapping?

KJL: Oh, well, *that's* over there. The stone-age mutes at least know a thing or two about pits and fire.

KGM: You don't say.

KJL: How do you mean?

KGM: The bodies.

KJL: Really?

KGM: Big ones, outside the cities. I watched them doing it.

[sounds of the ocean; whales rubbing against the pier; sounds of gulls crying]

KJL: Doubt they'll leave a care package for Maggie.

KGM: Yeah, doubt that. Let's walk.

[sounds of the ocean; whales rubbing against the pier; sounds of gulls crying; sounds of footfalls on sand, on rock, sandy shoes scratching on cement]

KGM: You sure it's mine?

KJL: Kevin.

[scratching on cement stops; sounds of the ocean; whales rubbing against the pier; sounds of gulls crying]

Yes.

KGM: Nobody else even possible?

KJL: No. Stop it. Turn that off.

KGM: Hold on. Let's keep it rolling for the record. 'Case I gotta go to court to fight paternity and child support.

KJL: *Kevin* . . .

KGM: She said with anger.

KJL: [sighs]

KGM: How far along?

KJL: We did it once. Rainy day at my place. That long.

KGM: How...do you know?

[sounds of the ocean; whales rubbing against the pier; sounds of gulls crying]

KJL: I just know.

KGM: Well, I mean, how? Did the kids take you to a drugstore to get a pregnancy test kit?

KJL: No.

KGM: So, how? Explain it to me. The assumed father must know these things.

[sounds of the ocean; whales rubbing against the pier; sounds of gulls crying]

KJL: I've been pregnant before.

KGM: Oh—

KJL: Yeah.

KGM: So, you just, know.

KJL: Yeah. They've been taking extra special care of me because of it, I think. They know. Kids know a mother. It's in their body language. A general genuflecting.

KGM: It's only been a few weeks. Can you really be so sure?

KJL: Brutal morning sickness.

KGM: You've been spending your days with whale carcasses. Could make you wanna barf.

KJL: I'm craving stuff I don't like. For example, you know I'm a vegetarian. But I'm wanting steak. Werewolf-hungry for it. I'm peeing a lot, shortness of breath, tits hurt. Missed my period. Let's see, what else?

KGM: Okay, all right. Condom failure, huh?

KJL: It happens. Also, get this. That morning, the day of, when you came to find me at the store, besides the baseball bat, the other thing I had in my hand was a pregnancy test.

[sounds of the ocean; whales rubbing against the pier; sounds of gulls crying]

I was opening the store that morning, right? But that morning turned out to be what it was and so I didn't go in at the usual time. I mean, Eric and Sarah Jane were standing in my yard and my parents were gone and the TV news freaking out and—[deep quick sigh] you remember.

KGM: No, I don't. Remember? I saw nothing, no footage of anything. Nothing except for a little of this guy on Univision in Spanish before the camera tilted over. All I got was…hearsay. From you and Bass and Mr. Fleming. I told you this.

KJL: Anyway, I texted you and went there because that felt safe to me. Being back in that storeroom, listening to the radio until you got there. That felt safe. And I just grabbed one of those tests kits, shoved it into the pocket of my fatigue shorts, and I don't know, I just . . .

KGM: As the world was falling apart you shoplifted a pregnancy test.

KJL: It's like I *knew* I'd need it. You know? I know you know what the intuition felt like.

[sounds of the ocean; whales rubbing against the pier; sounds of gulls crying]

You're nodding. Besides, you know I'd been having dreams too, mostly in the summer. They stopped after around July Fourth or so, but, I just knew that I'd be pregnant in the fall and that it would be important to know right away. That's all I knew.

KGM: Huh. June dreams, you say?

KJL: Yes, mostly. Same time as you, huh?

KGM: Filled with doom, the future?

KJL: The future, yes. Doom...not really. Not scary. About being pregnant.

KGM: Mine were. Wrote a short story based on the way it made me feel.

KJL: A story called...?

KGM: *The Late Bloomers.*

KJL: *Shit.*

[sound of door swinging open; scratching footfalls; outside sounds disappear]

KGM: Those tests any good? I mean, they cost a dollar. You're ignoring me. You're giving me a look.

KJL: Here we are. Home sweet home.

KGM: Where's the food?

KJL: Oh, here, this way. Usually they leave me something at the front door.

KGM: Maggie, stay.

KGM: [WHISPERING] THERE'S A FEW cars in that parking lot.

KJL: Uh-huh. Why are you whispering?

KGM: We could do it. Drive back to Utopia. Perfect place.

KJL: Keys?

KGM: You seen kids go anywhere near the cars?

KJL: No. But I don't watch them twenty-four seven.

KGM: The dying didn't take their car keys.

KJL: Say we make it to the parking lot. You know they're going to stop us. They stopped me every time I even feigned running off, day and night. They just appear. You know this.

KGM: I know, I know.

KJL: They want us here, Kevin. It's their world.

KGM: Kodie, we can't stay here. You can't live out your pregnancy here. Give birth here. Raise the child in a natural history museum eating packets of charred fish?

KJL: I don't see a rational choice. I've done nothing but think about this since I've been here and lucid enough to think. I've gone through different scenarios. You being here included.

KGM: But did you ever plug into your formula that I have this gun? And Maggie? She owes me and she knows it.

KJL: You're looking at her. What happened between you two?

KGM: Later.

KJL: Kevin, you're wasting time trying.

KGM: Did you see what was happening down there tonight?

KJL: You mean the flaming whales and all that?

KGM: Yeah, all that. Have they ever lit whales on fire since you've been here?

KJL: Not that I've seen. I've been in here quite a bit.

KGM: I didn't see any burnt ones down there today.

KJL: Maybe they did on some night when I was asleep up here and they burned it completely and dumped the rest in the bay.

KGM: Why are you so resistant? You're defending them again. Their apologist.

KJL: I don't—

KGM: But you are, you do. At every turn.

KJL: You're overreacting. I don't like this any more than you do. Yes, of course, I'd love to escape but I'm just trying to be reasonable. It's impossible, Kevin.

[long pause]

KGM: Johnny tell you that? You're nodding. What else?

KJL: Nothing.

KGM: What else has he told you?

KJL: Nothing . . .

KGM: It's not nothing. What are you so afraid to tell me? [pause] Why are you...?

KJL: They won't let us leave, Kevin.

KGM: You've already said that. You're being so evasive.

KJL: I'm not.

[long pause]

They just won't. I'm afraid for my baby. If we try to leave, they'll—

KGM: Kill us?

KJL: [sigh] I don't know what they'll do.

KGM: You know something, Kodie. The fact that you won't even tell me... [long pause]

The night I arrive, they light the whales on fire. They dance around the fires. They sing and hum like I've never heard them do before. It's not in my head like before. Because it's not for us. It's for them. They're celebrating. It's the freaking Whos in Whoville down there.

[long pause; distant sounds of singing-humming]

KJL: Maybe you really are their savior, Kevin.

KGM: I'm really tired of that conversation. Dead horse, dead end. They don't need me.

KJL: Okay. [sigh] What Johnny said was...he said you can help them remember.

KGM: I'll help them over a damned bridge. Yes yes.

KJL: Won't you even consider that? I mean, that's why I asked you about Bastian's ghost. Can you even consider it? Something that's beyond reason? Kevin, this whole experience, that morning, the world dying off as it has. That's not something you or I or Dr. Jespers or anybody would've thought possible. So why can't you? You came here on a kayak for days and days. Don't tell me you don't somewhat get this.

KGM: Is that what Johnny wants you to do? Talk me into it?

KJL: How can I possibly talk you into it? [long pause]

KGM: Whales on fire. They dance. Celebration. That thing, out on the water....

KJL: I haven't seen anything. What are you talking about?

KGM: Something's happening tomorrow. I know it. It's—

KJL: What? What are you talking about?

KGM: It's the thing I can't see, they haven't let me see.

KJL: What what what?

KGM: What Simon was talking about. Tomorrow's the beginning.

KJL: The beginning.

KGM: Before I saw you running up the pier, I was looking at the drilling platform out there thinking I saw something on it.

KJL: On it.

KGM: Yeah. Something really big that moved.

KJL: Moved.

KGM: When I looked at it through the binoculars, nothing there. Just the platform, a rig coming up out of it.

KJL: So what's the—

KGM: When I look out there again with just my eyes, I see it. Sitting there. I've been seeing it, iterations of it, since the morning of.

KJL: Kevin, it's, what? A mile out there in the open ocean.

KGM: Something there.

[long pause]

KGM: Remember that morning? Bass naked with the gun? You're nodding. Right before he turned to shoot that boy at the door, do you remember what happened?

KJL: You were talking to him, telling him to put the gun down.

KGM: Well, yes, but more specifically. After that. You're shaking your head. Everything went black for a moment. Remember that? Not just clouds but like a full eclipse.

KJL: I...remember turning my head to the door because of that boy there. I remember screaming. His face...moved.

KGM: You don't remember that wink of darkness?

KJL: Huh-uh. I can't really—

KGM: Well I do. And whatever it was that made it dark moved quickly away, then Bass shot the boy through the door. Whatever that was that blocked out the sun for that brief moment, that's what's out there on that platform watching us like the weasel watches the hen.

KJL: I don't know what to say, Kevin.

KGM: [quietly, recounting to himself] Always indirectly, I see it. Saw its tail on the trail. Saw its shadow riding the wave. Saw it at MoPac, standing on the other side of the train cars. On Forty-Fifth behind the kids. Now it's out there.

KJL: You've not told me any of this.

KGM: I didn't want to believe it. If I admitted seeing it to you, it'd've seemed real.

KJL: Kevin.

KGM: It waits.

KJL: For what?

KGM: The beginning.

KJL: Kevin . . .

KGM: What, Kodie? *Won't you even consider it?*

KJL: Okay, okay. Point taken.

KGM: The dark smiling teeth. This is its lieutenant. Kodie. I know you know what I'm talking about. You won't look at me.

1 KGM: [QUICK WHISPERING] You're here. Now I'm here. A million of them
2 are here. They've been waiting. They could have taken us out at any time. At
3 any time at all.

4 KJL: You're scaring me, Kevin. Blink, Kevin.

5 KGM: Time's on their side.

6 KJL: Are you awake? You're sleep-talking. Kevin, wake up.

7 KGM: Whatever's out there, it's not just out there on that platform. It's
8 everywhere. It's vast. Like what Jespers was saying. [sound of ripping Velcro,
9 zippers, paper shuffling] "This thing (his word) hides in plain sight like
10 dark matter in space. It's there, it's so everything, so everywhere that we
11 geneticists don't think to see it. We don't know it's there, like a fish doesn't
12 know it's in water." On the platform out there it shimmers. Like it's there but
13 it's not.

14 KJL: Hey. Enough now.

15 KGM: Like the white stuff. It's always been within us. Hasn't it?

16 KJL: Kevin. Please, let's sleep.

17 KGM: Dark side of the helix. [whispering] *Cerca, cerca, cerca.*

18 [whispering, talking to himself, to the recorder; sounds of footsteps, KGM
19 pacing the floor]

20 KGM: My God—the kids have been trying to tell me all along. Johnny
21 was trying to tell me. Because I *did* know. I wouldn't admit it. I took those
22 feelings and bent them into fiction. I absolutely knew, and I did nothing.
23 [more pacing sounds]

24 I ask you, dear reader, what was I supposed to do? I mean, tell Mom, the
25 school counselor, Mr. English? Tell them what? That I'm having vivid visions,
26 dreams, my brother mumbles things to me when he sleepwalks and pees on
27 the floor which I clean up so he's not embarrassed, and because of these
28 things I'm certain the world is ending soon, like right around Halloween
29 sometime? *Pffft.* They'd've put me on psychotropics faster than you can say
30 "selective serotonin reuptake inhibitor".

You just tried to say that fast didn't you? That's why I like you. You're hanging in with me, more than anybody.

Maggie? What? C'mere. Lie down. You feel it. Don't you, girl? My anxiety, that they stir in their sleep.

KGM: [VOICE PANICKED, WHISPERING] KODIE. Kodie. They didn't pick me to save them. They didn't pick me.

KJL: Hmmm? What are you talking about now? You're sleep-walking again. Come back to bed.

KGM: No! [still whispering] Kodie. That thing out there. They're doing *its* bidding now. I've felt all along that they're conflicted. Professor Fleming, is this why you didn't want me to know about Jespers's work? "The dark side of the helix" isn't just a turn of phrase, is it? You knew if I knew...I'd know too much.

KJL: Why do you keep waking me up? I thought you said—

[sound of skin slapping skin]

KJL: Hey! Why'd you do that? That hurt.

KGM: Gotta wake up. We've got to get out of here. Before dawn breaks. It's their float zone. They're not as...aware just before dawn breaks. I've watched them. They go into this collective REM sleep spasm thing. We can get away. [sound of Velcro ripping; metal snapping] We've got this glock, this dog.

KJL: What are you doing?

KGM: I've been thinking. Maybe the old world picked me, picked us. Like Fleming and Jespers tried to tell us—we've got the conch, we're supposed to keep the flame of the *old* world. We're supposed to save *us*, but not by staying here. You and me, Eve. We've got to try. You're nodding. You know I'm right.

KJL: Okay. [voice broken; sniffling]

KGM: C'mon. We can do it. Yeah? Okay? You okay? I need you.

[sniffling loud and close to the microphone; scratching sounds[29]]

---

29 It's believed they are hugging here, as is ratified by KGM's next statement.

1 Dear reader, her face is buried in my chest and she's nodding her head. This
2 is when you go *awwww*.

3 [KJL laughs quietly, sounding loud in the microphone]

4 [sounds of sirens; very loud][30]

5 KGM: THE SOUNDS! THE KIDS are—

6 KJL: —same as the morning of . . .

7 [sounds of running footfalls; heavy breathing; dog barking]

8 KJL: Same sounds! What is that?!

9 KGM: Coming from out there!

10 [the loud siren-like sounds[31] augment; the recording becomes unclear; their
11 voices indecipherable]

12 [sounds of running footfalls; heavy breathing]

13 KGM: The kids are...the sounds! This is...good! They're totally confused
14 right now.

15 KJL: Kevin, look out!

16 [sound of gunshots] *pop pop pop pop*

17 KGM: Maggie! Go!

18 [sound of dog barking; those sounds continuing but receding]

19 [squealing sounds; dog barking maniacally in the distance; siren-like sounds
20 continuing]

21 [sounds of fast footfalls]

22 KGM: [breathing heavily] God, listen to that. They're shrieking! [sounds
23 of children; sounds of car door opening; car[32] door chiming] This one's got
24 keys! Get in! Get in! Get in!

25 KJL: Why are they shrieking like that?

26 KGM: I don't know! [sound of car door slamming shut; car door chiming]

30 By the recording time stamp, it is believed to be dawn.

31 It is believed that these sounds are the "whalesounds" KGM described hearing at the start.

32 2014 white Chevrolet Impala, specialty Texas license plate BB01B, "Texas State Parks"

KJL: Oh, shit! [sound of car door slamming shut; car door chiming stops; engine starting up; engine stalling] There they are! Oh, Jesus! They're coming. Hurry!

KGM: Trying. Engine's cold. Car's been sitting here. [sound of car engine turning over] Okay!

KJL: *Kevinnnn!*

KGM: Okay okay okay. [sound of engine starting] Here we go.

KJL: Here they come—!

KGM: [sound of car put into gear] Look! Maggie's heading them off! Look at her! Oh, man, look at her—

[sounds of dog barking] [sounds of engine revving; tires squealing] [siren-sound continuing]

KJL: Go go go go go!

[sounds of dog barks receding]

KJL: Careful. More of them. Bound to be. They'll try to get in front of us.

[sounds of engine revving; tires squealing]

KGM: Look. Maggie's got them. Down on the beach. They're not... We're gonna make it!

[sounds of car engine; tires squealing; acceleration]

KJL: We're going to...oh my God it's...they're not...there's not enough of them! Ha-haaaaa!

[sounds of car engine; tires squealing; acceleration; heavy breathing; coughing]

KGM: No no no no no. They're [sound cuts in and out; knocking sounds] the road. We're on Sixth. We've got to turn into town. Aw, shit! Can't go west!

KJL: Why?

KGM: River's flooded all up and down there. Gotta go east for bit, then cut back. Hold on. Gotta U-y.

1   [sounds of tires screeching; acceleration]

2   KGM: More up there. Dammit. We've got to—

3   KJL: Turn down—

4   KGM: I can't do that! I—

5   KJL: Go!

6   KGM: Gotta ditch and hide before they get here.

7   KJL: Look look look. Pull in, pull in.

8   KGM: Good idea.

9   [sounds of tires squealing; engine turning off; car doors opening; car door
10   chime]

11   [sounds of footfalls]

12   [sound of a roaring[33] and slam]

13   KJL: Where should we go?

14   KGM: In there.

15   [sounds of car doors slamming]

16   [sound of interior door opening; footfalls]

17   KJL: They saw us. [sounds of heavy breathing of two people]

18   KGM: No they didn't. Let's just stay here awhile. [sounds of heavy breathing
19   of two people]

20   KJL: They did.

21   [sounds of heavy breathing of two people]

22   KGM: FYI, IT'S BACK ON.[34]

23

---

33 It is believed this sound is the sound of a garage door closing. The car (type footnoted above) was found in an auto repair facility, Advanced Auto Repair, in Bay City, Texas, approximately twenty-one miles north of the Natural History Museum parking lot at Matagorda Bay. KGM's boat bag was recovered from inside the car. Dr. Warren Jespers's draft paper and the notes from Professor Kenneth Fleming and KJL were found inside, copies of which are attached as Exhibits B and C.

34 By time stamp, it is almost evening.

KJL: Uh, okay. Not really a priority right now, Kevin.

KGM: Let's recap for dear reader.

KJL: Let's not. Let's get out of here.

KGM: Real quick. Okay. We've been in this oil-smelling office since this morning. Blinds shut. Hunkered down and still.

KJL: We napped.

KGM: You napped.

KJL: I napped. I'm a little bit preggers. Sleepy.

KGM: They didn't even come up this street. I sat here and thought about everything again, how things relate. You remember all those copies of *Lord of the Flies* Jespers had?

KJL: Yeah.

KGM: Remember that Bible citation on his board?

KJL: Yep. Matthew 16:23. Uh, something like get behind me, Satan. You don't have God in mind, only things of men.

KGM: Yeah, something like that. You know what "lord of the flies" translates to in Greek and Hebrew?

KJL: Waiting for you to tell me.

KGM: Beelzebub.

KJL: Dammit. Get behind me Beelzebub. Don't remember learning that in ninth grade. [pause] So, you're saying Jespers…what? He's a scientist.

KGM: Dunno. He was reaching, he was having premonitions, putting puzzle pieces together, looking outside of science. All scientific discovery starts with wild what ifs, right? What I was saying about Grandma Lucille earlier? I *just* wrote an extra credit essay on *Lord of the Flies*, a story about children all alone, no adults; *just* wrote that story about late bloomers based on vivid dreams of me and you and Bass looking at a sea of kids; Johnny's night terrors; I go up to Mount Bonnell apropos to nothing that morning. Me, you, Bass, Fleming. No—

KJL: —coincidences . I'm with your Grandma Lucille. Wish I'd met her.

1 KGM: Me, too. She died this summer. Missed all this fun. Listen, as soon
2 as it's dark, we'll drive up to Utopia. Or somewhere in the Hill Country,
3 somewhere where they can't box us in. Wait out the winter there.

4 KJL: Kevin?

5 KGM: What?

6 KJL: Feel that?

7 KGM: What?

8 KJL: That…[whispering] There's someone here.

9 [sounds of heavier, quicker breathing close to the microphone]

10 KGM: Who's…who's there?

11 [sounds of heavy, quick breaths close to the microphone continues]

12 NEW VOICE[35]: It's only me, brother. No other.

13 [KJL screams]

14 [muffling noises; popping on the microphone]

15 [SOUNDS OF CHILDREN HUMMING ONE note; loud close surf]

16 [sounds of the ocean; whales rubbing against the pier; sounds of gulls
17 crying]

18 JLM: Good morning, brother. Here, take this thing.[36] Let's finish your story.
19 We want it to be complete, don't we?

20 [sounds of the ocean; whales rubbing against the pier; sounds of gulls
21 crying]

22 KGM: [scratchy, confused voice] Johnny?

[long pause]

Where's Kodie? What have you done with Kodie?

---

35 This voice belongs to Jonathan Livingston March ("JLM" hereafter), KGM's younger brother,
Johnny; me, transcriber and editor herein.

36 JLM, like Nate before him, speaks here in that "wet, flangey" voice. Around the world during
that early period of weeks to months after the "day of" (now known as New Day or "ND"),
though scant accurate records exist supporting this with this recording being the strongest. It is

JLM: She's fine. She's over there.

KGM: Over where? Kodie! *Kodie!*

JLM: Stop.

KGM: [breathing heavily] We can help you, Johnny. I came here because you all asked me to. To help you.

JLM: [his voice wet and flangey here] Sure. That's why you two were trying to escape. You wanted to help us.

KGM: If you need our kids to grow and breed with yours, if that's what's going on then, okay, I can see that and—

JLM: No no no. Not at all. That's not it at all.

KGM: Johnny's pacing. My brother paces back and forth. He's agitated, he's—

JLM: Stop. Always talking. All you ever did. Your world. Talk talk talk.

[sounds of children humming one note; loud close surf]

[sounds of the ocean; whales rubbing against the pier; sounds of gulls crying]

KGM: Yes. We talked. I talked. I had to tell the story.

JLM: Why?

KGM: I can't explain it.

[children's humming falls away]

JLM: Yes you can. Tell us.

KGM: He waves his hand like a game show host over the huge crowd of kids surrounding us.

[sounds of the ocean; whales rubbing against the pier; sounds of gulls crying]

To understand, I guess. To try to understand. To make a record so we can remember what happened.

believed that no more than a few children were speaking, JLM and Nate among them. It is not yet understood why during this "transition period" the population did not speak. The "thing" referenced here is the digital voice recorder KGM has had with him throughout.

1   JLM: Blah blah blah.

2   KGM: You're holding your head. [sounds of children humming low]

3   JLM: I don't want to remember. Stop making us . . .

4   [sounds of the ocean; whales rubbing against the pier; sounds of gulls
5   crying]

6   KGM: Why did you bring me here, then?

7   [long pause]

8   KGM: You're looking around. Your face is desperate. The faces around you
9   look back with cold indifference—

10   JLM: —I don't want to do this!

11   KGM: Do what, Johnny?

12   JLM: You want me to explain? You want me to *talk*? So you can
13   *understaaannnnnd*? Well, I won't do that. [JLM sniffing[37]] We do. Kevin? Do
14   you understand? We just do. We take care of each other. Each and every one,
15   all the time. We know each other's faces intimately. We don't have names
16   for each other. Do you understand what I'm saying? Do you get what that
17   means? You call me Johnny because that's all you know and I respond to it
18   with words right now because I have to.

19   [long pause]

20   [sounds of the ocean; whales rubbing against the pier; sounds of gulls
21   crying]

22   KGM: You think this will last?

23   JLM: It just is. There's no thinking to do. The morning of, as you call it, it all
24   changed. Simple.

25   KGM: Simple.

26   JLM: That's right. But you can't understand that.

27   KGM: It'll break down, Johnny.

28   JLM: There's nothing to break down. We just are, and we just do. We exist,
29   we sing and then we die. So simple.

37 In my normal voice, I sound upset here.

[sounds of the ocean; whales rubbing against the pier; sounds of gulls crying]

[long pause]

JLM: [the voice wet and flangey] It's time.

KGM: Johnny? All these kids are milling around. Lining up. Johnny?

JLM: It's time. And that's all.

KGM: [voice sounding clipped and panicked; sounds of heavy breathing] Why not just let me and Kodie go? What's it matter?

JLM: Because we can't.

KGM: Why? Is this the beginning?

JLM: No. You were lied to. No. This…. this is the end. And that's all.

KGM: We can do this together. Or you can let us go and we won't bother you. We promise.

JLM: It's not a task I want, Kevin. You must know that. I *need* you to know that.

[long pause]

[sounds of children humming]

[sounds of KGM's amazement; a quick intake of breath; the ocean wind booming hard on the microphone; voices obscured]

KGM: That thing out there…it's moving…oh, it's…oh, Johnny what is that thing?

JLM: [whispering] Don't look at it, Kevin.[38]

KGM: *WHAT IS IT?!*

JLM: It doesn't matter.

KGM: Does it come for me?

JLM: It doesn't matter.

---

38 I say this in my normal voice.

1   KGM: [ocean wind cuts out the voice] You're [unintelligible] Johnny.
2   [unintelligible] just happen. You can't [unintelligible] won't let you
3   [unintelligible] controls you.[39]

4   [sound of many many children humming, growing into a note] It needs you
5   to [unintelligible].

6   KJL: [her voice far away; some of it lost in the wind] What is that? Jesus
7   Christ, Kevin! Johnny!? What is that out there? [her voice a shriek]

8   JLM: It doesn't matter. [very flangey voice now]

9   KGM: *Kodie! I'm here!* Let me see her! No! Move! They won't let me by.
10   [speaking into the microphone] Johnny's eyes are fluttering, closing...he's
11   raising his arms like he's done before, like, heh, his goddamned Wayne
12   Rooney poster on his wall...the thing out there...it moves, dear reader.
13   Mom! Dad! Martin! Mr. E!

14   [pause; heavy breathing]

15   [whispering loud and close into the microphone] Grandma Lucille—*help*
16   *me!* It moves. No such thing as luck. Oh my God, it moves so terribly.

17   [the humming note rises, changes form, rises again]

18   It's...coming. Close close close.

19   [the microphone cuts out]

20   [SOUNDS OF THE OCEAN; SOUNDS of gulls crying]

21   JLM: Kevin. It's over now. Kevin, wake up.[40]

22   KGM: [voice groggy] What?

23   [long pause]

24   JLM: It's time.

---

39 I have listened to this innumerable times and have employed different techniques to bring up
the sound clarity. Knowing my brother's voice, vocal inflections and what he was trying to say, I
am confident that what he said here was: "You're a liar, Johnny. Things don't just happen. You can't
talk about it because it won't let you. I know it's not you. It's making you do this. Just remember
that. It controls you. It needs you to need it."

40 I believe I hold the recorder and have started recording.

KGM: [pause] It's not...Where'd it go?

JLM: It's time.

KGM: Time? Time for what?

JLM: It's time.

KGM: I don't understand.

JLM: It isn't to be understood. It just is.

KGM: What?

[the mass of children begin humming again; a different, darker note, unlike any other on this recording]

KGM: [voice cracking] Why? Oh no no no no. God, *why?*

[voice emotional but collected] My brother holds a plastic grocery bag. [sound of sniffing] *Oh god* he's tearing it open.

[pause] [sounds of sniffing] [sounds of the ocean; sounds of gulls crying]

He holds the stone. The price sticker from the HEB...

[pause] [sounds of sniffing] [sounds of the ocean; sounds of gulls crying; children humming low and thick]

KGM: Johnny, wait. Can I...Will you let me play a song? Can someone get my trombone? It's...I don't know. Somewhere.

[long pause] [sounds of sniffing] [sounds of the ocean; sounds of gulls crying]

[close sounds of KGM opening the trombone case; sniffling]

JLM: [voice wet and flangey, through crying] Play, Kevin.

KGM: Where's Kodie? [Kevin sounds strong now, resolved]

JLM: She couldn't watch.

KGM: [big deep sigh]

[sounds of the ocean; sounds of gulls crying]

As I'm about to raise my horn to my lips I see ten thousand children step aside together to reveal many small piles of stones. They each stroll over

1 and pick one up. Each of them with a smooth brown stone. [voice hitched,
2 sounding surprised] *Ah, oh*—[breathing quickly] they snap into a line that
3 goes down the beach. They all put their hands behind their backs. Johnny
4 steps up to within several feet of me. I will now raise my horn to my lips,
5 dear reader, and I will play for you "When the Saints Go Marching In". The
6 jazzier, snappy version Grandma Lucille really liked.

7 [loud and close to the microphone,[41] the song[42] plays]

8 [TUSSLING SOUND; SCRATCHING ON THE microphone]

9 KGM: [his voice clear and loud directly into the microphone[43]] Dear reader!
10 You! Don't keep this between me and you! Don't you do that! You've got to
11 know what happened. You must remember. And you must fight back! This
12 isn't the way it has to be! It can't be! You've *got* to remem—

13 [sound of a single loud thump[44]]

14 [sound of the recorder falling into the sand]

15 [sounds of less loud thudding]

16 [sounds of the ocean; sounds of gulls crying and the continuous sounds of
17 stones thudding into the body of Kevin Gabriel March]

18 [the very last sounds of the recording are of the faraway sounds of Kodie
19 Janine Lagenkamp, screaming]

---

41 Apparently I hold the recorder close to the mouth of the trombone.

42 Also known as "The Saints." Though KGM plays an instrumental, the opening lyrics to this famous song of the old world are as follows:
Oh, when the saints go marching in
Oh, when the saints go marching in
Lord I want to be in that number
When the saints go marching in

43 KGM has snatched the recorder from me and speaks into it.

44 These early days—especially once I left the late bloomers with Rebecca to be with the children—are very foggy in my memory, nearly a blackout, but the memory of that moment on that morning on the beach is sharp enough. I do know, I do remember, though it hurts my head like memories of the old world still do, that it was my stone that knocked my brother unconscious. It struck him just above his right occipital bone.

*** END OF RECORDING ***

Acknowledgments

Thank you:

Robert J. Peterson

Andrea

Stella

Elizabeth

About The Author

Mark Falkin is the author of the novels *Days of Grace* and *Contract City*. Though he remains a card-carrying member of the Texas Bar, he is a literary agent by day and oftentimes by night. He lives with his wife and daughters in Austin, Texas.